****

Fire and Maneuver:
1981
Soviet Endgame—Book Two

****

By Alex Aaronson and James Rosone

****

Published in conjunction with Front Line Publishing, Inc.

Copyright Notice

ISBN: 978-1-957634-67-8
Sun City Center, Florida, United States of America
Library of Congress Control Number: 2023901395

Table of Contents

Dedication

To Lacey, whose love and support are instrumental to the writing of these novels, and to Shannon, Ana, and Caroline. A father couldn't ask for better daughters.
Special thanks to Rick Ahlstrom, Miranda Watson, Roel Martinez and Master Sergeant Owen Schultz, (USMC Ret)

Chapter 1

1 January 1981
Czechoslovakian-German Border

Major Dmitriy Bogdanov was one of the fastest men in the world. Tonight, in the skies above the Czechoslovakian border, he was going to bet his life on the speed of his MiG-25R.

The Soviet Air Force, the Voyenno-Vozdushnye Sily, or VVS, launched a massive sweep into NATO airspace. Aircraft from bases all along the frontier were launched in "coordinated chaos." The first to get into the air were the fastest planes on the battlefield: the Mig-25 Foxbats. These planes were sent into NATO territory to get as much information as they could on enemy air defenses. They flew without weapons and instead relied on their electronic sensors to provide the Soviets with the vital intelligence that they would need to deal with the NATO surface-to-air missiles (SAMs).

This gave Bogdanov a unique view of the battlefield. Between his electronic intelligence, or ELINT screen, his own radar, and the radio communications between units, he could see everything happening for hundreds of miles. He could see all the way to the Germany-Luxembourg border, where an E-3 Sentry airborne warning and control system (AWACS) plane flew lazy circles. He imagined the American radar operator watching his display as a mass of contacts were picked up in Czechoslovakian and East German airspace.

The Sentry stood guard over the skies of West Germany and was no doubt relaying the contacts to NATO commanders on the ground. The first of those contacts to come racing across the border was Major Bogdanov. Behind him were the rest of the 1st Squadron, 931st Independent Guards Air Regiment.

Major Bogdanov's mission was to fly directly at the NATO air-defense installations. He knew that there were missile batteries out there, and his job was to find them so that his brothers in the VVS could kill them. Most pilots thought the men of the 931st must be insane. No rational man would fly directly into the hornet's nest, begging the enemy to engage, all while being completely unarmed.

Bogdanov wasn't crazy, he was well trained. He knew that with his MiG-25, he could get into the enemy's backyard, collect the electronic intelligence he needed, and get back out before the Americans or Germans could engage. He'd picked up the nickname *"Germes"* when he'd first been assigned to the MiG-25 nearly ten years ago. Bogdanov was affectionately known as the God of Speed.

The Soviets originally designed the MiG-25 as an interceptor with the mission of stopping the American SR-71 Blackbird, or the potential B-70 Valkyrie. Both USAF aircraft could fly at speeds more than Mach 3. The Foxbat could keep up with the Valkyrie and could get close enough to the Blackbird to fire one of its massive R-40 air-to-air missiles. Bogdanov's MiG-25R didn't have any missiles. Instead, the Soviets had built it for pure speed. The MiG pilot settled in at his patrol altitude of ten thousand meters and steeled his nerves as the war began.

Germes knew that the American airmen in the E-3 Sentry would vector interceptors toward the threat. F-15 Eagles or F-4 Phantoms would close with the Soviet forces near the Czechoslovakian border to the south and the inner-German border to the north. Those few fighters would be all that stood in the way of the massive onslaught rising from the Soviet airfields. From his glowing cockpit, Bogdanov marveled at the intricacy of it all.

The air battle was nearly a living thing. The complexity of the operations contained millions of tiny variations that would change the result of an action of a given aircraft, and variations in the actions of an aircraft would change the actions of a squadron. The actions of the squadrons would change the actions of an entire battle force. When you then added the culmination of all of the enemy's actions, the chaos that resulted could never be predicted in detail. This phenomenon was best summed up by Prussian Field Marshal Helmuth von Moltke when he said, "No battle plan survives first contact with the enemy."

It was in this chaos that Bogdanov watched a pair of Eagles stumble into a flight of what he assumed were Su-17s. The Soviet planes were attacking a NATO Hawk SAM battery in Grafenwöhr. This was bad news for the Soviet flight. Within minutes the Americans had dispatched four of the Fitters with their AIM-7 Sparrow missiles.

When the Eagles moved in closer to engage with their shorter-range AIM-9 Sidewinders, *Germes* saw a flight of MiG-23s light up their RP-23 air-intercept radars. Within seconds, the F-15s turned south. *The better part of valor*, thought *Germes*. *No doubt they will rearm and be back before this battle is over.*

Across Germany, F-15 Eagles and F-4 Phantoms were being launched. *Germes* knew that NATO controllers would send every airframe they had, and they wouldn't want to risk losing the pair of Eagles on a suicidal charge into the enemy formations.

Along the northern battlefront, Soviet Su-24 attack planes had launched long-range antiradiation missiles at the air control radars across West Germany. These radars weren't the primary target of the Soviet attack squadrons, but they could provide the enemy with real-time intelligence on Soviet aircraft. The known fixed position of the radars made them easy targets. The mobile Hawk batteries were the real target, and the real challenge for *Germes*.

Major Bogdanov flew his MiG-25 over the German town of Grafenwöhr. He had every reason to believe that six miles below, there was a NATO SAM itching to take a shot at him, or any of his brothers in the VVS. At 2344 local time, Bogdanov picked up the AN/MPQ-46 fire control radar of the Hawk site. The NATO forces had been ready for the incoming Su-17s that had been reported by the combat air patrol. As soon as the radars came online, the Hawk sites started to spit missiles at the incoming attackers.

The math in this fight was against the Soviets. They had to close within six miles before they could launch their Kh-25 missiles against the NATO forces.

The Hawk launchers, on the other hand, started firing at the Su-17s from twenty-two miles away. Due to the proximity of the SAM sites to the border, by the time the engagement began, the Fitters were already in range. The race was on. Could the three separate clusters of SAM launchers take out the incoming Soviets before the Kh-25 missiles destroyed their radars or launchers?

The MIM-23 surface-to-air missiles left the rails and screamed toward the Soviets. The Su-17s dove for the deck to evade. The Fitters neared their launch point and started to fall from the sky. SAMs exploded, taking Soviet planes and pilots out of the battle. It was in vain. The attackers had too much speed and too many aircraft to be stopped.

As the enemy cleared the six-mile radius, each fired their antiradar missiles. The Kh-25 missiles homed in on the radiation emissions of the NATO defenders. The main radar truck was struck by some of the first missiles to reach the area. Additional missiles hit the other emitters located with the missile launchers themselves. The first Soviet salvo had taken out two of the three Hawk firing positions.

Even after the Su-17s had launched their missiles, the Hawk units continued to prosecute them. As they turned to run back to Pilsen, they were chased by NATO missiles.

By the time the shooting was finished, only a single Su-17 had survived the attack. The F-15s and Hawk missiles had destroyed the other fourteen aircraft in the flight.

****

While the battle over Grafenwöhr raged, the Il-76s of the 175th Military Transport Aviation Regiment formed up west of Bechyně, Czechoslovakia. The forty-five planes that were carrying the men and equipment of the 345th independent Guards Airborne Regiment took time to get off the ground and ready for their drop. All the while, there was nothing for the men inside to do but wait. Sergeant Mikhail "Misha" Kozyrev tried to relax.

"Sergeant," said Private Andrei "Andrusha" Koshelev, "how can we be sure that our brothers in the VVS will be able to destroy all of the NATO SAM sites?"

So much for relaxation, thought Misha. They were going to conduct a combat airdrop over Giebelstadt Air Base, west of Grafenwöhr. It was imperative that the NATO SAM batteries be taken out to maximize the Desantniks' chances of getting through.

"Andrusha," replied Misha, "most of the air battle over this sector of Germany is likely dedicated to that objective. Having the initiative in combat meant that our forces can choose the time and place of the engagement. That means that we can concentrate the men and equipment needed for success."

Andrusha didn't look convinced, so Misha continued, "NATO forces now have to guess and react. Without knowing the specific objectives of the mission, they can't commit all of their defensive resources. At the time of the attack, NATO defenses would only know that an attack was underway. Units on the ground across the frontier would report advancing Warsaw Pact forces crossing the borders. For NATO, these first minutes would be dedicated to defending the skies over the battlefield and trying to establish air superiority over the entire battlespace. The VVS would be attempting to hold air superiority over selected areas."

"There are rumors in the ranks" said Andrusha, "that our objective hosts a NATO SAM battery."

"I can neither confirm, nor deny that, Private. But it doesn't matter either way. We will sit here until it's time to walk down the ramp." Misha hoped his tone conveyed to the young man that the conversation was over. Andrusha had no follow up questions, so it must have worked.

****

Miles away from Misha and the 345th VDV, *Germes* had just watched the failure of that first flight. He called in the danger of the still-active SAM site to his ground controllers, who then relayed it to the second flight of attack planes. This flight was originally tasked with striking the radars and missiles protecting the landing zone for the airborne assault.

Instead, many of the attacking strike planes were forced to engage the targeting radars outside Grafenwöhr that were tracking them. Again, a duel between the ARMs and SAMs played out. Again, by force of numbers, the Soviets pushed past the defenders. The remaining missile launchers were just too few to stop the onslaught.

The strike planes approached their objective from the southeast. They were moving north to avoid reported NATO fighters when they were suddenly painted by a fire control radar northeast of them. The missile battery had been hiding near one of the air control radars at Vilseck Airfield. It was pure happenstance that the air control station hadn't been taken out during the initial wave of missile attacks. The panicked Su-17s broke formation, with each trying to get past the missile umbrella. Each of the remaining five attack planes was destroyed before they were close enough to fire their missiles.

A second wave of attackers headed toward the landing zone. It was imperative that they neutralize the air defenses before the VDV could be dropped. The first aircraft to enter the SAM coverage area were MiG-23 Floggers that were conducting a fighter sweep. Those aircraft presented no threat to the missile batteries, but there was no way of knowing that from the ground. Unable to distinguish between a fighter sweep and an incoming ground attack, the battery hurled MIM-23 missiles at the Floggers.

The flight of MiG-23s were alerted to the incoming attack as alarms sounded in the cockpits of each of the fighters that was targeted. The formation immediately broke up, with each plane taking evasive actions to try and break the lock of the incoming missiles. Missiles rushed at the Soviet fighters, and the fighters danced to avoid them, spitting out aluminum chaff bundles and pulling tight, high-g maneuvers. In the end, three of the MiGs were destroyed, with the remaining five evading to the north, away from Giebelstadt.

The immediate effect of this encounter was to put several of the Hawk launchers out of position to defend against the second set of attacking aircraft. The incoming Su-17 attack planes popped up from their extreme low-altitude approach and loosed their Kh-25MR antiradiation missiles. With four of the five Hawk batteries still rearming from the attack on the MiG-23s, the easternmost battery was unable to overcome the incoming swarm. The launcher and associated radar facilities were destroyed, but the air-defense network protecting Giebelstadt remained robust. While the Fitters ran home to the east, the air over the drop zone remained incredibly hot.

With time running out for the operation, the last remaining flight of attack planes was closing on the airfield. These were the MiG-23s of the 85th Fighter Regiment. Instead of the standoff guided missiles that were used by the dedicated attack planes, the MiGs were loaded with unguided general-purpose bombs. They had been intended for use against any base defenders to soften them up for the VDV troops, but now they were being pressed into service against the missile launchers.

Major Bogdanov could see that the search and fire control radars were still active near the airfield. Even worse, the enemy had managed to vector fighter cover to the airspace west of Nuremberg. At this rate, two NATO F-4 Phantoms would be in position to intercept the incoming flight of Il-76s. If that were to happen, it would be a massacre. With a full load of missiles and 20mm cannon rounds, those two planes could take out ten to twenty of the transports. Knowing that it would probably cost him his life, the God of Speed pointed his MiG at the enemy fighters and advanced the throttle.

As *Germes* flew at the enemy, the MiG-23s overflew the air base. They were greeted by MIM-23 missiles from the Hawk launchers.

The missiles struck incoming attackers, depleting their numbers as they advanced. The surviving MiGs passed over, and each released eight FAB-100M bombs. The bombs scattered across the platoon of three SAM launchers. Two of the three were destroyed, and the MiGs extended to the south to get some distance before turning back for East Germany. As with the previous attacks, the SAM launchers reached out to swat at the Soviets after the drop. By the time the 85th Fighter Regiment had cleared the coverage area, only a single MiG-23 remained. With the loss of two Hawk launchers, NATO still had seven defending the field.

NATO air defenses had dissected the airspace over the battlefield and divided it between SAM defense and combat air patrols. The concept was to keep NATO forces from getting shot down by their own SAM batteries. In the fury of battle, there would be no time to distinguish friend from foe. At least, not with any reliability. The Soviets were aware of this tactic, and they were trying to exploit it. They could make out the basic SAM zones based on the ELINT information coming in from the reconnaissance Foxbats. Now the ground controllers were trying to vector the Il-76 transports along the edge of the SAM zone, to try and keep the NATO fighters at bay.

Germes pointed the nose of his MiG down to gain additional speed and to put him at the same altitude as the NATO fighters. The Phantoms, seeing the MiG bolting right for them, broke off their run and turned to engage what they thought was an enemy interceptor. As the Foxbat blew past them, they kicked on their afterburners to give chase. If they were lucky, they could get a trailing missile shot as Bogdanov banked to the west, away from the transports.

There was no way the Phantoms could hope to catch the Foxbat. Bogdanov was aware of this, but he was also aware that they didn't need to. His mount could outrun any plane on the battlefield today, but it couldn't outrun the AIM-7 Sparrow missiles that the Phantoms were carrying. His only hope was to put himself far enough away from them that by the time they got a lock on his aircraft, he'd be too far away for them to bother with. He knew that the only way that would happen was if something distracted the Phantoms, as he had distracted them from the Il-76s. He also knew there was no hope of that.

Bogdanov's radar warning went off, telling him that his number had come up. There were two AIM-7 Sparrows trailing his Foxbat at four times the speed of sound. Running all out, Bogdanov engaged his emergency throttle levels. His plane pushed past Mach 3. At this point, he was aware that even if he made it back to base, his engines wouldn't survive. His speed increased, and with every second, he flew further into NATO-controlled airspace.

The missiles were covering nearly a mile every second. And each second they gained 175 meters on the fleeing Foxbat. Bogdanov could feel the aircraft straining under the thrust as he squeezed every last bit of speed out of her.

The alarm continued to blare, telling him what he already knew: time was running out. The Sparrows were closing. Within seconds, they would detonate and take out the rear of Bogdanov's plane. He braced for the explosion, and his left hand drifted from the throttle to the handle of his ejection seat.

Then, as quickly as it had started, the alarm stopped barking at him. Behind him, first one, then the other Sparrow ran out of fuel and fell from the sky. Though he couldn't outrun them, he'd managed to outlast them.

Germes had lost sight of the Phantoms that were hunting him, but he wasn't worried about them now. Instead, he was fully focused on trying to get his MiG-25 back to Merseburg. He banked the plane to the right and made a gradual turn to the northeast. He assessed his instruments and came to the unfortunate conclusion that his route home would take him right over Giebelstadt. From what he could see, Giebelstadt had been the target of the airborne assault. The Il-76 transports were turning back for Czechoslovakia, and every enemy plane in the sky was looking to get some payback on them.

****

On board the Il-76, Misha was only aware of the battle raging around him in the abstract. He knew that the VVS would send fighters and attack aircraft ahead of the Desantniks. He knew the Americans would send fighters to destroy them. He knew vaguely that there would be a duel between the attackers and defensive missile batteries. He tried to keep the thoughts of that battle out of his mind. There was nothing that he could do about it. Instead, he reviewed his tasks, and the tasks of his men.

The first men of his platoon to hit the ground would be Taras and Tisha. They would take the "Devil's Taxi" to the battlefield, being air-dropped while sitting in the BMD. Parachutes would slow the vehicle, and when it approached the ground, retrorockets would fire to slow the descent even more. Any failure of the chutes or the rockets would spell doom for the two men. Misha hated the thought of riding a coffin into the ground. If the chutes failed, Taras and Tisha's contribution to the battle would be an impact crater and smoking debris.

After Taras and the regiment's heavy equipment had dropped, the rest of the men in the regiment would drop. Misha's priority was to get the four other men of his squad rallied together so they could set out to find their BMD. Of all the men, his most junior trooper would be the most important to track down. Private Novikov had possession of the squad's search receiver, which would lead the squad to the BMD.

Once the squad mounted up, Misha would get on the radio to receive orders. Depending on how many defenders there were, and where the various companies had landed, he would either be assaulting the airfield or setting up a defense. If he were a betting man, Misha would lay money on the former. He and his platoon would assault the airfield at Giebelstadt and destroy all of the NATO defenders.

The transport plane suddenly dropped altitude and banked to the left. This wasn't the normal turbulence that Misha expected during transits. No, this was the beginning of the end of his flight. Maybe they'd be shot down, maybe they'd make the drop. One way or the other, Misha and First Squad would be on the ground in a matter of minutes.

The flight of Il-76s approached the airfield without knowing how much damage the attackers had dealt the air defenses. The sudden appearance of incoming SAMs gave them the answer: not nearly enough. Hawk missiles streaked up toward the massive formation of forty-five transports. Knowing that they would never make it to the primary drop point, the pilots were turning for an alternative drop point that the commanders had selected for this exact contingency.

During the turn, a Hawk missile connected with the fuselage of the northernmost aircraft before exploding. The transport split in two with each half falling to the earth, taking the crew and the six men in their BMDs with them.

The 175th Military Transport Aviation Regiment completed the turn and started the drop. Two more of the Il-76s fell to the incoming

SAMs before they could get their cargo released. As the men dropped following their heavy equipment, a SAM blew the wing off another transport. The plane spiraled toward the earth while men still scrambled to get out before the centrifugal force pinned them to the bulkhead. The sky filled with white bouquets and the Desantniks of the 345th Independent Parachute Regiment floated to the ground.

With chaos surrounding them, Misha yelled to his men to focus only on the compartment, the drop sergeant, and the drop light. Misha hadn't pissed himself, but he knew that several of the men had. Their bodies had engaged the "fight or flight" reflex, where their subconscious brains told their bodies that they didn't need to expend any energy holding on to liquid waste. This just added to the sense of terror that accompanied their first opposed drop.

The one hundred and twenty-five paratroopers had rehearsed this action many times. They had worked it out on the ground, using benches and chalk outlines. They had rehearsed it from the aircraft while stationary on the runway. They had even practiced twice at altitude in a moving aircraft. None of that could fully prepare them for today.

There were three points of egress from the aircraft: two side hatches, forward of the wings, and the rear cargo ramp. In the front of the plane, the drop light changed from amber to green. Troopers poured out of both hatches and into the night sky. A static line opened their chutes as soon as they were clear of the airframe.

While the men at the front of the plane were jumping, Misha watched the rear jump light change from red to amber. The massive cargo ramp lowered, letting the cold air whip into the cramped compartment. Misha and his fifty closest friends stood and waited for the light to turn green. Once the last of the troops had cleared from the front hatches, the light switched to green, and the left side of the rear compartment began their long walk down a short ramp. Misha waited patiently.

His was the last column to leave the aircraft. With each waiting second, he could feel panic rising in him. Each second was one more second that something could go wrong. Each second meant a missile could swat the plane from the sky. His need to get off the plane was building. It took all of his training and discipline to keep him steady and ready.

At last, he could see the last man leave the left column and he felt the jostle as his column began its advance. Finally, when he thought he couldn't take it any longer, he stepped off the edge of the ramp and into the darkness. He felt the drop as he left the ramp and was almost immediately snapped back as his chute deployed.

Hanging from his harness beneath his open chute, Misha could see more of the transports being shot down by missiles, the glow of the fires illuminating the falling debris. In the distance, he could see the fiery jet exhaust of more aircraft to the west. For the sake of the transports, he hoped that they were friendly, but he had bigger things to worry about as the ground rushed up to greet him.

Chapter 2

1 January 1981
Soviet Battle Cruiser *Kirov*
450 Miles Northeast of São Miguel
Atlantic Ocean

The vastness of the dark ocean spread out in front of Captain of the First Rank Fyodor Mikhailovich Serebrov. Looking forward, he could see nothing but the blackness of the ocean at night. The vast emptiness suddenly felt quite small as he thought about his mission. A mission for which he was about to reach the point of no return. He looked to the port side of the ship, where the Soviet destroyer *Odarennyy*, a Kashin-class destroyer, launched her Ka-25 ASW helicopter. He returned his gaze forward as he addressed his executive officer, Captain of the Second Rank Grigoriy "Grisha" Vasin.

"How long do you think it will take for them to get a solid fix?"

"If our exercises are anything to go by," replied Grisha, "we'll have a firing solution on the American within the hour."

Now it was time for the waiting. Waiting for the helicopter and two frigates to locate and destroy the American submarine that had been shadowing the task force. Once that was accomplished, *Kirov* would take her leave from the escorts. While the destroyer and two frigates would make a dash for Angola, *Kirov* would turn into the heart of the Atlantic to become a thorn in the side of the American forces trying to get to Europe. The escorts didn't have the endurance to remain on station. The *Kirov*, with her two nuclear reactors (in addition to two gas turbines) could loiter in the ocean for weeks. She would run out of food before she would run out of fuel.

Kirov was a tiny speck on that vast ocean. With satellites, aircraft, submarines, and other surface ships, Captain Serebrov didn't think that he would be able to hide out for long. But that was his mission. To occupy as much of the Americans' attention as possible to help pull resources away from their escort duties. *Kirov* had been designed from the start to be able to operate independently, and this mission would be the ultimate test of that design philosophy.

Kirov had a state-of-the-art S-300 air-defense system. This was easily the best SAM system in the world. This would provide *Kirov* with a shield against incoming aircraft or missiles. His Ka-25 ASW helicopter working in coordination with hull-mounted and towed sonar arrays would protect him against enemy submarines. And best of all, the latest antiship cruise missiles, the mighty P-700 Granit, would deal with any surface vessels he came across. *Kirov* was the most powerful ship in commission. The American *Virginia*-class cruisers were a shadow in his presence.

When Serebrov had first received these orders, the whole mission concept had reminded him of Operation Rheinübung from the Great Patriotic War. In that operation, the Germans sent the battleship *Bismarck* into the Atlantic with orders to find and sink enemy commerce. In response, the Royal Navy mobilized every available asset to search for and destroy the German battleship. By the time the British sank the *Bismarck*, they had deployed one aircraft carrier, four battleships, four cruisers, and seven destroyers. Yet, even with all of that firepower being drained from other areas, the raid didn't achieve any meaningful results. It didn't sink any commerce, and there was no increase in the effectiveness of submarine attacks along the convoy routes.

There was a lesson to be learned here, and we seem to have learned the opposite, thought Serebrov.

After twenty minutes of waiting, they were interrupted by the radioman.

"Sir, the *Odarennyy* reports a faint contact. They are prosecuting."

"Very well, Starshina Khalturin," replied the captain. He knew that this was just the beginning of the process. After a moment, he continued, "Khalturin, does the enemy submarine show any indication that they know they are being hunted?" There was a pause as Khalturin passed the question to the destroyer and awaited a response.

"Negative, sir, the contact is continuing on course, with no change in aspect or behavior." Antisubmarine warfare (ASW) was paradoxically exhilarating and boring at the same time. The process was slow and methodical, which caused a certain apathy. The life-and-death stakes, on the other hand, kept one from being too casual about the affair.

Here in the middle of the Atlantic, Captain Serebrov had no idea what orders the American submarine had. If word of the imminent Soviet invasion had reached the Americans, the attack submarine might be attempting to gain a firing solution on the *Kirov*. They could very well be in a fight for their lives, without even knowing it. Another twenty minutes passed before Khalturin interrupted his thoughts again.

"Sir, they are about to go active."

Up to this point, the Soviet hunters had been relying on the passive mode of the Oka-2 dipping sonar on board the Ka-25 to listen for the submarine. From the faint contact they'd first found, they had narrowed the location of the trailing sub using passive sonobuoys. To get a solid firing solution, the helo was about to go active with their dipping sonar. This would ensure that the American submarine would know that they were being prosecuted. Of course, the submarine might already be aware, having heard the hovering Ka-25, or the splashes of the sonobuoys, but once the chopper pinged them with the active sonar, there would be no remaining doubt.

From the bridge of the *Kirov*, Captain Serebrov couldn't hear the actual ping, but he could see the result of it. The night was shattered by a burst of orange fire to the port side as one of the Krivak frigates fired a URPK-3 missile. The solid rocket motor would deliver a UGMT-1 torpedo to the location of the submarine pinpointed by the Ka-25. At the same time, the helicopter was dropping its own torpedo.

"*Odarennyy* reports that the American has performed a crash dive and has started a rapid acceleration," said Starshina Khalturin.

I bet they have, thought Serebrov. *Right now they are so focused on their self-preservation, they won't be able to attack us. If we don't manage to sink them with this opening move, things might get very tricky.*

"Helmsman, come to two-seven-zero, and go to flank speed," said the captain, heading due west and putting as much distance between himself and the embattled American as he could. The escorts would continue to prosecute the sub, then head for Africa and the protection of friendly air power. With that detail attended to, *Kirov* began her hunt in the Atlantic.

****

1 January 1981
Polish 20th Armored Division
10 Miles East of Meiningen

The Hussars of the Polish 20th Armored Division had established their position on the east side of the inner-German border. They had started this deployment a month ago and were standing on the line in place of the Soviet 79th Guards Tank Division, which had been pulled back to the Polish-German border. Of all the non-Soviet Warsaw Pact forces, the Polish were the most highly trained. The Hussars were the elite of those Polish forces. Even so, they had no idea how important their role would be in the coming days.

"I don't care what he says about representing the workers, Lech Wałęsa is a traitor to the state and should be shot," said Senior Sergeant Alfons Knopik, the tank commander of this T-55A tank. "If he were here, I'd shoot him myself."

"You don't have to be so bold, Sergeant. There isn't a party official within a hundred yards of the tank," replied his gunner, Corporal Bronisław Kohutek.

"Bah. I'm not just repeating the party line. I mean it," replied the sergeant. "Wałęsa is putting *his* workers ahead of the rest of *our* people. Why do they deserve special treatment? Because they are skilled laborers? Let's see that goat fight this tank."

"You're making too much of this, my friend. This whole Solidarność business will be over long before we return home from our deployment." The two men had been crewing the same tank for over a year now. They were the senior members of the crew, which also comprised Privates Leon Dębiński and Grzegorz Adamiak, the driver and loader, respectively.

"My uncle Aleks works at the Lenin Shipyard," said Dębiński. "He said that conditions there were fine. He never complained."

"See, there is a Polish citizen? A man of the people. Keep him in mind, young Dębiński, there's a role model for you." Before the conversation could continue, there was a rapping on the turret. Sergeant Knopik popped open his hatch and looked down at the private who had summoned him.

"Sergeant, the lieutenant has passed the word to load the Kastet and get the tank started." Knopik gave the soldier a nod and the young man ran down the line to the next tank. The sergeant slid back down into the tank and looked over to Adamiak. "Private, load a Kastet," he said, then to his driver, "Dębiński, begin the start-up." He looked to his gunner. "Something is afoot, Borna." It was unusual for the unit to keep

20

a round in the gun. The negative outcome of a negligent discharge far outweighed any benefit of having a gun "hot."

"It all makes sense, Comrade Sergeant," replied the corporal. "They never would have given us those new missiles if they didn't expect us to use them." The unit had been outfitted with brand-new 9M117 "Kastet" missiles, which could be fired from their main 100mm cannon. They had spent the better part of the last two weeks integrating the weapons system which had originally been intended for their Czechoslovakian counterparts.

"You can't be serious. The lieutenant is just running us through the paces to make sure we're all paying attention," said Knopik. "Hopefully he'll at least let the engines run long enough to heat up this coffin," he added, patting the metal skin of the tank. The temperature had just dipped under freezing.

After ten minutes, the engine was heating up and they were just getting some warmth inside when the R-123 radio crackled to life.

"This is Crusader Two-One to all Crusader Two units. Form a staggered column on me, heading two-six-five."

There was silence in the tank as everyone processed the order. Then, after that brief hesitation, Knopik ordered, "Driver, course two-six-five, form up on the lieutenant."

The tank jerked as Dębiński made a stationary turn to the course heading and then advanced the throttle to follow the lieutenant's tank. Knopik stood and extended through his hatch and was amazed to see the entire company in motion, forming up by platoon. He looked to his driver. "Dębiński, once you have the lieutenant, we need to button up. If we remain on this heading, it won't be long before the shooting starts."

Dębiński nodded, and Knopik dropped down and slammed his hatch shut.

"OK, men, I don't know what's going on any more than you do. But we must assume the best-case scenario is that we've been chosen to drive the fascists out of Germany," Knopik said with a bravado that he didn't feel. The men could sense it. "But we are the best unit in the People's Polish Army, and we will make an account of our presence on the battlefield. Our fathers killed fascists forty years ago, and now we have our chance. Our fathers and uncles never had a mount like this"— he again slapped the steel skin of the T-55—"and the enemy will feel the wrath of the Hussars!"

With his men whipped up, he continued, "Borna, what can we expect from NATO?"

His gunner responded without hesitation. "They'll have dismounted cavalry at the border. Maybe a few armor units like their Sheridan light tanks. Unless they are expecting us. Then they will meet us with massed M60 tanks. If we hit a German unit, it'll be mostly the same, but with the Leopard or M48 tanks in place of the M60s. Either way, the real danger will be from their antitank missiles."

"Since the lieutenant ordered us to load the Kastet," said Sergeant Knopik, "we need to focus on identifying enemy armor. I don't want to waste that missile on one of those APCs they shuttle around in."

"Understood, Comrade Sergeant."

Traveling from the outskirts of Meiningen to the southwest at top speed, the Polish 20th Armored Division crossed into NATO territory at the Meiningen/Eußenhausen road crossing. Artillery had destroyed the western border guard post long before Knopik's tank crossed over. From his limited view inside the tank, he could see the fiery wreckage that remained of the building and wondered how far forward the protective artillery could reach. In the very limited periphery from his view port, he could also see incoming and outgoing fire from the head of the line. Streaks of red illuminated the valley as missiles crossed paths. Explosions along the hills marked the end of defensive units.

"Keep your eyes wide, Borna," said the sergeant. "Once we fire the Kastet, we'll load M8s, and keep loading M8s until I say otherwise. I expect us to be engaging armor all night long." The 3BM8 projectile was a hypervelocity armor-piercing discarding-sabot round. Of all the rounds the Hussars were carrying, this one had the best chance of penetrating the front armor of the American M60 Patton tanks. Sergeant Knopik knew that he'd rather fire an antitank round at a concentrated infantry position than be stuck with a high-explosive round when he needed to punch through a tank.

The radio boomed to life above the sound of the tank engine. "We have contact, two hundred twenty degrees. Multiple tanks!"

Without hesitating, Borna rotated the turret to the right. "I have them," said the gunner.

"Fire!" ordered Knopik.

The Kastet missile shot out of the main gun and headed toward the concentration of German M48s. The Americans were focused further up the line, and the Polish missile caught one completely unaware. The warhead penetrated the side armor, and Knopik watched in awe as the turret exploded into the sky.

"Load M8!" said the tank commander.

"M8, understood," replied Private Adamiak, the loader.

"Borna," said Knopik, "keep putting rounds into those tanks until they are destroyed."

"Understood, Sergeant," replied the gunner.

After two more rounds, and many more from the rest of the platoon, the M48s had had enough.

"Sergeant, the enemy is withdrawing. They have dropped into the valley to the southwest."

"I see that. Keep your eyes wide for any additional targets. It's going to be a long war." Having survived the crossing had given Sergeant Knopik the slightest of hopes that they might survive the night.

Chapter 3

1 January 1981
White House
Washington, D.C.

"Mr. President, we have to move! Now!"

President Jimmy Carter was awoken from a sound sleep to the yelling of his security detail. He hadn't quite oriented himself before he felt the arms of his Secret Servicemen pulling him from his bed and setting him upright on the floor. As two men hurried the President out of the room, a pair remained behind, collecting clothes and sundry items from the bedroom. They would reunite the President and his belongings once they reached the Presidential Emergency Operations Center, a bunker under the East Wing of the White House.

"What's happening?" asked the President, catching up to reality.

"There's an emergency in Europe. The NSC is assembling to brief you, sir."

"And what about Rosa?" asked Carter.

"She's being taken to a separate bunker. Once we have a feel for things, I'm sure you'll see her again." The men scrambled downstairs, going from the second floor to the state floor, then on through the ground floor and into the basement. The President was now fully awake and aware.

"Do you have any information on the emergency?" asked the President.

"Negative, sir, this is all just coming together now. If I had stayed around long enough to find out, I wouldn't have been doing my job."

"I see," replied Carter. "That makes sense." The three men entered the Presidential Emergency Operations Center.

"Mr. President, I have a representative from SACEUR on the line," said an aide, handing the President a phone receiver.

"Why isn't General Rogers on the line?"

"General Rogers is dead, sir."

Carter's heart sank. Rogers's predecessor, General Alexander Haig, had survived an assassination attempt a year and a half ago, but the idea that the Supreme Allied Commander, Europe, was dead seemed unreal.

"This is the President."

"Mr. President, this is Brigadier General Frederick Willis. At 0650 local time, massed tank formations of the Soviet, East German, Polish and Czechoslovakian armies crossed into West Germany. Soviet and Warsaw Pact air forces have also conducted massive air operations over the country. There have been tremendous losses on both sides." The blood drained from Carter's face.

"Who's in charge over there?" asked the President.

"There is a lot of chaos out here, sir. East German Diensteinheit IX and Soviet Spetsnaz operatives infiltrated the city and have been killing off leadership. General Rogers is dead, sir. He was one of the first targets."

"Yes, I heard. What else do I need to know?"

"Sir, we have intelligence that indicates the Poles, the Czechoslovakians, the Romanians... Hell, the entire Warsaw Pact is involved. Pact forces are even moving through Austria, in violation of Austrian neutrality."

"Is there any good news, General?" asked the President.

"We have seen no indication of the use of chemical, biological or nuclear weapons. Other than that, it's all bad news today, sir."

"General, I need you to fight this war. We'll keep the lines of communication open, but for now we both have a job to do. God protect you, General."

"Thank you, sir, may God protect us all," replied General Willis.

Carter felt like he was finally catching up with the situation, but the horror of it all was still just too great for him to fully conceptualize.

"Sir, the NSC is ready for you," said a blurry-eyed Hamilton Jordan. Carter turned to see the members of his National Security Council seated at the table, waiting patiently to begin the meeting. Carter sat at the head of the oval table and looked to Zbigniew Brzezinski.

"Zbig, give it to me straight. What are we looking at?" asked the President.

"Mr. President, we are at war. This morning, Warsaw Pact Troops crossed into West Germany along the length of the inner-German border, as well as Czechoslovakia and Poland. We have lost contact with the Berlin Brigade, but we anticipate establishing contact with them in the near term."

"I don't understand," said the President. "If the Soviets overrun them, how are we going to get in contact with them?"

"Mr. President, in accordance with our defense of Germany plans, Detachment A of the Special Forces in West Berlin will go underground and begin guerrilla operations against the Soviet occupation. This will give us insight into the situation behind enemy lines, as well as disrupting Soviet operations in the city and surrounding countryside."

"I see," said the President before Brzezinski continued.

"Our latest intelligence indicates that the Soviets are moving with a slower pace of action than we expected. This is likely due to the use of older, slower units on the frontier. As you recall, the Soviets made a big show of moving their premier units off the line prior to the attack. The Poles and Czechoslovakians who are spearheading the attack are not nearly as proficient as the crack Soviet units they replaced."

"I suppose that counts as good news," said Carter. "What about the situation in the air?"

"Sir, I can speak to that," said Harold Brown, the Secretary of Defense. "The initial onslaught was brutal. The Soviets had the advantage of choosing the when and the where, so we were caught flat-footed. Our air-defense systems blunted their attack, but many of the positions on the frontier were overwhelmed by sheer numbers. We could only fire so many missiles, and there were some indications that the Soviets sent in Polish and Czechoslovakian fighter squadrons as bait to get us to commit our missiles and show our positions before committing their crack units. That last is unconfirmed, sir, but I have high confidence in the assessment."

"And at sea?" asked Carter.

"From what we can make out, the Soviets have sortied most of their submarine fleet. Even the older Foxtrot-class diesel boats are making a dash at the GIUK gap—"

"Excuse me," interrupted the President, "the what?"

"Sir, the Greenland, Iceland, United Kingdom Gap. It's the Soviet front door to the Atlantic Ocean. Every NATO Navy is currently attempting to intercept them."

"And the Soviet surface fleet?"

The question caused Secretary Brown to lower his gaze and look to Robert J. Hermann, the Director of the National Reconnaissance Office, who spoke up.

"Sir, we were tracking a surface action group, out near the Azores. We had the USS *Batfish* trailing them, but we've lost contact. More concerning, we have lost contact with our KENNEN satellites."

"I'm sorry, Mr. Hermann, what exactly does this mean?"

"The KH-11 KENNEN satellites were the only satellites capable of giving us real-time imagery. These were instrumental in keeping Soviet maritime moves under surveillance. As of this morning, we don't have contact with those assets."

"Mr. President," interrupted CIA Director Stansfield Turner, "we have a working theory on this." The President nodded for Turner to continue. "The Soviets have been working on a 'killer satellite.' It's a fairly harmless-looking orbital vehicle that's packed with explosives. They'll maneuver the satellite near one of ours and detonate it, destroying both. It's a crude but apparently effective system."

"Surely we've deployed our own killer satellites to counter their spy satellites?" asked the President. There was silence for a second before Secretary Brown spoke up.

"Sir, we don't currently have an antisatellite weapons program. Our previous operation programs were all nuclear-based. The last of those came off-line three years ago. We had some theoretical programs based on lasers, but with our funding shifts to more conventional projects like the XM-1 tank, the Aegis cruisers, and the MX missile... it just wasn't a priority."

"So, we're blind. What does that mean for today?"

"Sir, it means that we've lost track of that Soviet SAG. They could be operating in anywhere in the North or Central Atlantic Ocean."

"I see," said the President. "I'm sure Admiral Hayward and his men will put together a plan to address that. What about our allies?"

Harold Brown took the question. "The British Army of the Rhine along with the rest of the Northern Army Group are just as engaged as we are. They're also being pushed west, just like our units in the Central Army Group. We expect the line to settle after this initial thrust, but we're not sure how far the Pact forces will make it. The rest of the NATO states have begun mobilizations, but it's going to take time for those units to get to the front. Oh, and we haven't heard from the

French yet. That's not too surprising since they aren't a part of the joint NATO command structure. However, we anticipate that they'll be mobilizing as well."

"What about outside of Europe?" asked the President.

"Our forces in Nicaragua haven't noticed any unusual activity. The 101st Airborne has secured Estelí and is pushing south, while the Marine Corps is driving toward Managua from their beachhead in Corinto. Pockets of resistance are being dealt with, but the locals don't have an appetite for the fight. We have the voice of America down there blasting the airwaves with the story of Soviet betrayal.

"In the Middle East, fighting has broken out between the Soviet Naval Infantry Brigade on the Caspian coast and the 82nd Airborne. This was clearly coordinated with the Iraqis, who are making a renewed push in Southern Iran. The Soviets are outmanned there, so unless they reinforce those Marines, I can't see how they'll achieve anything of tactical or strategic interest."

"You mean, other than tying down the 82nd Airborne Division?" asked the President. "That seems to be of significant tactical and strategic interests."

"Yes, sir. That's true," replied Secretary Brown.

"What about the Pacific?" asked Carter.

"The Soviet surface fleet is still in port at Vladivostok, but the submarine pens in Petropavlovsk are mostly empty. It looks like they've sent a massed sortie of their nuclear attack submarines. Our best evidence suggests that they're going to stay on the defensive out there. We think they're trying to keep Japan out of the conflict."

"What about their treaty obligations?" asked the President.

"Sir, if the Soviets don't attack our facilities in Japan, there is no treaty obligation under the Treaty of Mutual Cooperation and Security."

President Carter furrowed his brow at this news.

"Mr. President," said Secretary of State Jeane Kirkpatrick, "we have our diplomats in Japan pressing the Japanese for a commitment, but we haven't gotten far. It's still early, but we'll keep the pressure on them."

"Thank you, Madam Secretary."

"On the Korean Peninsula," said Secretary Brown, continuing with the run-down, "there hasn't been any activity. Our sources in-country believe that the North Koreans were as surprised as we were. This was likely due to the Soviets not trusting the North Koreans to keep a secret, as best we can tell. Lastly, there hasn't been any movement of forces between Pakistan and India. We don't anticipate Pakistan making a move, what with India holding the nuclear sword over their head."

"The long and the short of it, Mr. President," said Brzezinski, "is that we must focus on the war in Europe. I recommend that we look for solutions in Iran and Nicaragua to get our units disengaged so that we can redeploy them to Europe. This will go a long way to assuring our NATO partners that we are fully committed."

"With respect to Dr. Brzezinski," said Secretary Kirkpatrick, "if we leave our business in Nicaragua unfinished, there's every reason to believe that we'll have an even worse situation waiting for us after this war in Europe."

"Thank you for your insight," said the President.

"If we don't secure NATO's position in Europe, we'll have much more to worry about than Latin American communism," said Brzezinski.

Kirkpatrick started to respond, but the President held up his hand.

The President said, "I understand the situation. You will have time to continue this argument in the future, but right now, I need to contact my counterpart in each of the NATO countries, then we'll expand to our allies. Dr. Kirkpatrick, we'll start with Prime Minister Thatcher, then work our way through the rest. Please, give me a brief on anything I need to know before we make that call." With that, the National Security Team started the process of catching up to events as they unfolded.

Chapter 4

1 January 1981
21st Special Air Service Regiment
Lübeck, West Germany

Trooper Trevor Pearce looked at his cards. The king of diamonds and the two of hearts. Corporal Willis, the dealer, was showing the five of spades. It was a no-brainer.

"Oi, I'll twist," said Pearce. He looked at the card and tossed the other two on the table with disgust. "Bullocks!" The ten of clubs caused him to bust, and play moved down the line. Lance Corporal Cooper stood fast while Trooper Baker twisted a card. Play moved to Willis. He flipped his down card over, showing the queen of spades, giving him a total of fifteen. He twisted another card and drew the ace of diamonds. He sighed, twisting another card. The king of clubs busted Willis.

"Shit," said Willis, tossing his cards down. Cooper and Baker turned their cards over. Baker had managed to hit twenty-one, while Cooper had a respectable eighteen.

"All right, hand 'em over," said Baker as Willis paid out both him and Cooper.

"Pearce," said Cooper, "what happened with that blonde German number you slipped out with last weekend?"

"What do you think happened?" replied Pearce. There was something about Trooper Trevor Pearce that the local women found irresistible. He had a charm that none of his squadmates could define, but every one of them envied. Pearce himself believed that it had a lot to do with his natural confidence, a trait shared by anyone who managed to get into 21 SAS, and his fluency in Holsteinisch, the German dialect spoken in Lübeck.

"Oh, I can just imagine," said Cooper.

"And that's all you'll have," replied Pearce, "an active imagination." The other men of the squad laughed at Cooper's expense.

"The next time Coop gets a shag in," said Baker, "he'll be thinking about Pearce boffing that blonde the whole time." More laughter erupted.

Wanting to change the conversation away from his love life, Pearce asked, "Willis, how's the family back home?" The corporal's wife and six-year-old son were back in Leeds while Willis served out his contract in Germany.

"They're good," said Willis. "Henry likes his new school… Well, as much as Henry's going to like any school, that is."

"A chip off the old block, then?" said Pearce.

"More than you know," replied Willis, chuckling. "Lara's going after it with my mum, but that's nothing new. Those two will be fighting their own kerfuffle while the world's ending. But it's good."

"What are you going to do when you get out?" asked Baker.

"My old man got me on at the Meltog plant in the Southeast."

"What the hell is a Meltog?" asked Cooper.

"Thank you for asking," laughed Willis. "Ahem." He cleared his throat before breaking into what was clearly the backside of a company flier. "Meltog Manufacturing produces high-Quality metal packaging machinery as well as both filter tube manufacturing machinery and a range of industrial shredders."

"And that," said Cooper, "is what you've chosen to do, instead of going on further adventures with this lot?"

"Don't take this personally, lads. I just need to spend more time with the family. I've had the time of my life up to this point, but I know what it's like to grow up without a father around and I don't want that for Henry."

"Hey, are you arseholes playing or what?" asked Baker, sensing the discomfort creeping into the conversation as it brushed too close to Willis's personal life. Willis smiled and started dealing out the next hand. Pearce looked at his first card. The three of clubs. He dropped a thirty-pence bet, the lowest bet allowed in today's game. Cooper looked and bet three pounds, the maximum.

"Someone's looking at an ace," said Pearce.

Before Cooper could reply, Willis broke in, "Shhh. Shut it."

Everyone went quiet, straining to hear whatever had caused the corporal to halt the game. The faint sound of sirens echoed.

"Bloody hell," said Pearce as the troopers collected up their money and Willis gathered up the cards.

"All right, men," said Willis, "we've done this drill a hundred times. You get to the Rover with your kit, and I'll report to Captain Clarke for orders."

Pearce and the other two troopers headed out of the barracks and down to the motor pool, where they would get their Land Rover Series III ready for the drive into the wilderness south of town.

The role of 21st SAS was to take cover in underground "Military Engineering Experimental Establishments," or MEXE shelters, and await the coming Soviet war machine. When the Soviet forces reached them, they would do... nothing. 21 SAS would hide in their underground bunkers and let the Red Army storm right past them. They were what was referred to as a "Stay-Behind Unit," or SBU.

After the enemy passed them over, they would emerge from their hiding holes. They would be behind enemy lines and would conduct operations against the enemy's rear. Their missions ranged from rescuing downed airmen to assassinating enemy leadership and providing targeting coordinates for strategic targets like fuel and ammo depots. They would do all of this with no direct support from the Army, and limited support from local "Stay-Behind Organizations."

The men hit the motor pool and went through the vehicle checklist for their Land Rover. As they were wrapping that up, they heard a rumble in the distance.

"The hell?" asked Pearce. "Is that artillery?" The question was answered by the explosions lighting off in the surrounding area. Corporal Willis rejoined them right after the first of the rounds landed.

"Get in!" he shouted. "This ain't a drill!"

"No shit," said Cooper. "What was your first clue?" The men clambered into the Range Rover and joined the queue of other vehicles heading to the gate. With traffic building up, an enterprising squad in a Ferret armored car made a run at the fence, knocking it down and creating a second exit. Cooper turned the Rover and headed for the new exit.

Once clear of the fence, the squad sped to the south. There was a prearranged hiding spot for the Rover. They would dump the vehicle, then hike to their shelter about two klicks into the woods. As they drove, the sounds of artillery faded, but they never went away.

"I know it don't seem like it, but we're some lucky bastards," said Willis from the front passenger seat.

"How's that?" asked Cooper.

"Whatever is coming at us is running late. This attack started in the CENTAG half an hour ago. Units along the border in the south didn't get any warning. They were decimated on the ground before they even knew there was a war on."

"Good Lord," said Pearce. The situation was playing out so quickly. He'd been on autopilot from the time they'd heard the sirens until Willis had confirmed that they were at war. "I reckon this is the big one, innit?"

"It's big enough," replied Willis. "Just focus on your small part of it. There's nothing you can get by worrying about anything outside of our mission."

The drive to the drop point was uneventful. They watched as planes streaked across the sky. There were flashes in the distance as missiles found their targets. Those aircraft were all busy with other errands. None of them were concerned with a single Land Rover in the middle of the German countryside. They found the depression right where they knew it would be. As they had practiced countless times, they pulled the camouflage tarp from the boot and spread it over the Rover. While Willis and Cooper secured the tarp, Pearce and Baker gathered downed branches and foliage to help conceal it further.

With the Rover secured, Willis took the lead as the squad made their way into the forest. Any of the troopers could have found the MEXE shelter, but Willis was responsible for getting them there, and he wouldn't put that on anyone else. Within twenty minutes, Willis stopped short. Everyone knew that they'd reached their destination.

"Eh, Pearce, get the hatch, would you?" ordered Willis.

Pearce dutifully bent down and brushed at some of the dirt and leaves, exposing a small handle. He lifted, pulling the hatch out of the ground and exposing the hole that was the entrance to their new home. "All right, lads, let's get in and get comfortable." Pearce spent enough time in exercises to know that the first few hours would be the least oppressive.

The four men would share these cramped confines for at least the next few days and possibly weeks. Each day would add to the filth. Once command was sure that the Soviet and Warsaw Pact forces had overtaken them, they would ring them up with orders.

Pearce dropped in first. The shelter was dug down two and a half meters.

Once in the shelter, Pearce turned on his torch. He looked down the eight-meter main operations area and everything seemed in order. They had six weeks of food, a cache of weapons, and the radio equipment. He walked to the end of the main corridor, where two side tunnels formed a T, as the rest of the squad dropped in.

"Everyone get comfortable. It's going to be a while," said Willis. "It's not likely that Ivan's going to roll over the British Army of the Rhine so easily. Might as well get some rest."

In the darkness of their hole in the ground, the men of 21st SAS began their covert role in World War III.

Chapter 5

1 January 1981
82nd Airborne Division
Tehran, Iran

"Everybody up!" The sound was both familiar and unwelcome to Specialist Marlon Reeves. He and the rest of his squad scrambled out of their racks. This was not the usual start to the day. This felt like boot camp.

"What the hell's going on, Sarge?" asked Reeves.

"Get your gear and get into formation ASAP," said the patrol leader, Staff Sergeant Felix Watkins.

It was clear from his tone that Reeves wasn't going to get a sneak preview of what was happening. He scrambled to get everything he needed. It would be just his luck that'd he'd forget something and end up in Watkins's doghouse.

"Hey, Davis, give me a once-over," he said to PFC Sebastian Davis. The soldier looked over his comrade, going through a checklist of items.

"You're good, man," said Davis once he finished. "Now you do me."

Reeves repeated the process and slapped the private on the shoulder. The two of them jogged out of the room and out into the Persian night.

The whole company was forming up, and Reeves looked at his watch. *Dammit, I should still be asleep*, he thought. He saw Sergeant Herman Becker, the translator that was still attached to his squad. "Becker, what's the word?" asked Reeves.

"How should I know?" replied Becker. "I just crawled out of my rack same as you."

Reeves would just have to wait and see what the company commander had to say. It didn't take long for the company to assemble, and Captain Patrick Foster took his position front and center.

"Men, there's no use in beating around the bush. We are at war with the Soviet Union." There was no gasp, no reaction. Just men standing at attention.

But Reeves's heart leapt in his chest. He was at once excited by the prospect of battle and also worried. Up until yesterday, they'd been running joint foot patrols with Soviet Naval Infantry. Then, yesterday morning, they'd awoken to find the Soviets gone. Reeves and Watkins had even gone over to the Soviet outpost looking for them. They had just vanished.

Captain Foster gave the company the details he had on the invasion of Germany. Then he turned his focus to his unit and their mission.

"I'm not going to lie to you—this is not where I want to be right now. I want to be on the front lines, in Germany. But we don't get the missions we want. We get the missions that the Army needs. And today they need us to rid Iran of the Soviet presence here. Once we do that, we'll get our next mission. And we will complete that mission and take on the next. This is our life now, gentlemen. Division command staff is working on the puzzle, and as soon as they have orders, we'll be taking it to Ivan. The news from the German front is grim. Let's be sure that the 82nd Airborne Division gives America some good news." With that, he dismissed the formation.

"Holy shit, man," said Davis as the squad broke up and returned to the barracks.

"You can say that again," replied Reeves. "I never in a million years would have guessed that this would happen. I mean, we were working so well together. This whole 'peacekeeping' mission was really bringing our two sides together."

"We need to get that out of our heads, man," said Davis. "They're the enemy now, and we need to go find them and kill them."

"Amen, brother. Amen."

****

1 January 1981
Rama, Nicaragua

Carlos Rodriguez focused on the target. As he lined up the shot, he thought that he'd been out of the action too long. He lacked the confidence he'd once had. Back when he was at Camp Lejeune, this would have been routine, but if you don't train, your talents atrophied.

He knew that his men were counting on him. He had to make this shot count.

Sweat beaded on his forehead. He knew he was stalling. He had to take the shot.

Thunk. The dart missed its mark, landing on the 1 instead of the 20.

"Dammit, Carlos!" came the groans from his friends.

"Dude, that was twenty bucks!" said Sergeant Jimmy Mason. "When did you start sucking at darts?"

Pedro "El Tiburón" Gálvez scooped up a pile of money before saying, "We don't give your friend much time for fun and games." With that, he winked at Carlos.

"Oh, we play a lot of games," interjected Fred Poole, the head of the local CIA mission that was running a group of Contras against the Sandinista government and their Soviet partners. "They're just much more fun, and for much higher stakes." That made Pedro and Carlos laugh, while Mason and the other Marines at the table shared sideways glances. The Marines had been in-country for six weeks, but this was the first chance they'd had to take in some R&R. In fact, this evening at a local bar was more or less sponsored by the CIA, with Fred pulling some strings to make it happen. It was just past midnight, and things were really getting going.

"So, Carlos... What the hell are you doing out here?" asked Staff Sergeant Dominic Page, Carlos's former platoon sergeant. "The last time we saw you, you were clearing out your gear at Lejeune and taking some civvy job."

"What's the mystery, Dom?" replied Carlos. "This is that civvy job. I provide security services for Southern Air Transport Company. Sometimes that includes palling around with drug lords—"

"Retired drug lords," corrected Pedro.

"Excuse me, palling around with *retired* drug lords and shooting communists." Again, the Contra men laughed out loud and toasted each other while the Marines were still trying to make heads or tails out of it.

Carlos looked across the room, where Clara Gálvez sat at a table drinking a beer with some of Pedro's men. Clara was Pedro's niece, and a former member of the Sandinista People's Militia. It seemed like a million years ago that she had taken him prisoner and brought him to her uncle, which had started this cooperation between El Tiburón and the CIA. *I wonder how different this fight would be if we hadn't gotten into that first firefight*, Carlos thought.

"Whoa, whoa, whoa," said Page, catching Carlos's wistful expression. "What do we have here?" Carlos broke his gaze away from Clara. "Is Sergeant Carlos Rodriguez back in the game?"

"Dude, no. It's not like that," replied Carlos defensively. "That's Pedro's niece, Clara. She's not like any of the girls back home. She's pretty badass."

Fred, overhearing this, added, "Oh yeah, she's enough of a badass to capture this mean green former Marine."

"There are no 'former' Marines," said Carlos.

"Yeah, yeah, whatever, buddy," replied Fred.

"So, fellas," said Carlos, eager to change the topic, "how did the assault go down? I talked to a few of the guys in Lima Company, but things were still playing out and they had no idea what you were up to."

"It was pretty straightforward," said Page. "Jimmy and First Squad were with the LT and Headquarters. We didn't meet much resistance along the west side of the airfield. In fact, the only major action was your old squad."

"Yeah," interrupted Mason, not wanting to be left out of the conversation. "Second Squad ran into some heat taking a POL installation. They had to ride out a Sandi counterattack and Strickland caught hero disease." Carlos raised an eyebrow toward Page.

"It's true. Strickland had been catching hell since the Manz," said Page, referring to the battle of Manzariyeh, where Kilo Company had fought off a mixed force of Iranian fanatics.

"I remember," replied Carlos. "He was catching blame for a lot of the casualties out there. I really didn't think that was fair."

"It wasn't," said Page, "Leadership tried to put an end to it, but that just drove it underground. Anyhow, by the time we got here, Strickland was wound tight. I talked to Oliver in an off-the-record after-action briefing, and it seems that when Strickland's A-gunner was killed, he lost it. He took over the defense, and when his M60 was out of ammo, he just charged the enemy with his .45. From what Oliver says, he zonked two or three of the Sandis before they gunned him down."

"Damn, what a waste," said Carlos.

"I don't know," replied Page, "from the way everyone's telling the story, Strickland saved the operation. The captain's putting him in for a posthumous medal, but nobody can decide what it'll be. I bet they'll settle on a Bronze Star. And he earned it."

"Amen," said Carlos before raising his beer. "To Strickland!"

"To Strickland!" echoed everyone, even Pedro, who had no idea who Strickland was.

"You mentioned Oliver," said Carlos. "How the hell is that shitbird? I miss having him around."

"You wouldn't recognize him, man," replied Mason. "I don't know what Corporal Evans did, but Oliver is squared away. I've always figured he'd burn out, but he's starting to talk like a lifer."

"That's great to hear," replied Carlos. "I was worried after Mack bought it." Corporal Lionel Mack was Oliver's team leader who had been killed in Iran. "I thought he and Evans would come to blows at some—"

"Shhhh. Shut up," said Pedro. He turned to the bartender and said in Spanish, "Turn that up!" as he gestured to the radio in the corner. Carlos focused on the broadcast from the radio, which had been playing music up until the last minute or so.

"—itial reports are very broken. All that is known at this point is that there is fighting in West Germany. We have lost contact with our correspondent in East Berlin, who had been filing reports on the progress of the workers' manufacturing efforts in the German Democratic Republic. Western outlets are reporting fierce air and ground combat taking place along the inner-German border."

"Holy shit," said Carlos before noticing that everyone was staring at him. It took him a second to realize that none of his friends spoke Spanish. "Fred, we've got to get back to base. The local radio is reporting war in Europe. They don't know what's going on, but they're saying there's fighting breaking out between East and West Germany."

"Oh, shit!" said Page, standing up too quickly and knocking his barstool to the ground. "Mason, we need to get back to camp."

"I have a driver who can take you," said Pedro as he motioned to one of the other patrons in the bar. He spoke quietly to the man before turning back to the Marines. "Manuel will take you back. Please ensure that your sentries don't kill him." That last comment elicited a panicked look from Manuel. Pedro just winked at him.

Carlos stood and put an arm on Page's shoulder. "Take care of yourself, Dom. I don't know what's happening, but this may be goodbye."

"Oh, don't give me that crap, Carlos. You know that when this is all said and done, I'll see you in hell."

Chapter 6

1 January 1981
West of Giebelstadt, West Germany

Germes knew he was in trouble. Ever since his Mach 3 dash, he was flying on borrowed time. Now fate had come to collect. An alarm blared in the cockpit, alerting him to the rising heat in his left engine. The overstressed metal in one of the cooling components had failed, which set off a chain reaction that would inevitably lead to the failure of the engine.

Now *Germes* had to ride the fine line between easing off the throttle to try to keep the engine going and just pushing through to see how far he could get before the engine died. Every second took him closer to his side of safety.

Before he spent too much time dwelling on it, his Foxbat made the decision for him. With a terrible roar, his left engine failed. The metal tore itself apart and the continued flow of jet fuel added to the streak of fire that engulfed the rear of the aircraft.

Without thinking or hesitating, *Germes* yanked his ejection handles. The rocket motors activated, and the thrust pushed him deep into the seat as he blasted into the open night. The motor cut off, and the seat fell away, leaving *Germes* floating in a seemingly silent night. The wind still whipped, and there was still a battle underway, but after the sound of the exploding engine and the two rockets just a few hundred centimeters under his ass, the night was quite calm.

He looked around to get a feel for what he was dropping into. He could make out the airfield at Giebelstadt. He turned to his left, looking south, and could see the white pillows of silk carrying the last of the VDV paratroopers down to the battlefield.

Germes decided that if he should make it to the ground, he would take cover and try to link up with the attacking Soviet unit. With a little luck, he could catch a ride back to his base once the VDV began flying in supplies for the base.

****

South of Giebelstadt, West Germany

The drop had been uneventful for Misha. The drop zone was mostly farmland that sat empty in the late autumn. *If you land in a tree out here, you would have to be aiming for it*, he thought. He used the time spent in the air to go over the plan. *This is the southern alternate zone*, he thought. *There's a copse of trees just west of the village of Gaukönigshofen. That's First Platoon's rally point.*

He looked out over the landscape and could make out the lights of the village. *Lucky for us, they haven't thought to black out.*

He absorbed the impact of landing with his legs, then tucked into a roll. Once on the ground, he quickly gathered up his gear and scanned the area, looking for his men. In a lucky break, he ran down Private Novikov, who had been right behind him on the Il-76.

"Novikov, over here," called out Misha. "Quick, we need to get to the rally point, get the rest of the squad, then we can head out to find Taras and Tisha."

The young private nodded his understanding and broke into a run to keep up with his squad leader. It was a quick trip to the rally point, which was good because the same flat openness that had made this an ideal landing zone was now working against them as it provided very little cover or concealment. Others in the platoon had landed closer to the tree line, and were already assembling and preparing to set out for their vehicles.

In the distance, Misha could hear rifle fire. Novikov looked at him with concern.

"I think those are some dismounted elements that landed closer to the base. We need to get assembled and go relieve them before the fascists push them back." Misha then called out, "First Squad, assemble here." A murmur went through the paratroopers as the word was passed that First Squad's sergeant had arrived.

"Sergeant," said Private Andrei Koshelev, the squad's machine gunner.

"Congratulations on your safe landing, Andrusha," said Misha.

"I've got some bad news, Comrade Sergeant. Private Chernyavsky failed in his landing. He's down with a broken ankle." Misha shook his head.

"Even after all the training over the last six months? Where is he?"

"He's about a half a kilometer that way." Andrei pointed to the southwest. "I left him hiding in some bushes."

"All right." Misha turned to a senior sergeant who was assembling his own unit.

"Sergeant Pankin, please pass the word for a straggler. I've lost a private in the drop." The man nodded, and just like when Misha had called his squad to assemble, the word went through the grapevine. He turned back to his assembling squad and saw Corporal Rodya Shuldeshov shaking hands with Andrei. "Private Novikov, get the box."

Misha watched as Novikov took off his pack, opened it, and removed the radio receiver that would lead them to the BMD.

"Comrade Sergeant," said a private that Misha didn't recognize. "Private Starodubov from Second Platoon, Third Squad, reporting."

"Good timing, Private," said Misha. "Let's get to the tank!" Everyone turned to Novikov, who oriented the receiver and set off at a jog to the north. Misha looked across the battlefield, where other dismounted units were running across the open German fields. In addition to the chitter of rifle and machine-gun fire, Misha heard the booming report of the 73mm cannons on the BMDs.

Novikov led them to the outskirts of Gaukönigshofen, two miles from the objective. There, on the edge of town, were the platoon's three BMDs. All three had survived the drop. Misha climbed on top of his vehicle and banged on the command hatch.

The hatch popped open and Junior Sergeant Tisha Dezhnyov, the vehicle gunner, poked his head out and verified that it was Misha, and not some mixed-up vehicle commander from another squad.

"Welcome, Sergeant," said Tisha. Not even the war could quell his enthusiasm. "With the family all together, we shall kill fascists!"

"In due time, Tisha," replied Misha. "Let me first get our orders from the lieutenant." As he slid into his command seat, he greeted his old friend Taras. "I'm very happy that you aren't lying at the bottom of a smoking crater, my friend."

"And I love you too, Sergeant," replied the burly paratrooper who was the vehicle's driver. Misha grinned as he flipped on the R-123 radio and tuned to the company frequency.

"Saber One, this is Saber Two-One, ready for action."

"Saber Two-One, this is Saber One," replied Captain Sedelnikov, the company commander. "Await orders from your platoon commander."

"And now we wait," said Taras.

Not satisfied with waiting, Misha switched to the platoon frequency.

"Saber Two-Two, this is Saber Two-One, over."

"Saber Two-One," replied Sergeant Yuri Aleksenko, the squad leader for Second Squad, "this is Saber Two-Two, receiving."

"Saber Two-Two, any word from the lieutenant?"

"Negative, Saber Two-One, we haven't had any contact."

"Dammit," said Misha to himself. According to doctrine, he was required to wait for the lieutenant. He didn't have a battle plan other than the vaguest "assault the air base" objective. Was his unit supposed to feint from the south while the rest of the company made an assault from the east? He didn't know. He couldn't know, and that lack of knowledge led to an impotent feeling as the platoon sat next to a German village waiting for a lieutenant who might well have died half an hour ago.

"I hate sitting here, Taras," said Misha.

"Take it easy, Sergeant," replied Taras. "I'm sure we'll head out to the slaughter soon enough."

"Contact!" shouted Tisha as he dropped down into his seat and slammed the hatch closed. "Low-flying aircraft, ten o'clock. I think it's a helicopter." It was as if Taras had summoned the threat with his warning.

"I'm not going to sit here waiting to die," said Misha, picking up his mic. "This is Saber Two-One to all Saber Two units. Form a wedge on me and advance on course three hundred. We have helicopters approaching from the west."

"Understood, Saber Two-One," replied Yuri.

"Negative, Saber Two-One," said Sergeant Shishov, Third Squad's leader. "We wait for the lieutenant."

"*Govno!*" muttered Misha. "Taras, advance on a course of three-zero-zero, maximum speed." Over Misha's right shoulder, Tisha turned the main gun turret to face the oncoming threat. As they ran, he kept turning the turret to the left, tracking the helicopter's approach.

"He's going for Shishov," said Tisha.

"He made his choice," said Taras, knowing that Misha was going to blame himself for whatever happened to Third Squad.

As the helicopter came closer, Tisha called out, "It's a UH-1." He had trouble pronouncing the word Iroquois. "Engaging!"

Misha could hear the 12.7mm machine gun open and imagined that the other two BMDs were doing likewise.

"*Da nu!*" exclaimed Tisha. "The American has unleashed a rocket attack on Third Squad and is withdrawing to the south."

With the immediate threat over, Misha got back on the radio. He switched to the company frequency.

"Saber One, this is Saber Two-Two, over."

"Saber Two-Two, this is Saber One, receiving."

"Sir, we are under helicopter attack. Third Squad is hit and damaged, possibly destroyed. We have not made contact with the platoon commander and are advancing on the objective." There was a brief silence on the other end, and Misha feared the worst—that he would be ordered to return to the rally point.

"Saber Two-One, you are to advance to reference point Ivan Four and await orders to advance. Continue to monitor this frequency. We'll command you from here."

Misha switched the frequency back to the platoon. "Saber Two-Two, come to heading two-eight-zero. We are advancing to reference point Ivan Four." He then switched back to the company frequency and waited.

****

West of Giebelstadt, West Germany

Germes crouched low in the brush. His best guess was that he was a mile and a half from the edge of the airfield. Unfortunately, there was a swift stream flowing between him and the base. He was sure that he wouldn't have any trouble crossing it, but he wasn't looking forward to wearing a wet flight suit on a freezing night.

Nevertheless, he knew he had to push on. He had just watched a helicopter make a pass at some unseen targets, so he was keenly aware that the enemy response was underway.

He had only put a kilometer between himself and his chute. Although he'd tried to hide any signs of his landing, there was no doubt in his mind that Americans or Germans were searching for him. He needed that motivation to keep him pushing. He could hear a vehicle approaching from the road behind him. His hesitation at the stream might just cost him his freedom, or even his life. He got as small as he could and hoped that they would drive right by.

To his horror, he heard the vehicle come to a stop thirty meters away. *Germes* drew his Makarov pistol and quietly chambered a round. He heard two doors open and close and the muffled conversation between two men. He spoke neither German nor English, but it was clear that they were looking for something.

Flashlight beams cut through the darkness to his left, south of his position. There was more chattering between the men. *Germes* watched the lights flicker down from the road and onto the stream bank. The lights shone to the south, away from him, and he felt a glimmer of hope.

Within ten seconds of that hope, he was again horrified as the two men turned and began walking in his direction. He slowed his breathing, forcing his body into a calmness that he didn't feel. He overcame the urge to dash across the stream, or make a break across the road.

The beam of the flashlight cut through the brush in front of him. The men kept walking. *Germes* steadied himself for action. He needed to kill both men before they could return fire. He was confident that so long as they closed to within twenty meters, he could do it. *Why didn't I spend more time on the range?* he thought.

A beam of light swept across him, and the men stopped. *This is it*, he thought. But the light was held steady a few feet to his right. There was another brief exchange between his assailants.

Before they could pursue him further, there was a massive series of explosions coming from the direction of the airfield. The men's radio crackled to life, and a panicked radio operator issued orders that *Germes* assumed were letting the guards know that the base assault had begun. Both men broke out in a run back to the vehicle and tires screeched as they fled the scene. *It's time to get wet*, thought *Germes*, eyeing the stream.

****

Reference Point Ivan Four
South of Giebelstadt

"This is Saber One to all Saber units. Commence the attack," said the captain.

"You heard the man," said Misha, and Taras grunted an acknowledgment as the BMD lurched forward. "Keep your eyes peeled, Tisha. We're not expecting any armor, so you're looking for defensive strongpoints and any targets of opportunity."

Misha and Yuri were on the captain's right flank, protecting that side of the company's main thrust. Command had tasked the 9th Company with clearing out the aircraft revetments along the southern edge of the base. On some occasions, helicopters would have taken up those protective slots. Today, however, they were more likely to hold defenders looking to stop the Soviet onslaught.

Misha's view of the battle was limited to the thirty degrees on either side of his view port. The crew had kept the BMD buttoned up ever since the helicopter attack that had taken out Third Squad. Misha shook his head at the thought of Shishov and his crew. They had tried to raise them on the radio, to no avail. Tisha reported that he hadn't seen any survivors after the rocket attack. But that was the past, and they had a battle on their hands in the present.

There was another thrust coming from the east side of the airfield, and Tisha had to maintain fire discipline within his assigned sector. Any firing to the right side of his assignment could easily hit a friendly unit advancing ahead of pace.

"I have movement along that berm, ten degrees right," said Misha.

"I see it," replied Tisha. "Engaging!"

The thundering boom of the 37mm cannon echoed through the vehicle. Something caught Misha's eye to the left. He turned just in time to watch a streak of fire strike one of Headquarters Platoon's BMDs.

"Tisha, there's a TOW launcher out there to the left."

"I'm not worried about that one," said Taras. "It's the other ones that haven't fired yet that have my attention." Illumination shells exploded over the airfield, throwing shadows in all directions as each tiny sun turned the night into day.

"*Govno*," said Tisha as the gun thundered again. "Multiple targets, I'm engaging as they come to bear." The overlapping fields of fire allowed the Desantniks to ensure that nothing got through as they advanced, but it also meant that in some cases, multiple BMDs would engage the same target. The turret of the miniature tank pivoted from the left to the right as Tisha cleared out everything he could from his sector.

"Don't forget the second line of revetments!" said Misha as he watched a team of defenders scrambling from the first row to the second.

"I see them," said Tisha. They were about two hundred meters from the second row when the team popped back up from behind the revetment they had just scaled.

"Tisha, now!" Misha knew that there was nothing that Tisha could do. The autoloader could only move so fast. To his dismay, he watched as a man pointed a tube at them.

"Incoming!" shouted Misha when he saw the flame leap from the tube and head straight for them.

Boom! The noise of the rocket hitting the BMD dwarfed the sound of Tisha's gun.

"It didn't penetrate," said Misha.

"Really?" said Taras. "I hadn't noticed that we aren't dead." Taras then gave the BMD a quick turn to the left, then right. "Controls are all in order. I'm not sure what happened, but we are still combat-ready." The thunder of another outgoing round emphasized the point.

"It must have been an RPG," said Misha. "It bounced off the angled front armor." He couldn't help but feel that they had just cheated death. They were getting closer to the defensive positions when the radio broke the tension.

"All Saber units, come to course three-three-zero and form a line."

"I heard him," said Taras, preempting Misha's repeating of the order.

"Understood," replied Misha, confirming the captain's order.

The plan was for the company to run parallel to the runway and the line of revetments and destroy anyone who remained. They knew they didn't have the manpower to hold the facility as well as care for a lot of prisoners of war. Better to kill them in the fight before they had a chance to surrender. Misha found this distasteful, but he understood the utility. Half of the company would be focused on pulverizing the defenders in the exposed revetments, while the other half would be focused on protecting the company from a counterattack from the north.

The captain ordered the turn to course zero-seven-zero, and the surviving BMDs from the 9th Company began a slaughter. The defenders had been flanked and now had enemy armor in the rear. Headquarters Platoon, at the head of the line, pounded every defensive position as they pushed northeast.

From his view port, Misha watched as a missile streaked out of one of the revetments. It struck the side of the third vehicle in the line and punched through the weaker side armor, destroying it. Misha could tell from here that there would be no survivors.

The remaining BMDs concentrated fire on the position as they parted to the left and right to pass their dead comrades. First Platoon was the second in the line, after HQ. By the time Tisha was passing by the positions, there were no living defenders to contend with.

Occasionally, there was movement and he fired a round to be sure, but he couldn't tell if he was shooting at anyone or just the flickering shadows caused by the flares and the fires that broke out from the combat.

Once HQ Platoon passed the last of the revetments, the captain ordered the tanks to a course of three-three-zero and issued the order: "Prepare to deploy." With the primary defenses wrecked, the Desantniks would now have to clear out the remaining enemy forces building by building.

"Everyone get ready," said Misha on the vehicle intercom. He had a good squad. Most of them had combat experience from Afghanistan. He knew who he could count on. But he had a few wild cards as well. *How will Novikov and—what's his name? The new guy from 2nd Platoon—do under fire?* he wondered. He didn't have a choice. Good or bad, he was about to find out.

The vehicle came to a sudden stop, and Misha commanded, "Go! Go! Go!" As he popped his own command hatch and scrambled down the side of the BMD, the rest of his shooters climbed out of the hatch over the engine and hit the ground. Within seconds, the five men were running toward the first building in their area of responsibility.

It appeared to be an administrative building. The squad scrambled to the entryway and took defensive positions, looking for targets as Misha tried the door. It was locked. He fired a burst from his AKS-74 rifle into the door frame next to the locking assembly, then planted a solid front kick on the damaged door.

The kick sent the door crashing in, and while Misha covered the opening with his rifle, his squad slipped into the building. Misha followed and uselessly closed the door behind them. It bumped against its frame and reopened behind the squad.

"Don't get bunched up, and clear each room before you pass," said Misha as his men went to work. Storming an admin building at dawn was just as rewarding as it sounded. There was nobody there. And Misha was quite happy with that. He would complete his orders, whatever they might be. Here, he'd caught a break with a safe assignment.

There was a sudden commotion ahead. Misha heard a man scream out in a foreign language. He could tell that it wasn't German, so he assumed it was English. He rushed forward to assist, chastising himself for not taking the lead again once they'd entered the building.

When he got to the office that was being cleared, he could see Private Novikov pointing his rifle at an unarmed soldier. From his uniform, Misha was certain that he was an American. The man was talking at a rapid pace, and the whole situation was boiling over.

The American reached down toward his desk, and Novikov fired a burst into him. Misha had no curiosity. He didn't care what the American had been reaching for. He was already considering the report, if there would be one. The American could have been reaching for a box of chocolate and a "welcome to Germany" card. It didn't matter. The report would state that Misha believed he was reaching for a weapon.

There were no more surprises in the office. He positioned the squad in defensive positions, then sent Rodya up to the roof to attach the squad's VDV flag to the building. It was bad OPSEC, but it was great for morale. They would now hold their new possession.

If the Americans wanted anything in the building, they would have to fight through First Squad of First Platoon, 9th Company, 345th Independent Guards Airborne Regiment.

****

1 January 1981
Jacksonville, North Carolina

Nancy Rodriguez had spent the day in a haze. From the time she'd clocked in at the credit union, there had been reports of war in Europe. Everything was fragmented. The nascent "Cable News Network" was trying to keep up with the facts as they came in, but they simply didn't have the infrastructure. It was impossible to verify all the data that was swarming the wires. Much of it was contradictory, and that which remained was quickly overtaken by events. And so, she'd shut it out of her mind during her shift. It was deposits and withdrawals, and nothing in between.

Once she'd picked up Jennifer, returned home, and made dinner for Duane, she was ready for Walter Cronkite. She needed to understand what was happening as the world fell apart. The *CBS Evening News* banner ran across her screen, and she watched Cronkite sitting at his donut desk, looking seriously at the camera. He launched into the news without hesitation. Across the country, Americans tuned in to be assured that though the news was bad, there was still hope.

Cronkite explained that the Soviets and their Warsaw Pact allies had invaded Austria and Germany. The Soviet war machine had unleashed air and missile strikes against the United Kingdom, Iceland, Norway, and the Low Countries. He further explained that our troops and our allies were standing firm against the Soviet aggression, and though nobody could predict how this would turn out, we would fight on until we had defeated the communist invaders. Cronkite concluded his report, and the screen faded to black.

The *CBS Evening News* was replaced by the seal of the President of the United States. That image too faded out and was replaced by President Carter, seated at a desk, looking directly into the camera.

"My fellow Americans. The world is at war. The global push for self-determination has been a hallmark of my administration. We believed—in fact, still believe—that when given a choice, the people of the world will choose freedom. We stayed out of the Nicaraguan revolution when the socialists took over. We did not intercede when the socialists took power in Turkey. We did not even offer military assistance to Iran until we did so under a joint United Nations Security Council Resolution.

"What we offered as peace has been taken for weakness. The Soviet Union stands in direct contrast to our vision of self-determination. Mr. Brezhnev knows that the people of the world will choose freedom. It is what he fears most. That is why the Soviets overthrew the governments of Nicaragua and Turkey. That is why the Soviets instigated a war between Iran and Iraq. That is why they have invaded Western Europe.

"We offered them peace, and they gave us war. So be it. Now that they have made that choice, we are committed to defending our allies in Europe and our homeland. There will be dark days ahead of us. There will be defeats as well as victories. We have suffered losses and we will suffer more. But as God is my witness, we will not give up in this fight. We will continue to fight for the freedom of the world. The light of freedom will not be extinguished."

As the screen went back to the CBS news studio, Duane crossed the room and turned off the TV.

"What do you think?" he asked.

"I don't know what to think," replied Nancy. "It was bad enough knowing that we were at war in Nicaragua. This is crazy. I'm afraid. I am deathly worried that the world is about to end. I don't know how to take care of Jennifer when the bombs drop. I mean, what are we supposed to do?"

"Baby, we can't get too crazy. Nobody is talking about nuclear war—"

"Are you insane!? How do you think this ends? At some point, one side or the other is going to start losing, and then it's all over. Carlos was clear—"

"Baby, listen, Carlos was a sergeant in the Marine Corps. They don't tell him everything. In fact, they tell those guys a lot of wild stuff to keep them motivated. He doesn't know that this will go nuclear, and neither does anyone else. We need to keep our heads and not panic."

Nancy put on her jacket. "I'm going to the A&P. Make sure Jennifer goes to bed on time."

Nancy regretted that she hadn't stocked up sooner. By the time she made it to the supermarket, the run had already begun. Thanks to Carlos's rantings, she knew to avoid perishables. While there was a run on meat and dairy, she was gathering powdered milk and canned goods. She pushed her shopping cart through the aisles and was shocked at the empty shelves. The war was barely real, and chaos was rolling through the grocery store.

Nancy heard a loud whistle burst the air. There was a commotion at the entrance to the store.

"Hey, you didn't pay for that!" yelled a man.

"Go to hell, I need it!" came the reply.

Nancy ducked her head and pushed toward the cash register. She waited in line as sirens went off, and two police officers showed up to try and calm the situation. She wondered how many cops were deployed to all of the retail stores in Jacksonville tonight.

Finally, she made her way to the cashier. After she unloaded her groceries, she pulled out her checkbook and waited for the total.

"I'm sorry, ma'am," said the checker, "we can't take any checks tonight. This is cash only."

Nancy tilted her head in surprise. She always paid by check at the A&P. Luckily, she'd made a habit of keeping cash on hand in case she needed it to smooth a transaction at the credit union, and was able to cover the costs.

We're going to tear ourselves apart at this rate, she thought as she left the store and headed for her apartment.

Chapter 7

2 January 1981
Gwangju Air Base
Republic of Korea

Captain Sun Young-ho sat in the cockpit of his F-5E Tiger II. Captain Sun and the rest of the 102nd Fighter Squadron of the ROK Air Force had been on a constant alert ever since the Soviets had initiated hostilities the previous day. There was no guarantee that the North Koreans would take advantage of the global instability, but there was no reason to think they wouldn't.

As the second hour of his alert slid into the third, Sun wondered if his unit, or even the Air Force as a whole, was ready for what might be waiting. The Air Force's state of readiness was questionable. South

Korea had been in political turmoil for the last few years. The corruption and infighting in the government did little to help morale in the ranks.

At least we managed to upgrade our fighter force, Sun thought as he looked around the cockpit of his Tiger. These newer F-5Es were a significant upgrade over the F-5As they'd replaced.

Sun's radio came to life. "This is Hallasan Control to all Magpie units. Scramble. Scramble. Scramble." Sun keyed his mic and acknowledged the order as he pushed his throttles forward and raced down the runway.

"This is Hallasan Control. We have multiple contacts in DPRK airspace, heading south. There is massive shelling outside of Seoul. We suspect the enemy air activity will be in support of those efforts. You are to prioritize enemy strike aircraft."

Again, Sun acknowledged the order. "Magpie Eight, this is Magpie Four."

"Magpie Four, I'm receiving."

"I know command wants us to focus on the Su-7s, but we need to be ready for a fighter sweep. We'll be the leading edge of the response, and we have to assume they'll be ready for us."

"Understood, Magpie Four. We'll need to be ready for MiGs. Over." Sun turned it over in his head.

The North fielded the MiG-21 as well as a Chinese version of the older MiG-19. The older aircraft wasn't as fast as the MiG-21, but it was a bit more maneuverable. Both fighters were armed with heat-seeking missiles. The American propaganda told Captain Sun and his fellow pilots that the F-5E was superior to either enemy fighter, but reports coming out of the Iran-Iraq war illustrated that they were very closely matched.

The two-ship formation picked up another section, giving them a flight of four Tigers approaching the battlefield. Sun could see the radar signatures of a pair of MiG-21s. They were blasting the air with their air search radar, practically begging the Magpies to engage them. *And to distract us from the attack planes that are undoubtedly out there hiding*, thought Sun. He checked the display: they were facing a force of eight MiGs.

The two forces entered the merge, where they would cross each other's path. The goal for each aircraft would be to get behind an enemy plane and stay there long enough to lock an air-intercept missile onto the enemy. The Tiger was more maneuverable than the MiG, but the MiG had a speed and acceleration advantage. That meant that the ROK pilots needed to end this fight quickly. The longer they turned and burned with the MiGs, the more of an advantage the enemy would have.

In this matchup, the MiG was almost like a grappler, trying to get leverage on his opponent. The Tiger was more of a striker, trying for a quick hit or two to take down the opponent before the MiGs could wear them down.

Sun followed behind and above his flight leader, Major Sam Seung-gi. This "welded wing" position wouldn't last long as the fight evolved, but sticking together and keeping the major's six clear was the most Sun could do right now. As the planes crossed each other in the sky, the MiGs started an aggressive climb, trying to take the fight vertical, where their superior thrust-to-weight ratio would give them an advantage.

Major Sam pulled a high-g turn and Sun watched in awe as the MiGs flattened out and tried to turn into the Tigers. The MiGs were playing right into their hands! Within seconds, Major Sam fired an AIM-9 Sidewinder at the lead MiG. The missile raced from the rail to the enemy in an instant, exploding behind the aircraft and destroying the engine.

Before Captain Sun could react, an orange burst of light exploded and another MiG slashed in front of him. He watched in horror as the major's Tiger was split in two by what must have been the 23mm cannons from one of the MiGs.

The battle was a living thing. He'd entered with an idea of how it would play out, and that idea had survived all of five seconds. Now it was a chaotic fight to the death. Sun pushed his throttle to the walls and tried to get a trailing shot on the second of the two MiGs he and Major Sam had originally engaged. The missile left the rail, but the MiG was doing what it did best: it ran.

With the afterburner engaged, the MiG raced away before cranking hard and dropping a line of flares. Sun was already pulling a split-S maneuver, where he rolled his plane onto its back and pulled back on the stick.

This extreme maneuver gave him a quick change of direction and allowed him to build up some speed, which he'd drastically depleted during the first pass. With his cockpit pointing at the earth below, he noticed a formation of aircraft below him. It was too dark to make them out, but he was sure they were ground attack aircraft. He pointed his nose in front of them and began his intercept. He knew that he was being targeted by at least one of the MiGs, so he wouldn't have long to make his attack.

Sun pushed down on the stick a bit, sending him into a slight negative-g dive. His seeker locked onto one of the enemy aircraft and the formation scattered. He launched his remaining Sidewinder at the enemy, knowing he was running out of time. He cranked his stick to the right and dropped a string of flares, just in case.

Sun didn't know how, but he was alive, and his plane was fully responsive. He dove for the deck and ran. Without any more Sidewinders, he needed to put some distance between himself and the fight. As he flew south on the deck, he could see more aircraft flying into the fight. He'd been one of the first to the fight, and now his brothers in arms were rising to the challenge.

Chapter 8

2 January 1981
Mount Weather Emergency Operations Center
Rural Northern Virginia

In the hours since the first news of the invasion had come in, President Carter had been working the telephones nonstop. Every ally across the globe needed assurances that the United States would honor their treaty obligations in the face of this unprecedented invasion.

In the entire history of the human race, there had never been anything like this. The start of the Second World War was nothing in comparison. The combined armies of all eight Warsaw Pact nations were slamming into NATO defensive lines. That was to say nothing of the looming nuclear threat.

With the unprecedented threat came an unprecedented response. The President and key members of the government were whisked away to several secret bunkers to ensure the continuity of government in case of the worst. At Mount Weather, the President couldn't be expected to survive a direct hit by a nuclear weapon, but he would have a fighting chance at anything short of that. While congressional leadership had been moved to a separate bunker in Pennsylvania, the President's executive team was with him here.

"Mr. President," said Secretary of State Jeane Kirkpatrick, "I've spoken to Ambassador McHenry in New York. His Soviet counterpart isn't taking any calls. We're not sure what, if anything, the Soviets will say to justify this attack."

"I think there are two things that we can be sure of," said National Security Advisor Zbigniew Brzezinski. "First, that they will tell us that the invasion was necessary to break the chains of the workers in Western Europe, to save the people from the tyrannical leadership of the West. Second, that this will be a lie. This is and always will be nothing more than the forceful continuation of the Worker's Revolution."

"What, then," asked President Carter, "am I to make of that?"

"Only," replied Brzezinski, "that there will be no negotiating with them. They do not have reasonable demands. The Soviets and their allies will take this fight as far as they can go. The soonest we can hope to stop them is after they have overwhelmed Germany, Austria...

Perhaps Greece. If we can inflict enough casualties on them during this drive, we might be able to negotiate with them. Short of this, they will continue the drive and this war will grind on."

"I have some bad news on that front," said Secretary Kirkpatrick. "The Turkish ambassador from the socialist government there has indicated that they will not be honoring their Article 5 commitments. They intend to remain neutral during this war. I think that goes to Dr. Brzezinski's point about Greece."

"Those sons of bitches," said President Carter. "This has to be coordinated. There's a left-wing coup in September, and now three months later, they've decided to sit this one out?"

"I agree," said Brzezinski. "There is a clear connection here. We have to assume that this is not the last diplomatic surprise we're going to get today."

"Do we have any news from SACEUR?" asked the President. There hadn't been a real update since the initial phone call with General Willis at the onset of the attack.

"Yes, sir," said Stansfield Turner, the Director of the CIA. "The Pact forces have advanced quickly along the entirety of the inner-German border. The deepest penetration has been outside of Würzburg, some forty miles inside NATO lines. A Soviet Airborne unit captured an airfield there. We believe the intent is to draw our forces away from the main attack while the paratroopers dig in and wait for the ground assault to catch up to them."

The President furrowed his brow at the news.

"If there's any good news," said Dr. Turner, "it's that the British Army of the Rhine has completely foiled an East German tank attack on the North German Plains. Also, the Italians have held off a Yugoslavian attack along their border. Yugoslavian mechanized infantry forces ran into a group of Italian Armored Division who just happened to be conducting training in the plains east of Udine."

There was a commotion, and an aide pulled Turner aside and whispered a report to him. Turner nodded gravely and turned to the assembly.

"The DPRK has initiated a massive bombardment against US and ROK forces." There was a pause as everyone took in the new information.

Secretary of Defense Harold Brown was the first to speak. "This changes things for sure. However, most of our response plans have assumed that North Korea would be a belligerent in any future global war. The bigger question, of course, is what will Deng Xiaoping in China do?"

"To that point," said Dr. Kirkpatrick, "I imagine Xiaoping will take a wait-and-see approach. China would gain nothing by acting impulsively that they couldn't get later by waiting."

"What about South Korea?" asked President Carter. "How ready are they to take on the North Koreans?"

"The South has begun an initiative to take on more of their own defense," said Secretary Brown. "But that movement is in its infancy. They wouldn't stand a chance without the 2nd Infantry Division and the Pacific Air Forces backing them up. To make matters worse, since our announcement that we would begin withdrawing American forces from the peninsula, the DPRK has gone on a major military buildup. They've been preparing for this for years."

"It doesn't help," said Dr. Brzezinski, "that South Korean President Chun Doo-hwan is dealing with considerable unrest. While the invasion may rally the nation behind him, there's just as much of a chance that a fifth column will undermine his leadership."

"OK," said President Carter, "all this speculation is good and well. What's the bottom line on Korea?"

"To start with," said Secretary Brown, "we need to get our forces in Japan into the fight. Our priority needs to be getting as many of our aircraft as possible moved to air bases on the peninsula. We need to get the Marines up from Okinawa and have the Navy get supplies moving out of Sasebo. That's just to slow them down. We're going to need more men."

"We have two entire Marine divisions tied down in Nicaragua," said Dr. Brzezinski.

"And they have a mission to accomplish, Dr. Brzezinski," said Dr. Kirkpatrick icily.

"I hear what you're saying, Jeane," said President Carter. "And for now, I agree with you. But things are changing quickly out there. There may come a time when we need to shift our focus. But we will not forget what's going on in Latin America, and we will not tolerate a communist infestation." The words he had just spoken sounded alien to

Carter. He had never in his life thought he'd sound like a reactionary. *I can't let the craziness of today sweep me up. I need to stay grounded,* he thought.

"OK," said the President. "Jeane, I need you to reach out to the Chinese and see where they are on this. Stan," he said to Turner, "I need you to use whatever means you have to see if we can tell China's intentions in case they stonewall us. Now, moving beyond Korea, where are we on getting new satellites launched?"

"I spoke with Dr. Hermann from the National Reconnaissance Office. They have a new KH-11 satellite ready to go, but they still need to ship it from Sunnyvale, California, to Vandenberg to launch it. Additionally, the Air Force had to stand down the Titan rocket that was on standby for a national emergency. They were getting some anomalous readings on a launch test, and since they only have one shot at this, they're taking a second look at everything."

An aide brought a sheet of paper to Secretary Brown. He read it and shook his head slightly.

"What is it?" asked President Carter.

"Sir, a cargo ship has been sunk exiting Charleston Harbor in South Carolina. From what we can make of it, we believe it struck a mine."

"How the hell did the Soviets mine a US port without us having any idea that it was coming?" asked the President.

"Sir, our best guess—"

"I don't want guesses, dammit. I need actual answers."

"Sir, I—"

"I'm sorry, Harry, there's a lot coming at us, and I understand that you're doing the best with the information that you have. We need to get ahead of something for once."

"I understand, Mr. President. We believe that they pre-positioned a submarine offshore to mine the harbor. I will check with the Naval Security Group to see if they have any tracking on the Soviet VLF air—"

"I'm sorry, Harry, the what?"

"VLF, sir. It's shorthand for the submarine communications aircraft. Right now, we're operating under the assumption that this isn't a one-off. We're going to find these mines in the shipping lanes of the Eastern Seaboard. The only way they could have coordinated this is if they could give the subs a simultaneous order. That could only happen with a VLF aircraft in the area."

"What are we doing to counter the threat?" asked the President.

"The Coast Guard is shutting down the sea lanes. They're diverting incoming traffic to Canada and the Caribbean. The Navy is working on clearing out their port facilities, then they'll move out to cover the civilian ports. In addition to the active-duty mine warfare forces, they've activated the naval reserve force training mine warfare ships. That will give us an additional twenty minesweepers once they are up and running."

"How are we doing with REFORGER?" asked the President, referring to the Return of Forces to Germany.

"The first personnel flights are en route to their pre-positioning points in Europe. That's the good news. Additional heavy equipment is being loaded at the port of Beaumont, Texas, and Bayonne, New Jersey. But those ships are going to be buttoned up in port until we can clear the mine threat. Once they're out of the ports, they still have the challenge of crossing four thousand miles of ocean."

"With Soviet submarines, aircraft, and that damned *Kirov* hiding along the way," concluded the President.

Chapter 9

4 January 1981
Rama, Nicaragua

Major Jason "Ripsaw" Thomas and his copilot, Phil "Snow" White, had fallen into the routine of this new war. They'd eat an early breakfast before the sun rose. They'd get the daily briefing, telling them what the day's mission would be. Then they'd get all the details they needed and head back to the "Vulture Nest," where the helos were stored to get the CH-53 ready for duty.

As they went through checks and double checks, they would inevitably be met by a young Marine lance corporal who had approximately a million questions about the life of a pilot and the operation of the Sea Stallion.

At first, the officers were taken aback by the curious Marine. It had only taken Lance Corporal Oliver a few minutes to win them over. Ripsaw chuckled, remembering that first encounter.

"Hey, Captain," said Oliver. "How come the major has a badass call sign, and you got stuck with a Disney movie?" The two pilots looked at each other.

"The balls on this kid," said Ripsaw.

"Ripsaw ain't a badass call sign when you know where it came from," said Snow.

"Bullshit," replied Rip. "They call me Ripsaw because I cut through the enemy like a radial arm saw tears through a plank of wood."

"Dude," said Snow, "you fly a transport. No, kid, he got the handle because during his first deployment he snored so loudly, nobody wanted to bunk with him."

"That's a bunch of lies and you know it," said Ripsaw, not conceding the point. "What can we do for you, kid?"

"I just wanted to learn about the helo. Ya know, we fly in these things all the time, and I have no idea how they work."

"That ain't your job, son. Your job is to jump out the back and shoot communists."

Oliver looked crestfallen. Rip had seen the same expression on his own twelve-year-old son when they'd had to cancel a family trip to Disneyland when he'd deployed to Iran.

Rip said, "Tell you what, kid. You can hang out here while we prep the helo. Don't touch anything, don't say anything, and try not to think too much."

Oliver's face brightened. "Thank you, sir."

"Shhhhhh," said Snow.

In the time between that introduction and today's mission, the two pilots had taken Oliver on as some kind of pet or mascot. Each morning, they would take about ten minutes to explain something about how the helicopter operated. Rip started with an explanation of basic flight controls. Then Snow took him aside to show him the differences between aerial navigation and land navigation. Oliver impressed both pilots with his ability to retain the information they gave him. Sometimes Rip thought the kid surprised himself with how well he could learn new things.

This morning, Rip was giving Oliver a tour of one section on the instrument panel when the grunts came jogging in for today's assault.

"Gotta go, Rip," said Oliver. "Thanks for the lesson."

Rip watched him scamper out of the cockpit and out the door to rejoin his squad.

"What do you think about today's assault?" asked Snow.

"Doesn't matter what I think," replied Rip. "But since you asked, I think this will be the last of the easy ones." Snow gave him an inquisitive look. "Look at your map. Santo Tomás is right on the eastern edge of the Amerrisque Mountains. Those mountains are the last barrier between our eastern thrust and Managua. If I oversaw the other team, I'd be getting my Alamo ready on the other side of those mountains."

"Damn, Rip," said Snow, "they should make you a Soviet general with that kind of thinking."

"You know I'm right," said Rip, shaking his head.

****

"You have fun with your new friends?" asked Corporal Darrell Evans.

"Dude," replied Oliver, "did you know that the fuel selection levers on the top of the instrument panel—"

"Let me stop you right there, Oliver," said Evans. "Part of the deal was that you can come hang out with the bus drivers if they'll have you. In exchange, you keep on the new guys to keep them sharp, and I don't have to hear about helicopters all day. A simple 'yes, Corporal' is all I need from you."

"Yes, Corporal," said Oliver dutifully. The squad loaded onto the CH-53 with the rest of the platoon and secured themselves to their seats. "Hey Riley," said Oliver to the team's juniormost member, "buckle your strap, man. I don't want you bouncing around like popcorn when some Sandi takes a shot at us with a MANPAD."

Embarrassed, the private grabbed both sides of the safety belt and strapped himself in.

Oliver knew that they'd have just over half an hour in the air, so he pulled a notebook out of one of his blouse pockets and started making notes from his morning's lesson. Once he was back at camp, he'd transfer the information to a growing stack of flash cards he'd made. He had told no one, but he was going to figure out a way to get a commission and fly.

The ride was uneventful. The Sandis had shown little backbone in the east. Oliver had heard that there was some serious fighting in the north, where the 101st were fighting. They'd run into some of the Soviet Spetsnaz forces as they pushed south from Honduras. The 1st Marine Division, pushing in from the northwest, was hitting stiff resistance as well. In the seven weeks of battle, the circle around the capital city of Managua was getting tighter and tighter. With each mile they gained, the resistance increased.

The scuttlebutt going around was that all three units would converge on the city in the coming weeks, as soon as they shored up the supply lines from this latest hop. Oliver didn't believe that. It just seemed like too many people in too little space. He'd let the big brains in the Pentagon worry about that. As Rip had pointed out earlier, he had some commies to shoot. He could feel the attitude of the helo change as it neared the ground. The Marines efficiently egressed and took up defensive positions along the LZ.

The LZ was situated just southwest of the town. Second Platoon was tasked with perimeter security, and Evans and his team fanned out to cover the northeast corner, facing the objective. Oliver took up a position in a tree line that overlooked the village. His team was already tracking for targets as the CH-53s lifted off to make room for a second wave.

Oliver caught a burst of flame rising from within Santo Tomás, streaking toward the LZ. He was trying to locate the source when he heard the explosion. He turned in time to see the tail boom of one of the helos explode, separating the tail rotor from the cargo compartment. The helicopter immediately spun. The sudden shift in course sent the helo into the flight path of one of the second-wave CH-53s. There was a loud crumpling sound as the two giant helicopters collided in midair, supplanted by the screeching of metal tearing and a loud explosion as the helicopters slammed into the ground.

The organized, routine drop slipped into chaos. Marines were running into the debris, trying to find their brothers to pull them to safety. Oliver knew that there was nothing he could do, and his mission was to protect the LZ until the entire force of Marines was on the ground. If there was a soldier in that village with a MANPAD, what else might be waiting for them?

As if in answer to that question, Oliver noticed a single explosion drop about fifty meters to his left. It seemed out of place. Then there was another explosion, about thirty meters out. Then it clicked.

"Incoming!" shouted Oliver. "They've got mortars in the village." What little order had been regained since the helicopter crash evaporated. Oliver could see Lieutenant Beck on the radio, but everyone in the LZ was putting as much distance between themselves and the helicopters as they could. If Oliver ran away from the LZ, he would charge into a hostile village.

"Get small!" yelled Evans, answering Oliver's silent question. He pulled out his entrenching tool and started digging. He knew it was too little, too late, but he had to do something.

The artillery fell all along the LZ. The last of the CH-53s had departed, and the only aircraft in view were AH-1 Cobras that were hunting for the mortars. Another MANPAD came out of the tree line to the north, but the targeted Cobra banked right and dumped a series of flares. The missile took the bait, and the Cobra returned to the hunt.

The ground around Oliver and the rest of Fire Team Three rumbled as round after round of small-caliber mortar fire struck. From what Oliver could tell, the focus of the bombardment was more centered on the LZ, striking where the Marines had originally assembled and not spreading out to where they were currently hiding out.

Rookies, thought Oliver. *They can't adjust fire. They're just pounding the empty ground at this point.*

There was a flash in the distance, and Oliver looked toward the village to see a stream of rockets leap from a Cobra, exploding on the ground. He suspected that in a minute or so, the firing would trail off. As far as he could tell, his team was the most forward-deployed. If the enemy came pushing out of the village, they would have to hold them off while the rest of the company advanced.

"I've got movement," said Evans. "Looks like squad strength, about fifteen. Hold your fire. Oliver, when the lead element is about a hundred meters out, drop a few 40mms in the middle of them. As soon as those grenades go off, fire at will. Holmes and Riley, work left to right. Oliver and I will work right to left." With the plan laid out, they just had to let the enemy get closer.

They didn't have to wait long. Another AH-1 flying over the battlefield spotted the advancing squad and tore into them with its 20mm nose-mounted cannon. The organized advance broke into a panic, and the Sandis that weren't gunned down outright withdrew into town.

The open area between the LZ and the town would be impossible to traverse undetected without heavy smoke. Oliver wondered if they would continue the assault or withdraw to an extraction point and come back with another plan. Right now, his team was cut off, and they'd have to hold on to their piece of dirt with both hands.

It was midmorning before they saw movement to the rear. Teams and squads were emerging from the trees, having assembled in the jungle that surrounded the LZ. It looked like a good chunk of Kilo Company had survived the landing. Oliver wondered who they'd lost in the helo crash, and if Rip and Snow had been the CH-53 that was hit by the missile. Lance Corporal Murphy, from Second Platoon's Headquarters Squad, was the first of the Marines to reach Evans and Oliver.

"Hey, the LT is putting together a raid," said Murphy. "We're going to set up a feint"—he pointed off to the east of their position—"over there on the south side of town. We're getting some artillery and a ton of smoke. We're going to shake the nest and see what comes out. But it's all for show."

"What are you distracting them from?" asked Oliver.

"From you," replied Murphy. "LT wants you guys to slip through the trees and set up an OP on that hill with the mine." Oliver remembered the mine from the briefing this morning.

"And if it's occupied? I mean, it's on top of a hill, Murphy. If it's a good OP for us, it's a good OP for them."

"LT said he's had eyes on the hilltop, and they haven't seen any movement, but approach with caution. Anyhow, we need you up there and observing before they send in the next wave. I heard the colonel get on the radio and let the LT know we were taking this village today no matter what it takes. Oh, here. Take these." He handed a pair of binoculars and a PRC-77 radio to Evans.

"Thanks, Murph," said Evans. "Pass the word. We'll be ready when the smoke drops. Riley, put this on." He held the radio out toward the private.

Twenty minutes later, they were once again treated to a hammering. This time it was their own guns making the fire and the fury. High-explosive and canister rounds exploded south of the village. After several minutes of sustained fire, the smoke shells started to create a wall of haze that made movement difficult for the enemy to detect.

"Let's go, Marines," ordered Evans, and the team moved out to the east. Oliver heard the bark of rifle fire mixed with the staccato chittering of at least one M60.

The LT's really putting on a show, thought Oliver. Fire Team Two had to cross two hundred yards with little cover. If the LT was wrong about the mine being abandoned, they could be in trouble. If the wind picked up, or the shelling just wasn't quite enough… He put the thought out of his mind.

They made the approach without contact and found themselves at the bottom of the hill. The uneven earth gave them something to work with as far as cover and concealment, but it still wasn't ideal. If they ran into anyone, they'd be assaulting uphill.

Evans halted the team and signaled to them to split into two teams. Holmes and Riley would advance while Evans and Oliver covered. Then they would leapfrog, with Evans and Oliver taking the lead while the other two Marines covered. They would continue in this fashion to what they had called the "operations building" in the briefing.

Near the top of the hill, with fifty yards to go, Evans signaled for the team to halt. He crossed over to Oliver and asked, "You see anything in there?"

"Negative, Corporal. I think the LT is right. They've abandoned this place."

"It just seems like a trap," said Evans.

"Yeah, it does. But it's not like you have a choice," replied Oliver.

"Good point. Keep an eye on the building. I'm going to relay the plan to Holmes."

"Hey," said Oliver. "I'd like to know the plan too."

"Damn, sorry, Phil," said Evans, with a rare use of Oliver's first name. "My brain's going a hundred miles an hour. We're going to have Holmes and Riley cover from left and right. Call it a thirty-degree cone of fire on the front of that building. Then you and I are going to go up there and kick in the door and kill anything inside. They'll protect the flanks in case there's trouble."

"Roger that, Corporal." Evans passed the word and the two Marines split off to the left and the right. As soon as they signaled they were in position, Evans turned to Oliver and said, "OK, we're going to take it slow for the first twenty-five yards, then we'll sprint the second half."

"I'm with you, boss. I won't get lost," said Oliver, thinking back to when he'd first met Evans, and what an a-hole he thought he was. It seemed like a million years ago.

The two Marines moved toward the building. Oliver was sure with every step that he'd hear a rifle crack, signaling a new battle. He watched Evans break into a run and followed suit. Oliver noticed a tunnel carved into the hill to the northeast of the building. *I don't like the looks of that*, he thought.

The twenty-five-yard dash ended with the Marines slamming against the wall of the building, trying to present as small a target as possible to any unseen enemies. They scanned the area and couldn't see anything. Evans tried the door, and it was open.

"You were saying something about a trap?" asked Oliver. Evans grimaced as he pulled a flash-bang from his vest, pulled the pin, and tossed it in. As soon as the explosion went off, the Marines were in the office, moving from room to room, checking for any hostiles.

"Clear," said Evans as he walked through the third and final room. Oliver took stock of their new building. It was a shithole. Maybe it kept the sun off you, but it kept the wind off you too. He moved over to the window facing town. It gave a decent view of the town, much better than they'd had previously from the LZ.

"I think this might have been worth it after all," said Oliver. Evans motioned to Holmes and Riley to join them. Oliver turned to see the two Marines trotting up from their firing positions. He heard the crack of the rifle, and before he could react, he saw Holmes go down.

More firing came from the northeast side of the building, and Evans ran to that side, looking for a firing position. Oliver poked his head out the door, looking for the attacker while Riley dragged Holmes toward the building before being struck himself.

"Shit," said Oliver.

Evans came back, saying, "There's no window on that side. We need to figure out what we're up against before we can go get them." He gestured toward the two stricken Marines. "You go left, I'll go around wide right. On my signal we both converge on the tunnel."

After a few seconds, Oliver heard Evans roar, "Oorah!"

From a kneeling firing position, Oliver peeked around the corner and pumped a 20mm grenade in the direction of the hole before pulling back. As soon as he heard it detonate, he went prone and turned back to the tunnel, firing two three-round bursts before stopping to look for targets. He saw none.

"Cover the hole. I'm going for the men," said Oliver.

When he got to the spot where Holmes and Riley had been gunned down, he could tell that it was too late for Holmes. He was about to turn Riley over to check him out when Riley said, "Damn, Oliver, I thought I was going to die right here."

"Can you get up?"

"It's my leg, man." Before he could even finish the sentence, Oliver was picking him up and walking him into the operations building. Oliver pulled Riley's first aid kit, and his own Ka-Bar knife.

"Where's it at?"

"Left calf," replied Riley. Oliver cut the pant leg off at the knee and pulled it down to expose the wound.

"Damn, went right through," said Oliver as he pulled Riley's field dressing from his first aid kit. He pulled it open and wrapped the sterile side around Riley's calf, then tied it off and grabbed his rifle. "Put pressure on that, unless you want to lose it. And call the LT on that." He pointed to the radio the private was wearing. "And get Doc up here," he said before he returned to his perch to see how Evans wanted to handle the cave.

"What're you thinking?" called out Oliver.

"I know there's more in there, so we can't turn our backs on them."

"Well, I ain't going in after them," replied Oliver.

"No shit. Keep your rifle on the hole, I'm going to place a special order." With that, he slipped back around and into the building. Oliver kept his eyes peeled on the entrance to the mine. He could have sworn he'd seen movement, but he could never be quite sure. He went ahead and fired off a burst, just to let the bad guys know that he was still there.

After a few minutes, the area behind the beleaguered fire team was again battered by smoke rounds from the Marine artillery. Again, there was a mass of fire coming from the south of town as the lieutenant shot up the town and made enough noise to draw attention away from the tiny post on the hill.

A few minutes more and Oliver could see what had happened. He watched as a lone figure ran through the smoke and into the building. He wanted to turn and find out what was happening, but he couldn't. He had to keep his gun on the tunnel.

"Hey, pal, how the hell are you?" asked a voice from behind Oliver. He didn't turn his head, he was mission-oriented.

"I'm fantastic, Doc. How the hell are you?" he asked.

"I'm making a house call, but first, I get to do something I've always wanted to do." Oliver heard the sound of something sliding, and then an audible click. He knew that sound. His suspicions were confirmed as Doc Watts said, "Backblast area clear!"

A streak of flame shot over Oliver's right shoulder as the M72 light antitank weapon flew past him and into the mine. Another streak from the left flew in. Clearly, Evans had acquired one of the rockets as well. Oliver added the weight of fire of his own M203 grenade launcher. He pumped two rounds into the shaft before the entire front of the structure collapsed. The explosives were just too much for the wood-reinforced earthworks.

With the threat neutralized, the Marines fell back into the building, where Watts could tend to Riley and Evans and Oliver could start bird-dogging the village for the next wave of the assault.

****

4 January 1981
20,000 feet over Santo Tomás
Nicaragua

Lieutenant Junior Grade Samuel "Pharaoh" Bell looked to his forward left to see his section leader, Lieutenant "Rhodie" Charters. The two A-7E Corsairs were flying over the battlefield, waiting to put bombs on target whenever the Marines below placed an order for ordnance.

"Charger Four, Chieftain, over," called the Marine Corps Tactical Air Control Party, or TACP.

"Chieftain, Charger Four. Copy," came Rhodie's reply.

"Charger Four, this is Chieftain. I have a priority target. Approximately twenty men dug in two point two five kilometers southeast of reference point Alpha Two. Elevation, three hundred meters, will mark with smoke. Over."

"Chieftain, Charger Four, mission received. Out."

"All right, Pharaoh, let's go lighten our load," said Rhodie over the squad net. The two Corsairs banked left and started shedding altitude. "Once we see the smoke, we'll line up our run from south to north. I'll make the first pass just east, you follow me in just to the west. Dump everything you've got on the target. We'll cover a ton of space with sixty of these Snake Eyes." Rhodie was referring to the low-level Mk-82 bombs that they were dropping on the Sandinista troop concentration. Each five-hundred-pound bomb would leave the hard point, then deploy four drag-inducing tail fins on their way to the target.

"Roger that, Rhodie, let's melt that hilltop." Pharaoh was making a bit of an assumption, but the three-hundred-meter elevation should qualify as a hill. Besides, if the enemy was concentrated, there would have to be some tactical reason for it. He scanned the ground. He spotted the town center, otherwise known as reference point Alpha Two, and looked southeast.

"I've got cherry smoke, three hundred thirty degrees," said Rhodie. It annoyed Pharaoh that his section leader had found the target before he did. "OK, Pharoah, we're setting up the run, south to north."

Pharaoh followed Rhodie as he rolled right, heading south-southeast. When he reached a point due south of the target area, Rhodie cranked hard to the right and headed north. The two planes flew almost on top of the smoke now billowing on the hilltop before pushing over and diving.

Rhodie hit the east side of the hill with a string of bombs, and the hill disappeared in the fireball. Pharaoh followed, pickling his bombs as he dove on the west side of the hill. With his ordnance expended, he pulled out of his dive.

As he raced away from the hill, he checked over his shoulder to ensure he wasn't being chased by a missile. To his shock, Rhodie could see the contrail of a missile rushing at his fleeing Corsair. He banked hard and dropped a string of flares.

The aircraft buffeted as the missile detonated behind it. Pharaoh was sure that he was dead. He nearly punched out of the aircraft, but he hesitated. He still had control.

"Rhodie, once we're clear of the battlefield, can you give my aircraft a visual inspection? I just took a MANPAD hit, but everything seems to be working."

"Roger that, Pharaoh, let's get feet wet and see what we can see." The two Corsairs headed west, toward the Pacific. Once they were over the ocean, Rhodie dropped back and looked at his wingman's aircraft. "Yeah, you definitely got peppered. It looks like minimal damage to your elevator and vertical stab. It doesn't look like anything that'll keep you from getting back to the ship, but keep an eye on your instruments. There's no telling what might have shaken loose in there."

"Understood, thanks, Rhodie." The two continued on course toward *Coral Sea* in silence. Rhodie remained abaft Pharaoh, keeping an eye on the younger aviator.

After ten minutes of flying, the silence was interrupted.

"Rhodie, Pharaoh. I'm getting a hydraulic leak indication. Can you see anything back there?"

"Negative, Pharaoh. I've got nothing. How's your hydraulic pressure?"

"It's within standard parameters, but dropping. I'm switching to the secondary."

"Understood. That missile probably cracked a line and it's just taken a while to develop into a real leak. Just keep an eye on the backup. We're getting close. And try to relax."

Pharaoh wasn't too concerned. He knew that they had built the redundant systems into the Corsair for this exact reason. Any strike aircraft was going to put itself in harm's way. A fighter could fly twenty successful missions without encountering a SAM. A Corsair would be lucky to fly five. His thoughts were interrupted by the master caution light. A quick look at the hydraulic indicator told him what he already knew: he was in trouble.

"Rhodie, Pharaoh. I'm getting another hydraulic pressure warning."

"Understood, Pharaoh, let's call the boss and see what he wants us to do here." The two planes were still ten miles from *Coral Sea*, but some decisions had to be made.

"Mustang, Charger Four, over."

"Go ahead, Charger Four."

"Mustang, we have a developing situation here. Charger Nine took some damage from a MANPAD back there. He's bleeding hydraulic fluid from both systems." Rhodie and the Commander, Air Group, or CAG went over the particulars of the problem, with Pharoah adding the pertinent details regarding the rate of loss and the responsiveness of the aircraft.

"Try not to maneuver too much," said Rhodie. "There's no telling if you're going to make it worse."

"Charger Nine, CAG. We're going to have you bring her in for a barricade arrest. Listen, son, you've got the training for this, and we're going to get you down. But we can't risk you missing the trap and having to come around. You're only going to get one shot at this, but we'll have you in the wardroom in no time. Charger Four, we need you shipboard as soon as you arrive on station."

It was unsaid, but Pharaoh knew that they were bringing Rhodie in first in case he missed his landing and damaged the flight deck.

Both aviators acknowledged the orders and Pharaoh went back to nervously watching his hydraulic fluid leak out of his aircraft. Commander Duncan, the CO of the Royal Maces, came on the radio and gave Pharaoh some words of encouragement. Several of his other squadmates came on to wish him luck, or in Heaver's case, to claim dibs on Pharaoh's collection of cassette tapes.

Pharaoh watched Rhodie land, then extended five miles behind *Coral Sea* to set up his own landing run. He dropped his tailhook and landing gear as the ship's landing signal officer, or LSO, guided him in.

"Looking good, Charger Nine. Throttle back a bit. Remember to cut power when you hit the deck. You can't bolt out of this one."

Under normal conditions, Pharaoh was trained to push his throttle to full military power as he touched down. This would allow him to get airborne again to make another pass. Today's first pass would be for all the marbles. He could see the barricade on the flight deck. The twenty-foot-tall barricade looked a bit like a giant white ladder lying on its side.

"Lift your nose a bit… That's good." The LSO's voice calmed Pharaoh.

If something is going to go wrong, it'll go wrong soon. As if he'd willed the issue into existence, the master caution light flashed again. He was suffering a complete hydraulic failure.

"Charger Nine, get your nose up." Pharaoh pulled back on the stick, willing the mechanism to respond. "Nose up! Nose up!" the calls from the LSO echoed in his ears.

Without warning, he was thrown forward in the cockpit as his tailhook caught the first wire, and he was brought to a halt in the webbing of the emergency barrier. Deck apes swarmed the plane, clearing the barricade and ensuring the young lieutenant could get out of the aircraft.

"Next time, let's not get hit by the bad guys, Pharaoh," said Rhodie, waving from his cockpit across the deck. "Welcome home."

Chapter 10

7 January 1981
Houston, Texas

It was a rare occasion for the Bush family to gather outside of the holidays. For George Bush, this was more important than Thanksgiving and Christmas combined. The nation was at war. He knew that one day this war would end.

And when the question was asked, "What did you do in the war?" the answer would be "Everything that we could." His campaign for the presidency in 1980 was hardly over, but he was already planning for 1984. To that end, he had gathered the family in the wealthy West Oaks suburb of Houston to ensure that the rest of the family would be doing everything that they could.

After dinner as a family, the men retired to the sitting room, where the elder Bush held court with his sons.

"Boys," said the elder Bush, "this war is going to define the rest of this century and the next. I don't want any of you thinking that this is anything like what you've seen before. This is not Vietnam. Communism has always been an existential threat to our nation and our way of life. When we fought the wars against the communists in Korea and Vietnam, we had the luxury of staying out of them personally." At that, he glanced at his eldest son.

"But this is different. This war is coming for us, and we must be prepared to fight the Soviet war machine in Europe. When I was younger than any of you, I was faced with the same decision that you are now. I chose to join the Navy as an aviator to fight fascism. Tonight, I want to know what your intentions are. What will you be willing to do to serve your country in the face of this immeasurable threat?"

There wasn't an immediate response, and he continued, "George, if you're interested in reactivating your Texas Air National Guard Commission, I can make some calls."

"I don't know, Poppy," said George Jr. "It's been years since I've flown, and I didn't exactly leave with a sterling record."

"Now listen, son," said the elder Bush. "You loved to fly, and they're going to need all the pilots they can get. I'll look into what it's going to take to get your commission reinstated, but you need to get yourself in the mindset of a pilot. Things have changed a lot in the past six years, but you'll still be ahead of a fresh recruit. With some familiarization training, you should be able to integrate into a unit quickly."

The younger Bush looked at the glass of bourbon in his hand but didn't argue.

"And you, John?" asked George Sr. "What are your plans during our nation's struggle?" John Bush, affectionately called "Jeb" by his friends, didn't have a previous military background to fall back on.

"I thought that with my background in Latin American studies, I might apply for a commission with Army Intelligence. I think I could do some real good for the people down there, and help with the war effort in this hemisphere."

"I appreciate your reasoning," said George Sr. "But things on the ground move more quickly than the bureaucracy does. By the time you're trained and commissioned, there may not be a war in Latin America. Then again, the Army will find a use for you, and if you can get into Intelligence, you'll be well placed." The senior Bush knew damned well that if the son of a former CIA director like himself wanted to join Army Intel, someone would find a spot for him.

"What about you, Neil?" asked George Sr.

"I've been thinking about it since the war broke out. I've decided to follow in your footsteps and join the Navy. I'll go wherever they send me, but with my MBA, I'm guessing it'll be supply and logistics."

"There are certainly worse places to be. And don't be fooled, supply and logistics are just as important as any other aspect of the battle plan. The strength of our forces in the Second World War was logistics. We could bring more people and equipment to the fight than our enemies."

"I'm joining the Marines," said Marvin, the youngest brother. The room got quiet. "I've been thinking about it, and to be honest, I think that this is where I can do the most good. I've already been to the recruiter, I've had my physical, and I'm scheduled to head to OCS in three weeks."

The elder Bush was taken aback. He knew that he could expect his boys to do their part, but he hadn't expected one of them to put themselves so directly in harm's way.

"That's a hard life, Marvin. I've known many a Marine in my time, and I know that the Corps will make you a better man." He raised his glass. "Boys, there will be dark days ahead. I'm proud of each of you for standing up and answering our nation's call in this terrible time. May God bless you in your efforts, and may God bless us all."

Chapter 11

8 January 1981
20th Polish Armored Division
Northeast of Schweinfurt, Germany

Corporal Bronisław "Borna" Kohutek saw the punch coming. The bear of a man in front of him might have been strong, but he was clumsy. Borna easily ducked the haymaker and drilled the man with a right cross to his exposed side. Even with the bear's thick uniform coat, Borna knew he'd feel that one. The bear fell to the ground, but not before grabbing onto Borna's sleeve, bringing him down with him.

Now Borna was in trouble.

The bear pulled Borna in close and started to squeeze the air out of his lungs. With each cough, Borna pushed out air that he couldn't replace. Panicking, he clasped his hands together and started to beat at the bear's head, hoping for a desperate blow to dislodge the man—to free himself.

Then, as if by magic, he could breathe again. He sputtered as gasping breath after gasping breath put his body in order. He looked up to see Sergeant Alfons Knopik, his tank commander, standing above him.

"What the fuck is wrong with you?" asked Knopik, kicking Borna's hip and knocking him flat on the ground.

Still gasping, Borna pointed at the bear, who was being restrained by Private Grzegorz Adamiak, his tank's loader. "He was sleeping at his post and didn't want to be woken."

"Bullshit," spat the bear.

"Well, he's not asleep now, so everybody back to posts," said Knopik. Then, extending a hand to his gunner, he said, "You can't go beating people because you're bored, Borna. Save your fight for the fascists."

The first week of the war had been brutal for the Hussars of the 20th Polish Armored Division. The relief Sergeant Knopik had felt after surviving first contact with NATO forces was quickly ground down into the numbness he now felt. They had quickly overwhelmed the town of Mellrichstadt before NATO could mount a vigorous defense. But even the minor slow-down in operational tempo was enough to allow troops to dig in at Bad Neustadt an der Saale.

The advance was stopped in its tracks by massed antitank guided-missile attacks. The enemy had lain in wait, allowing the advance units to cross the Brend River before blowing the bridges and unleashing preprepared TOW missiles on them.

The T-55 tanks and OT-64 armored personnel carriers exploded under the missile barrage, and any men who managed to escape from the crippled vehicles were gunned down by machine-gun fire. Knopik shuddered at the memory.

With the bridges blown, the division was stuck on the north shore of the Brend. Because they were facing dismounted infantry, hidden in the town, they couldn't effectively engage them. Sure, they could fire round after round into a building until it came down, but by that point, the fascist ants would have infested another building. They needed to get across that river. Knopik's lieutenant informed the platoon that they were waiting for a company from the 7th Engineer Battalion to come bridge the river.

There was a rumor that one of the company commanders had ordered his men to mount the snorkels to their T-55s, but he was killed by a "stray bullet" before the order was carried out.

"Sergeant!" called out Private Leon Dębiński, Knopik's driver. The boy was standing in the turret of the tank, gesturing at the sergeant to come over. "The lieutenant is on the radio." *Finally, we're getting some orders,* thought Knopik. He climbed up the side of his tank and slid down through the commander's hatch.

"Crusader Two-One, this is Crusader Two-Two transmitting."

"Crusader Two-Two, I need all tank commanders to report to my vehicle now." *He could have just told Dębiński to pass the word,* thought Knopik as he hefted himself back out of the tank.

As an afterthought, he called back to Dębiński, "Stay with the tank. We're probably moving out soon." The only reason to report to the lieutenant's tank would be to get orders that were too sensitive to be transmitted in the open. Of course, any NATO spies listening in might make the same assumption and be eagerly awaiting the move.

At the lieutenant's tank, Knopik met the other two tank commanders from his platoon. Lieutenant Mirosław Stencel stood at the front of his T-55, with Sergeant Cyprian Lubomirski standing over his shoulder looking at a map that was splayed out on the sloped armor on the front of the tank.

"Sergeant Knopik, I'm glad you could make it," said the lieutenant. It was a mild rebuke, made in jest. Since coming to rest in this rear area of the fighting, the platoon had relaxed some of the tighter discipline that they needed in combat. So long as one crew member remained with a tank and the rest of the crew was within shouting distance, the lieutenant was content. "I hear that one of your men was in a bit of a dustup this morning?"

"It appears that fighting the Germans isn't enough for some of our men. I'll ensure that Corporal Kohutek is disciplined for his part."

"We can worry about that after this next mission." Knopik didn't like the ominous sound of that. "We're rolling in twenty minutes. We're heading out to these hills over here." He pointed to the foothills on the northeast side of the city. Knopik and Lubomirski shared a quick glance. They knew these hills well. The fascists had been using underground bunkers in those hills to hide and maneuver for harassing attacks along the Soviet flanks. Just like at Bad Neustadt an der Saale, it was the damned antitank guided missiles that were giving the Polish forces hell. Here, the man-portable M47 Dragon missiles were being deployed from these bunkers.

"Reconnaissance overflights have been unable to locate these bunkers, so we haven't been able to bombard them. We're going to go find those bunkers. Basically, gentlemen, we're bait."

Both sergeants muttered curses under their breath.

"You'll be taking on a load of D-412 smoke rounds. We will advance along this eastern valley, from the north to the south." The lieutenant drew a line with his index finger. "During our transit, you and your gunner will be on the lookout for bunker entrances. You are to mark any bunkers you locate with a smoke round.

"If you find a relatively close bunker, you need to mark it and then get as far away as you can. The Air Force will be dropping five-hundred-kilogram bombs on the targets you have marked, and I don't want you to get the paint on my tanks scratched."

The two men nodded.

"When we advance, I will be in the lead and will maintain a visual focus on the thirty degrees straight ahead. Knopik, you are to follow and scan the thirty degrees left of center line. Lubomirski, you will bring up the rear and scan thirty degrees right of center line."

Both men nodded again before the lieutenant added, "Look, I don't like these orders any more than you do, but we need to get these vermin out of those hills, and this is what the command has come up with."

"The sooner we get in there, the sooner we can be on our way to Würzburg," said Knopik, just trying to put a positive spin on a very negative morning.

Back at the tank, the rest of the crew had assembled.

"If we survive the day, the lieutenant will have your ass tonight, Borna." Borna just nodded in response. Knopik relayed the orders to his horrified crew.

"So, we're going to go into a den of missiles in broad daylight? That's suicide," said Dębiński.

"It's not suicide," replied Knopik, "it's orders. And keep your voice down. You know better than to display defeatism in the open."

Lowering his voice, Dębiński continued, "We need to cross into the valley, where there are known antitank missile forces. We're only supposed to shoot smoke shells at them, and then we have to hope that our air force doesn't accidentally drop a bomb on our tank?" He looked to the ground and shook his head.

"OK, look," said Knopik, "I agree that we can't go in there defenseless. Grześ, I want you to get the rounds set up so that you can alternate HE and smoke. If we come across one of these nests, we'll first hit it with the high explosives to keep their heads down, then we'll hit it with the smoke for the aircraft. You need to be fast. I don't want the lieutenant to notice that we're deviating from the direct orders."

The loader nodded in understanding. Given the limits of the T-55 loading process, which required the gun to be elevated before it could be loaded, this was a tall order. "And be careful with those smoke shells—they're probably older than you are."

With the housekeeping out of the way, they mounted up and readied themselves for the order. Twenty minutes later, they were approaching the entrance of the valley.

"Keep a sharp eye out, Borna," said Knopik, "I don't want to die surprised."

Both Borna and Knopik were pressed into their binocular view ports, staring out at the hills to the left of the tank. Knopik wondered what the enemy would make of the column of three tanks traversing the hostile battlefield in the middle of the day. The absurdity of the situation only drove home the desperation of the army to get past this obstacle.

Boom! The report of the 100mm cannon on the lieutenant's tank got everyone's attention. It was to the right of Knopik's field of vision, and he didn't dare turn away from his own search. Instead, he called down to his driver.

"Dębiński, what can you see?"

"The lieutenant fired a smoke round about fifteen degrees about three thousand yards."

Knopik wished he knew what the lieutenant saw. What did the target look like? A "bunker entrance" could look like anything.

"I have something, three hundred degrees. It looks like a cement mound, covered by brush and trees."

"Fire!" said Knopik without hesitation. The round went out, and immediately he ordered, "Reload smoke!" Borna raised the gun, and Private Adamiak slammed the smoke shell into the breech.

Fifteen seconds after the HE round was out, the smoke round followed. "Reload, HE!" Again, the barrel went up, and Adamiak slammed home the round. From outside the tank, they heard a terrible roar.

"Sergeant, the lieutenant's tank has been hit," said Dębiński. "It looks bad." With an actual threat in front of him, Knopik traversed the turret forward to see if they could identify what had taken out his platoon commander.

"I've got it," said Borna, firing off another round of HE at the new target.

"Reload smoke." As the men coordinated the reload, Knopik thought that having the HE round loaded might have saved their life.

"Firing," said Borna, but there was no pounding explosion following the words. "Misfire!" yelled the gunner.

"Something's wrong," called Adamiak. Smoke began to flood the fighting compartment of the tank.

"*Gówno*" shouted the four men, almost in unison. Each man popped their hatch, and they scrambled out of the tank as the vintage smoke round continued to billow.

"Take cover," said Knopik. "If those missileers recover from our HE round, they're going to be gunning for us."

"Maybe they'll see the smoke," said Borna, "and think that another unit took us out."

Then it dawned on Knopik.

"Run! We need to get as far away from this tank as possible!" The crew fell in behind him, everyone sprinting as quickly as they could, putting distance between themselves and their beleaguered tank.

"What are we—" started Borna before he was cut off by a massive explosion on the hillside they had marked just minutes before. It was suddenly clear that the tank was marked with the same smoke. They ran faster. Then they were flying. The blast wave hit them before the sound did.

Knopik couldn't hear anything except a buzzing in his ears. He couldn't see anything except the dirt in front of his face. But he could feel, and he felt pain. All over his body was a dull aching. He raised himself on one elbow and shook his head to try to clear the fog. After a minute, as his hearing returned he shouted,

"Sound off!"

"Gunner here," replied Borna.

"Driver here," said Dębiński.

Knopik looked around for Adamiak, spotting his prone body ten yards away. He ran to the young man and instantly knew that he was dead. A piece of shrapnel from their tank had embedded itself in his back. His open eyes stared off into the abyss.

"Damn." There was nothing more for Knopik to say. They still needed to get out of here before the NATO forces became bold enough to investigate. In the distance, he saw Sergeant Lubomirski's tank approaching them. The men ran for the tank.

As they got near, the hatch popped open and Lubomirski's head was exposed long enough for him to shout, "Get the tank, we're getting the hell out of here!"

Knopik's surviving crew climbed on the front of the vehicle as the remainder of the platoon fled the valley.

Chapter 12

8 January 1981
21st Special Air Service Regiment
South of Lübeck, West Germany

Trooper Trevor Pearce watched as Corporal Willis picked up the radio receiver. This was the first contact they'd had with the outside world since they'd crawled into their hole a week ago.

"Oscar Four-Three, this is Echo One-One." Normally, Willis would have transmitted a response. However, early in the development of SBUs, the Army had discovered that the enemy could use high-frequency direction finding, or HF/DF, to quickly pinpoint and destroy the units. Instead, after Echo One-One repeated the call, they transmitted a series of letters and numbers.

Pearce listened as Command issued coded instructions. Willis and Cooper were both jotting down the alphanumeric message. Once Command signed off, Cooper and Willis compared their copy. Since there was no discrepancy between the two copies, Willis began the process of decoding.

"Looks like we've got a long-range recon mission," said Willis. "We've got some coordinates of a suspected fuel depot. No idea how they got these, but they want us to confirm the location, then get the message to our SBO contact in Mechow."

"Seems pretty straightforward," said Cooper.

"I should say so," replied Willis. "The kicker is that these coordinates put the enemy depot less than two and a half klicks from here." The men in the bunker exchanged a tense glance with one another. The Soviets were right on top of them. But that was the mission they'd signed up for.

"I'll take Pearce with me. Coop, you're in charge until we get back." With that, he and Pearce sat down at the table to go over the specifics of the operation. Once Pearce answered all of his questions and assured him that he had a grip on the mission, Willis grabbed his L1A1 rifle and headed for the tunnel hatch.

Pearce followed. "Coop, give me a sweep before we head topside."

Across the tunnel, Cooper peered into a small green periscope. He made a clockwise turn, searching for anything out of order.

"Looks good, Chief," said Cooper. Willis carefully climbed the few rungs, slid open the hatch, and pulled himself out. Pearce followed him out, and they resealed the hatch and concealed it with dirt and brush. With their friends once again hidden, the two troopers headed out to the northeast. They maintained silence as they pushed on through the forest. Any sound could give them away. Because they didn't know much about enemy positions, they had to assume that the enemy could be behind every tree and every rock. This slowed their progress considerably.

After several hours of cautious progress, Willis motioned for Pearce to come to a halt. They were on the northeast edge of a rise, looking down on Highway 208. Pearce kept his rifle at the ready, seeking out any possible targets as Willis raised his binoculars.

After a few minutes, Willis patted Pearce's shoulder and handed him the binoculars. Pearce raised them to his eyes and scanned the horizon.

Across the highway, he saw a massive operation. There were fuel bladders on the ground, with fuel trucks lined up around the corner. If he had to guess, he'd say the bladders had been airlifted in by helicopter, and now the trucks were moving the fuel to the front lines. The Soviets had taken a real gamble with this, but so far it was paying off.

We'll have to see about that, thought Pearce as he tapped Willis and returned the binoculars.

Willis motioned to Pearce, indicating the path they were going to take. Pearce was a bit confused as they were heading in the opposite direction from their contact in Mechow. This didn't upset him. To get to Mechow, they would have needed to cross right through that Soviet force. After they made it a kilometer away from the hillcrest, Willis signaled for Pearce to bring it in.

"Whoever put together this mission," said Willis in a hushed tone, "must have just looked at the closest SBO safe house without regard for our starting position. There's no way we're going to just waltz through the entire damned Red Army. I'm exercising tactical control, and we're going to our alternate point in Salem." Willis didn't need to tell Pearce what was up, but he appreciated that he did.

It took them over three hours to cover the five kilometers between the hill and Salem. The tree line ran right up to the tiny hamlet, and the safe house was on the northeast edge. The two troopers gathered what concealment they could and observed the scene. They were looking for any indication that the house had been blown, and what Soviet activity was in the area.

After an hour on the hill, Pearce was convinced that they were clear. None of the prearranged deterrent signals were present. Should the house be compromised, the blinds would be halfway drawn, or the welcome mat would be upside down. With neither of those conditions being present, they knew they were in the clear on that account.

As for Soviet activity, that too was in their favor. There was nothing in Salem to attract the Soviets, and the major refueling operation just a few kilometers to the north meant there was no reason for a large occupation force here. There was light traffic along Kammberg road, and the occasional foot patrol, but nothing else.

They waited until sunset, then, when the patrol passed by, Pearce slipped out of the trees and made a dash for the house. Speed was of the essence, but operational security demanded that he use the passcode.

He knocked on the door.

"*Wer ist da?*" came the reply from the other side of the door.

"*Es ist Hecke,*" said Pearce, finding it odd to refer to himself as a "hedge." The correct pass code having been provided, the door opened. Pearce quickly entered, and they retreated to a windowless closet.

Pearce explained everything in detail and provided the exact coordinates of the fuel depot, as well as the approximate amount of fuel present and the number of fuel trucks at the time of the report. Once this was completed, he returned to the front room of the house and peered out the window. He opened and closed the blinds, leaving a slit open for him to see out. Then he waited.

He wasn't sure how long he'd been watching when he saw a single glowing red torch turn on and off once. Willis had signaled to him that he was clear. Pearce stepped out of the house and had taken about ten quick steps into the open when he saw headlamps in the distance. *Bloody hell, there's a car turning onto Kammberg*, he thought. There was no way he was going to make it to the trees. He was screwed. He threw himself on the ground, hiding his painted face in his right elbow.

His ten steps carried him across the road, and about ten yards passed. He might as well have been in the middle of the road. Pearce watched as the headlights turned and passed right over himself. He waited for the sound of gunfire and fingered the safety on his L1A1. *I doubt I'm going to even get a shot off*, he thought. But he knew that staying as still as possible was his only move here. If he were to try and position himself to get a shot, there was no way the enemy wouldn't see him. Sweat beaded on his brow despite the cold temperature. His heart pounded in his chest.

The lights continued to pass by as the vehicle on the road continued its turn. As it continued off to the north, Pearce caught a glimpse of it. It was a Volkswagen Golf. He had no idea if the people in the car were German civilians or Soviet/Warsaw Pact soldiers. But either way, he was alive. He waited for the car to pass in the distance, then completed his sprint to the tree line.

"I thought you were as good as clipped out there," said Willis. "I can't have you leaving the team this early in the war," he added with a smirk. The two then made their way back home to the MEXE shelter.

The following day, as they awaited further instruction, they were rewarded with a massive rumbling of the earth. One of the canvas roof panels tore open, and some dirt started to fall in, but Cooper was quick to make a repair with the fast application of duct tape.

"What the hell was that?" asked Pearce.

"I'd say that was Ivan's petrol station going up in flames," replied Willis.

Chapter 13

8 January 1981
Peretrusovo, USSR

Pyotr Nilovich Demichev, the Soviet Minister of Culture, watched a small boat float along the Volga River. It was innocuous at first glance, but Pyotr knew that the men on the boat were armed and dangerous. Security around this compound was unlike anything he'd ever experienced before.

It had been a week since he had been whisked out of his Moscow apartment and brought to this location between Moscow and the city of Tver. Since that morning, he'd had no contact with anyone outside of this facility.

"It's a brisk morning," said the Director of the KGB, Yuri Vladomirovich Andropov.

"Yes, a perfect December morning, Comrade Director," replied Pyotr. He didn't think he was being tested, but it was better to just be as positive as possible when dealing with Andropov.

"What was the latest briefing you have had on the war?" asked Andropov. Now Pyotr was sure he was being tested.

"I was at the general briefing this morning. The forces of our communist brothers in Poland, Czechoslovakia and Germany are as slow and inept as we expected, but NATO is even slower and more inept. Our only problem at the time is in the North German Plain. The East German 9th Tank Division's thrust was halted by the British Army of the Rhine. Our 1st Guards Red Banner Tank Army is in position to break through the lines there. Hanover is surrounded. The generals believe that Schweinfurt will fall today or tomorrow, and there is no expected NATO resistance between there and Würzburg."

Andropov nodded.

"At sea," continued Pyotr, "our submarine forces have sunk the occasional cargo ship crossing the Atlantic. However, the Americans haven't sent out a major convoy to this point, so we haven't really been tested, but that will change soon. The NATO air base at Keflavik is not operational, but it will be soon if we don't send in a follow-up attack in some form."

"That will be a challenge," said Andropov. "It was simple to send in a massed air assault when everyone was asleep at their post. With NATO on full alert, we will not return so easily. Thank you for the update, Comrade Minister. There is a lot to take in, and I am pleased that you are following everything in detail."

"Thank you, Comrade Director," replied Pyotr, thankful to have seemingly passed the test.

"Please, call me Yuri," replied the Director.

Pyotr tried to hide his surprise. There were only a few years between them in age, but given Andropov's position, he didn't expect to be addressing him by his given name.

"There are many things afoot, beyond the war, Pyotr," continued Andropov. "Even before we started planning the invasion, plans were underway to make changes in leadership. The liberals under Kosygin have destroyed our economy. Their refusal to implement more centralized control and their experiments with market reforms did nothing but set us on the course for total war with the West."

Pyotr found this surprising. The spat between Kosygin and Andropov was well known. But by pushing the "liberals" out of power, Andropov would be parting ways with friends and political allies. Pyotr was unsure if he should test his new relationship, but he needed specifics.

"Does this include Comrades Gorbachev and Ryzhkov?" asked Pyotr, referring to the Secretary of the Central Committee and the First Deputy Chairman of the State Planning Committee, respectively. These two men were the most reform-minded in the Central Committee, and Gorbachev was a friend of Andropov's.

"Yes," replied Andropov after a moment's hesitation. With that one word, he sealed his friend's fate and promoted the Minister of Culture to the de facto second-in-command of the Soviet Union.

****

8 January 1981
Mount Weather Emergency Operations Center
Rural Northern Virginia

The massive amounts of information flowing into and out of the executive compound were daunting. Between the volume and the speed of operations, it became difficult to remember what day it was. Had the war been going for a day? A week? A month? All seemed equally likely to President Carter.

"Who's next, Ham?" Carter asked his Chief of Staff, Hamilton Jordan.

"It's Secretary Brown, sir," replied Jordan.

"Let's get this over with," sighed the President. The briefings from his Secretary of Defense were always depressing. Carter looked around at the sterile, white walls and the fluorescent lighting. "We need to get something on the walls in here. Maybe a plant or two also."

"I'll see to it, sir," said Jordan as he and Dr. Harold Brown traded places.

"Harold, it's good to see you," lied the President. "How about today we start with the good news?"

"Well…" Dr. Brown hesitated before continuing, "The Soviet invasion isn't moving nearly as quickly as our analysts predicted."

"Does anyone know what's causing this?" asked the President. Before Dr. Brown could answer, he continued, "Is it due to the use of the Polish and Czechoslovakian armies at the front of the attack?"

"That's certainly a part of it," said Dr. Brown. "But there's more to it than that. The effectiveness of our antitank guided missiles is greater than we expected. Infantry units can ambush charging armored vehicles from hidden spaces, then withdraw before the tanks can respond effectively. We believe this has had a lot to do with a slowing of the assault."

"Well, that is good news," said Carter.

"In other good news, there have been no reports of chemical or biological weapons use. When the tempo of operations slowed, we feared that the Soviets might try to use chemical weapons to break up the concentrations of missile-armed infantry. Instead, they seem content to take the losses at this point."

"Anything else? This is the most positive briefing we've had in the past week."

"Yes," replied Dr. Brown, "the Navy is reporting that they've secured everything south of the Fortieth Parallel near the Azores. Keeping the sea and air clear of Soviet forces will be essential to getting the convoys through."

"And when will those convoys be departing?"

"They'll be heading out in the next day or two," replied Dr. Brown before switching gears. "Let's start the bad news in the Pacific. The DPRK has pounded Seoul and the surrounding areas nonstop since the start of the war. They have surged over the demilitarized zone from east of Seoul to the Sea of Japan. We knew that they had been building some massive infiltration tunnels, but we underestimated how advanced those projects were. They were able to bypass some of our more fortified units and attack them from the flanks. There were even reports of what appeared to be prison labor being forced to drive civilian vehicles across minefields with the motivation that if they got to the other side alive, they would be pardoned."

"That's barbaric," said the President.

"Kim Il-sung has never been known for his humanity or compassion, but yes, this is bad, even for him. There's also some civil unrest in South Korea, but I'll let the professors handle that." Brown referred to Zbigniew Brzezinski and Jeane Kirkpatrick, the National Security Advisor and Secretary of State respectively. Brown had earned a PhD in physics when he was twenty-one, but he wasn't included in the nickname.

"In Europe," continued Brown, "as I mentioned, the advance in Germany has slowed, but Austria has been overrun without resistance. It seems the shock of the attack and the disregard for their neutral stance left them incapable of an organized defense. This has increased pressure on the Italian front, as Warsaw Pact troops are now attacking through Austria as well as Yugoslavia."

"I'll talk to Jeane and Zbig about getting Turkey to commit," said the President. "Creating an eastern front could really relieve some of the pressure on the Italians."

"I don't have much hope for that, sir," replied Brown. "But I understand that we have to do whatever we can to turn this situation around." Brown glanced at his watch "I'll let you get on with your day, sir." Again, Brown and Hamilton Jordan swapped places.

"Who's next?" asked Carter.

"Actually, it's me," said Jordan. "We need to talk about this." He slid a copy of the *Chicago Tribune* across the table. It was opened to the opinion section, and the headline read "Jenny Get Your Gun" by Phyllis Schlafly. He read the entire piece, though he didn't really need to. He knew exactly what she was going to say. It was basically a five-hundred-word "I told you so."

Carter set the paper on his desk and asked, "Well, what are the real-world effects of this?"

"It's too soon to tell," replied Jordan. "There are a lot of people moving on this. We have women showing up to register for the Selective Service, we have mothers of sons calling their congressmen, demanding that women be added to the draft. There are even feminists weighing in supporting adding women to the draft."

"Where do we stand on this legally?"

"I've spoken to Civiletti about that," referring to the Attorney General, Benjamin Civiletti, "and he thinks that with the Twenty-Seventh Amendment in place, any of these groups will have standing and will likely prevail in court. He believes that while we can stall this thing, in the end, we'll have to include women in the draft."

"What about logistically? How are we going to manage this?" asked the President.

"I haven't gotten with Harold and the Joint Chiefs, but it's in the works. I'm going to ask them about what roles women can cover in each of the services. Functionally, there are many roles that women will be equally, if not more, equipped to handle. Think of the nursing corps in World War II as an example. Obviously, we can't just dump all of our drafted women into that field, but that's my starting point."

"That makes sense," said the President, "but there are other considerations that we need to take. What about families? We can't draft both a mother and a father at the same time. We need to account for that."

"I agree. There's a waiver process in place for things like college deferments, and conscientious objectors. So, there's a starting point. I think we should also consider allowing a family member—I'm thinking husband or brother here—to take on the draft burden for their wife or sister."

"That's an interesting approach," replied the President. "It will be interesting to see how this plays out."

"In the end, we need to field the best army we can within the constraints of the law. If we need to add a Twenty-Eighth Amendment excluding the draft from the ERA, we should start working on that now."

"I don't think that's going to happen, Ham. But if it comes to that, we'll deal with it."

"OK, that's all I had. I pushed the professors off to walk you through this. I'm sure they're antsy to get your ear."

"Send them in," said Carter.

As soon as the door was opened to let Jordan out, the professors were making their way in.

"Jeane, Zbig, I hope the day is treating you well," said the President. He tried to vary the greetings of each of his staffers to avoid falling into monotony.

"Unfortunately, Mr. President," replied Zbigniew Brzezinski, "the day has not been kind." Carter could see by the look on Jeane Kirkpatrick's face that she agreed.

"Well, let's not waste time, let's get into it." Dr. Kirkpatrick took the visitor's chair while Dr. Brzezinski stood. This had quickly become the pattern when they'd started delivering joint briefings. Occasionally, Brzezinski would have a separate meeting, but for the most part the National Security Advisor and the Secretary of State maintained a united front.

"Turkey won't budge," said Dr. Kirkpatrick. "The socialist government that took power in September continues to ignore their Article 5 obligations under the NATO treaty."

"What is their justification?" asked the President.

"That the oppressive conditions of the proletariat in the west is what provoked the war. Essentially, they're mirroring the Soviet talking points. They're saying that they cannot participate in a war that was caused by the actions of NATO governments."

"That's absurd," said the President.

"And yet, it's true," replied Dr. Kirkpatrick. "At this point, Turkey is at best a neutral party, at worst a Soviet client. I believe that they're waiting to see where the war goes before they commit. If we can stop the Soviets in Germany, they'll come to our side. But as long as the Soviets are advancing, they'll sit on the fence."

"Until they actively join the Soviets," added Brzezinski.

"Is there nothing we can do?" asked the President.

"Ambassador McHenry is going to give a speech in the United Nations General Assembly calling them out for failing to abide by their agreements, but nothing will come to it. We're basically just putting it in the record so that when we've won this war, they can't pretend that this didn't happen."

"Anything else on the situation with Turkey? Harold said there was something going on in South Korea."

"No, sir, that's it on Turkey. As for South Korea, Dr. Brzezinski was taking the lead on that."

"Yes, Mr. President," said Dr. Brzezinski. "As we feared, the fragile hold of the Chun Doo-hwan regime is fueling significant resistance in South Korea. There are paramilitary forces coalescing around deposing the current government. Obviously, we have suspicions that this is a well-funded psychological operation, but we don't know whether it's coming from Deng Xiaoping in China, or Brezhnev in the Soviet Union."

"Speaking of Deng Xiaoping," interrupted the President, "has there been any indication as to whether or not the Chinese will intervene in Korea?"

"Not yet," replied Dr. Kirkpatrick. "Just like in 1950, they'll wait until the DPRK starts to lose before committing." Carter nodded at that, and Dr. Brzezinski continued.

"These new factions in South Korea are causing significant logistical problems. They have attacked rail hubs and blown bridges and overpasses, slowing down our ability to get men and equipment to the front."

"What can we do to combat this new threat?" asked the President.

"There's not much that we can do, sir," replied Dr. Brzezinski.

"There is one thing," said Dr. Kirkpatrick. The President clasped his hands, waiting, and Brzezinski looked away. "We can give them what they want. We can replace Chun Doo-hwan."

"Do you believe that will help the situation?" asked the President.

"I do. In fact, I've taken the liberty of talking this out with Director Turner. The CIA has had plans in place since the Gwangju Uprising back in May. Mr. President. We need to confront the reality that there are no outcomes available where Chun Doo-hwan is the leader of South Korea by the end of next year. There will be new leadership in the Republic, and we are simply deciding whether that will be Kim Il-sung or someone more to our liking."

"Mr. President," said Dr. Brzezinski, "our administration has made it a hallmark of our governing philosophy that we do not prop up or overthrow the governments of sovereign nations."

"This is different, Zbig," replied the President. "We're not going into South Korea to overthrow the will of the people. Chun Doo-hwan is a brutal dictator. If we need to throw him out of the way to save the country, then so be it."

Dr. Brzezinski was taken aback. "Jeane, who does Director Turner have in mind as a replacement?"

Dr. Kirkpatrick's face showed no indication that she had just won a major point in her battle with Dr. Brzezinski. "They're leaning toward Kim Dae-jung. He's currently slated for execution, so he may not be available." The coldness with which Dr. Kirkpatrick referred to the man's death was unnerving. "If that's the case, Turner believes Kim Young-sam would agree. Either one of these men should quell the general unrest, leaving only the die-hard communists and foreign interlopers."

"I see," said the President. "I want both of you to work with Turner on this, and get me a plan by tomorrow. We need this enacted as soon as possible."

"As you say, Mr. President," said Dr. Brzezinski as Dr. Kirkpatrick rose and they exited the room.

Chapter 14

9 January 1981
Minskiy Komsomolets
East Atlantic Ocean

Captain of the First Rank Dmitriy Usatov was in command of a revolutionary Soviet submarine. The concept of *Minskiy Komsomolets* was like the previous Project 670 *Skat* submarines. The difference was in scope. While the *Skat* boats could carry eight P-120 antiship cruise missiles, the *Minskiy Komsomolets* carried twenty-four P-700 missiles. These state-of-the-art missiles were just now coming into service in the Soviet Navy. Only *Kirov* and *Minskiy Komsomolets* were armed with them. With a maximum speed in excess of Mach 2 and a range of over six hundred kilometers, the missile could outperform anything NATO was fielding at the time.

Captain Usatov knew that the Soviet Union created his boat with one purpose in mind: to sink American aircraft carriers. From his earliest days in the Soviet Navy, sinking an American carrier had been the pinnacle achievement that a submarine commander could hope to accomplish. With his current mission, he might get his chance. It was all about exploiting that chance and making it count.

"Lieutenant Krivov," said Usatov, "what's the status of the Nakat?"

"Sir," replied Krivov, the watch officer, "the Nakat has been tested and is ready to receive signals."

"Very well," said Usatov. *Minskiy Komsomolets* deployed the Nakat, an ELINT, or electronic intelligence, mast from periscope depth. This device would allow them to detect any enemy radar signals from two hundred and fifty kilometers away. It was always risky operating near the surface, even in the open ocean. However, their last burst communication from North Fleet Headquarters had sent them to this time and location to monitor the airwaves.

Usatov knew the broad strokes of the plan. *K-162*, an older cruise missile submarine, was operating out to the east of *Minskiy Komsomolets*. If the older submarine could get into firing position, she would provoke a response from the Americans. The twenty-year-old P-5 missiles on board *K-162* were modified to be launched on a simple line of bearing. They would be fired in the general direction of the enemy. Though the P-5 missiles were out of date, they were enough of a concern that the Americans would be forced to respond. Once the Americans lit up their fire control radars, *Minskiy Komsomolets* would pounce.

Now though, it was a waiting game. Intelligence indicated that there was an American carrier in the area. Usatov didn't know where the intelligence had come from. Was it a satellite? Perhaps another submarine, or a maritime patrol aircraft? It didn't matter to Captain Usatov. He had been ordered to be at this location at this time, and that was what he was doing.

"I'm deploying the periscope," said Usatov.

"Deploying periscope, understood," replied the watch officer.

Usatov put his eyes to the view port of the periscope. Unlike the old periscopes of the past, he didn't have to rotate it manually. Instead, he used thumb controls to spin the unit three hundred sixty degrees to get a full view of the surrounding ocean before retracting it. Now the ship's computer and analysts would take the data gathered by the sweep and see if there was anything useful.

After five minutes, it was clear that there wasn't.

****

USS *Ainsworth*
East Atlantic Ocean

Lieutenant Todd Jones looked at the readout again. There was definitely something out there. Was it a Soviet submarine? That he didn't know. He knew it wasn't what the carrier battle group was looking for. They were hunting the Soviet battle cruiser *Kirov*. This was underwater.

"*Ike* confirms there are no known friendly submarines expected at that location," said the sailor on the radio to his right. "They have a Viking airborne. They're sending them out to make a pass with their MAD gear."

The S-3 Viking was the mainstay of the carrier-borne ASW aircraft. The plane would fly low over the water and turn on its magnetic anomaly detection gear to see if they could detect the metal submarine hiding in the water. The Viking could also drop sonobuoys to listen for the submarine, and, if it was detected, the Viking could engage it with air-dropped torpedoes.

"It's probably another Foxtrot," said Lieutenant Junior Grade Harold Powell. Since the start of the war, the battle group had already engaged and destroyed three of the ancient Soviet attack subs. Jones worried that they were getting complacent. They didn't have a range on the contact, just a line of bearing on what was believed to be mechanical noise. Nobody else in the battle group had heard it, so they didn't have a chance to triangulate the contact.

"Get the captain to the CIC—this could be something," said Jones. He then tuned in to the ASW net.

"Nike One, this is Top Hat Three. Approaching the patrol zone." Jones imagined the aircraft dropping to very low altitude to allow the MAD gear to operate. There was a brief pause before the radio exploded back to life. "Holy hell! Nike One, Top Hat Three, contact, submarine on the surface. Engaging."

"Why the hell would it be on the surface?" asked Powell.

"Maybe it's in distress?" replied Jones.

"Nike One, this is Top Hat Three. You have missiles inbound. It looks like an Echo—I'm dropping now."

"Sound general quarters," said Jones, just in time to greet the captain.

"What do we have, Jones?" asked Commander Gregory Robinson, the ship's captain.

"Sir, there's a Soviet Echo out there firing missiles at us." The ship's klaxon rang out, sending men scrambling to their battle stations. "The S-3 from *Ike* is engaging."

"Understood, Jones. I have the conn," said the captain.

"The reason the sub is on the surface," said Jones, leaning over to Powell, "is the Echo can't fire its missiles while submerged." The men stared at the NTDS, where two upside-down V shapes appeared, and started moving toward the battle group. These icons represented the incoming SS-N-3 missiles.

Almost immediately, two upside-down U shapes appeared southwest of *South Carolina*. These icons represented the missiles sent to intercept the Soviet attack. The *California*-class nuclear-powered guided-missile cruiser could fire two standard surface-to-air missiles every eight seconds. A second pair appeared before the first reached their targets.

"Torpedo is homing," said Top Hat Three. The first set of SAMs intersected with the incoming antiship missiles and one of the ASMs disappeared.

Everyone in the CIC held their breath as the second set of SAMs approached. A third pair left *South Carolina*. They weren't needed, as the second pair took out the other ASM.

"Why'd they only shoot two missiles?" asked Powell. "I thought they had eight."

"They do," replied Jones. "But they can only fire them in pairs."

"Thank God for that," replied Powell.

"Amen."

****

Minskiy Komsomolets
East Atlantic Ocean

"Deploying the periscope," said Captain Usatov.

"Deploying the periscope, understood," replied the watch officer. Usatov made his sweep, and they waited for the data to be processed.

"*Da nyet!*" exclaimed one of the sailors examining the incoming information. "Sir, we have multiple radar contacts. Type-48 radars. Bearing seventy-five degrees, range three hundred and ninety-two kilometers."

"Number of contacts?" asked Usatov.

"Six," replied the seaman as he updated his computer, and the enemy units appeared on the display screen. There were three units in the front of the formation, two trailing, and a big fat target in the middle.

"Weapons, target four *Granits* each at the leading ships, then eight for the middle contact. Split the final four, two each for the trailing ships."

"Understood," replied the weapons officer, who immediately began punching in the required inputs to unleash the most advanced antiship cruise missiles in the world. The boat shuddered as the twenty-four missiles left their forty-degree tubes on either side of the long sail of the boat.

Usatov considered the missiles for a second. Each flight of missiles would fly at sea level toward the course programmed by the weapons officer at launch. When they neared the anticipated area of the targets, one missile from each flight would climb to a higher altitude and go active. The active radar would send updated targeting data for each of the missiles in the flight. If the Yankees managed to shoot down the active missile, the next missile in the flight would take its place. On and on until the missiles were all destroyed, or they found their targets.

"We have done well, Captain," said Captain of the Second Rank Yermolovo, the boat's political officer.

"We'll see, Comrade Captain," replied Usatov. "We likely won't know until we get home. Once we pull into port to rearm, we'll find out if we're heroes or goats."

"You doubt your weapons or tactics?" asked Yermolovo.

"No, but I take nothing for granted either," replied Usatov. "Now we just have to survive the trip home."

****

USS *Ainsworth*
East Atlantic Ocean

"Nike One, this is Bluetail Two. Vampire, vampire, vampire! Contact bearing two-five-two." Powell looked at Jones.

"It's the AWACS bird," replied Jones, referring to the E-2C Hawkeye Airborne Warning and Control System aircraft that was patrolling the skies looking for threats.

"Nike One, Bluetail Two. We have multiple missile contacts. Range one hundred twenty-two miles. Speed one thousand fifty knots. I count twenty-four incoming missiles." The two officers looked at the NTDS screen and saw the new threats appear.

"This can't be good," said Powell.

"There's nothing for us to do," said Jones. "We can't even defend ourselves." That much was true. *Ainsworth* didn't have any surface-to-air missiles. There were plans to add a Sea Sparrow system to the *Knox*-class frigates, but that had yet to happen. Now she was a sitting duck.

"At least there are a lot of other targets out there bigger than us," said Powell. It might have been impolite, but it was true. *Ainsworth* wasn't much to look at on radar.

Looking at the NTDS, they could follow the battle. Bluetail Two vectored a pair of F-14 Tomcats toward the threat. Nobody had ever tried to take out an antiship missile with an AIM-54 Phoenix before, but they'd give it a shot.

To the west of *Ainsworth*, the guided-missile destroyer USS *Farragut* was the first to engage the incoming missiles. SM-1 surface-to-air missiles raced off her twin missile rails as fast as they could be loaded. She took out the lead "radar" missile of the group, but the remaining three flew right past her, on their way to a second target. With the first flight of missiles behind her, she started working on the second flight. Again, *Farragut* took out the first missile, but this time her number came up. The second missile in the flight penetrated the deck on the starboard side, forward of amidships, where the main superstructure met topside. The sixteen-hundred-pound warhead tore the ship in two.

The delay in the transmission of data between the operators and instruments meant that the men in the CIC of *Ainsworth* had no way of knowing that *Farragut* was lost. Even if they knew, they were far more interested in following the missile tracks that were steadily approaching their ship. The first flight of P-700s that overflew *Farragut* struck the defenseless *Ainsworth*. The ship lurched to the port side, and simultaneously, there was a tremendous sound, and the lights in the CIC went out.

"Everyone, keep your shit together," boomed the captain. "Get some lights on in here."

Several of the sailors had flashlights at the ready, and they began to get their heads back into the moment. The captain got on the 4MC and called out, "This is the captain, I need a report immediately."

As soon as the words left his mouth, there was another screaming sound followed by a thundering explosion. A ball of fire tore through the CIC, killing every man in an instant.

The scene was being revisited across the battle group. The *Spruance*-class destroyer USS *O'Brien* fired all eight of her Sea Sparrows at the four P-700s heading her way. She popped chaff during a hard-to-port turn. It wasn't enough. A single missile pushed through her defenses, striking just aft of amidships at the waterline. She began taking on water immediately.

While her escorts were fighting for their lives, *Ike* faced more missiles than any of her escorts. The Soviet captain had correctly selected his main target. With eight missiles bearing down, and no support from her escorts, who were committed to the first three flights of missiles, *Eisenhower* could only bring eight Sea Sparrows to bear. One SAM for each ASM. It was a bet that no commander would willingly make.

The first missile struck along the flight deck, tearing the metal into the air, and leaving a massive hole, exposing the hangar deck. That was bad, but if the fires could be contained, *Ike* could survive the day. The second missile struck below the massive island, tearing into the heart of the ship, and flooding the middle decks with fire.

Damage control crews immediately reacted to stop the fires and save the ship. The third missile struck the island itself, wiping out the tower, and all of the radar equipment. The fourth missile struck aft along the waterline. *Eisenhower* was mortally wounded.

In the end, *Farragut, Ainsworth, O'Brien, Eisenhower,* and *Virginia* were sunk. The only surviving ship from the task force was *South Carolina*, whose position left her with only two missiles to defend against.

Chapter 15

10 January 1981
USS *Arkansas*
Gulf of Mexico

Arkansas smelled new. Captain Aaron Stewart wasn't sure if this was in fact true or if it was all in his mind. The ship had been commissioned just two months prior and had been performing her shakedown cruise off the coast of Virginia when the war had broken out. She was about as new as an active warship could get. They still had engineers from Raytheon working on her AN/SLQ-32 electronic warfare suite, but the Navy needed her for convoy duty.

He raised his coffee cup and took a sip as he looked out the forward windows on the bridge of the nuclear-powered guided-missile cruiser. Captain Stewart and his crew had joined up with several other destroyers and frigates to escort a massive fleet of transport ships from Beaumont, Texas, to Brest, France.

Ever since he'd received the orders, Stewart had considered the danger of the passage. Intelligence reports indicated that every Russian submarine that could sail was in the Atlantic, waiting for them. Additional harassment could be expected from the air, where Soviet Tu-22M Backfire bombers were expected to cause problems. As if that weren't enough, the Navy was still chasing the Soviet battle cruiser *Kirov*.

Captain Stewart thought *Kirov* was an interesting issue. The search for the beast was using a lot of resources. P-3s from Halifax to the Azores to Bermuda were beating the ocean with radar, looking for her. But the ship had simply vanished. There were some gaps in the coverage provided by the maritime patrol bases, and the aircraft carrier USS *Eisenhower* had been sunk trying to cover some of those gaps. There were rumors that it was *Kirov* that had sunk *Eisenhower*, but Stewart wasn't convinced. His suspicion was that *Kirov* was hiding out in the South Atlantic, doing more good by disappearing than she ever could in combat.

"Skipper, XO," squawked the intercom. It was Earl Brown, the ship's executive officer, calling from the ship's combat information center or CIC. Stewart picked up the handset.

"What have you got, Earl?"

"*Pharris* is reporting a weak contact north. Commander Langley is sending his Seasprite to take a look."

"Thanks, Earl," replied the captain. "Keep me updated." This last was added out of habit. Clearly everyone in the CIC would keep the captain updated on the ASW situation.

Pharris was one of the *Knox*-class frigates that were providing the ASW screen for the task force. Though smaller than the cruiser and conventionally powered, the frigates were strong antisubmarine warfare platforms. The SH-2 Seasprite supported by the frigate extended the search range of the fleet, deploying a dipping sonar to listen for enemy submarines. Once a contact was detected, the helo could prosecute it, or *Pharris* could fire a RUR-5 ASROC or antisubmarine rocket from six miles away.

Stewart looked at the Navy Tactical Data Screen and saw the three-sided yellow square that represented an unknown underwater contact. It was north of the task force, and only one hundred and fifty miles from the Florida city of Destin. It had never occurred to Captain Stewart that there would be a threat so close to the homeland. His brain couldn't make sense of it.

Ten minutes later, the intercom squawked again.

"Skipper, XO."

"I'm on my way." Captain Stewart was heading to the CIC regardless of the message that Commander Brown was about to give him. He made his way down and aft and entered the "dungeon" as the men of *Arkansas* called it. Glowing screens filled the dark room. Digital readouts fed a constant flow of information to the crew, who would then act and react to it. This was the brain of a combat ship.

"What'cha got, Earl?"

"They've definitely found something," said Brown. "*Peterson*'s sent her helo in as well." With two helicopters dipping their passive sonars in the water, they would be able to triangulate the target in the event they both picked up the same signal.

"She's running!" said a sailor monitoring the ASW frequency. There was a slight delay as the data was collected and transmitted to the NTDS. The yellow square turned into a red upside-down V.

"What do you think, Earl?" asked Stewart. "What are we looking at?"

"This deep in the Gulf, and that close to shore? It's gotta be a nuke. Call it a Victor." Commander Brown was referring to the NATO designation of the mainstay of the Soviet nuclear attack submarine fleet.

"One thing's for sure—the boys in Jacksonville are going to get torn a new one once this contact report gets out." Naval Air Station Jacksonville was the home of several patrol squadrons, which were responsible for picking up this submarine before the task force came through.

"Yeah, after those close approaches on the opening day of the war, I'm sure their asses are about as chewed as they can get." While this conversation was occurring, there was a life-and-death struggle going on to their north, hundreds of feet under the water. With each new piece of data, the NTDS would update.

"Well, I'll be damned," said the captain when the submarine ID came through.

"Wow, how long has she been sitting out here?" asked Commander Brown. The submarine in question was what NATO referred to as a Tango. It was a diesel/electric boat.

"I'm guessing she charged up her batteries in Cuban waters before making her run at the coast. If she was on her way to the port of New Orleans…" The captain turned to the map board behind him and did a quick calculation. "If she started in Cuba and was heading to New Orleans, I think those helos picked her up while she was snorkeling."

Unlike their nuclear counterparts, diesel submarines needed to charge their batteries after a period of time. To do so, they would need to suck in fresh atmospheric air and eject the exhaust caused by running the diesel engines. This meant that while the electric boats were quieter than the nukes when they were running on batteries, they were noticeably louder when running the engines. Stewart had heard about new systems that could charge the batteries without snorkeling, but they were still years down the road in development.

"They've dropped on her, sir," said the sailor monitoring the ASW frequency. Sure enough, after a few seconds, a blue U appeared on the screen, almost on top of the red V. The bridge went silent as everyone who wasn't staring at their own instruments was fixated on the screen.

"I have a detonation," said the sonarman who was monitoring the waters around the ship. The sub was too far away for *Arkansas*'s

AN/SQS-26 sonar to pick it up, but the explosion came through loud and clear.

"Sir, Trident Two is reporting secondary explosions. They're marking that down as a kill."

A quick cheer went up before Stewart said, "Knock it off. This is just like scoring a touchdown. Act like you've been in the end zone before. There are going to be a lot more of those in the coming weeks." He left the CIC in silence and headed back up to the bridge.

****

11 January 1981
USS *Arkansas*
Off the Coast of Beaumont, Texas

Captain Stewart looked out the portside window on the bridge of USS *Arkansas*. Between his ship and the horizon were dozens of ships. There were twenty-five cargo and transport ships accompanied by ten escorts.

"Any word on getting any additional assets once we get out of the Gulf?" asked Commander Earl Brown, *Arkansas*'s executive officer, Stewart's second-in-command.

"We're going to rendezvous with the *America* battle group once we cross over into the Atlantic. She's steaming south from Virginia. She'll make most of the crossing with us, but she's turning back once we get under NATO air cover."

"That'll give us a few more cruisers and destroyers in addition to the air group. Have they updated the threat assessment?"

"Not much," replied Captain Stewart. "Really, our main concern is going to be those submarines. *Forrestal* will be taking a convoy across on the northern route. They'll have to contend with more of an air threat as they get closer to the continent. For us, it's the subs, and of course *Kirov*."

"I'm beginning to think *Kirov* is a red herring, if you'll pardon the pun," said Brown. "I wonder if she was even fully functional. Maybe she put to sea without operational missiles, or radar or something. Now she's just a ghost. A spooky bad guy to keep us up at night."

"It's not going to keep me from getting shut-eye. Those submarines are already doing that. The Tango we picked up yesterday was a stark reminder of how slippery those bastards are."

****

12 January 1981
USS *America*
Off the Coast of North Carolina

"Courage, this is Aardvark Three. I have two contacts, possible missiles. Inbound to your position. I am engaging."

Everyone in the ship's signals exploitation space, or SSES, of *America* went quiet. The NTDS screen verified what the radio had already told them. The two contacts were then updated to four. Lieutenant JG Richard Rogers was shocked. The inbound missiles had come out of nowhere. One second the skies were clear; the next, four Soviet missiles were hurtling toward the battle group.

"Fox three," said the F-14 pilot, indicating that he'd fired an AIM-54 Phoenix missile at one of the targets. This was repeated by the pilots until they fired all four of the Phoenix missiles they were carrying. The missiles appeared on the NTDS screen. They were on an intercept heading. The symbols representing the air-intercept missiles merged with those of the antiship cruise missiles.

There was a collective sigh of relief as all four of the incoming missiles were shot down by the combat air patrol or CAP fighters.

"Courage, this is Aardvark Three. We're RTB, Winchester," said the pilot, letting the carrier know that they were returning to base because they had fired their primary weapons. Two fresh Tomcats would be launched to replace them on the patrol.

"Courage, Screwtop Two. You have four more missiles inbound." Screwtop Two was an E-2C Airborne Warning and Control System aircraft from VAW-123. A quick look at the screen confirmed this.

"This is Lion Six. We're intercepting now." A second pair of Tomcats were engaging the new threat. This time, they were only able to stop two of the approaching missiles. The second pair was shot down by

SM-1 missiles fired from the USS *Biddle*. Lieutenant Rogers sighed with obvious relief as the final incoming missile disappeared.

"Tell me, young Rogers," said the lieutenant standing to his left. "What do you make of the attack?"

"Well, sir, it had to be an SSG," replied Rogers, referring to the Soviet class of guided-missile submarines.

"Obviously," replied the lieutenant. "Do you have any more insights?"

"No, sir, I'm not sure what you're getting at."

"When you look at a situation, you need to look at all of the data you have. Then drill down. How many missiles were there?"

"Eight," said Rogers.

"That's right. What does that tell you?"

"That the submarine most likely only had eight missiles."

"That's right. Now, it could be that they have more missiles and are retaining some of them, but everything we know about Soviet tactics tells us that they will fire a full broadside if they get an advantageous position. They want to overwhelm our missile defenses. Who knows? If those Tomcats weren't on station, they may have... But I doubt it."

"So, eight missiles. There's a Charlie down there?"

"Hey, look at you, analyzing the data." The lieutenant laughed. The only sub known to carry a payload of eight missiles was what NATO codenamed Charlie. "Now, was it a Charlie One or a Charlie Two?"

Rogers thought about the differences between the two boats. "It's a Charlie Two."

"Why do you think that?"

"Because the missiles were subsonic. The Russkies traded speed for range when they put in the new SS-N-9s in place of the SS-N-7s," explained Rogers.

"Bingo. Good job, Rogers. Now we know that there's a hostile submarine out there. Even with her missiles expended, the Charlie still carried torpedoes, and those'll poke a hole in your ship just as well."

The *America* battle group was steaming south to meet up with the convoy heading for Brest, France. With this attack, and the clear knowledge that there was a Soviet Charlie II out there, the battle group was turning course to the east to give the ASW birds out of Jacksonville a better chance of locating and destroying the submarine.

The routine of the transit was punishing. There was a constant buzz of activity on the flight deck. SH-3 ASW helos and fixed-wing S-3 Vikings were constantly coming and going. They were flying to assigned sectors then dropping sonobuoys, or in the case of the helos, lowering their dipping sonars to listen for the Soviet threat.

Eight hours after the missile attack on the battle group, general quarters again sounded throughout the ship. It was noon, and Rogers was hustling from his stateroom back to the SSES. He'd been sent to his rack to get some sleep after having been up for over twenty-four hours. As the juniormost intelligence officer, he was getting baptized by fire during the start of the transit. As he entered, his eyes went straight for the NTDS.

On the screen, he immediately saw the problem. Among two blue circles in the southwest quadrant of the battle group were two red V shapes. He made his way over to Lieutenant Edward Diaz, the man who had been quizzing him earlier.

"*Josephus Daniels* was about to UNREP with USS *Mars* when they detected incoming torpedoes," said Diaz.

"Courage, this is Lilac Bravo," came the call from the supply ship, USS *Mars*. "We've taken a torpedo aft. There is catastrophic flooding. We are abandoning ship." There was a hush in the SSES as everyone realized that they had taken their first casualties of the transit. The quiet was shattered as the radio burst back to life.

There were no clear words, just the sounds of a klaxon sounding and men shouting over one another. After a few seconds of obvious chaos, someone finally transmitted, "Courage, this is Rover, we have had a torpedo detonation. We're doing what we can." *Rover*'s noncommittal response wasn't very reassuring.

On the screen, a new icon appeared near *Josephus Daniels*. The red V shape represented the submarine that had attacked the battle group. Under the V was the label "Victor." Rogers leaned over toward Diaz.

"Do you think the Charlie intentionally pushed us toward the Victor?"

"It could be," said Diaz, "but coordinating while hiding out under the water is a real challenge. It could have just as easily been that they were patrolling in separate stations, and we just got lucky enough to hit them both."

The two officers watched as the USS *Biddle* launched an SH-2 ASW helicopter to prosecute the Victor. The Victor ran at flank speed into the battle group, while the carrier and her escorts sprinted away to the east.

"He's hoping to get off another shot. Gutsy call," said Diaz. "He probably should have cut and run."

Diaz's analysis was confirmed minutes later when the SH-2 reported dropping a torpedo, then hearing the impact, and finally listening to the sounds of the hull collapse in on itself, killing anyone who had survived the initial explosion. There were no cheers at the news of the Soviet submarine's demise.

"Dear Lord, Diaz," said Rogers, "this is just day one. We've still got four thousand miles of this ahead of us."

****

14 January 1981
USS *Arkansas*
Mid-Atlantic Ocean

The rendezvous with the *America* battle group went smoothly. With the loss of the *Belknap*-class cruiser *Josephus Daniels*, the escorts now numbered seventeen. P-3 Orions flying out of Naval Air Station Bermuda extended the range of the ASW screen.

News of yesterday's losses had reached the mess deck, and the genuine risks of the transit were weighing on the crew. And now Captain Aaron Stewart had even more to worry about.

"OK, Hank," said the captain, "walk me through it from the top."

"Captain, one of the SIGINT satellites picked up a short voice radio burst. Once the linguists worked on it, they determined that it was Soviet flight operations. Based on the location, and other unspecified factors, command believes that it's *Kirov*." Stewart nodded for the man to continue. "That's the good news. The bad news is that we only have the one satellite to base anything on."

"Which means we've only got a line of bearing?" concluded Captain Stewart.

"That's right, sir. Given the satellite's position when the signal came in, *Kirov* can be more or less anywhere along this line here." The ship's intel officer used a straightedge to draw a diagonal line across the Atlantic.

"That's not a lot to go on," said Commander Brown.

"You're not kidding, Earl," replied the captain. "But it's better than nothing. Hopefully the CAG on *America* has a plan for this, because there ain't much we can do from here." *Arkansas* couldn't come close to the standoff capabilities of the Soviet cruiser. There weren't any ships in the Navy that could.

Eight months earlier, Congress had authorized funds to activate the battleship USS *New Jersey*. Stewart heard rumors that when she returned to the fleet, *New Jersey* would be armed with Tomahawk antiship cruise missiles. Those were slower than the Soviet missiles but would be a considerable improvement over the existing SM-1 standard missiles that *Arkansas* would have to rely on for both anti-air and antiship defense.

Right now, *Texas* was getting Harpoon missiles added to her arsenal, but it would be a while before *Arkansas* would be so lucky. With the war on, Stewart wondered if they'd be adding Tomahawk missiles to her bag of tricks. *That's years away*, he thought. *I need to focus on getting my crew through the next few days.*

"Sir," a seaman said, interrupting his train of thought. "Peterson's bird has a faint submerged contact east. They had solid engine noise before it went quiet. They're running it through the computer now."

"Very well," replied the captain. There wasn't anything else to say. He'd have to patiently wait for information. Such was the nature of convoy duty. You had to exercise patience. Sometimes antisubmarine warfare was like trying to catch a bubble. If you tried too hard, you'd pop it. Peterson's helo would work to reestablish contact, and until then, Captain Stewart would have to wait.

"Sir, Peterson is reporting the contact came back as a Juliett."

"Not exactly sending their best," commented Brown in reference to the age of the Juliett-class boats, which had first put to sea in the early sixties. The design was obsolete when compared to modern attack submarines, yet she was still a threat.

"I'm not superstitious," said Captain Stewart. "But I wouldn't tempt fate like that. Has the helo reestablished the contact?" he asked the seaman.

"Negative, sir, they're still working it, but it's gone cold."

Dammit, thought Stewart. *It's bad enough knowing that one might be out there. It's another thing altogether knowing for certain that there's one out there.*

With every minute that passed, the submarine put distance between itself and the point of contact. Every mile it could move increased the search area. In a race between time and distance, the submarine had the advantage. The minutes turned to hours with no sign of the Juliett.

"Contact!" The announcement rang through the CIC.

"What've we got?" asked the captain.

"Unidentified contact, bearing zero-nine-five, range fifty-two miles."

"That can't be our Juliett," said Commander Brown.

"Yeah, it's way too close," replied Captain Stewart. Everyone waited for the analysis to come in.

"Sir, it's a Zulu."

"Wow, bringing out the classics," quipped Brown. The Zulus were ten years older than the Julietts. "How the hell does an old rust bucket like that get to within fifty miles of our convoy?"

"Best guess, Earl," replied the captain, "is that they're sitting in the shipping lanes without moving. Just sitting there circulating the air and listening for us." He looked at the NTDS screen and watched an inverted U shape approach the new red V. The U was an S-3 Viking from *America*.

The fight followed a predictable pattern. A torpedo hit the water, and the Zulu tried to get underway. She was barely making five knots when the torpedo detonated, destroying the 1950s-era boat.

"It's absolute suicide to set out in one of those," concluded Commander Brown. Nobody in the room disagreed. With the death of the Zulu, the weight of the missing Juliett returned to everyone's thoughts.

If that boat is heading toward us, it would be in missile range by now, thought Captain Stewart.

"Whatd'ya think, Earl?" asked the captain. "If you were driving that Juliett, what would you do? How would you make your approach?"

The commander thought about it for a few minutes. "I can only answer that question if we make some assumptions."

The captain raised an eyebrow.

"First, I need to assume that the Juliett knows that we're here. That Zulu was oblivious when we found her."

"Fair enough," replied the captain.

"Second, we need to assume that my primary target is the convoy, not the carrier."

"Agreed."

"In that case, I'd go deep, let the convoy come to me. Creep and drift. Keep everything as quiet as possible. Then, once I was in torpedo range, I'd fire a spread of torpedoes and my missiles. Once I've smashed the Yankee forces, I'd get lost in the noise of sinking, dying ships. Then I'd work my way home for caviar and vodka."

"Not a bad plan, XO," replied the captain, "but there is one flaw." Brown tilted his head. "You'd have to surface to fire your missiles, and it'll take you five to ten minutes to get them off. I don't know that our ASW birds would let you get that shot off. Plus, if you're in torpedo range, you're definitely in ASROC range, not to mention that since you're on the surface, I'd personally take you out with an SM-1."

"I guess it's good that I'm not a Soviet sub skipper," said Brown, chuckling. The conversation waned and the crew continued working through the night.

Captain Stewart was thinking about getting some sleep. He'd been at it for eighteen hours since he'd last gotten any shut-eye. With the missing Juliett, he was reluctant to leave the CIC.

On the other hand, they might never find that submarine. For everything they knew, it could be moving north and would miss the convoy completely. He wouldn't be doing himself or his ship any favors wearing himself down this early in the crossing.

Fate resolved the question for him.

"Contact! Torpedo in the water!" All eyes were on the NTDS screen. A torpedo contact appeared right next to USS *Camden*, a fast combat support ship.

"Looks like we've got a fox in the henhouse," said Brown. "Unless that torpedo's a dud, we're about to be down a ship." Another submerged contact showed up on the display.

After a few seconds, the mystery was solved. It was the missing Juliett.

"It looks like you weren't too far off," said Captain Stewart. "I think the sub crept up on us and executed your torpedo attack. But I don't think he's going to make the missile run."

"But why did he only fire the one torpedo?" asked Brown.

"It's possible that this was the only good firing solution he could get," replied the captain. "But I think you'll have to ask the Soviet skipper."

"Better be quick, because I don't think he's going to be around long," said Brown. Within ten minutes, both *Camden* and the Juliett were on the bottom of the Atlantic.

Chapter 16

15 January 1981
Mount Weather, Virginia

Without a doubt, these had been the longest two weeks of Jimmy Carter's life. The constant stream of bad news was wearing him down. He felt helpless. There was nothing he could do to stop the Soviets or North Koreans. He listened to his admirals and generals, and he issued the orders they needed to prosecute the war. But it seemed so distant. So... disconnected. He addressed the nation on an every-other-day rotation. That seemed to be having a calming effect on the citizenry.

Yet there were still conflicts within the nation. Except for a small contingent of isolationists and communists, the nation was coming together in support of the war. Regarding the draft, however, there was a lot of disagreement. The passage of the ERA in October of 1980 was the root of the conflict. For the first time in history, the United States was going to draft women into the military.

"Congress won't touch this with a fifty-foot pole," said Hamilton Jordan, the President's Chief of Staff.

"They don't have to," replied President Carter. "They know that I'll have to issue an executive order amending the Selective Service system again, like we did over the summer." Carter was referring to Proclamation 4771, whereby he had used an executive order to reinstate the registration of men aged eighteen to twenty-six in the Selective Service. Those very men were now being sent to basic training units across the country. Soon they'd be joined by their sisters.

"There's really no way around it. But we need some guardrails on this. I've talked to the Joint Chiefs of Staff, and they're all in agreement that a military made up of fifty percent men and fifty percent women wouldn't be an effective fighting force. Even if it could be, none of them are willing to take the risk during a shooting war with the Soviet Union."

"I can't blame them," replied Carter. "You can't take this risk this significant without a very real potential reward. There's no such reward here. What are they suggesting?"

"Right now," said Jordan, "each branch has commissioned a project to review their military occupational specialties to see which ones would be best suited for women. When those efforts wrap up, we'll see where we stand. Most estimates I'm hearing are that the military will take on a composition of fifteen to twenty percent women."

"I imagine that someone will challenge that on constitutional grounds, but we can delay that in the courts. Hopefully, we'll have won the war by then and we can deal with this issue during peacetime."

"From your lips to God's ear," said Jordan as he rose to leave. Before the door closed, Secretary of Defense Harold Brown entered.

"Good morning, Harry," said the President. "Have a seat."

"Thank you, Mr. President. I know you're busy, so I'll get right to it." The President nodded appreciatively. "The 82nd Airborne has pushed the last of the Russian Marines out of Iran. They have also been coordinating with the Shah's army to start pushing back on the Iraqi incursions in Khuzestan Province."

"That's good news," said the President.

"It's not bad news, that's true," said Brown. "On the other hand, we have evidence that the Soviets more or less withdrew to Azerbaijan and Armenia. We suspect they plan on sitting back and playing defense there."

"Fair enough. We'll let that play out for a while longer, but we need a plan for the 82nd once this tidied up."

"True enough," agreed Brown. "We haven't seen any movement yet, but the NSA is reporting that Turkey is going to open the Bosporus to allow the Soviet Black Sea Fleet access to the Mediterranean. Right now, the USS *Kennedy* battle group is steaming in the Med, so they might be looking to engage. *Kennedy* has been pounding Yugoslavia to give the Italians some relief. If the Black Sea Fleet sorties in the Atlantic, we'll have to redirect to face the threat."

The President nodded.

"Moving on to Asia," continued Brown, "the situation on the Korean Peninsula is grave. DPRK forces have advanced a hundred miles into the south. The fighting is around Daejeon, and it's not going well. We're moving the 3rd Marine Amphibious Force from Okinawa to Busan to get them into the fight. That's just under thirty thousand Marines. That doesn't look like it's going to be enough. With operations winding down in Nicaragua, the Commandant of the Marine Corps is asking to redeploy the 1st Marine Division to the Pacific. I'm inclined to agree with him, sir. The 101st Airborne and the 2nd Marine Division have Nicaragua in hand. I'd even consider sending some of the 2nd over to Korea, but for now, let's focus on moving the 1st."

"I think the situation in Nicaragua has finally reached a point where even Dr. Kirkpatrick will agree that we can spare the men. Especially given what's happening in Korea."

"Speaking of Nicaragua," said Brown, "we're closing in on Managua. I can't imagine that the remaining Sandinista, Cuban and Soviet forces will hold out much longer. That said, we still don't know where the Sandinista leadership has withdrawn to. There's clearly someone still in charge, but we have no idea where they are. The CIA has a team down there, so hopefully they can piece something together soon. Once we figure that out, I think we can work with the locals to establish a new government."

Carter furrowed his brow at this last bit. He wasn't a fan of "establishing" a new government. That was for the Nicaraguan people to do.

"As long as it's a provisional government that will allow for a free and fair election after the war," said Carter.

"Understood, sir," replied Brown. "The situation in Germany seems to be stabilizing. We're gearing up for a counteroffensive with the Central Army Group. We first need to solidify our lines south of Würzburg—then we think we can hold the city itself. There's been some renewed Soviet efforts against the British Army of the Rhine outside Hamburg. We're going to have to watch that closely. We may be able to shift some air support to help out the British, but there's not a lot we can do up there.

"Finally," said Brown, "on the home front, with the National Guard units being federalized, there's a major effort to backfill the stateside presence for air defense. F-4 Phantom units are being deployed to the European theater, and the Air Force is pulling the F-106s out of mothballs to retake their role as interceptors. They are putting training squadrons together to get those units up and running as quickly as possible."

"How effective will those be?" asked the President.

"They'll serve the role well. They were built from the drawing board as interceptors and their older Falcon missiles are up to the task of taking out incoming bombers. They won't do much against a more agile aircraft, though."

"I suppose that'll have to do," said the President. There was a pause as he waited to see if Brown would continue. When he didn't, the President said, "Thanks, Harry, I'll see you tomorrow unless something urgent crops up."

****

15 January 1981
Giebelstadt, West Germany

Taking Giebelstadt had been easier than expected. Though the losses in the air were dramatic, once the force was on the ground they had quickly overwhelmed the defenders and taken possession of the air base. With the air war in full effect, the Soviets were able to cover the approach and landing of a squadron of AN-22 transports. These transports brought the unit's artillery and heavy equipment. It was hoped that the D-30 122mm howitzers would give the Desantniks the firepower they would need to repel the inevitable counterstrike.

Sergeant Misha Kozyrev thought back to the night of that counterstrike. It was grim work, but the Americans had come at them piecemeal. It was as though they had hoped that by getting to the battle quickly, they could overwhelm the Soviets before they were prepared.

The intel spooks later said that the force attacking was a dismounted air assault force whose helicopters had been largely caught on the ground at nearby Kitzingen. Even with limited armor and air support, they were ill prepared for the fully mechanized force that was occupying the air base.

That was the second night of the war, and there hadn't been a serious attack since then. Sure, there had been nearly nonstop harassment, and the occasional artillery barrage. The airfield was completely unusable at this point, but once the Soviet armor relieved them, the engineers would have it up and running in no time. Until then, they were vulnerable. And Misha knew that the Americans wouldn't make the same mistake twice. The next time they came for Giebelstadt, they would be coming in force.

Tonight, he was sitting in the command seat of his BMD-1, waiting for that attack. His platoon was positioned on the north side of the base, looking toward Würzburg. If the Americans were feeling the pressure of the Soviet advance, they could withdraw forces from Würzburg and use them to take back Giebelstadt. They could then link up with advancing forces from Frankfurt to reengage the Soviet advance. At least, that was what the lieutenant had told them during the mission briefing.

There was a commotion in the vehicle, then Junior Sergeant Taras Knyazev popped up through the driver's hatch, in front of Misha. Taras was turned around to face his friend.

"You're quiet tonight, Comrade Sergeant," said Taras.

"I didn't realize that talking a lot was a prerequisite of this mission," replied Misha.

"It's not, per se, but it certainly helps with staying awake. What's on your mind that you don't want to share with us?"

"Nothing unusual, just thinking about how quiet the war has been for us, and how when that changes, there will be carnage. It's as though the longer we live through this calm, the worse the storm will be."

"Bah," replied Taras. "Worrying about the next battle is like carrying water in a sieve. It's just pointless. Instead, worry about Private Starodubov's integration with the squad." Private Nil Starodubov was a late addition to the squad. In the chaos of the landing, he'd joined with Misha's squad for the assault. His own squad hadn't assembled, so he had been used to backfill for one of Misha's men who had broken his ankle during the landing.

Since then, they'd learned that Starodubov's squad had been killed during the landing. Now, he was having trouble adjusting to life with Misha's squad. He was full of anger and hatred, and Misha's easygoing command style wasn't working for him.

"He just needs some time, Taras. Remember how we all were after Valya and Tsezar bought it in Kabul." Misha recalled two of their squadmates who'd died during the invasion of Afghanistan.

"Sure, we were angry," replied Taras. "But we had Afghans to kill. We paid them back tenfold the day it happened, and then tenfold again in the days following. Starodubov isn't going to get right until he has a chance to swim in the blood of the Americans."

Before Misha could reply, air raid sirens started screaming at them. Both men slid down into their seats and slammed their hatches shut. They were dug in deep, so realistically only a direct hit from an incoming round would destroy them now that they were buttoned up. The radio came to life.

"This is Saber One to all Saber units. Sit tight and wait out the barrage. Be ready to redeploy." Taras automatically began the start-up procedure for the BMD.

"I think the captain is telling us something," said Taras. "This could be that storm that you were so worried about."

"I think you may be right," replied Misha as the sound of explosions filled the night. After an eternity of waiting to die, the incoming fire slackened, and the radio came back to life.

"Saber One to all Saber units, redeploy to reference point Anna Two and prepare to repel an enemy assault."

"Taras, get us out of this hole, then come to a course of—"

"Two-seven-zero," said Taras, completing the sentence for his sergeant.

Misha wondered how many men would be left to defend the north in case additional units moved in from Würzburg. It didn't matter; his mission was to move to defend an attack from the west. He looked through his viewfinder and could see the captain's BMD ahead of him. He knew that the rest of Company 9 was moving along with him. After the invasion and the earlier counterattack, Company 9 was down to seven of their original ten BMDs.

Outgoing artillery rounds tore into the sky on their way to the NATO forces. The explosions lit the sky downrange.

"Hang on, everyone," said Taras, "we're almost to the hole." He spun the tank 180 degrees, then backed it in. The tank dropped into the fighting position and lurched to a halt.

"Tisha," said Misha as the gunner rotated the turret to face the rear, "keep an eye out for APCs and infantry concentrations. Don't fire on any armor unless you have to."

The 73mm cannon on the BMD was a very effective weapon against most targets. Technically, the high-explosive antitank or HEAT rounds could penetrate the frontal armor of US and German main battle tanks, but the current plan was to leave the tanks for the antitank guided-missile teams. The BMDs would only engage the tanks if there were enough of them to threaten to overwhelm the missileers.

"Contact!" said Tisha. "tank, bearing fifteen degrees, range ten kilometers."

"Hold your fire," said Misha, not wanting his excited gunner to blow the plan from the jump. Misha looked through his view port and found the approaching enemy. Almost as soon as he found the M60, it exploded. The Russian minefield would slow them down, but Misha had no doubt that engineer units were moving to the front to deal with it. They would have to demine the field under the constant barrage of Soviet artillery. The initial American barrage had taken out several of the cannons at the airfield, the survivors were joined by massive 203mm 2S7 self-propelled artillery guns that were supporting the main front lines at Kürnach on the outskirts of Würzburg.

Keeping his eyes on the countryside, Misha knew that the Americans were using the many valleys and basins to the west to marshal forces for the assault. The hills would protect them as they gathered, but once they were in the open they would rush at the airfield with all of the speed and ferocity they possessed. There were more explosions in the distance as the Americans were demining the fields.

"Get ready," said Misha. "It won't be long now." Above the horizon, he saw streaks of fire in the sky, undoubtedly NATO and Warsaw Pact aircraft trading missiles and gunfire in the skies above Giebelstadt. The battle was building to a crescendo.

"Contact, M60, three hundred forty-five degrees," said Tisha.

"Hold." Misha watched as a stream of the tanks burst from behind the hills. Tension filled the BMD. With the enemy rushing at them, it seemed mad not to engage.

"Dear God, that's a lot of tanks," said Tisha.

"Taras," said Misha, "be ready to get us out of here if we get the order to reposition."

Trails of flame streamed out of the defensive positions, leading to the tanks. Misha watched as the 9K111 missiles exploded against the approaching enemy. "Tisha, keep an eye out for the infantry. Don't get distracted by the tanks." *Do as I say, not as I do.*

"Saber One to all Saber units," said the captain. "Engaged the armored threat, but prioritize any infantry targets of opportunity." The words were hardly out of his mouth before the report of Tisha's gun rocked the tank.

The autoloader slammed another 9K111 HEAT round into the chamber, and another 73mm round went downrange toward the oncoming Americans. Every seven and a half seconds, Tisha put another round on target.

The Americans weren't defenseless. The M60 tanks hurled 105mm shells into the defenders. They punished the Soviet line in a relentless push.

"Steady, everyone," said Misha as the tanks closed on them. His nerve faltered in the face of the onslaught, but he couldn't break ranks.

A string of bombs exploded along the attacking column. Misha couldn't see it, but he knew that one of their close-air support aircraft had survived the air battle long enough to add to the carnage before him. Toward the rear of the attack, he could see American M113 armored personnel carriers joining the fray.

"Tisha, APCs to the rear. Engage them!"

"Understood, engaging," replied the gunner. What was left of the American tank column was passing to either side of Company 9. Misha prayed to a God he didn't believe in that the flanks would hold. They were being enveloped. The APCs were taking major losses and unloaded their troops at about two kilometers from the Soviet line. The small infantry units could more effectively use the terrain to mask their movement and preparations. Soon, TOW and Dragon antitank guided missiles would hit the Soviet lines.

"Saber One to all Saber units, withdraw to our original positions. We need to fall back!"

"Taras, hit it!" ordered Misha, but Taras had already gunned the engine and the BMD leapt out of its firing position. Looking over the back of the BMD, Misha watched a missile strike the captain's vehicle.

"Give us some smoke," said Misha, hoping to create some kind of concealment as they moved in the open.

They had made it about one kilometer from the western line when there was a tremendous booming sound, and the vehicle rocked hard to the left.

"We're hit," said Taras. "We've thrown a track."

"Everyone out of the tank!" ordered Misha as he popped his hatch and scrambled over the top.

Taras, Tisha, and machine gunner Andrei Koshelev hit the ground and started sprinting northeast, looking for cover.

Misha ran to the rear of the BMD to help the rest of the team out of the troop compartment. One look told him everything he needed to know. The explosion that had taken out the left track had also penetrated the compartment. There was nothing left that resembled a living being. Misha took off after the remaining men of his squad.

Chapter 17

16 January 1981
USS *Arkansas*
Mid-Atlantic Ocean

Captain Aaron Stewart was in the CIC of *Arkansas*. He was thinking about heading up to the bridge to get some fresh air.

"Sir, they've got another signals hit on the possible *Kirov*." It had been days since they'd first picked up the Soviet battle cruiser and this was the only other contact they'd gotten. This time the line of bearing was much closer to the convoy.

"That's a bit disconcerting," said Commander Earl Brown, the ship's XO.

"Yeah, I have to say, I'm not a fan of it," replied the captain. "Hopefully *America* will send something along that line to take a look."

After a few minutes, it was pretty clear that a pair of Tomcats was flying to the southwest along the line of bearing. If the intel guys were right, they'd be flying directly toward one of the most advanced air-defense systems in the world.

"Why'd they send those Tomcats?" wondered Brown. "They could paint half the Atlantic with those E2-Cs they have."

"If I had to guess," replied Captain Stewart, "I think they're trying to preserve the element of surprise."

"I don't follow," replied Brown.

"Right now, there's no reason for *Kirov* to think that we know where she's at. If we fly a Hawkeye down there with its radar blasting away, *Kirov* will know that their cover is blown. If we send a pair of Tomcats out at thirty thousand feet, with their radars off... It'll be a lot easier for the tiny fighters to find the giant ship than for the ship to find those dots."

"Of course, if the Russians do see them, they're as good as dead."

"True, but as soon as *Kirov* lights up her radar, she'll have the full weight of Carrier Air Wing Eleven on her ass. One way or another, if she's out there, we'll know soon."

When the call came in, it was good news for the Tomcat pilots. Steaming thirty thousand feet below them was the world's most powerful surface unit. They were able to get in, get *Kirov*'s location, and get back out without being detected. That was the good news. The bad news was that nobody knew the range of the SS-N-19 missiles she carried. Right now, she was over three hundred miles from the convoy and steaming toward them.

"What do you think, skipper?" asked Brown.

"I think they have a pretty good idea we're out here. Don't forget, they still have satellites. For all we know that last SIGINT hit we got was Severomorsk telling them all about us," said Captain Stewart, referring to the headquarters of the Soviet Northern Fleet. "Either way, she's here to play and we're going to need to be ready."

****

16 January 1981
USS *America*
Mid-Atlantic Ocean

"What do you know about the SS-N-19?" asked Lieutenant Edward Diaz.

"Nobody knows much about it," replied Lieutenant JG Richard Rogers. "Some think it's an updated version of the SS-N-12; others believe it's a brand-new system." There was a pause. "After what they did to the *Eisenhower*'s battle group, I think we're dealing with something much more than an updated SS-N-12," he concluded.

"I think that's a fair estimate," replied Diaz. "What about their air-defense capabilities?"

"It has a layered air-defense system consisting of two separate but integrated SAM systems, plus point defense cannons. *Kirov* is the first ship equipped with the SA-N-6 surface-to-air missile—"

Diaz grunted, interrupting the younger man. "Well, sure. There is that Kara-class cruiser where they performed sea trials if you want to count that."

"I do," replied Diaz. "I like to be thorough."

There was a knock at the door. It was a seaman neither of them knew. "The skipper wants you in the briefing room ASAP." The two officers shared a sideways glance before following the young man out of the SSES. When they entered the briefing room, they were greeted by the carrier's leadership team. This consisted of the ship's captain, the commander of the air group, or CAG, the operations officer, and the COs of each of the three attack squadrons.

"Thank you for joining us," said Captain Darren Ingram. "We're putting together the strike package for *Kirov*. I want you on hand for questions. That's your role today. I don't want to hear from you unless and until I call on you, understood?"

Both men nodded and said, "Aye, sir."

"OK, we're dealing with a SAM system that we've never dealt with before. CAG, what's your estimate of what we're looking at?"

"My experience in Vietnam dealing with SA-2 missiles won't translate much here. These new systems are light-years ahead of what the North Vietnamese were throwing at us. However, the operational concepts are the same. Diaz, what can you tell us?"

"Thank you, sir," replied Diaz. "First, we're dealing with two separate systems. The older SA-N-4 system is used for close range and point defense. The newer SA-N-6, however, is the real wild card. We know that it's using a powerful phased-array radar. Intel reports indicate that it could have a range of around fifty miles. We don't have an exact figure on that."

"I'll let you know when I get back," quipped Dave Stevens, the CO of VA-195.

"It's also important," continued Diaz, trying not to react, "to know that the Soviets are employing a unique vertical launch system. Instead of using launch rails fed by a missile magazine, the Soviets have dozens of launch tubes built into the deck of the ship. This allows *Kirov* to fire massive salvos of missiles nearly simultaneously."

When it was clear that Diaz was done, the CAG said, "We have two possibilities here. First, we swarm the target with enough targets to overwhelm it. Second, we use antiradiation missiles to blind the ship, then we can clean up the rest once the radars are down."

"This might be easier if we'd been equipped with those new Harpoon missiles," said the CO of VA-95, the A-6 Intruder squadron on *America*.

"Dammit, Glen," said Captain Ingram, "I don't need you adding noise to the signal in this meeting. I don't care about what you can't do, I need to know what you *can* do."

"Sorry, sir," replied the man sheepishly. "We really lack the ability to deliver a massed swarming attack. In fact, the best that we could do on that front is try to swarm them with AGM-78s," he continued, referring to the large antiradiation missiles carried by his Intruders.

"OK, so we load up the Lizards," said Ingram, referring to the squadron's nickname, Green Lizards, "with every ARM they can carry. Then we follow that with the Dambusters and Dragons"—referring to VA-195 and VA-192 respectively—"loaded up with Mk-84s."

"We're going to want to stagger the attack," said the CAG. "As you mentioned, we don't know a lot about this new SAM system. If the AGM attack fails to take out the radars, it'll be a bloodbath out there."

"I think you're right. We want to be bold here, but not brazen. What's the flight time on those missiles?"

"If we fire them from extreme range, and I intend to, they'll take about two and a half minutes to reach the target."

"Alan, Dave, I need you to bring your birds in five minutes after Glen's boys make their pass. If *Kirov* fires even a single SAM after the ARMs have impacted, I want you to abort. We can't risk having you trying to drop those bombs inside that SAM umbrella."

"Understood, sir," said Alan Garner, the CO of VA-192.

"OK, get it written up and briefed. We need this to happen ASAP." With that, the room emptied out and Diaz and Rogers went back to the CIC to follow the battle on the NTDS.

The race was on. *Kirov* was steaming for the convoy. At some unknown point in time, she'd be in range to fire her missiles. Before that happened, Carrier Air Wing Eleven needed to take her off the board.

It took over an hour to get the mission ready. Plans were drafted and disseminated. Aircraft were armed and fueled. By the time the first A-6E Intruders were hurtling down the flight deck, the urgency of the race was building to a crescendo. The three squadrons formed up and began their approach. As they got near to the target, the CAG vectored the E-2C Hawkeye toward *Kirov*.

"See that, Hawkeye?" asked Diaz.

"Yeah, what's it doing out there?" replied Rogers.

"They're going to light up *Kirov* on radar. That's going to do two things. First, It's going to give the attack planes the exact location of the ship. Second, it's going to tell *Kirov* that we're onto her."

"Don't we want to use the element of surprise?"

"Not today," said Diaz. "We need them to activate their radars in order for the AGM-78s to lock onto their radars. If they don't turn on the radars, we can't launch on them."

"Hold up," came a voice over the murmurs of a dozen private conversations. "We're getting painted," said a sailor at the electronic warfare, or EW, station. "Big Bulge Radar, bearing one-two-one."

"Comms," said Captain Ingram, "get on the horn and find out who else is picking this up. I want it triangulated and I want to know how far it's penetrating the convoy."

"What do you know about the Big Bulge radar?" asked Diaz. Every moment was a training opportunity.

"It's an airborne surface search radar. It's carried on the maritime surveillance variant of the Tu-95—"

"Which model is that?"

"Bear D," replied Rogers. Diaz nodded and he continued, "And the Ka-25 Hormone-B."

"That's right. And guess what ship carries at least one of those?"

"*Kirov*," said Rogers.

"That's right. And right now, she knows exactly where we are. There's only one reason she'd send up the helo."

"To get targeting data?"

"Yup. We'd better hope we blend in with all these tankers." After a few minutes, the various ships in the fleet triangulated the signal and had a good idea where the helicopter was operating. A pair of Tomcats were ordered to intercept, but the tiny helo had already accomplished its mission.

The Green Lizards were nearing their launch point. Rogers put on a headset and tuned to the squadron frequency.

"Magnum," said Commander Hopkins as he released the first of his four AGM-78s.

Instantly, the call was ringing out on the squad channel as each of the twelve aircraft launched its payload. In less than a minute, a second call came in. "We've got SAMs inbound. Evade and duck out west. Let's get the hell out of here and get back to the ship."

It was almost morbid to listen in. A couple hundred miles away, chaff was popping, and the A-6s were crankin' and bankin'. But in the CIC on board *America*, there was a quiet murmur.

In the back of his mind, Rogers knew that there was a good chance that his own life was in danger. He had no reason to doubt Diaz about the incoming missiles. But the frantic calls of pilots and their bombardier/navigators punching out brought out the reality of the life-and-death struggle.

Rogers looked at the NTDS. A string of new air contacts rose from *Kirov* to meet the incoming missiles. Even from the onset, it looked like it was going to be a close call. More and more of the ARMs disappeared as the flock of them continued toward the target.

Before the data screen caught up with reality, Rogers heard over the radio, "This is Skyknight One-Zero, I've got a confirmed impact."

"Copy that, One-Zero, anyone else?" asked Hopkins.

"This is Skyknight Seven, pay dirt."

"Outstanding, Seven. We'll let the kids know they can start their run."

"Will two missiles be enough to take out the SAM system?" asked Rogers.

"I honestly don't know," admitted the older officer. "I guess we're about to find out."

Rogers counted the icons of VA-95 and came up with only seven. With two men per plane, ten of the Green Lizards wouldn't be coming home. He switched over to VA-195 to continue monitoring the battle as the A-7 Corsairs began their bombing run.

"This is Chipper Actual to all Chipper units," said Commander Stevens, CO of VA-195. "We're crossing the SAM threshold."

Rogers thought back a few hours, when Commander Stevens said he'd let them know the new SAM's range when he got back. As soon as *Kirov* engaged the incoming A-6s, the US Navy had an estimated range of the SA-N-6.

"Tallyho, incoming SAMs," said an unidentified pilot.

"Break, break, break. Abort the attack run," said Stevens. Because they didn't have to stay on target as they launched missiles, the two Corsair squadrons were able to outdistance the incoming SAMs. As the Americans flew northwest for the carrier, *Kirov* raced south to get out of harm's way.

"Missiles inbound, starboard side," came the call from the 1MC.

"This is it," said Diaz. They watched on the screen, indicators appeared, showing the incoming SS-N-19s.

At first glance, none of them seemed to be heading for the carrier. They continued watching as the combatants raced to put themselves between the incoming missiles and the convoy. The slow pace of the American SAM response was agonizing when compared to how quickly *Kirov* was able to get her missiles out.

It was quickly apparent that the convoy was going to take some losses. Ship icons flashed, showing missile hits.

By the time it was over, five of the cargo vessels were outright sunk, with three more burning and dead in the water. In addition, the USS *Semmes*, a *Charles F. Adams*–class destroyer, joined the cargo ships on the ocean floor.

Chapter 18

17 January 1981
4.5 Miles Southeast of Würzburg
West Germany

Misha and his squadmates had been on the run for two days. In that time, they'd only managed to cover five and a half miles. They were slowed considerably, trying to avoid detection. With the loss of the airfield at Giebelstadt, whatever was left of 9th Company was behind enemy lines.

"There are worse places to be stuck," said Taras.

"You say that now," replied Misha, "but you won't be saying that when the Yankees dig us out of here."

The squad had taken refuge in a densely forested area on the banks of the Main River. It was an idyllic place. It reminded Misha of springtime along the Volga in his hometown of Tver. As much as he wished to stay here for the rest of the war, he also knew that every moment they remained behind the lines, the more likely it was they'd be captured, or killed.

The immediate problem was the Main River itself. They could see that the battle for Würzburg was well underway. From what they could make of it, the Soviets held the town east of the Main, while NATO held everything to the west of the river.

So, it was just a matter of crossing one hundred meters of swift-flowing river in the dead of the German winter. *What could go wrong?* thought Misha. He knew that if they crossed during the day, the Yankees would figure out who they were and shoot them. If they tried at night, the Soviets would assume they were NATO sappers and shoot them. Maybe staying here forever wasn't such a bad idea...

"Shhh!" said Taras, raising a hand. He then pointed to his ear and motioned for everyone to get down.

Lying prone, Misha looked toward his friend, who pointed to the south. Misha strained his eyes and ears, desperate to pick up any indication of what had Taras on edge.

Then he heard it. Someone was coming. Misha drew his Makarov and quietly switched off the safety. He wished that he'd salvaged his AKS-74 when NATO knocked out his BMD.

He could make out the form of a man. It looked like he was alone, but he could just be the point man on an attacking force, so Misha waited. Plus, he was still a good twenty-five yards away. Misha was more of a rifleman. Pistols weren't his strong suit.

He was just about to take the shot when something odd stuck out to him. The man didn't have a helmet on. And there was something off about the contours of his uniform. Then it struck him. The man was wearing a jumpsuit. He wasn't a normal infantryman. Misha didn't quite relax, but he was more willing to let this play out.

The man appeared to be trying very intentionally to avoid making noise. This was funny to Misha, because he was so clearly bad at it. Each step crushed a branch, or kicked a rock. He even heard the man wince once as he stumbled. As the man drew closer, Misha finally could make out enough of his uniform to recognize that he was a Soviet pilot.

"*Poluchit na zemle!*" said Misha, ordering the man to drop to the dirt. Without hesitation, the intruder complied. Misha wasn't sure, but he thought there was some relief in the man's collapse.

Misha cautiously approached the pilot with his gun drawn and aimed at him. "Who are you? What are you doing here?"

"I am Major Dmitriy Bogdanov, of the Soviet Air Force. They call me *Germes*."

Maybe it was a trap. Maybe this "Bogdanov" was a NATO infiltrator. *No, that's ludicrous. You've been reading too many ministry reports*, thought Misha.

"Comrade Major, how did you find yourself behind NATO lines?" asked Misha.

"I was flying over the battlefield on the first day of the war and was shot down. I was able to make my way to Giebelstadt, but once there, I was stuck."

Misha listened to the man's story, weighing its truthfulness.

"I thought I'd get a flight out of Giebelstadt, but by the time I got there, flight operations had halted. Every day I thought I'd be able to catch a transport out, but every day it was the same. The Fatherland couldn't risk a transport to rescue a downed MiG-25 pilot."

"And when NATO took the airfield, you ran?" asked Misha.

"Of course," said *Germes*. "What was I supposed to do? End up in a Yankee concentration camp?"

At that, Misha smiled and stuck out his hand. "Welcome to our little oasis. I am Sergeant Misha Kozyrev, and this is what's left of First Squad, 9th Company, 345th VDV Regiment." He gestured toward Taras, Tisha, and Andrei. "We took the airfield, and for a time, we held the airfield. But now we're reduced to bandits, living off the land."

"You have done well to survive this long," said *Germes*. "I can hardly believe that I've stayed ahead of the Yankees."

"I've seen you move, Comrade Major. I think that luck has more to do with it than anything else," said Taras, laughing. There was a tense moment when everyone waited for the major to explode on the junior sergeant. But it never came.

Instead, *Germes* laughed quietly. "You have no idea how true that is, Comrade Corporal. You have to believe in luck if you're going to fly a MiG-25R."

The joke was lost on the Desantniks, but they recognized the attempt at humor and gave a sympathetic laugh.

"Tell me, Sergeant," said *Germes*, "do you have a plan?"

"Unfortunately, Comrade Major," replied Misha, "I've been weighing our options, and they aren't good."

"And what are those options, as you see them?"

"We either try to cross the river and get back to friendly forces, or we wait here for the Red Army to come to us."

"I can see the disadvantage of crossing the river," said *Germes*. "I doubt there's a single bridge remaining, and we'd likely freeze to death trying to swim it. I don't suppose any of you have a raft?"

Taras looked like he was about to say something, but Misha quickly cut him off.

"We don't have much in the way of supplies at all. We lost almost everything when the Yankees destroyed our BMD. We have no raft, and we don't really have the tools to make one, especially not if we're trying to hide while doing it."

"It seems to me," said *Germes*, "that our decision is made for us. Unless we can figure out a way across that river, we're stuck here. What are the disadvantages of hiding out?"

"Every day we stay here, we risk getting detected and captured or killed. The Americans that pushed us out of Giebelstadt will probably move to reinforce Würzburg. They might decide that this forest is useful. Even if they don't, our brethren over there"—he gestured to the east bank of the Main—"will soon push the defenders out of the city. When they do that, some of the fleeing troops will probably come through this area. This forest will look just as appealing to them as it did us."

"It looks like there are no good options," said *Germes*.

"Our only option is to get really good at hiding," replied Taras grimly.

Chapter 19

18 January 1981
Puerto Morrito, Nicaragua

The CIA had taken over a warehouse near the dock on Lake Nicaragua. Over the past two weeks, the noose had tightened around the capital city of Managua. The 101st Airborne had linked up with the 1st Marine Division and most of the resistance had collapsed. The war was nearing an end, and Fred Poole was trying to figure out where the last battles would be fought.

Reviewing the situation, Poole said, "Signals intelligence hasn't been able to pinpoint the command and control facilities for the Ortega regime. They've gone underground, but we have no idea where."

"We know, Fred," replied Carlos. "We've been over this a hundred times."

"And we'll go over it a thousand times if we don't figure it out." Everyone's nerves were fraying as the frustration built up.

"You know, there are sharks in the lake," said Pedro, changing the subject.

"I thought it was fresh water?" asked Carlos.

"*Sí*, freshwater sharks," replied Pedro. "Bull sharks—they are ferocious. It is as if they are angry at being cut off from the ocean. This is why I got my name. You had to be ferocious to fight off the Colombians when it came to smuggling. When I was a younger man, I would fish for them." El Tiburón had a gift for captivating an audience.

"One time, my cousin Hector and I were fishing in a skiff off Ometepe Island when one of those monsters capsized us. I assure you, *señor*, I am a brave man. But on that day, I practically flew out of the water back onto the boat. We waited for three hours before we had the courage to flip the boat back over." Pedro laughed at the memory, and everyone joined in. "We spent the night on the island and didn't sail home until the next morning."

Poole looked at the map spread out on the table in front of them. Ometepe Island was thirty-five miles to the west, across the largest lake in Central America.

"What's on the island?" he asked.

"The coastline is populated with fishing villages. There are small farming communities at the low slopes of the volcanoes. But not much after that."

"Any military presence?"

"Nothing that I know of," replied Pedro. "There's not much infrastructure out there. No airport, and just a small seaport at Moyogalpa. It's totally out of the way, with no real military value."

"No, but that might be exactly what gives it value today," said Poole. "We need to get on that island and have a look around. That's about the last place in this country where we don't have a steady presence."

"What does that look like?" asked Carlos. "You want to get on the horn and put some Recon Marines or Navy SEALs out there?"

"I don't know," said Poole. "I think we have the right group here. You and Pedro can move around on the island without suspicion. You can mix in with the population and find out what's really going on out there. Then you can report back, and if there's anything to this, we can send in a combat force to deal with the situation. If it turns out to be nothing, we'll just keep working on the problem."

****

Ten Hours Later

Carlos had grown up on the beach and had put in many hours on boats. Even so, after Pedro's story about the bull sharks, he was more wary than usual. He looked across the boat and watched the wind blow Clara's short black curls behind her. It was rare that he saw her in civilian clothes, and it occurred to him that she was stunning. Maybe it was the fact that the war seemed a million miles away. Maybe it was the perfect seventy-six-degree morning and the boat zipping along the water. Maybe it was all of those things.

"What are you going to do after the war?" asked Carlos, trying to get her attention. She looked at him and furrowed her brow.

"Well, Norte," she replied, "that all depends on if we survive the war." Carlos knew that it was bad luck to talk about an uncertain future, but he didn't know where else to take the conversation.

"No, hear me out," he continued. "My war is going to continue after this. I don't have a light at the end of the tunnel. As soon as we're done here, I'll ship off to Germany or Korea, or some other battlefield, and I'll look back fondly on the war we fought here. Do you know how cold it gets in Germany or Korea?"

She smiled at that. Carlos hoped that it was because she found him charming, and not because she was imagining him freezing to death in a snowy trench somewhere thousands of miles away from her.

"You, on the other hand," said Carlos, "might not even pick up a rifle again. What does your life look like when things get normal again?"

Clara considered that. "I don't know what normal even looks like," she said. "I thought I would return to Ayapal and go back to teaching. But now I don't know. I've learned that I missed my family. Once the shooting stops, I'm going to try to reconnect with my parents. They're up in Honduras, but now that the Sandinistas are gone, perhaps they'll come back. I think Uncle Pedro can talk some sense into my father."

"Do you think your parents will get their plantation back?" asked Carlos.

"I don't know. I imagine there will be a lot of people demanding a lot of property when the dust settles. I think my family will get their land back, though. They can prove that it was theirs, and that the Sandinistas took it from them. It really just depends on who takes the place of the government. If it is someone as corrupt as the Somoza regime, they'll probably just give everything to their cronies, and we'll be right back where we started."

"I don't think the US will let that happen," said Carlos.

"Ha. Norte, listen to yourself. That's the problem." She fixed him a stern gaze. "You think that your government can fix my nation. I'm not saying that the United States is responsible for every bad thing that ever happened in Nicaragua, but they certainly are responsible for a lot of what went wrong over the past fifty years. The only way that we're ever going to fix our situation is if we have a chance at self-determination. You and your government will need to accept what we come up with, even if you don't like it."

This was getting away from Carlos. This conversation was going south fast.

"I agree," he said, trying to salvage the situation. "I've learned a lot since I first came down here. Somoza was a bastard, and we really shouldn't have been supporting him. I don't know what happened with the Sandinistas and the Russians, but I think you're right." Before she could find something else to argue about, he continued, "Will you go back to teaching?"

"I don't know," she admitted. "There will be a lot to do when we start rebuilding the government. I might get involved with education at a higher level. I haven't given it enough thought."

"Heads up," said Pedro, "we're coming up on Puerto de Moyogalpa. Once we moor the boat, I'm going to head into Altagracia to meet a contact I have there. You two stick around Moyogalpa and see if you can find out about any unusual activity on the island over the past year or so. Tonight, we'll decide how to proceed once we've collected some information."

"When did you start running intelligence operations?" asked Carlos.

"I'm just telling you what Fred told me," said Pedro with a chuckle. "If anyone asks, you've been displaced by the fighting in Managua. Clara knows enough about the geography to make that stick."

Carlos considered that. It was plausible, but there weren't many refugees heading to the island. There was a fear among the population that the Americans were herding people to the island, where they would then cut them off and operate it as a concentration camp. Carlos didn't know where those rumors were coming from, but they were incredibly effective. In fact, some of the islanders were finding reasons to return to the mainland while the fighting intensified.

"Oh, and tell people you're newlyweds. That'll buy you some goodwill with most people," he concluded with a wink.

"*Tío!* You're the worst," said Clara.

"There are worse things in the world than to be married to me," said Carlos.

"Is that how your ex-wife feels?" shot Clara. Carlos winced as the comment landed.

"You two certainly fight like a married couple. You'll want to at least act like you get along if this is going to work."

Pedro navigated the boat into the tiny harbor, then glided it effortlessly to the pier. Carlos scrambled to the port side to tie the boat to a mooring. Carlos secured the bowline while Clara took care of the stern.

The three of them climbed up out of the boat and headed into the small village. They only covered a block and half before a car pulled up next to Pedro.

"This is where we part ways," he said. "We have reservations at the Hotel Nicaraus. I'll meet you there around sundown." With that, he climbed in the battered Ford and drove off to the north.

Clara and Carlos were now embroiled in what should be a thrilling espionage caper. But in reality, they just stood around a tiny harbor town with no real idea where to begin.

"I guess we may as well start at the hotel," said Carlos. The haphazard nature of this operation was unlike every other aspect of his fieldwork. For some reason, Poole was playing this one close to the vest. Carlos wasn't sure his bosses in Langley knew that he was on the island. Clara stopped a passerby and got directions to the hotel. It was about a kilometer away, a few blocks east, then a few more south.

They checked in, and Carlos was surprised to find a message waiting for them. He opened the card and read in Spanish:

Mr. and Mrs. Rodriguez,

Congratulations on the happy occasion of your marriage. I regret that your timing was less than perfect, but in life, things seldom are. I'm sure you are making the most of your time together. I hope that you have time to visit Mount Concepción. It has been years since I've been there, but the view to the southeast of the summit is breathtaking. Have fun, and I look forward to seeing you soon.

    Regards,

    Federico

    P.S. I had a few things sent to your room.

"I suppose that's something," said Carlos, handing the note to Clara.

They made their way to the third-floor room. On the king-sized bed lay two Samsonite suitcases. In one, they found hiking boots, several changes of clothes, two pairs of binoculars and a stack of Nicaraguan córdobas, the local currency. The second suitcase contained all manner of firearms and explosives.

Clara took one look and said, "You were saying something about never picking up a rifle?"

Carlos did his best to ignore the comment. "OK, this is coming together now. We're on our honeymoon, we're tourists, and we're going to hike the volcano."

"This is a very American cover story," replied Clara.

"This is all happening on the fly," said Carlos. "We've just got to take it as it comes."

The two took turns changing into something more appropriate for the hike, then, armed with a .45 M1911 each, they headed out.

The clerk at the front desk told them that the best trailhead for ascending the mountain was at San Ramón, and he had a cousin with a jeep who could take them there for a good price. They grabbed an early lunch before heading out to the volcano.

****

Rama, Nicaragua

Lance Corporal Oliver sat in his tent outside of Rama, Nicaragua, and ran through his deck of flash cards again. He'd been working on learning everything he could about the CH-53 for three weeks now, and he was amazed at how much he had memorized. He was almost ready to ask Captain White to quiz him on the instrumentation, but he hadn't gotten the courage to ask him. More than anything in the world, he didn't want to disappoint the pilots. The tent flap opened, and Corporal Evans entered.

"You want the good news or the bad news?" asked Evans.

"I guess let's get the bad news over with," replied Oliver.

"You ain't getting promoted to corporal," said Evans.

"What the hell? I just put on lance two months ago. What are you talking about?"

"Yeah, so about that. You're in charge of Fire Team Two. That's the good news. I was trying to get you the chevrons to go with it, but the captain wouldn't budge. He didn't think he could push it up the chain of command, and even with the war on, he thought you could use more time in grade. So, you get all the duties and responsibilities of a corporal, but not the extra twenty bucks a month."

Oliver thought about it for a second before replying, "So, are you squad leader? And are we getting two cherries to replace you and Holmes?"

"Those are the right questions, Oliver," replied Evans. "And, yeah, I'm getting the squad, and"—he looked at his notebook—"Lance Corporal Saunders is rotating in from stateside, and Private Harrington is a total cherry. They're supposed to be here tomorrow, so you have that long to figure out how to 'corporal.'"

"I've learned from some pretty effective corporals," replied Oliver.

"Yeah, I love you too, pal, don't get too excited."

"I was talking about Mack," said Oliver with a grin.

"Yeah, well, in all seriousness, you've earned this. Now don't screw it up."

"Thanks, and congratulations, Sergeant." The two shook hands and Evans excused himself. Oliver thought back to the ride through the haboob into Iran on the way to the Manz. That had been eight months ago. Since then, he'd lost Mack, Yates, Holmes, and Strickland. Estrada and Palmer were both wounded enough to get rotated out. He didn't even want to think about how bad it was going to get once they were done here. If they were shipped to Korea…

He put the thought away and went back to his flash cards.

****

It was six p.m. and the sun had fallen behind the horizon. Carlos gave the landscape another sweep with his binoculars. For as far as he could see, there was nothing but the trees. *Why couldn't Fred have given me a bit more detail into what I'm looking for out here?* he thought. He set the binoculars down and took a drink from his canteen. The hike to the summit wasn't difficult, and they'd made good time. They were now camped out on the southeast edge of the volcano's caldera.

Carlos had never seen a real volcano, much less climbed one. It was nerve-racking to think that he was so close to a force of nature that could destroy the surrounding countryside with little effort.

"I think I have something," said Clara, sitting to his left. "There was a dim flash of light on the side of the mountain."

"Where?" asked Carlos.

"Just to the left of center, about three-quarters of the way down."

Carlos raised his binoculars and tracked to where she directed.

"I've got nothing," he said.

"It was real quick. Hang on, there," she said as a quick flash lit the surrounding area. Carlos wasn't quite on the spot, so he could make out that there was a flash, but he had no idea what had caused it. "I think it's a door," said Clara. "When they open the door, the light inside is coming out."

"Don't these guys know anything about light discipline?" asked Carlos.

"We don't even know who this is," said Clara. "Wait… I think, yeah, one of them just lit a cigarette."

"Wow, some dipshits sneaking out to take a smoke break. OK. We need to mark this position." He had found the area in question and watched as a lighter flared up another cigarette. He did some quick calculations and made a notation on his map of the island. He raised his binoculars again in time to watch the door open again. He could make out the shape of a man going through the door before it closed, blocking out the light.

"I don't know if this is everything they sent us to find, but let's keep an eye on this for another half hour. Then we're going to have to get back down the mountain to meet up with Juan," said Carlos, referring to the hotel desk clerk's cousin who would meet them for the return trip.

They met Pedro in the small hotel restaurant. He had ordered several appetizers and was reading the paper when they arrived.

"Ahh, the happy couple," he said, rising to greet them. He gave Clara a hug and shook Carlos's hand. "How was the countryside?"

"Beautiful as always," said Clara. They were alone in the restaurant. The tourist industry had been hard hit by the war, and the rumors that Ometepe was to be a concentration camp had more or less emptied out places like this. They sat at the table and got to work.

"My contact has really proven his worth," said Pedro. "Starting eighteen months ago, there was a lot of construction activity on the island. Most of it was near Mount Maderas, and none of it was done by locals."

"Could he tell who was doing the work?" asked Carlos.

"No, just that none of the local construction firms were brought in. There were some rumblings that it was the Cubans, but that was never confirmed. After construction started, there were several *blancos* on the island. They would come and go like tourists, but they never seemed to stay at any of the tourist traps like this place. Nobody paid them much mind until the war started, and by then, what was the point?"

"We may have a lead on that construction," said Clara. Pedro raised an eyebrow. "I'm one hundred percent sure that we found a hidden entrance to a bunker dug in under Mount Maderas." Carlos made sure there were no lurkers nearby and pulled out his map, setting it on the table.

"There's something here." He pointed to where he'd marked the location of the door. "I'm sure that's not the only way in or out, but that's what we found after following the lead Fred gave us. We're going to need to get this information back to the Agency so we can decide how to proceed."

"I agree," said Pedro. "First thing tomorrow, we'll head back to Puerto Morrito. We'll get some sleep and head out around four o'clock." Pedro tossed a stack of córdobas on the table to pay for his meal, and they rose to leave. As they approached the stairs that would take them up to their room, Pedro stopped Carlos.

"Oh no, Junior, you're staying with me," he said with a smile. "I'm sure my *pollita* will sleep much better with you under my watchful eye."

Carlos considered reminding Pedro that Clara was the one who'd held *him* prisoner but decided to let it go.

****

18 January 1981
Jacksonville, North Carolina

Nancy sat in a pew in Antioch Presbyterian Church, waiting for Reverend Patterson to begin his sermon. She looked around at the congregation. The church was packed, as it had been last week. Nancy couldn't say about the week before. Like many of the parishioners, she hadn't been a regular attender for years. She and Carlos tried attending Church when they were expecting Jennifer. They both wanted Jesus to

143

be a part of Jennifer's life, but they had a hard time figuring out how to make that happen.

Carlos had grown up Catholic, while Nancy grew up at Antioch. She gladly attended Mass with Carlos, but was turned off by what she felt were "magical" elements of the Mass. She couldn't for the life of her understand how a wafer was transformed into the literal body of Christ. Not that she'd be able to take communion anyhow. And that bothered her. She was a Christian. She was baptized, and confirmed. She felt she had every right to take communion and couldn't accept a church that didn't accept her as a Christian.

That was to say nothing of the fact that the Catholics wouldn't allow women to be ordained. While it was still uncommon to find a female Reverend, it was at least possible. This latter point really rubbed Carlos the wrong way. He'd insisted that she was mixing her politics with religion, and that they were two totally separate things. They just couldn't see eye-to-eye on this.

After the disastrous mass, Carlos grudgingly attended a service at Antioch. He didn't seem as opposed to it as she had been, but he didn't like how much singing there was, and he really didn't like the lack of kneeling. Thinking back on it, Nancy decided that this ludicrous critique was just to keep from having to go back. She frowned, realizing that his ploy had worked. That was the end of their search for a church.

"Before I start my sermon proper," said Reverend Patterson, "I wanted to begin with a word of caution. I have received many letters and phone calls concerning Matthew, Chapter Twenty-Four, Verses Six through Thirteen. While I'm aware that we've already had our readings for today, I want to add this for reference."

"You will hear of wars and rumors of wars," he read from the bible on the podium, "See that you aren't troubled, for all this must happen, but the end is not yet. For nation will rise against nation, and kingdom against kingdom; and there will be famines, plagues, and earthquakes in various places. But all these things are the beginning of birth pains." He looked up to ensure the congregation was engaged before continuing.

"Then they will deliver you up to oppression and will kill you. You will be hated by all of the nations for my name's sake. Then many will stumble, and will deliver up one another, and will hate one another.

Many false prophets will arise and will lead many astray. Because iniquity will be multiplied, the love of many will grow cold. But he who endures to the end will be saved."

He looked up from the book, and addressed his flock. "People come to me with these words and with grave concerns. They want to know if the end times are coming." He paused to let that sink in. "But they are missing the entire point of this scripture. Since Matthew wrote these words, there have been countless wars. Countless famines. Countless earthquakes. Did the Franco-Prussian War of 1870 presage the coming of the Christ?"

Another pause.

"Of course not. But what of the false prophets of the Godless communists? Surely, they are the ones to whom we'll be handed over and persecuted. I imagine the same was said when Hitler and the Third Reich were massacring the Jews and the Slavs. What makes this different? 'But Reverend, they ask'" continued Patterson, "'just because it wasn't true last time, how can you say that it isn't true this time? What if this is the beginning of the end times?' Then I say, rejoice, for the Kingdom of God is at hand. There is nothing that can be done to us that will be remembered when Christ returns. Be faithful and not afraid. As Matthew specifically instructed, 'See to it that you are not alarmed,'" With that, he closed the Bible and started into his intended sermon.

Nancy considered Reverend Patterson's words. She hadn't spent a lot of time considering that this war would be the end of the world. She was aware that it could escalate into a nuclear conflict that might kill everyone on the planet. When that didn't happen in the initial days of the conflict, it faded from her mind. The world hadn't ended, and she still had to live in it.

Now that Reverend Patterson had caused her to reconsider the end of the world, she grew concerned. She was still terrified of dying. She didn't want to leave this world and it made her ashamed. She couldn't rejoice in the coming of Jesus when she was so afraid for her own life. She questioned whether she was a strong enough Christian if her faith couldn't get her through this challenge.

Chapter 20

20 January 1981
20th Polish Armored Division
Estenfeld, West Germany

Sergeant Alfons Knopik had been out of the fight for nearly two weeks. In that time, the Soviet 3rd Shock Army had overtaken the Polish 20th to become the vanguard of the Soviet attack. That was fine with Knopik. The Polish 20th Armored Division had taken horrendous losses in the invasion of West Germany. Knopik counted himself lucky that he still had three-quarters of his original crew. When his tank had been destroyed and his loader killed, he hadn't been sure what his war was going to look like. Mostly, he feared that he and his crew would be executed for cowardice.

Instead, they had been greeted as heroes. Their recon mission had exposed enough of the bunker infrastructure to enable the VVS to neutralize it. They had finally allowed the Soviet forces to get through Schweinfurt and attack Würzburg. That the Soviet 3rd Shock Army was the force making the attack didn't matter to Knopik. He was just thankful to have survived this long.

Today, his crew was receiving two new additions. The first was Polish. Private Rafal Krok was fresh out of basic training and would serve as his new loader. The second was Russian. It was a "new" T-55 tank. The tank that he'd lost had been a fully modernized Polish-built T-55AM2P. The Army had trained him on that tank from the day he'd passed basic training. This tank was… less than that. He could fight this tank, but it would be a challenge. The gauges were in Russian, and though they were mostly the same, Knopik just wasn't quite sure. Any hesitation could prove fatal. The Army had taught him that lesson in training, and it had been proven in the field.

"Borna," said Knopik, "grab Dębiński and meet me at the motor pool." The "new" T-55s had just been off-loaded from railcars that morning. Knopik had no idea how the Soviets were still pushing trains through, yet the tanks were here, so clearly some of the trains were running. Knopik wondered how many of these tanks the Soviets had built. He also couldn't help but wonder how long this war would go on before they ran out. *Just focus on surviving each day, you fool*, he thought.

The three soldiers reported to the motor pool, where a queue of men waited for tank assignments. They took their place in the line and waited among the other tankers. After a twenty-minute wait, they were finally at the head of the line.

"Sergeant," said a Soviet junior lieutenant sitting at a table with a ledger in front of him. "The T-55 requires a four-man crew."

Knopik said nothing, waiting for this to play out.

Sighing, the lieutenant continued. "There are only three of you. I cannot assign a tank to an incomplete squad."

"Comrade Lieutenant," replied Knopik, "my loader was killed, and we have yet to receive a replacement. In fact, once we have secured the tank, I will be heading to personnel to retrieve our new private."

"Sergeant," said the lieutenant with deep condescension, "you cannot just choose to do things out of order. Everything has to happen according to established procedures. That is the only way that this war will be won. Get your man, then you can get your tank."

Inside, Knopik was furious. He didn't need a loader to drive the tank back to his platoon's staging area. There was no real justification for keeping him from getting the tank. It was just a bureaucratic tangle. But like so many people behind the Iron Curtain, he had long ago learned to keep that on the inside.

"Of course, Comrade Lieutenant. We will return with a full squad. I apologize for wasting your time." Knopik hoped that his sacrifice at the altar of bureaucracy would be enough to keep him out of trouble.

"Very well. Make sure you have everything in order before you return." It seemed the god of institutional power was assuaged.

As they shuffled off toward the personnel tent, Borna leaned in and said, "By the time we get this new meathead, all the best tanks will be taken."

"Hmm," replied Knopik. There wasn't much to say. Borna was right. The tank crews would pop into the tanks, give them a once-over, and pick the best one. It was absurd that a system that required a regimented order to things would allow for such a chaotic distribution method.

An orderly distribution must not feed anyone's ego or ambition, thought Knopik, recalling the sound of the Soviet lieutenant's voice.

At the personnel tent, he had better luck. Private Rafal Krok was not only there, he was ready to move out. That was a good sign. Knopik stuck out a hand.

"Sergeant Alfons Knopik."

"Private Rafal Krok, reporting as ordered, sir."

"Don't call me sir, Private. Don't they teach you anything in basic training?"

"I'm sorry, si—Sergeant. I'm just nervous," said the young man. Knopik looked him over. He was a classic Polish peasant. His hazel eyes under dirty-blond hair reminded Knopik of half a dozen of his own cousins.

"Don't worry about it right now. Just do your best. When did you graduate basic?"

"Ten days ago, Comrade Sergeant," replied Krok.

"Holy hell," said Borna. "This one's a real pup."

"This is good news," said Knopik. "This means that nobody has had the chance to teach you all the wrong ways to do things. How much experience do you have with the T-55?"

"None, Comrade Sergeant."

"What did you do before you were drafted?" asked the sergeant.

"I wasn't drafted, sir"—Knopik lowered his glare—"I mean, Sergeant. But I worked on a state agricultural farm as a water hauler." With his broad chest and thick arms, Knopik believed the man.

"When we get to the tank, you're going to have to learn quickly. As of right now, you're a loader on a T-55 crew in the Polish 20th Armored Division, the Hussars!"

"Hussars!" added Borna and Dębiński.

A grin spread across the new soldier's face as he felt more comfortable in his surroundings. Knopik had no doubt that the young man feared being thrown into a sadistic crew that would abuse him. The horror stories that ran through the personnel tent were well known. Some tank commanders ruled with an iron fist and a quick temper.

"Learn your job, perform your duties, and you'll get along well here," said Knopik.

When they returned to the motor pool, things went much better for them. They were able to get into the tank corral and, after popping into a few different vehicles, selected one.

Knopik climbed the turret and motioned for Krok to do the same. When the private was in position, Knopik pointed into the turret, to the right of his own position.

"Down there is your station. You need to climb in, get past Borna's chair, and smash yourself into that space. Do you understand?"

The soldier nodded and climbed into the gunner's hatch. Dębiński followed through the commander's hatch and burrowed his way into the driver's position. Knopik knew that Dębiński would be going over his checklist, getting the tank ready to start. This was always critical for ensuring equipment quality, but it was doubly important for an unfamiliar vehicle. Any potential issue would need to be discovered as soon as possible if the crew wanted to avoid being blamed for it.

Borna was about to slide into his seat, but Knopik stopped him.

"We have time," said the sergeant. "Dębiński will check and double-check everything before we move out. I'm in no hurry to pin myself in just yet."

"There is a brisk breeze," said Borna. "It's a nice day for January."

"What do you think they'll do with us now?" asked Knopik.

"Throw us as the Germans. What else would they do?"

"I suppose there is that, but with the Soviets in the vanguard of the attack, where do we fit in now?"

Borna thought about that for a few seconds. "It could be that we are used for the pacification of conquered territory. But I think that we proved ourselves more valuable than the Soviets originally thought we were. I think it's wishful thinking to believe that we'll stay off the front lines for much longer."

"I think you're right, my friend. This is going to be a long winter... if we survive. We'd better teach young Krok how to load the damn gun," said Knopik, who then slid into the tank commander's seat.

****

21 January 1981
Battle of Würzburg

"I don't like this, Sergeant," said Borna.

"What's to like?" replied Alfons Knopik. "These orders are shit, but they are still orders. So, get the snorkel out and get it ready. We need to get across the river, and the only way that's going to happen is with the snorkel."

"We're going to die in that river," replied Borna.

"We'll die on the bank of the river if we don't go forward. The Russians will drop a grenade into the compartment, then clean us out with a hose."

Borna shook his head, but he made his way to the equipment compartment to retrieve the snorkel and ancillary equipment. Normally, Knopik would grouse along with his gunner. But he knew that everyone in the tank feared drowning. It was a near-universal reaction to people who had seen "quality" equipment fail all too often.

Today's orders were near insanity. The Soviet 3rd Shock Army hadn't managed to get across the Main River. Instead, they were trapped on the east bank, fighting an artillery duel with NATO defenders. With all the bridges blown, the Soviets needed to get bridging units down to affect a river crossing.

In order to accomplish this, the 20th Polish Armored Division would first cross the river under cover of darkness and establish a beachhead on the west bank of the Main. The Soviet bridging effort would take place while NATO was counterstriking the Polish advance.

I don't appreciate being expendable, Knopik thought.

"How many tanks do you think will survive the crossing?" asked Borna.

"All of them," replied Knopik. "Look, Borna, the Main isn't even that deep. We probably won't even need the snorkel."

That was somewhat true. Even at its deepest, the Main wasn't much deeper than the T-55 was tall. But that didn't matter. Knopik just needed to get his team to accept that they had died two weeks ago and that every second they remained on the earth was a blessing. They were on borrowed time, and they owed death their very souls.

"Seriously, though. I think that enemy fire will wipe out, say, ten percent before we get across. So, that's twenty-five tanks. That leaves two hundred and twenty or so, depending on how depleted we are."

Borna nodded.

Knopik continued, "The real question is how long we'll have to hold that riverbank before the Soviets get across. We'll be all on our own south of the city, while the Soviets begin their crossing to the north."

The division was camped in a forested area a kilometer from the crossing point. The wide and open bank would allow the division to cross ten abreast. The crossing would be preceded by an artillery barrage, and a lot of smoke. This would advertise the location of the crossing, but it was all part of the ruse. It took the crew twenty-five minutes to get the snorkel attached. When they were done, Borna spent another twenty minutes double- and triple-checking it.

"We have done everything we can, my friend," said Knopik. "Now we wait."

The balloon went up at 0200. The thunder of artillery announced the beginning of the operation. The tanks rumbled to life, giving the shells time to land and spread out smoke before they lumbered out of the forest. Two hundred and fifty Polish T-55s rolled on toward the river. Counterbattery fire could be seen exploding out of the west side of the city. *At least I hope that's counterbattery fire*, Knopik thought.

Knopik looked through his view port and saw the tank in front of him. He moved the turret left, then right, taking in the view of the latest charge of the Polish Hussars. It was tanks for as far as he could see. Granted, it was dark out, but it was still an impressive sight. He was in the tenth rank back, so nearly in the middle of the formation.

"I wish we were in the lead," said Borna, sitting to Knopik's right.

"Yes, I agree. By the time we get there, the enemy will no doubt know what we're doing." Knopik scanned the horizon and was pleased to see additional smoke rounds dropping to the north of their position. These might keep the Yankees guessing and take some of the pressure off the attack. The tank lurched to a halt.

"Sorry," called Dębiński, the driver. "The column is bunching up as we near the river." The statement made the moment all the more tense. Not only would they have to wade across the water at an agonizing two kilometers an hour, they would have to wait, exposed and in the open, just to get to the water's edge.

Jets screamed over the tank formation, dropping bombs in the city. Unseen fighters above them fired missiles at the attacking Soviet close air support planes. Knopik watched as a Soviet attack plane popped a string of flares and cranked hard before being destroyed by a missile.

"They're going all in on this attack," said Borna.

"Maybe we're not so expendable after all?" said Knopik.

Forward and to the left, a tank exploded. Knopik thought of calling out that they were taking fire, but it was pointless. Borna and Dębiński could both see the hit, and there was no sense in frightening poor Private Krok.

With so many tanks on the riverbank, they were begging for an artillery strike. Knopik prayed to the god of chance that he'd survive if it came to that. There was nothing a tanker could do. Either a round hit you, or it didn't. You could be the best of the best, but you would be just as dead as anyone else.

"Missiles inbound," said Borna, as the crew watched the streaks of fire that followed the ATGMs as they raced for the Hussars. More tanks exploded. Dębiński inched the tank forward. More than once, they were bumped by the tank behind them as each driver tried to hurry the driver in front of them.

"The tank in front of us is dropping in," said Dębiński. "We're next." The combination of the fear of staying in the open competed with the fear of going underwater. Between the two, it was everything the crew could do to fight the tank.

"So far there's no opposition on the west bank," said Knopik, trying to raise the spirits of his men. An explosion rocked the tank.

"That was close," said Borna. "I think it was behind us."

"We're going over," said Dębiński.

"Time to put up a good face for a bad game," replied Knopik, citing the old Polish saying. The tank pitched forward, and the crew strained against their safety straps.

As they leveled out on the river bottom, Knopik warned, "Steady, Dębiński, watch your speed. I don't want to lose this snorkel."

It would take them three minutes to cross the one hundred meters of the river. They'd been in the water for just over a minute when they came to a crashing halt.

"What the hell was that?" asked Borna, verging on panic.

"We hit something," said Dębiński.

"What was it?" demanded Borna.

"I'm just as blind as you are, jackass," spat Dębiński.

"Cool it, both of you. If we panic, we die. Dębiński, try to push forward."

"No good, Sergeant. It's not moving." Knopik thought for sure that it was a dead tank, but he didn't want to add to the panic.

"We need to get around this obstruction," he said. "Back up and move to the left."

Dębiński did as ordered, and they hit something behind them as they backed up.

"Pivot left, thirty degrees, and move forward."

Again Dębiński complied. This time, something struck the tank on its left side.

"We are bouncing off each other down here," said Borna, stating the obvious.

"Turn right, thirty degrees," ordered Knopik. Now they were back on course.

"We're taking on water," shouted Borna. Knopik looked at the gunner's position and could see a thin trickle of water coming in.

"Relax, Borna, I need you to calm down. It's a small leak, and going crazy over it isn't going to stop it from leaking." In all of his life, the inside of the T-55 had never seemed as small as it did on the bottom of the Main River while under fire. After another thirty seconds, the tank suddenly pitched back as they made it to the far shore.

"Borna, scan for targets," said Knopik as the water cleared from his view port. The Hussars of the 20th Polish Armored Division had successfully crossed the Main River. They had a beachhead. Could they hold it?

****

"This is something big," said Taras as he and Misha watched the artillery landing in Würzburg. "We haven't seen a shelling this big since we got here."

"I agree. We need to be ready for anything," replied Misha. "Everyone, gather up." The two other Desantniks and the pilot surrounded the sergeant. "Listen, if this is the major push that I think it is, this forest will no longer be safe. If our brothers liberate the city, the fleeing NATO soldiers may come through here. A NATO counterattack could roll right up on us. We're helpless and cold. But if we can hold out through the night, we just might survive this after all. Everyone move out to your hiding spot, and hold tight. Don't break cover unless you've been shot, or you're about to get run over."

Over the past three days, the men had used jagged rock fragments to scratch out shallow trenches to give them some degree of cover and the tiniest protection from the wind. With the addition of some sticks, twigs, and dirt, they were well hidden under the dark sky. Each man was given a quadrant to scan so that nobody would sneak up on the party.

I'd give anything for an Afghan afternoon, thought Misha, remembering the warmth that was one year and a lifetime in the past. He scanned the horizon to the north, wondering who they would encounter first. *Even if the Russians find us, they're just as likely to shoot us on sight, and I wouldn't blame them.* He was surprised to hear major action south of their position. He had thought that the main push would come from the north to the south, as the main thrust of the invasion had.

That's stupid, lazy thinking, he admonished himself. If the Soviets were flanking to the south, there was a good chance that they'd roll right up to this area. For the first time since abandoning the BMD, Misha felt hopeful. He just had to remain where he was and let the army come to him. He noticed himself nodding off. *Can't sleep, durak! You need to keep watch. You can't let your men down.*

Time stretched on into hours. Sunrise wouldn't be until eight o'clock. That seemed like a hundred years from now. Just when Misha thought that he'd drift off, he saw movement. He focused on the men who were approaching. There were four men moving quickly through the forest. Two of them were carrying something large. *They are moving recklessly. They are confident that they won't encounter the enemy here.*

Misha expected the team to rush right past his position, but to his horror, they stopped not four feet from where he was hiding. One of the men excitedly pointed past Misha to the south. They were speaking what Misha assumed was English. It didn't sound like German.

As he watched, the men set up what Misha assumed must be a missile launcher. One man put down a big tripod, while the other set a large tube on top of the tripod. Finally, Misha could make out the optical sight that was the last part of the assembly.

This confirmed Misha's belief that the Soviets were flanking to the south. It was a pity that he wasn't in a position to attack this missile team. If his squad had coordinated a plan, sure. But without a plan, it was suicide. On the other hand, these missile teams would break down their weapon and withdraw as soon as they launched it. So, all he had to do was try not to breathe too loudly for the next few hours.

****

"Target, three hundred ten degrees, machine-gun bunker," called Sergeant Knopik.

"Engaging," replied Borna, squeezing the firing handle of the tank's 100mm cannon. Since they'd climbed out of the river, the battle for the west bank of the Main River had devolved into teams of two and three Polish tanks linking up and rampaging along the southern edge of Würzburg. With the principal fighting taking place in the north for the past week, NATO didn't have enough concentrated defenses in the south. The Hussars were running free in the open, smashing targets of opportunity.

"We need to get organized," said Knopik, to himself as much as to anyone else. He picked up the radio and tuned it to the platoon frequency.

"Crusader One, this is Crusader Two-One."

There was silence on the other end.

"This is Crusader Two-One to all Crusader Two units. Report."

In the absence of the new lieutenant, Knopik took charge of the platoon. The other two tanks reported back, and he managed to get them formed up in an echelon left to protect their left flank, while the Main River protected their right.

"Crusader Two-One to all Crusader units. Advance on me, speed, five kilometers an hour. We don't want to get too far ahead of the main body and get cut off." He switched off the radio and called down to his driver, "Dębiński, turn left, heading three-three-zero. We need to get out of the river valley."

The tank clawed up the hill, leaving the river behind them. At the crest of the hill, Knopik discovered the next threat.

"Borna, there's a heavily forested area straight ahead. If I were a missileer, that's where I'd want to be."

"Understood. Should we load HE?" asked the gunner.

"No, we've done well leading with the M8s so far," replied Knopik as the platoon continued to slowly advance on the forest.

****

Misha watched the missile crew as they became more animated. He didn't speak a word of English, but he was fluent in infantry. They were clearly about to spring an ambush. He just hoped that they would fire the missile and relocate somewhere away from him. He wished that he could do something to stop them, but he didn't stand a chance against the four Americans.

Suddenly, their tone changed. With horror, Misha realized that one of the men was pointing directly at him.

Without hesitation, Misha's training kicked in. He leapt up, whipped the Makarov around and fired two rounds into the man. The other soldiers were startled by the paratrooper in their midst. One fell over the missile launcher, trying to get out of the way.

Another tackled Misha, knocking the pistol from his hand and taking him to the ground. The impact knocked the breath out of Misha, but he kept his wits. He reached down to his left boot and drew out his knife. He was sure that he was about to die, but this American would die with him.

He stabbed the man in the side. The warm blood on his bare hand was at once comforting and repelling. The sickening sound of the knife cutting through the man's uniform and into his flesh was repeated over and over until the man stopped moving.

Misha rolled the man off him just in time to see Taras grab Misha's pistol and fire twice at a man pointing a rifle at him.

The fourth soldier, the one who'd fallen over the missile launcher, was standing with his hands up. His rifle lay several feet from him, and he hadn't had time to untangle himself from the launcher before the fight was over and his friends were dead.

"Taras, keep him where he is. Everyone else, grab their weapons," said Misha. He then went to the corpse of the man who'd tackled him, removed a grenade from his harness and picked up one of the M-16s that were lying on the ground. Misha grabbed the rifle, pulling the bolt back, and spotting a round in the chamber. "Anyone know where the safety is on this thing?"

"It's on the left side of the trigger," said Andrei. "Flip it vertically and you're in semiauto."

"Thanks," said Misha as he walked over to Taras. "We don't really have the ability to take a prisoner."

"Should I just end it now?" asked Taras, raising the pistol to head height. The American soldier spat at him.

"You speak Russian?" asked Misha. The soldier just stared at him. "You"—Misha pointed at the man—"get the hell out of here." He gestured to the north with his free hand.

The man looked over at Taras, who had lowered the gun, and used it to gesture in the same direction. The man took off at a sprint.

"The next meal that man eats will be the finest meal of his life," said Taras, chuckling.

"Listen, we need to get out of here. These guys"—he gestured to the dead Americans—"were expecting contact to the south of here. We need to get down there and make contact without getting blown up."

With the rest of the unit moving out, Misha pulled the pin from his grenade, walked a good distance away from the missile launcher, tossed the grenade and called out, "*Lozhis!*"

The grenade exploded in the distance. Misha didn't know if he'd disabled the weapon, but he'd done his best.

The five men began working through the forest to the south. They moved quickly, knowing that the American they'd let go would report their presence as soon as he reached his unit. It was a bizarre race between the two sides. Each needed to find friendly forces before the other.

The Soviets made it to the edge of the forest.

"What do you see?" asked *Germes*, who had fallen behind.

"Tanks," said Taras. "Lots and lots of tanks."

"Ours?" asked *Germes*.

"Close enough," said Misha. "Anyone speak Polish?"

"I'm sure one of the Skis will speak enough Russian," said Taras.

"We'd better think of something quick. If they see us in here, they're going to shoot us."

"Don't you have some kind of signal, or secret code or something?" asked *Germes*, the pilot. "This can't be the first time this has ever happened."

"Even if we did, I don't think our Polish friends would know it," sighed Misha. "It's not like we can just flag them down."

"That's it!" said Tisha. "Just a minute." He reached inside his dirty tunic and pulled out the squad's flag. It was green and blue with a white parachute in the middle and two airplanes flying to either side.

"Even the Skis will understand this," said Taras.

"Knock it off with that, Taras." Misha turned to Tisha. "Give me the flag. If they decide to blow anyone up, it might as well be me."

With that, he raised the flag and walked out to see what fate would bring him. There was no thundering report of a 100mm gun. There was no fusillade of machine-gun fire. Misha just walked in the direction of the tanks. Soon, the rest of the squad joined him.

The lead tank pulled up to Misha, and a hatch popped open.

"What the hell are you doing out here?" hollered the tank commander in Polish-accented Russian. "This is an active battle zone!"

"We've been trapped behind lines for six days," said Misha. "We need to rejoin the line!"

"There's a casualty collection point that way." He jerked a thumb behind him. "Down by the river. You can't miss it."

"There was a missile team in there." Misha pointed behind him. "We took care of it for you."

The Polish tank commander lifted his hand in a two-finger salute. Misha returned the salute, and the two forces parted ways.

Chapter 21

25 January 1981
Jacksonville, North Carolina

Nobody would say that life had returned to normal in Jacksonville. So long as the men of the 2nd Marine Division were fighting in Nicaragua, it would never be normal in Jacksonville. But things had settled into a routine. The panic at the onset of the war had been brief. In some ways, because the Marines had already been at war at the time of the Soviet invasion of Germany, Jacksonville was better prepared for the situation they now found themselves in.

Nancy and Jennifer were spending Jennifer's birthday with her parents. Nancy knew that someday she wanted her own traditions for her own family, but this year she was thankful to have a home to return to. She always felt safer when her daddy was around. She had so many memories of her own here. She hoped that Jennifer would, too.

"Nancy, breakfast," called her mother from downstairs.

Nancy had been lying in bed, contemplating the war and how unimportant it made everything else seem. *What's the point of being a bank teller when the world could end any minute?* she wondered.

But President Carter had assured the nation that everything had to continue, even as the world changed. Those changes started with shortages. There was plenty of fresh food, but when it came to canned goods, or anything nonperishable, they were scarce. Massive amounts of food were now traveling from the production facilities in the heartland straight to the nation's ports to be shipped overseas for war relief.

Nancy rose and straightened out her nightgown before heading downstairs to greet the day. In the kitchen, she found her parents and Jennifer sitting at the breakfast table.

"Good morning, princess," said her father, Brad McNamara. "I trust you slept well?"

"Yes, Daddy," replied Nancy. "It was exactly what I needed. But now, this"—she reached for the coffeepot—"is exactly what I need."

"Like father, like daughter," said Janice, her mother, with a laugh.

"You know," said Brad, "I'd have sworn that by the time you were Jennifer's age, you were just wild about birthday presents. I remember when you got that Chatty Cathy doll. I swear, you would not let up until we had that party."

"Presents?" said Jennifer.

"Oh, Brad," said Janice. "That was when Nancy was five. I swear your memory is just one big hole." She playfully grabbed his hand and gave it a squeeze. Jennifer was eating a pancake in her highchair, and Nancy helped herself to a couple. Her mother passed her the orange juice.

"This was hard to come by," she said. "I hope that when the oranges come in during the spring, it'll ease up, but the frozen concentrate is just disappearing."

"We all have our burden to carry, Mom," said Nancy, though she loved OJ and also hoped for a good orange crop this year.

"Have you heard from Carlos?" asked Brad. Once upon a time, this question would have bothered Nancy, but with Carlos as their window into the war, she'd grown used to it.

"I got a letter from him on Tuesday. As usual, he can't say much. He's still in Nicaragua. He said that he ran into some of the old gang while he was down there. That really seemed to lift his spirits a bit."

"Is he going back to the Marine Corps?" asked Brad. "I never quite understood what he was off doing when he left here so abruptly."

"No, Daddy, he's going to stick with what he's doing, working private security. It sounds like it's every bit as dangerous and important as what he was doing. Maybe even more so."

"Well, I hope he stays safe either way."

"Nancy, I hate to pry, but did you take care of that thing at the post office?" Janice couldn't bring herself to say "register for the Selective Service."

"Yes, Mother," replied Nancy, "I signed up for the draft." Janice's face soured at the comment. "There's nothing to worry about, Momma. I'm sure there are exemptions and deferments for single mothers whose ex-husbands are off fighting the war."

"Speaking of," said Brad, trying to move the conversation along. "Did you see that the Henderson boy was called up already?"

"Greg?" asked Janice.

"No, the older one, Douglas. He's heading out to the Army at the end of the week. They told him he was lucky that they didn't ship him out immediately."

160

"How rude," said Janice. "I understand that we have to make sacrifices, but can't we just try to stay civilized about it?"

"If only the rest of the world had your sense of modern etiquette," said Brad with a smile as he reached out and returned his wife's earlier hand squeeze. It was one of the many endearing traits the couple shared, and it drove Nancy crazy that it seemed so easy for them.

"Presents?" repeated Jennifer.

"I suppose we need to move this along," said Nancy, pushing back her chair and crossing to pull Jennifer out of her highchair.

"That's hardly the festive birthday spirit," said Brad.

"I'm sorry, Daddy. Everything is just so strange this year."

"Well, I have just the thing for that." As the family moved from the kitchen to the living room, Brad went to the record player and began flipping through his stack. "The Beach Boys, or Dean Martin?"

"Let's go with Deano," said Nancy. "I know you only have the Beach Boys because of me."

As Dean Martin crooned, "I can't give you anything but love," Jennifer was presented with an Easy-Bake Oven, which had been one of Nancy's favorites when she was young.

"She's way too young for this, Daddy," said Nancy, imagining the girl sticking her hand on the hot lightbulb.

Seeing his crestfallen expression, Janice intervened, "I'm sure she'll grow into it. Until she's older, she can play with it unplugged. That's what we did for you."

That made Nancy smile, and for a few moments, on a cold January morning, the McNamara family was normal again.

Chapter 22

30 January 1981
Rama, Nicaragua

"How's it hangin', Major?" asked Lance Corporal Oliver.

"Hey, kid," said Ripsaw, "how the hell are you? Haven't seen you around so much."

"Yeah, the price of leadership. I think that's what Sergeant Evans called it. But hey, I brought you this." Oliver handed the major a crudely wrapped gift that was clearly a bottle of liquor.

"Tequila, or rum?" asked the major.

"Local rum. Really potent local rum," replied Oliver.

"Aww, thanks, kid. Damn, I didn't get you anything."

"Well… That doesn't have to be true, sir," said Oliver sheepishly. The major cocked his head. "You could let me do the preflight checks today. I've got it all down, and this'll be my last chance to do it."

"Let me get this straight," said Captain White, who appeared behind them. "You, a broke-ass E-3 without two nickels to rub together, paid good money to buy a gift so that you could bribe this rich O-4? And you are bribing him so that he doesn't actually have to do the job that the Corps is paying him to do?"

"Well, I… um. I got one for you too," said Oliver, handing over a second bottle to the captain.

"You know what?" said Snow. "Keep it. I'm sure Rip will be nice enough to share. But you'd better get on that checklist if we're going to be ready by go time."

With that, the two officers watched as their young mascot diligently went through the preflight checklist. There were one or two simple corrections, but by and large, Oliver felt quite proud of himself as he completed the task.

"You did good, Kid," said Ripsaw.

"Yeah, too bad you can't stick around," said Snow.

"And don't think I don't know what this is all really about," said Ripsaw. "You want to be a pilot. You should, it's the coolest thing you'll ever do. But there's a long road ahead of you. I tell you what, I'll take a look at commissioning options and let you know. You might have to cross over to the Army, but that's just a guess."

"Why the hell would I have to do that?" asked Oliver.

"The Marine Corps doesn't have any warrant officer pilots, and with a shooting war going on, I doubt they're going to send you off to college for four years."

"Hey, look on the bright side," said Snow. "Maybe enough of us will die in the next few months, they'll decide to open up a warrant officer pilot program in the Corps."

On that grim note, Oliver stood to leave. The major extended his hand, and Oliver shook it before shaking hands with the captain. Oliver returned to his team just in time to get his team ready for the day's mission.

He crossed from the Vulture's Nest back to the platoon's assembly area in time to hear Staff Sergeant Page say, "Glad you could join us, Oliver. Can we start now, or do you need to get some coffee?"

"I'm good, Staff Sergeant, I'll grab a cup afterwards," replied Oliver.

"Look, Marines," said Lieutenant Omar Beck, the platoon commander, "this is a weird one. We're providing security for some real James Bond shit. We will deploy from the CH-53s along the perimeter road on Ometepe Island. First Squad will deploy here"—he pointed to the map set up for this briefing—"at the northern tip of the southern circle. Second and Third Squads will deploy here." He pointed to a spot on the opposite side of the island. "The platoon will fan out and secure docking facilities on the island. Your squad and team leaders will have the exact positions. We're not expecting major resistance. However, the word is there's a bunker of unknown size on that mount." He pointed to the volcano that made up the island. "Recon is going to hit that bunker, and we're there to make sure that nobody gets off that island."

"And," added Staff Sergeant Page, "just because we're anticipating the main threat coming from the mountain, keep an eye seaward. We don't need anyone getting jumped from the lake."

With that, the platoon was dismissed and marched to the helos.

****

Ometepe Island

Carlos watched the CH-53s dropping Marines on each side of the volcano. On the one hand, he always loved a good helicopter assault. On the other hand, the Agency was insisting that he go along with the Force Recon team that was about to breach the bunker at the very door he'd spotted the week before. *Life is about tradeoffs, I guess*, thought Carlos.

The team of elite Marine Operators was in position. They were just waiting for the go-ahead indicating that the security teams were in position.

"Olympia." The word came through the radio, and without hesitation, the Marines sprang into action.

The breaching team blew the steel door and tossed in a flash-bang grenade. Carlos followed along as the team entered the building and spread out along the hallway. They moved forward quickly, looking for rooms or side corridors, anything to allow them to get more separation. The chaos in the hallway was amplified by the sound of an alarm blaring through the building. The flashing lights disoriented Carlos as he advanced.

The team came across several abandoned guard posts. It was almost as if they were late to the party. It seemed like a battle had already taken place. They continued to advance cautiously deeper into the lair.

After several minutes, they came upon a kitchen area. It was currently unoccupied, and it gave the team room to spread out. The Marines cleared the room, but before they could advance further, one of the Marines fired a burst from his CAR-15 rifle. Within seconds, the enemy returned fire.

When he first entered the room, Carlos observed three entry points. The one they'd entered through, then two sets of doors leading out. Right now, an enemy force was behind one set of those doors. That was what the Recon Marines were engaging.

The second door, however, was in Carlos's area of responsibility. He took cover behind some stainless steel cabinets and leveled his rifle to cover the door. The door opened a hair.

His finger was on the trigger. He was ready for action. The door closed again.

"I've got someone over here," shouted Carlos over the sounds of battle. One of the Recon Marines moved to his side.

"What've ya got, sir?"

Carlos was mentally taken aback by the *sir* but didn't hesitate. "There's someone on the other side of that door, but they aren't engaging. The door opened a crack, then closed."

"All right." The Marine looked over to the firefight on the other side of the room. "I'm going to cross and open that door. When I do, you're going to pour some fire in there, and we'll force that jackass to engage."

"Roger that, Staff Sergeant," replied Carlos.

The Marine waited for the volume of fire across the room to die down before he darted from his concealment and ran for the door. In an instant, he flung the door open.

Carlos had his rifle at the ready, finger inside the trigger guard, selector on burst. In the instant that he was to fire, he hesitated and lowered his rifle.

As the Marine came around the door, Carlos held up his hand. "No! Stand down," he shouted.

The other side of the door was a pantry. Among the food and cookware were three scared women wearing white aprons. Carlos slipped into the pantry and cleared it of any enemy fighters. In Spanish, he told them to get back in and stay down until someone came for them. They would be safe as long as they stayed there.

With the door secured, he and the staff sergeant turned to face the threat from the other door. By the time they were in position, the firing had stopped.

"We don't know if we've killed them all, or if they ran," said the team leader. The team advanced into the corridor and found three dead Sandinistas.

"You gotta give these bastards credit for commitment to the cause," said the staff sergeant next to Carlos.

"Yeah," replied Carlos, "they're fanatics to the end."

These turned out to be the last of the Sandinista fighters they would encounter. The base was largely abandoned.

In the main headquarters control room, they found the body of Daniel Ortega. He was dead from an apparently self-inflicted gunshot wound. The Makarov pistol that killed him was next to him on the floor.

The bullet had entered his right temple and left a massive exit wound on the left side of his head.

"I guess he had a change of heart in the end," said the team leader, handing Carlos a bloodstained note. "What's this say?"

Carlos read the note. "Fuck Marx, fuck Brezhnev, fuck Lenin, fuck every lying Russian in that godforsaken country." He looked up from the note. "I'd say that was a change of heart indeed."

The next day, Fred and Carlos went over the situation. Fred had some HUMINT sources that filled in the blanks. When the war was coming to its final stages and the Marines were clearing out the last of Managua, the Soviet "advisors" had turned on their Nicaraguan hosts. The Spetsnaz unit had slipped away in the middle of the night with not so much as a "so long." When the Americans had breached the compound, the Soviets were long gone, and the remaining troops had turned on each other.

From what they could tell, Ortega had been alive when the raid had started but had shot himself as soon as it was clear that it was over.

******

3 February 1981
21st Special Air Service Regiment
South of Lübeck, West Germany

In the three weeks and four days since the war had started, Third Squad, Fourth Troop, 21 SAS had run several missions. In addition to the targeting of the fuel depot, they had done force-level reconnaissance and roadside sapper operations, and Cooper had even had the opportunity to snipe a Soviet colonel from seven hundred meters. The squad was racking up success after success.

Trooper Trevor Pearce was collecting up his kit for the next mission. Control had radioed in that an RAF SEPECAT Jaguar pilot had bailed out in their vicinity. This would be the most challenging mission yet.

We'll be lucky if we can find the pilot and make contact without either getting shot by or shooting the Crabfat, thought Pearce, using the derogatory term for RAF personnel.

Then they'd need to get the pilot to a safe house to get him on the road home. All the while, they needed to keep themselves from running into the Soviets and find their way back home. It wasn't a surprise, and it wasn't a "suicide mission," but it was a challenge.

On this mission, Lance Corporal Cooper was in charge. Pearce followed him out of the hole, and they quickly melted into the forest. During the premission briefing, Cooper and Pearce had gone over the last known location of the pilot, and how to get there. It was a three-kilometer hike, but there was a one-klick gap in the forest.

"We're going to make that dash together," said Cooper. "There's no reason to double our exposure. I expect that you'll keep up with me."

Pearce smiled internally. He could best Cooper in any footrace. Coop could beat him swimming, but on land, it was no contest.

"I'll be right behind you," replied Pearce.

The two troopers poked through the forest before they came to an opening. The next kilometer beyond this tree line represented the most dangerous aspect of the mission. Once they crossed this (and if they could contact the Crabfat), they would be covered by the forest.

"OK, Pearce, this is the tricky part," said Cooper. "We need to get across this field without being detected. The enemy has to be on alert after all the hell we've raised. So, I need you to set the land speed record between this tree and that one." He pointed to the east of the clearing. Pearce watched as Cooper looked at him and counted down. "On three… One… two… three!"

The two troopers burst out of the tree line and into the clearing. With every step, Pearce felt vulnerable. Each step into the open filled him with dread. But surprise immediately displaced his dread. Lance Corporal Cooper was pulling away from him.

In the most important race in his life, Pearce was falling behind. He doubled down on energy that he didn't think he had, just to keep up with the lance corporal. Long before he made the tree line, he heard an ominous sound.

Thump-thump-thump. Pearce didn't look back. He just ran. He knew he was behind enemy lines. That had to be an enemy helicopter.

Pearce pushed harder than he ever had before. He was literally running for his life. He felt the downdraft as the helo overflew him. He expected to be dead at any second. He couldn't believe it when he and Cooper crashed through the brush at the edge of the tree line.

Both men went prone and scanned the skies, trying to make sense of what had happened. Pearce found the helicopter, still heading to the southeast.

"Oi," said Pearce, "I reckon that's a Gazelle. I'd know those lights anywhere." Pearce had spent enough time climbing into and out of those helicopters to recognize them, even at night.

"I think you're right, Trooper," agreed Cooper.

Before they could discuss the topic further, a streak of flame shot up from the ground and struck the helicopter. The brief illumination of the missile warhead exploding confirmed the men's belief that this was a friendly helicopter.

"What the hell was he doing out here?" asked Pearce.

"He was either sent in to give us some cover, or they sent him in after our Jaguar pilot."

"I doubt he was giving us any cover. In fact, the opposite. He's drawn attention to this neck of the woods." Cooper raised his binoculars and inspected the crash site. "Either way, I don't think we're going to be coming back here to pick the pilot up. There's no way he survived that." After a pause, he continued, "Anyhow, let's get a move on. Our flyboy still needs rescuing."

Cooper set off to the southwest, with Pearce in tow, turning away from the burning helicopter and toward their objective. They crossed the one kilometer between their entry point and the last known position of Captain Maddox Wright, Royal Air Force.

Cooper signaled for Pearce to halt, and the two troopers took a knee and listened. Pearce scanned the landscape, looking for any sign of the airman. He caught the flapping of something in the trees. He pointed it out to Cooper, who acknowledged it and rose, starting off again to the southwest.

They moved slowly now. Each trooper scanned the ground, looking for traces of their objective. Cooper found the track easily, and they quickly followed the trail until they were confronted by a man crouched next to a tree, pointing a Browning automatic pistol at them.

"Oi, take it easy, mate," said Cooper. "You call for a hack?"

Relief washed over the pilot's face. "I'm bloody glad to see you chaps," said Captain Wright. "I was starting to think I'd be speaking German for the next few years."

"Well, let's get a move on, then," replied Cooper. "We can't just wait around for Gerry and Ivan to come trotting along."

With that, Wright collected up his gear and fell in between the two troopers. They marched southwest through the forest. Dawn was approaching, and they needed to get to the safe house before the sun rose.

It was the same house that Pearce had used in his first mission. This time, however, they were approaching from the east instead of the north. The approach was a bit more difficult, but they were able to cross Seestraße without incident, then slip into the sleeping village of Salem. They moved through empty alleys and quiet side streets until they came upon the house. Cooper knocked on the door. After a pause, a voice came from the other side.

"*Wer zum Teufel will was von mir um diese Uhrzeit?*"

"*Es ist Schmutz*," replied Pearce. The door opened and the three men rushed inside. The contact was expecting them, so there wasn't any information regarding Captain Wright, but they did file a report about the downed Gazelle and the lack of any survivors from the crash. Once that was accounted for, Cooper pulled Pearce aside.

"Look, mate, it's almost daybreak. We're not going to make it back to the hole today."

"I won't complain about not being in the hole, but what's the plan?"

"We'll hole up here for the day," said Cooper. "Then once it's dark out, we'll make our way back. We'll take the direct route to the north, so I don't have to smoke you in a foot race again."

"What the hell was that all about?" asked Pearce. "I'm *always* ahead of you in the combat fitness test."

"Never spend more energy than you need to, Pearce."

"So, you're just lollygagging out there?" asked Pearce.

"Of course not," replied Cooper with a grin. "I'm accomplishing the mission within the required parameters."

****

3 February 1981
White House
Washington, D.C.

It had taken considerable persuasion to convince the Secret Service to return the President and his family to the White House. Carter was glad for it. The sterile walls and fluorescent lights of Mount Weather were grating on him.

His day was wall-to-wall briefings, as it was every day. He'd already gone over the draft situation with Hamilton Jordan. The Joint Chiefs of Staff had created their list of "acceptable" military occupational specialties or MOSes for women to serve in. To nobody's shock and surprise, these were primarily clerical and support roles. Areas where women were already *allowed* to serve, even if they were discouraged. This was where the military intended to stash the fifteen percent of the fighting force that happened to be women.

Now, Harold Brown, the Secretary of Defense, was sitting before him, putting papers together for the DoD brief.

"If we want some good news, or at least 'not bad' news, we can start in the Pacific. The Soviets still haven't made any moves there. They are boxed in at their naval bases in Vladivostok and Petropavlovsk. They aren't coming out. We still think that this is to reassure the Japanese and keep them out of the war."

"I don't like that the Soviets still have a major fighting force there," said the President. "Just because they haven't used it doesn't mean that they won't."

"That's true, Mr. President. Admiral Davis, the commander-in-chief of the Pacific Fleet, is putting together a plan to engage the main headquarters at Vladivostok, but until the Korean Peninsula is saved, it's going to be difficult to put together the resources to conduct such a strike." Carter knew that the Soviet naval base was less than one hundred miles from the border with North Korea, so this news wasn't too surprising.

"Speaking of Korea, any news from the front?" asked the President.

"Things on the peninsula might be stabilizing. The South Korean morale has improved considerably since the untimely death of President Chun Doo-hwan." Carter winced. To this point, no evidence had come out that linked the CIA to the explosion that wiped out the Chun Doo-hwan administration. Hopefully none ever would. But he knew the truth of the matter, and he thought it would haunt him for the rest of his life. "The fighting has stalled outside of Daejeon in the west and Gumi to the east. General Wickam believes that this pause in operations is to tighten their lines and prepare for another push. We believe that the addition of the 3rd MAU, which is currently in Busan, will help blunt that push. However, we may be in real trouble if we don't get the 1st Marine Division in place quickly."

"When can we expect that?" asked Carter.

"It'll take at least a month to get everything wrapped up in Nicaragua. Then we'll fly the personnel to Japan, then on to Korea. The heavy equipment will take a few more weeks."

"Will that be soon enough?"

"We won't know until it happens. The Eighth Army was on its heels at the onset of the invasion, but they're turning it around. I believe we'll see drastic improvement. I wouldn't be surprised if they have some success in counterstriking during the pause, based on some conversations I've had with the generals."

Brown shuffled his papers, then continued, "In the Mediterranean, it looks like the rumors of the Black Sea Fleet coming out to join the war were true. A Navy unit in Bahrain picked up SIGINT indicating they've sortied from Sevastopol with the bulk of the fleet today."

"What kind of threat are we talking about here?" asked Carter.

"For the most part, it's a cruiser-destroyer force. There's an emphasis on ASW. However, they do have a significant antisurface capability. USS *Kennedy* is redeploying from the Adriatic to engage. It's going to come down to detection, but the admirals are confident that *Kennedy* will be able to handle the threat.

"Moving on to Germany," continued Brown, "much like Korea, there's been something of a lull. The Soviets threw everything they had at Würzburg in the south. They managed to get a hold of the west bank of the Main River before our counterattack could relieve the forces there. The fighting was intense. Hanover is on the verge of collapse, but the British are holding out in Hamburg.

"Finally," said Brown, "we have Nicaragua. The cleanup of the bunkers is complete. It looks like Ortega took his own life when the

Marines attacked the facility. There was a brief firefight, but not too much resistance. Some of the prisoners taken after the battle claimed that there had been Russians in the facility until the beginning of December. Once the war in Europe started, they simply disappeared."

"It's no wonder Ortega killed himself," said Carter. "He must have felt terribly used."

"He was terribly used," replied Brown. "Either way, that really concludes combat operations in Nicaragua. We'll still leave some peacekeeping forces there. The 2nd Marine Division will be freed up for redeployment soon."

The door opened and Hamilton Jordan poked his head in.

"Dr. Brown, are you going to go over?" Jordan liked to keep everything working like clockwork.

"No, Hamilton, we're just finishing up," replied the Secretary of Defense as he gathered his papers.

Chapter 23

15 February 1981
Jacksonville, North Carolina

Nancy sat on the couch watching the *CBS Evening News*. Jennifer was playing with blocks on the floor.

It had been a long day, but like nearly everyone else in America, Nancy wanted to know what was going on with the war. Like many of her friends, she would tune into CNN when she had a chance, but as soon as Walter Cronkite took the stage, she was sure to be tuned to CBS.

"This is the *CBS Evening News*, with Walter Cronkite," said the television. As usual, Cronkite plunged into the news without delay.

"Today, the Chief of Naval Operations briefed the press on the Battle of the Eastern Mediterranean." The screen faded and returned with an image of Admiral Hayward in front of the Mediterranean Sea. There were symbols on the map to show the positions of the two forces. One, marked "Black Sea Fleet," was south of Turkey. The other, marked "Kennedy Battle Group," was located to the northwest of the Soviets.

"The Battle of the Eastern Mediterranean was an overwhelming victory for the US and our allies," said the admiral. "The Soviet Black Sea Fleet departed their base in Sevastopol and steamed into the Med with the intention of disrupting commerce and engaging NATO naval forces. They offered battle, and we obliged them." He used a pointer to help him illustrate the story.

"The Soviet fleet was detected by US aircraft at a distance of one hundred and twenty-five nautical miles on a bearing of one hundred and six." He pointed at a line connecting the two fleets. "The *Kennedy* was screened by a surface group centered around the cruiser *Richmond K. Turner*.

"As *Kennedy* was preparing an air strike against the Soviet fleet, they detected an incoming attack from Libya." He pointed to a spot on the map labeled "Gamal Abdel Nasser Air Base." "The Tomcats of VF-32 and VF-14 were tasked with intercepting this raid. The fighters succeeded in destroying many of the incoming aircraft. However, there were simply too many to stop them all. The Libyan attack resulted in the loss of the *Turner* as well as the guided-missile destroyer USS *Mahan*.

Of the fifty Libyan aircraft involved in the attack, forty-eight were destroyed." He paused a moment to emphasize the casualties.

"*Kennedy* responded by launching Attack Squadrons Thirty-Four, Seventy-Two, and Forty-Six against the Soviet fleet. The attack was successful, resulting in the sinking of two guided-missile cruisers, five guided-missile destroyers, and one helicopter carrier. Having been bloodied, the Soviets withdrew, making for the protection of Syrian air cover. During our pursuit, the Navy encountered and sank two additional ships, which were too damaged to keep up with the fleeing Soviets.

"This victory was not without costs. During the attack, we lost a total of twenty-seven aircraft. The identities of those lost are being withheld pending notification of the families. But do not let their anonymity take anything from their brave sacrifice. Those aviators are heroes, and we owe them a debt that cannot be repaid." The screen faded out and returned to the studio and Walter Cronkite.

"In other news, Warsaw Pact forces have secured the area surrounding the German city of Würzburg. This latest surge has pushed NATO forces—"

"Can we turn the channel?" asked Duane.

Startled, Nancy replied, "Oh, sorry, I didn't hear you come in."

Duane had been putting in long hours at the dealership. It was clear to everyone that they would be reducing staff, and Duane wanted to be sure to stand out as a hard worker. With US industry moving from civilian to military production, there wouldn't be many new cars to sell.

"Yeah, I just got here. After the day I've had, I'd rather not watch this depressing crap."

"Oh, what happened?" asked Nancy.

"They're shutting down the dealership."

"Oh, baby, I'm so sorry. What's going to happen to everyone?"

Duane walked into the kitchen. "Jeff pointed out that there were going to be plenty of jobs in manufacturing. I guess I'll have to figure something out." Jeff Larson was the dealership's general manager. "I guess he's out on his ass just like the rest of us."

"With my job at the credit union," said Nancy, "we should be able to get by for a while."

That seemed to cheer Duane up a bit.

"Yeah, that's true. I guess I've got some time before I really have to worry about this," said Duane as he cracked a beer.

"Why don't you grab today's paper and check out the classified ads?"

"I'll get to it later. I just want to relax right now." Duane flipped the switch on the TV, turning it from broadcast to cable.

"Hey, I was watching that," said Nancy.

"I'll save you the time," replied Duane. "The Russians are winning, we're losing. The end." He turned the channel to ESPN, where Chris Berman and Bryant Gumbel were discussing the upcoming Super Bowl matchup between the Dallas Cowboys and the San Diego Chargers.

"You don't have to be a jerk about it," replied Nancy.

"Don't you have something to look after in the kitchen or something?" asked Duane.

Nancy knew that there was nothing to do at this point but just give him space. She hated when he got like this and was worried that his newfound unemployment was just going to make everything even worse. She walked over to the kitchen. Duane seemed oblivious to her mood.

"Hey, babe, what do you think about the conspiracy theory out there that the government is manipulating the NFL playoffs?"

"I don't know, Duane, what's the conspiracy?"

"Well, there's no way the Dallas Cowboys should have overcome that Philly defense. No way. And don't even get me started on how Oakland was driving the field with two minutes to go and sure-handed Mark van Eeghen fumbles the ball, allowing Mike Fuller to recover it and run it back? Ridiculous."

"Why on earth would the government care who wins a football game?" asked Nancy.

"Think about it. The biggest game in the most American sport in the world is about to be played between 'America's Team' and the team with the biggest military presence in the NFL."

Nancy checked the chicken roasting in the oven and basted it with butter. "If that's the case," asked Nancy, "wouldn't it make more sense to make sure the Patriots were in the Super Bowl?"

"I bet if the Russkies had invaded a week earlier, they would have. But they were already out of the playoffs by the time of the invasion."

"I don't know. That sounds pretty farfetched to me. Anyhow, dinner'll be on the table in ten minutes." Nancy wasn't sure exactly what she'd expected of her new life, but this sure wasn't it.

****

1 March 1981
USS *Arkansas*
Her Majesty's Naval Base Devonport

Commander Earl Brown considered himself fortunate. His mission was to protect a convoy from Beaumont, Texas, to Brest, France. He'd done that. True, it would have been better had they not lost ten of the transport ships, and two combatants. To make matters worse, one of the Sealift ships lost carried with it the much-needed M1 Abrams main battle tanks of the 1st Armored Division. Brown preferred to focus on the fifteen cargo ships that had survived the crossing. Their equipment and supplies were vital to the war effort.

Now, his ship was docked at Her Majesty's Naval Base Devonport. This was the largest naval base in the Royal Navy. The impressive base spread across the horizon.

"I'm pretty sure Norfolk is bigger," said Captain Aaron Stewart, *Arkansas*'s commanding officer.

"That's probably true, but it's big enough," replied Brown. "Though, to be honest, I'd really like to get back to sea. I know we need to take on supplies, and they need to form up a return convoy for us to escort, but I just feel like we're wasting time here."

"I hear you, Earl. What do you think the return mission will be like?"

Brown wasn't quite sure how to respond. Captain Stewart was a good captain, but he tended to want to hear his own opinion repeated back at him. So now Brown had to try and guess at what Stewart was expecting.

"From the reports, sir," said Brown, "the westbound convoy casualties are essentially the opposite of the eastbound. The cargo ships are surviving, and the combatants are taking heavier losses."

"I suppose that makes sense," replied Stewart, leaving Brown to wonder if he'd guessed correctly. "No sense in wasting good torpedoes on empty ships. Better to take out an escort to make the next eastbound convoy less protected. So, what do you think, Earl? Why do you think they did it? Why now instead of back in 1962?"

"I suppose," replied Brown, "the war college answer is that this is just another resource war. What are you thinking?"

"I think it's more than that," replied Stewart. "I think that this is a clash of civilizations. The Soviet and Western systems cannot coexist. The West is based on liberty and the individual. Our successes come from keeping a tight focus on protecting the individual. The Soviets are collectivists. They believe that the individual is the root of evil in the world. They simply cannot allow us to continue. Bah, who knows? Maybe it's just that Brezhnev is so old he wanted to go out with a bang."

"It's frightening," said Brown, "to think that the fate of the entire world could be balanced on the whims of a seventy-year-old geezer in Moscow."

"And yet, that's exactly where we find ourselves," replied Stewart. "But, Earl, my friend, we're the warrior caste, and we were built for this. Men like us, career military men, will always be there to take the fight to our enemies. We were born and bred for this fight."

This caught Brown off guard. This was a point on which the two men didn't necessarily agree. For Brown, joining the military was the best move he could make as a young man. He had grown up in the Kensington neighborhood in Philadelphia. It was a hard, poor life. From a young age, he'd wanted to overcome poverty. It had soon become apparent that he wouldn't be able to escape based on his athleticism. He was slightly above average in most track and field events, so he knew he'd need to rely on his brain if he was going to make it.

He'd studied nonstop. At nights when his mother was at work, he would look after his younger sister and keep his nose in a book. His friends faded into the background as they started to get into trouble. He received threats for his refusal to run with the local pack of boys, but nothing ever came of it. Instead, he kept his head down and graduated valedictorian of Kensington High School. He was able to ride that success all the way to Temple University. He joined the NROTC program at Temple. The idea of having a career after graduating was simply too good to resist.

Earl Brown had never once regretted that decision. He loved the Navy, and he couldn't see himself doing anything else. But he wasn't born into it, and he didn't consider himself part of the "warrior caste." He wasn't even really sure what Stewart considered the warrior caste. Was it anyone who chose to serve? Was it second- or third-generation service members?

"Oh, I don't know, Skipper, I'm just here to do the job."

"And you're doing a damn fine job, Earl. I can't wait to get back out there. Hopefully we'll nab ourselves a few more Russki subs on the way."

"Roger that, sir," replied Brown. "We'll put 'em underwater for good."

Three days later, they had orders and were steaming west with a group of ten empties.

"It's amazing how high they ride when they're unladen," said Brown, looking out over the water.

"Let's get 'em filled up, then," replied Captain Stewart.

Though it was just beginning, the trip had been uneventful. On the one hand, the Royal Navy was sealing off the GIUK gap, the waterways that led from the Soviet bases along the Kola Peninsula to the North Atlantic; on the other hand, they didn't have the same ASW coverage they'd had when *America* was sailing with them.

That thought sent a shiver down Commander Brown's spine. It struck him that just because they weren't seeing the enemy didn't mean they the enemy wasn't there. The escort consisted of two cruisers, five destroyers and two frigates. If there was a submarine lurking under the waves, *Arkansas* would be a tempting target.

****

5 March 1981
Ellington Air Force Base
Houston, Texas

George W. Bush felt a sense of nostalgia as he drove onto Ellington Air Force Base. It had been over six years since he'd come through here as he processed out of the Texas Air National Guard. *A lot has happened since then,* he thought. He'd gone into business, running a moderately successful oil and gas firm. He'd run for, and lost, a congressional race. But he'd learned a lot and had grown a lot since the last time he'd crossed through the main gate of Ellington.

Bush drove to the main administrative building and stepped out of his truck. He straightened his uniform, grabbed his briefcase, and walked into the building where he would restart his Air National Guard career.

After standing in line in the waiting room, he was directed to another building just north of this one. There, he would receive a briefing on exactly what the next steps in the process would be.

It was a classic "hurry up and wait" situation. He spent the time talking with the others who had gathered there. They were all pilots, and, to Bush's surprise, they were all veterans of one of the services. It made sense to him that the Air National Guard would lump together recruits of similar experience in order to maximize the efficiency of training.

"Attention!" The men in the room went ramrod straight as the order was shouted by a staff sergeant. A lieutenant colonel strode to the podium at the front of the room.

"At ease, gentlemen," he said. "I'm Colonel Alvin Lane. I am your senior flight instructor for this project. And you are an experiment. US losses in the skies over Europe and Korea have been devastating. The need to replace Phantom airframes has required the Air National Guard to relinquish our Phantoms to frontline units. Most of our pilots are also being activated. This leaves a gap in the air-defense mission of the Air National Guard."

Bush considered this. He wondered what airframes they would use since they wouldn't have access to the F-4 Phantoms that were needed overseas.

"We need pilots, and we need them fast," continued the colonel. "You men have been selected for this accelerated class due to your previous experience. I know some of you haven't flown a jet in many years. I know some of you don't have much experience." Bush thought Colonel Lane's eyes lingered on him with this last. "But we will get you trained, and we will get you up defending our nation's skies. We will begin with familiarization training in the T-33. Once you have proven that you haven't forgotten everything the military taught you, we'll move on to the F-102 for supersonic training." Bush smiled at the memory of flying the Delta Dagger.

"And finally, if any of you meatheads make it this far, you'll go on to train in the F-106. This will be the primary air-defense fighter unless and until they are replaced. This training is going to be grueling. If we can't get you trained quickly, we don't need you. We have a direct threat to our south. Between Cuba and the Marxist movements in Central America, to say nothing of the Soviets operating from their bases, America is vulnerable. Now, fall in along that wall"—he pointed to the west wall—"and follow Staff Sergeant Barton, who will take you to get your uniforms and gear. We will be forming up for PT in four hours and you'd better be ready for it. Is that understood?"

"Yes, sir!" replied the recruits.

And just like that, thought Bush, *I'm going to be a pilot again. And this time, I'm going to make the most of it.*

****

15 March 1981
82nd Airborne Division
Manzariyeh Air Base, Iran

Specialist Marlon Reeves was packed into the cargo hold of a C-130 Hercules. He'd done this over half a dozen times, but today was the first time he would jump into combat. After six weeks of skirmishing with the Soviets in the mountains, the big brains at command staff had finally found the resources they needed to put their plan into action. Sergeant Becker had some friends over in the 313th Military Intelligence Battalion who clued him in on some of the operational details of the assault.

The Air Force would plaster the Soviet armor, while the Iranian Air Force was tasked with plastering two known artillery batteries. The attack helicopters of 1/82nd Aviation Regiment would open up on some of the naval infantry units in the mountains as a feint, to keep the enemy's attention on the south. In the chaos that would ensue, the 1st Brigade, 82nd Infantry Division would swoop in and take Noshahr Airport. They would secure the runways, and the rest of the division would follow via the established air bridge.

Now all Reeves needed was to survive the low-altitude flight and drop over the airport. To achieve surprise, the paratrooper-ladened transports would fly north toward Rudbar before turning northeast and weaving through the Saravan Valley. They would make a sharp turn to the southeast and hug the coastline all the way to the target. Reeves and his platoon would drop on the airfield, secure the runway and facilities, then prepare to repel the inevitable counterattack. That was it. No problem.

Reeves was left to his thoughts as the windowless transport flew him toward his destiny. He'd steeled his nerves. He'd read the reports and briefings about the course of the war in Europe, and he knew that the 82nd needed to get into that fight. Today was the first step in that journey. *Don't screw this up*, he thought. *You didn't come all this way just to fail when the moment comes. Just get down, and get busy killing Russkies.*

The Herc banked to the right and turned into the valley. So far, the run had been perfect. There were no indications that they'd been detected, and if everything was going to plan, the enemy would be expecting some kind of action in the mountains.

Reeves thought about his friends back home in Des Moines. They'd thought he was crazy when he'd joined the Army, and even crazier when he'd gone Airborne. He just couldn't sit around. He didn't harbor any ill will toward Des Moines, but he felt he needed to see what the rest of the world was about. The Army gave him that chance.

In boot camp, he'd realized he was good at being a soldier and wanted to be the best soldier he could be. So, he'd applied for Jump School. He'd excelled there and was proud of the work he'd put in and the level of expertise he had acquired. *And now to put that to use. Let's make sure Uncle Sam gets his money's worth out of you, soldier.*

They banked again and made a sharp right turn. They were making their final run now. Soon, the Russians would know what was coming. Reeves just prayed that he'd be on the ground before the response was too coordinated.

The jumpmasters opened the side doors of the Herc, and the wind whipped into the hold. Before they could issue any further instructions, the plane made a quick jerking roll to the left before slowly righting itself. The roaring of the engines and the wind made it difficult to hear, but there was no mistaking the sound of the explosion outside. The Herc started to lose altitude at an alarming rate.

"Brace for impact!" The order came from several voices all at once. The already low-altitude aircraft was getting even lower, and from the concerned look on the jumpmaster's face, Reeves was sure that the pilots weren't in full control.

Reeves grabbed onto his seat with both hands. He'd never been afraid during a jump, but he allowed himself the luxury of fear while he had no control of the situation. The Herc buffeted as it continued its partially controlled descent.

The force of the impact forced everyone forward. Yells and grunts broke out, along with several expletives. When the aircraft hit the earth, it rolled violently to the right, snapping the wing, and tossing its cargo with abandon. The left wing stopped it from rolling any further, and it slid, upside down, for another fifty yards. It was pitch black in the aircraft, except for the two open doors.

"Get the fuck out of the plane," shouted a voice that Reeves didn't recognize. "Let's go! Let's go!"

Those who were able stood as best they could and worked their way in as organized a fashion as possible toward the nearest door. Reeves moved toward the door, hoping like hell that he'd get out of the plane before the Russians decided to finish it off. When he reached the door, he saw Sergeant Becker helping lift paratroopers over the lip of the upside-down door and out of the plane.

"Any landing you can walk away from," said Becker as he lifted Reeves over the edge. Reeves was still disoriented and didn't have a witty reply. He hit the ground and saw another NCO herding soldiers.

"We need to establish a perimeter around the crash site until we can evacuate the wounded," said Staff Sergeant Watkins.

Reeves was putting things together now. He looked over at the crashed Hercules, then turned his head to follow the path of destruction that extended to the west.

"Reeves!" said Watkins. "You need to get your head together."

Reeves snapped to and saw Watkins motioning for him to deploy to a copse of trees to the south of the crash site. He nodded and ran off after another soldier who was apparently headed to the same location.

Reeves took cover behind a tree on a slight rise and looked over to see PFC Sebastian Davis.

"Hey, SeeBee, what's the situation?" asked Reeves, using Davis's nickname.

"I ain't seen anything yet, Reeves," said Davis.

"Well, they know where we are, and they'll be coming for us," replied Reeves. He looked to his left and right and saw soldiers taking up positions all along the perimeter. Anywhere there was cover and/or concealment, men were preparing to repel the expected Soviet attack. He pulled out his map and tried to get his bearings. It was pretty flat for as far as he could see. There weren't any landmarks, other than the Caspian Sea, which he estimated was about a quarter of a mile to the north. There were open fields surrounding most of the site and a row of houses to the east. He saw American soldiers taking positions in those houses and prayed that civilian casualties would be light.

He could hear the battle for the airport raging. His best guess was that they were about two miles from the objective. After a half hour that felt like an eternity, Staff Sergeant Watkins and Sergeant Becker trotted up to their position.

"OK, meatheads," said Watkins, "here's the situation. We lost twenty-three in the crash, not counting the crew. We've got wounded being tended to. It sounds like the rest of the battalion is having fun without us. Reports from the airfield are very positive. We're going to hold this position for another thirty mikes, then establish contact with friendlies at the airport."

"Roger, Sarge, we'll hold down the fort here." And with that, Watkins took off to pass the word down the line. Becker unslung his rifle and joined the other two soldiers at their position.

"Why haven't the Russians come for us?" asked Davis.

"I'm not sure that you were aware," said Becker, "but they're fighting for that airport right now."

"For all we know," responded Reeves, "they saw the plane go down and figured we were all dogmeat." The three men continued their vigil as they waited for the medics to stabilize the wounded.

"Movement, one o'clock, two hundred yards," said Davis. Reeves raised his M16 and looked downrange. Sure enough, some kind of armored car was moving down the road to their right. "What the hell is that?" asked Davis.

"BTR-60," said Becker. "Scout-recon vehicle. Whatever's about to happen is going to happen."

"You've got rank, Sergeant, but I think you should go let the bosses know what we're dealing with. Davis and I can keep an eye on the situation. But if you can have them send an antitank team to our position, it would make me feel a lot better."

"You've got it, Reeves, I'll see what I can do." With that, Becker took off back toward the rally point in front of the wrecked Herc.

"What's the plan, Reeves?" asked Davis. Reeves really wished he hadn't asked. He was still working it out in his head.

"I'm not gonna lie," said Reeves. "There ain't any solid plans for two riflemen versus that thing. Right now, I'm just praying that Becker can get us someone with a LAW to take out the vehicle—then we can contend with the crew."

"Ain't much of a plan," said Davis.

"You got a better one?" asked Reeves.

Davis was silent, and Reeves let it go.

The BTR was advancing cautiously. With all the fighting at the airfield, Reeves was confident that the Soviets had no idea what might be waiting for them. The BTR continued to close. Reeves looked to his right. The fire team set up on a slight berm to his west was also taking in the BTR. The Soviet scout continued to move forward, looking for any signs of opposition.

Suddenly the machine gun on the BTR's turret spun toward Reeves, and a burst of fire tore up the ground in front of his position. Reeves and Davis rolled backward, away from the incoming fire.

As Reeves gained his balance, he shifted to the right about ten feet before heading back to another area within the copse of trees. He heard the shrieking sound of a rocket being fired and watched as a flicker of flame raced toward the enemy vehicle and exploded on the left track.

The BTR made a sudden left turn and came to a halt. The turret spun toward the other fire team and unloaded several bursts of machine-gun fire. Reeves watched as soldiers poured out of the back of the vehicle and ran for cover.

"Don't let them reach cover," said Reeves as he opened fire with his M16. The heavy machine gun on the BTR continued to lay bursts at the team on Reeves's right. He fired more rounds at the fleeing scouts and noticed the turret rotate just in time to duck back down.

Rounds exploded into the earth and trees. There was a sickening thudding sound as several rounds tore into PFC Davis. Reeves didn't want to look at his friend. He just knew that he was dead. But he had to make sure there was nothing he could do. A quick glance told him all he needed to know. Davis lay on his back, eyes wide open to the sky, dead.

He shook his head and turned to the BTR. The troops that spilled out must have taken cover on the far side of the road. The machine gun was taking turns firing at the two positions, forcing the soldiers to take cover, and allowing some of the scouts to make it to cover.

Reeves heard someone approaching from behind him, but he didn't take his eyes off the enemy. If there were more bad guys behind him, he was done for anyhow.

"Oh, shit," said Becker. Reeves assumed he'd found Davis. Several soldiers took up positions in the copse. "I've brought some friends to the party."

"There's about eight Russkies taking cover on the far side of the road. The vehicle is disabled, but the machine gun is—" Reeves was cut off as a shoulder-fired M47 Dragon missile exploded against the side of the BTR, sending the turret into the sky. With their covering machine gun gone, the Soviet infantry withdrew.

The Americans were able to pick off a few as they fled, but they had orders to hold their position and couldn't pursue. It was another ten minutes before a runner came to relay the order to withdraw. They were making a push for the airport, two miles to the east.

Chapter 24

20 March 1981
White House
Washington, D.C.

Harold Brown sat across the desk from President Carter. Before the war, Dr. Brown's top priority was getting upgrades for all of the services' main weapons systems.

Since the start of the war, his top priority had been managing the addition of the new weapons while also keeping up with replacements for older equipment to fill the gap. The first of the M1 Abrams main battle tanks were sitting at the bottom of the Atlantic after being sunk during the REFORGER operation. That was bad news. The older M60 tanks were outclassed by their Soviet counterparts. The M2 Bradley infantry fighting vehicle, or IFV, wasn't in production yet, but it was being pushed through. The current M113 armored personnel carriers were being destroyed at a horrific pace.

The US Navy had the greatest warship afloat: the USS *Nimitz*. But the sinking of *Eisenhower* showed that, without proper escorts, the carriers alone wouldn't be enough. They needed the Aegis air-defense system, but they were currently years away from being able to deploy it. The USS *Ticonderoga* was about to leave the shipyard, but the second unit in the class, *Yorktown*, had just been laid down four months earlier. She wouldn't hit the water until late 1982 at the soonest.

Air superiority was the bright spot when it came to force comparison. The Soviets couldn't match the American F-15 Eagle and F-14 Tomcat. The best reports from the intel services indicated that the Soviets were years away from deploying anything that could touch them. The Air Force's F-16 Falcon was proving itself in combat, and the Navy's new "Strike Fighter," the F/A-18 was just coming off the production lines. Pilots were being trained as planes became available.

"What can we do to increase our fighter replacements?" asked President Carter. "Our losses have been much higher than expected."

"We've got a few things working here. Do you remember that Taiwanese request for upgrading the F-5 to field Sparrow missiles?"

"Yes, we killed it after those rogue Iranian Air Force generals sold some of our advanced missiles to the Soviets."

"That's right," said Brown. "Northrop is telling us that they can make the changes and have new F-5Gs rolling out of their plant in Hawthorne by the end of next month. That will go a long way to replacing Korean and Iranian F-5E losses. The training on the new missile system won't take long, not compared to trying to train them up on a totally new airframe. We've also told McDonnell Douglas that they can't convert their F-4 Phantom production lines over to the F/A-18."

"What does that mean for the F/A-18?" asked the President.

"Right now, it means that the Hornet will wind up something of a niche plane. We're thinking about limiting it to Marine Corps use only unless and until we can increase overall aircraft production. Having the Marines fly these off land bases reduces the time it will take to get them fielded."

"What impact will that have on the fleet?"

"We believe it will be negligible. The Hornet would be a 'nice to have' cost-reducing aircraft. Right now, the carrier air wings have a mix of airframes that can perform whatever missions they need to. The Hornet can't outfight a Tomcat in the air, and it can't outdrop an Intruder on the ground. In the end, there are US, British, and German squadrons that need those Phantoms."

"I see. What about the Navy? What can be done there?"

"As a Navy man yourself, I'm sure you can see the problem here. It takes time to build ships. You can't get around that. What we need most is air defense. The *Ticonderoga* can be pushed into service with a minimum of workups, but that's risky. She's a brand-new class, and though she shares some commonalities with *Spruance*, she's still an unknown."

"Is there anything we can do?" asked the President.

"I think you should request that Congress fund the CGN-42 project."

"I understand that you advocated that previously, but these ships won't be built any faster than the *Ticonderoga* class. How is this going to benefit us?"

"It's all about the shipyards. Ingalls will focus on the *Ticonderogas* while Newport News will focus on the nuclear Aegis ships." Carter looked at Brown skeptically. "Newport News just finished *Arkansas* right before the war. They're ready to move forward on the next in class, including the modifications to include the Aegis system. It won't help us today, but it will help us if, God forbid, this war goes on."

"What can we focus on in the meantime?" asked Carter.

"We're funding additional shifts at Bath Iron Works to increase the production rate of the *Oliver Hazard Perry* frigates. Those don't help much with the air war, but they're very effective antisubmarine platforms."

"Anything else on the naval front?"

"The last practical measure I can suggest is that we recall the *Iowa*s back into service."

"Those old battlewagons?" chuckled Carter. "Do they even have a place on the modern battlefield?"

"Absolutely," said Brown. "Without any upgrades, they can still act as command ships. The Marines will want those sixteen-inch cannons if there's even a chance that we make an amphibious assault. Beyond that, during the workups, the wizards at Long Beach and Avondale Shipyard will be fitting Harpoon missile launchers to her fantail. There's talk of adding armored box launchers to give her the capability of firing long-range antiship cruise missiles, but that's going to have to wait. We need them in the fight sooner rather than later.

"The last thing I have, sir, is that we have managed to push the Soviets out of Iran. The 82nd Airborne Division hit them hard five days ago. It looks like the Russians were expecting it, and they withdrew as many of their naval infantry as they could. But we still gave them a black eye before they could pull back."

There was a knock at the door, and Hamilton Jordan poked his head through. "Sir, I've got the professors ready for you."

"I'll see myself out," said Dr. Brown.

Chapter 25

21 March 1981
Gwangju Air Base
Republic of Korea

Captain Sun Young-ho taxied his F-5E Tiger from the revetment to the runway. The ROK Air Force had learned many lessons in the past month. One of the first was to transition the F-5 squadrons from the air-to-air mission to the close-air support mission. Both the F-4 Phantom and the F-5 Tiger were multirole aircraft, capable of either mission. The Phantom could carry twice as many bombs as the Tiger, but the Phantom could also do something the Tiger couldn't: engage enemy aircraft beyond visual range.

The Tiger lacked the ability to fire the AIM-7 Sparrow missiles that gave the Phantom this ability. In the end, even with a reduced bomb load, the Tigers were primarily being tasked with dropping iron on the DPRK's men and machines.

Today's mission was yet another attempt to break the siege of Daejeon. Forces from the ROK's 30th Armored Brigade as well as selected units from the US Army's 2nd Infantry Division were making an armored thrust into the DPRK defenses from the southeast. The 102nd Fighter Squadron was providing close-air support for that thrust.

The mission was a tough nut to crack due to the terrain surrounding the city. It was hills, trees, and rivers. This created defensible approaches that would be hard to overcome. But the defenders in the city needed supplies, and while the airlifts had helped sustain the forces, they needed more than could be flown in via an air bridge. So, the Army was going to punch a hole in the communists who had encircled the city. Each of the Tigers was carrying ten Mk-82 bombs to help ensure the Army was successful.

Captain Sun was lined up just to the left and the rear of Major Wu Chong-ho when the tower cleared them for takeoff. Both Tigers shot down the runway and leapt into the sky. They would join two other Tigers and head to their station twenty-five miles southwest of Daejeon. There, they would wait for the Army to call in an air strike. Given the hilly terrain, this would be a challenging mission.

One thing that would make it a bit easier was the anticipation that they wouldn't be facing a major SAM threat. Most of the enemy missile launchers were deployed on the northwest side of the city, where they could be better defended from a ground attack like the one planned for today. Sure, the occasional MANPAD might reach out for them, but on balance, the threat was minor.

As they flew toward the battle that was just getting underway, Captain Sun considered the mission. He had always been more of a dogfighter than a bomb dropper. Then again, he didn't know anyone who flew a Tiger that had joined to be an attack specialist. *No*, he thought, *we all joined to be Hwarang, fearless Korean knights. We wanted to ride our mount into combat with the enemy and defeat him in the air.*

There were rumors around the wardroom that the next version of the Tiger would be equipped with the AIM-7. Sun hoped it was true. If they could play the beyond-visual-range game against the North Koreans, surely they would move the Tigers back to the air-defense role. *Not that it matters today*, he thought. *It's going to take years before that happens. Either I'll be dead, or this war will be over by then.*

They had been on station for less than ten minutes when Sun's radio came to life. There was a concentration of infantry in a rocky crag overlooking the Army's line of advance. The enemy was harassing the advance with ATGMs and recoilless rifles. The 102nd was tasked with digging them out. *You may not love the mission, but orders are orders, and you're going to kill some communists.*

The four-ship formation streaked to the northwest. Sun looked at the map on his thigh. He knew exactly where they were going, but the visual reference helped him get his head in the right space. He checked his radar. There was an air battle going on to the north of the city. Phantoms and MiGs were mixing it up, just like they had over Vietnam seven years earlier. *Get your head out of the clouds. You have a mission down here to take care of.*

Because of the location of the target, the flight would need to make their attack approach from the southwest to the northeast. All other approaches were covered by ridges. It was a tricky attack, but Sun simply needed to maintain his place in the formation as Major Wu put the Tigers in position to lay down some death.

"Magpie Three, this is Tiger Control. Be advised you have fighters inbound. Get your ordnance down, but be prepared to defend yourselves." It occurred to Sun that he was now in the same position as the Su-7 he had shot down on the first night of the war.

"Magpie Three to all Magpie units. Stick with me, stay on target. Our mission is to eliminate the target. Once that's accomplished, we'll worry about the fighters. If anyone breaks off the attack, I will personally deal with you when we return to base." The four Tigers turned to the northeast and began the attack run.

"*Ssi-bal!*" cursed one of the pilots. "Here come the fighters!"

"Do not break off," ordered Major Wu.

Captain Sun was sweating now. He knew that at this very moment a heat-seeking AA-2 missile could be racing for his aircraft, and he wouldn't know about it until it exploded. He saw the smoke marking the ground target ahead. They were nearly on top of it.

One of the Tigers to his left exploded just before the release point. The remaining three pickled their bombs and broke out in a jailbreak. Each pilot was now on their own in the coming battle.

Sun pulled out of his dive as gently as he could, trying to preserve as much of his energy as possible, knowing that the enemy would have the altitude advantage. He rolled left and gave a little stick to feign a flat turn before rolling again and reversing course in a wingover.

As Sun climbed, he searched the sky for the enemy. His worst fear was finding a MiG on his six. He looked back and was clear. His second-worst gear was finding the MiGs at high altitude. His heart sank as he spotted a pair of the Soviet-built fighters perched several thousand feet above him.

Sun knew that the MiGs had a speed advantage. With the added altitude advantage, he was in trouble. Sun kept his head on a swivel, searching for additional threats but never looking away from the two vultures circling above. The MiGs must have found what they were looking for, because they rolled over and dove. Sun followed their flight path and could see that they were making a pass at one of his squadmates.

Since he now knew the destination of the enemy aircraft, he was able to plot an intercept course of his own.

"Seven, this is Nine. You have two MiGs diving on you. Break away from me if you can." The Tiger instantly banked and pulled away from Sun. Both MiGs followed, putting them right in front of Sun's

Tiger. The infrared seeker on his Sidewinder found the heat signature of the rear MiG and he fired.

The missile left the rail, engaged its motor, and raced after the MiG. Sun doubted that the pilot even knew he'd been under attack. Thinking about it made the hairs on Sun's neck stand up. He looked behind him in a panic.

Sure enough, there was a MiG diving on Sun. Sun rolled over on his back and pulled back on the stick, performing a classic split S. This maneuver got him out of immediate harm, but in so doing, it bled energy. Speed equaled life, and altitude equaled options. Sun was low on both. He needed to get out of the furball. His mission was accomplished, and with only a single Sidewinder left, he wasn't in a position to add too much more to this fight.

He pushed the plane into a shallow dive, trying to get as low as he could. Sun checked his fuel gauge and frowned. He couldn't afford to light his afterburners.

The Tiger had really short legs when fully loaded. He was extending to the southwest, toward home. He was nearly untangled from the fight, but he noticed a dot closing on him rapidly. He had no doubt what was happening. The MiG had watched him break out of the fight and was now swooping in, hoping for a quick kill on an unaware enemy.

Sun stayed steady on his course. Pulling a lot of g's here trying to get his nose around on the MiG wouldn't do him much good. Now it was a balancing act. Sun needed to lure the MiG in close if he wanted a chance to engage. But he couldn't let him in close enough that he got an easy shot on the Tiger. He suspected that as long as the enemy pilot thought he was undetected, Sun would continue to close, setting up the "perfect" shot.

Instinct told Sun it was time to act. He dipped down and right just a hair, then cranked down and to the left. He knew that as soon as he jinked, the MiG would fire a missile on him. He executed a loose barrel roll, dumping flares as he did.

The maneuver had two results. First, it spoiled the MiG's shot. The missile bit on one of the flares. Second, it drastically cut Sun's speed. The MiG shot past him and extended up and away. Sun pulled back on his stick hard. He was playing the last card he had.

The Tiger was approaching stall speed. Sun watched the MiG desperately running. The stall warning was blaring in the cockpit, but then he heard the tone that indicated the missile had locked onto the MiG. The Sidewinder was barely off the rail when the Tiger pitched over and began to spin. At altitude, this wouldn't be a big problem, but this close to the deck, Sun needed to get out quickly. He kicked the rudder to the left while cranking his stick to the right. The world was spinning in front of him. Each rotation brought the ground closer. He was going to have to bail if—

His wings dug into the air, and he had lift! The Tiger straightened out, and Sun immediately searched the sky for the MiG.

He was alone. He didn't see any wreckage and thought that the enemy must have been uncomfortable flying this far into South Korean–controlled airspace.

"Magpie Three, this is Magpie Nine, over." There was a moment of silence.

"Magpie Nine, this is Magpie Five. Three is down. So's Seven. It looks like it's just the two of us." Sun pointed his plane for home, and the empty calm of having survived another dogfight spread throughout his body.

Chapter 26

29 March 1981
20th Polish Armored Division
Oberzent, West Germany

The advance in West Germany had slowed to a crawl since the Battle of Würzburg. Warsaw Pact forces were occupying the vast open areas between Würzburg and Mannheim. Sergeant Alfons Knopik was convinced that his division was going to be sent into Mannheim. He wasn't looking forward to the battle. *I can't complain*, he thought as he leaned on his T-55 tank. *It has been two months since I've been shot at.*

"There are rumors," said Knopik's gunner, Borna Kohutek, from the turret above.

"What are you hearing?" asked the sergeant.

"With the Czechoslovakians falling behind to the south, and the Soviets unable to break into Frankfurt, we will be sent north to help encircle the city."

"Bah, that's just gossip," said Knopik. "We've heard the same thing for a month now."

"Corporal Sobański seemed pretty convinced."

"Szymon Sobański would believe anything. He's very simple. As they say, a yokel can leave the village, but the village will never leave the yokel."

"Yokel or not, I think Sobański has a point. There's no way they let us sit here and enjoy the war."

"Oh, is that what they are doing, Comrade Corporal?" said Knopik with a snicker. "We aren't the only pieces on the board. They are just moving everything else around us right now. We covered a lot of territory, and you know from the reports that the NATO air strikes have been hitting our supply depots. We're not here to enjoy the war. We're just waiting for the machine to get wound up again so that we can be thrown into the fire."

"In other news, did you hear about Lech Wałęsa?"

"Yes, I did. I know that I've said he should be shot, but I have to admit that I wish they hadn't executed him. I've seen more death than I'd care to since that day."

"Indeed, we all have," replied Borna. "But what harm could Wałęsa and Solidarność really do?"

"I'm just a tank commander in the People's Army," replied Knopik. "But even I can see that the communist system, though imperfect, only works when we work together toward a common goal." Borna raised an eyebrow at that. "The Council of State," continued Knopik, "was elected to decide on that direction. When people like Wałęsa choose a different direction, they are saying that they are more important than you and I. They don't have to follow where our leadership takes us. I don't think that Wałęsa is so special that he deserves to change the rules for the rest of us."

"But what if Wałęsa is right?"

"What if he is? What if Solidarność has the right plan for paying the shipyard workers? Or the maximum hours they should work? How much time and effort do we lose while he bickers with leadership?" Knopik paused to let the point set. "How much weaker do we become while he tries to wrangle a few more *złoty* out of the treasury?" said Knopik, referring to the Polish currency. "Look around you, Borna. The West Germans are paying the price of a splintered population. Sixty million individuals are finding out that they cannot stand up to the singular will of the state."

"It certainly helps that we have more tanks," replied Borna. "I think you exaggerate the point, Alfons."

"Sergeant," called a runner, interrupting the debate. "The captain needs to see you immediately."

"Looks like Sobański was right," said Borna. "We're getting orders today."

"Let's wait and see on that, Borna."

Knopik followed the runner back to the headquarters tent. He approached the captain's desk and rendered a two-finger salute. Captain Zygmunt Drozd returned the salute.

"Please, Sergeant, have a seat." He motioned to the chair across from the desk. This was unusual. Typically, Captain Drozd would have Knopik remain standing when passing down orders. Knopik looked around and noticed that he was the only tank commander in attendance.

"Sergeant Knopik, I have taken notice of your performance during the course of the war. You made the most of a bad situation in Schweinfurt. That was a difficult mission. You also performed well in the Battle of Würzburg. You commanded the platoon well after the loss of Lieutenant Kalata. You didn't hesitate, and your initiative was instrumental in securing the beachhead."

Knopik shifted in his chair, uncomfortable with the praise. As a rule, he tried to blend in where he could.

"For these actions, I am putting you in for the Cross of Valor. Your actions are a credit to the company, and the Army. I believe that you have earned this."

Knopik couldn't believe what he was hearing. He hadn't done anything special. He'd just done his duty to his country.

Captain Drozd rose and motioned for Knopik to do the same. "Additionally, it is my duty and my honor to inform you that you have been selected for promotion to the rank of sublieutenant. Effective immediately." Knopik's jaw dropped as Drozd continued. "Commiserate with your new rank—you are also hereby assigned as First Platoon's commander. I have no doubt that you will succeed in this role." Drozd reached across the table with his hand out. When Knopik reached to shake it, Drozd palmed him something.

"Thank you, Comrade Captain," said Knopik as he looked down. In his hand was a uniform insignia with two small stars. "I won't let you down."

"I'm sure you won't. There's a leadership meeting in two hours. Be early for that."

"Understood, sir," said Knopik before he saluted again, turned, and left the tent.

****

1 April 1981
345th Independent Guards Airborne Regiment
Langenselbold, West Germany

Misha looked at the roster in front of him. It was filled with names he didn't recognize. *I can't believe how few of us remain,* he thought.

The second battle of Giebelstadt had been an unmitigated disaster. Three squads had withdrawn from combat when the western line was breached. They'd scattered eastward. Luckily, the Americans had abandoned the helicopter base at Kitzingen. This had allowed the BMDs to slip out undetected. There were a few more stragglers like Misha and his squad, but by and large, NATO had decimated Company 9.

"Have you gotten your replacements?" asked Sergeant Yuri Aleksenko, the squad leader for Second Squad.

"Yeah, Zlobin, Silivanov, and Uralets."

"I know Zlobin. He's a good soldier from what I hear. Of the other two, I have no idea."

"They are total virgins," replied Misha. "Straight from the factory."

"Hopefully," said Aleksenko, "they last long enough to get to know them."

"That just all depends on when we get orders," said Misha, who then excused himself and headed to the motor pool.

"What's the verdict, Taras?" asked Misha as he approached his driver and their newly acquired BMD fighting vehicle.

"It's shit," said Taras. "Whoever maintained this thing before did us no favors. In a perfect world, I'd take a week to break down the engine and rebuild it."

"And in the real world?" asked Misha.

"I'll have to give it the best tune-up I can tomorrow. I need some supplies before I can get to it."

"Understood, Taras. Before you do anything, I need to check with the new lieutenant and make sure that we can take the tank off-line."

"Make sure he understands that this is critical maintenance. If we don't take care of the tank—"

"The tank won't take care of us," interrupted Misha. "I'll let him know." Taras backed away from the engine and stood up, wiping his hands on a shop rag.

"You're not here just to talk about the tank, I assume?"

"Just checking in generally. How's the squad?"

"The new guys," replied Taras, "are blending in. Zlobin has been regaling the new privates with tales of combat from Afghanistan. Tisha and Andrusha have made it a point to be welcoming. Every once in a while, there's a reference to Tsezar and Rodya. That gets a little uncomfortable, but there's nothing to do about that."

"No, not really. I suspect everything will be a bit off until we're bloodied in battle with the new guys."

"On that note," said Taras, "have you heard anything about when that's likely to happen?"

Misha raised his hands in mock surrender. "Hey, I'm just a sergeant. They don't tell me anything until just before I tell you." Taras grunted at that. "The word around camp is that we're going to be used in a big push on Frankfurt soon. Command is cooking something up and we're going to be a part of that stew."

"I hope we can stick to the outskirts of town. I do not relish getting into dense urban warfare."

Misha understood that. While he and the shooters in the squad would deploy into the buildings to fight, Taras and Tisha would remain with the tank. In the confines of the urban battlefield, it would just be a matter of time before someone with a missile would try to take out the BMD.

"I assure you, Comrade Junior Sergeant, I will do everything I can to ensure that the tactical situation is to your liking," said Misha with a wink.

"Ah yes," replied Taras, "you are mastering the trade of the senior enlisted: making promises you have no way of keeping."

"Ours is but to do and die," replied Misha as he left to track down the lieutenant.

Lieutenant Krylov was a harsher man than Lieutenant Kadtsyn, whom he was replacing. Misha wondered how much of that had to do with Krylov receiving his command during wartime. *We'll never know, but I imagine that has a lot to do with it*, thought Misha. He found the man at the company HQ.

"Good morning, Lieutenant," said Misha.

"Sergeant," replied Krylov. "What do you need from me?"

"Sir, my mechanic has inspected our new BMD, and he's very concerned about the maintenance on the vehicle. I request permission to take the vehicle off-line tomorrow to give him the time he needs to perform the maintenance."

"Denied," replied Krylov.

"Sir, with respect—"

"Sergeant, are you and your mechanic questioning the competency or the industry of the vehicle's former maintenance team?"

"No, sir."

"Are you questioning the patriotism of the men who certified that this vehicle was ready for duty?"

"No, sir."

"Do you have special knowledge of when we will receive orders to advance?"

"No, sir."

"Then don't question my orders on this. That tank will remain online and ready for battle. Dismissed." With that, Krylov went back to leafing through a report at his desk.

Back at the motor pool, Misha broke the news to Taras. "You'd better figure out what you can do without taking us out of the fight. The lieutenant just railed at me just for asking."

"That man," spat Taras, "you could sharpen an ax on his head."

"With that as it is, what can we do?"

"First, if I can run down supplies, we'll change out the fluids today. I'll clean out the fuel system as best I can, without taking anything apart that can't be put back together in ten or twenty minutes. I'll just keep doing what I can, one piece at a time."

"And if we have to drive into Frankfurt tomorrow?"

"In that case, we try to keep the RPMs down and just baby her as much as we can, without falling out of position."

"With this new lieutenant, I don't think that's going to be possible. We're going to go charging in like Tennyson's Light Brigade."

"Indeed," replied Taras. "Ours *is* but to do and die."

****

2 April 1981
Jacksonville, North Carolina

There was a massive construction boom going on in Jacksonville. In addition to the new shopping mall there were several manufacturing plants that were being expanded or even being built from the ground up. This brought a swarm of new workers to the area.

It seems like anyone who isn't fighting the war is here putting up buildings, thought Nancy Rodriguez. The effects of this boom were swift. The increased demand for housing and no time to build it caused rents to jump drastically.

Nancy frowned at the thought as she carried another box from her car to her old bedroom at her parents' house. It just made sense that she move back home, but she was proud of the independence she'd achieved. Losing it was a real blow to her sense of self. In the end, she convinced herself that this was for the greater good. She had another place to stay, the construction crews didn't. She was putting in her part for the war effort.

"Has Duane found a new place?" asked Janice McNamara, Nancy's mother.

"Yes, mom. He's staying with Paul and Steve until he can figure something else out." Nancy's parents weren't happy when Duane moved into Nancy's apartment. There was no way that he was moving into their house when Nancy returned.

"Has he found a job yet?"

There it is, thought Nancy. She'd wondered how long it would take. She set the box of books on her bed and said, "Yes, *Mother*, he's been working in construction this week. The money's pretty good, but he says that it's really aggravating his asthma."

"Well, he's going to need to find some way to make money now that he's back on his own."

Nancy knew her mother was right. Duane had made a shift at some point. Even before he lost his job, he was starting to enjoy having two incomes without picking up any of the slack around the apartment. When the dealership went under, he made some token attempts, but he just really didn't seem to want to be there.

"I know, Mom. I know." Nancy started back to the car for another box. "I suspect you won't have to worry about Duane for much longer. He's been mentioning some friends he has out in Raleigh and some 'great opportunity' they have out there in one of the factories." She made air quotes with her fingers.

"Well, as long as he takes care of himself, that's what's important." The barb was effective. Nancy cringed at it. It was true. At the end of the day, Duane would take care of Duane, and if you were lucky, you'd get something out of it as well.

"Did you hear about Doug Henderson?" asked Nancy, changing the subject.

"Oh no, what happened?" asked Janice with concern in her voice.

"Oh, nothing to be worried about," replied Nancy. "Mrs. Henderson came into the Credit Union today. He's graduated from Bootcamp, and he's got orders to some place in Texas where he's going to train to be a medic."

"Oh, that's nice," said Janice. "That could come in handy after the war."

"I don't think anyone is thinking that far ahead mom."

"Nancy Anne McNamara," said Janice sharply. "We simply *must* think of the future. The moment we stop thinking of the future, we begin to accept that there may not be one. That is something that I refuse to do."

Nancy was taken aback. She'd been so busy living in the moment, that it hadn't occurred to her that her mother could be feeling any existential fear.

"Oh, Momma, I'm sorry," she said, reverting to a very childlike manner. She turned to embrace her mother. "I've been so very caught up in my own problems, that I haven't considered what you might be going through."

Janice returned the embrace. "Baby girl, you are so young. You were just a baby back in '62 when we all held our breath waiting for the world to end. When the Russians tried to run the blockade of Cuba, your father and I just knew that there would be a nuclear war and Jacksonville was too good of a target for the Russians to skip us. I told myself during those weeks that I will never consider that the world will end. As a Christian, I know that it will. But I also know that there is nothing I can do to stop it. All I can control is how I act. All I can do is pray, and believe that there will be a tomorrow."

"Is everything all right?" asked Brad McNamara.

Nancy dabbed at her eyes with the collar of her blouse. "Everything's great daddy. I'm just happy to be home," she lied. There was no point in bringing her father up to speed on the conversation. He'd just try to rationalize everything and impose a logical order to the issue. That was the last thing she wanted, and she suspected that her mother felt the same way.

"Say," said Brad, "did Duane ever find a job?"

"Honey," replied Janice, "let's not worry about that right now. Let's just be happy that our baby girl is home, and we can spend some time with Nancy and little Jennifer. We are blessed, and we should never forget that."

Chapter 27

5 April 1981
Minskiy Komsomolets
Southeast of the Denmark Strait

Captain of the First Rank Dmitriy Usatov knew that this was the riskiest aspect of his journey. Since the sinking of the American carrier, he'd kept clear of the main sea lanes, trying to avoid contact with NATO forces. But now, he didn't have a choice. He was approaching the Greenland-Iceland gap.

As *Minskiy Komsomolets* made his way home, Usatov received a burst communication ordering him to transit through the Denmark Strait between Greenland and Iceland.

"It's going to be an agonizing transit," said Captain of the Second Rank Sakharov, the boat's executive officer. "Five knots... We'll be practically standing still."

"Patience, Arseni," replied Usatov, "I'm sure Moscow knows what they are doing when they override my own intuition and issue orders like these. They know what's going on up there, and we're blind." Usatov wasn't sure how much he believed his own words, but surely Moscow had a reason to dictate the time and place that his submarine would be during the transit. Nevertheless, he knew better than to question the wisdom of the *Stavka*, the Soviet Military High Command, when the boat's political officer, Maks Yermolovo, was nearby.

"Captain," called one of the sonarmen, "I have a new contact, bearing zero-two-three degrees." Usatov waited for the man to continue. What was he hearing out there? Another submarine? A Royal Navy frigate out hunting for them? "Contact is a sonobuoy splash, sir."

"And so it begins," said Sakharov.

"Indeed," replied Usatov.

"The buoy isn't transmitting, sir. It's passive."

"Thank you, Senior Seaman Yurasov. That would be the United States Navy, rolling out our welcome mat." Usatov knew that US Navy P-3 Orions flying out of Keflavik would be holding a constant vigil along the Denmark Strait. *And God only knows what else is up there waiting for us*, he thought.

"Helm, take us to three hundred meters." He wanted to get under the thermocline, which could help prevent the American hydrophones from detecting his approach.

The Denmark Strait was where cold water from the Arctic Ocean ran headlong into the warm water of the Gulf Stream. This made for significant changes in temperature. The thermocline was the point at which the water would rapidly cool. This cooler water could deflect sound waves. The mechanical sounds of the boat would be reflected to the seafloor, and active sonars above the layer would be reflected to the surface. It wasn't a guarantee of stealth. After all, the Americans would surely program some of their sonobuoys to listen under the layer.

I think it just feels safer when we go deep... putting distance between the enemy and myself, Usatov thought.

The submarine continued to creep to the northeast. Overhead, more sonobuoys splashed into the water, then disappeared as they went silent. As long as the buoys remained passive, they could be fairly sure that they hadn't been detected. But everyone on the bridge knew that if the Americans dropped an active buoy, the tension would be ratcheted up a notch. An active buoy would mean the Americans had a contact and were prosecuting it. That didn't necessarily mean that they'd been detected, but it very well could.

"What are the Americans thinking up there?" asked Sakharov.

"They are thinking that today is another day at the office. We're the only ones out here burdened with the knowledge that things could go crazy in a heartbeat. To them, today is probably exactly like yesterday, and the day before."

"Hopefully they didn't prosecute and sink a Soviet submarine yesterday," said Sakharov ruefully.

****

6 April 1981
HMS *Bristol*
Denmark Strait

Lieutenant Teddie Anderson was standing watch on board the air-defense destroyer HMS *Bristol*. *Bristol* was a part of the Royal Navy's ASW task force in the Denmark Strait. She oversaw protecting the newest British aircraft carrier, HMS *Invincible*. Unlike the carriers of the US Navy, *Invincible* was limited to carrying Harrier vertical/short takeoff and landing (V/STOL) aircraft and Sea King ASW helicopters.

The helicopters were the key to the current mission. They would fly from the carrier and sweep the seas with magnetic anomaly detection, or MAD, gear. They would drop sonobuoys to listen for the enemy. When they found them, they would prosecute the contact and dispatch the enemy with Mk-46 torpedoes. If the helos detected a submarine, *Bristol* would be there to defend the fleet from any missiles fired.

According to today's briefing, the threat of air attack was low. The Soviets hadn't sent their Tu-22M Backfire strike planes near Iceland for several weeks now. The USAF had transferred a squadron of F-15 Eagles to the island, and this had helped convince the Soviets that they needed to find a new mission for the Backfires.

The task force was making five knots and running a zigzag pattern from the Greenland coast to Iceland and back. They would speed up to twenty knots to reposition along the zigzag, then drop off to five knots. This "sprint and drift" technique allowed them to cover a lot of water while also allowing the ship's sonarmen to monitor the depths with the relative quiet of the five-knot transit speed. Considering there was a war on, this mission was about as "routine" as you could get for *Bristol*.

"Captain on the bridge!" The call startled Anderson. The old man hadn't spent much time up here, preferring to command the ship from the CIC.

"Anderson, what's the word?"

"All clear, sir. We're making five knots on a heading of one-three-zero. The skies and seas are clear of unknown contacts. In addition to the fleet's helos, the Yanks have some patrol planes flying to the south of us, outside of our exclusion zone."

"Fantastic news. To be honest, I just came up to get some air and stretch my legs." Anderson raised his binoculars and returned to searching the surface of the sea for anything unusual.

"Bridge, CIC. We need the captain to the CIC. One of the helos from *Invincible* has picked up something." The captain took his leave after only being on the bridge for five minutes.

****

Minskiy Komsomolets
Denmark Strait

Minskiy Komsomolets had entered the strait over a day ago. They continued to catch the splash of sonobuoys now and again, but it had lessened quite a bit.

"What do you make of the absence of sonobuoys?" asked Sakharov. "Are we through the worst of it?"

"We're too far south for me to feel comfortable," replied Usatov. "My guess is that they haven't given up on us, they are just using a different means to look."

Sakharov raised an eyebrow.

"I think," continued Usatov "there is probably a surface ASW group up there. They have helicopters with dipping sonars and their own hull-mounted sonars. I guarantee that there are plenty of men and machines looking to kill us up there."

The boat continued his methodical transit. Usatov had fallen into the routine of it all. He couldn't let the tension wear down himself or his crew. The passage would take more than three days at this speed. Everyone would eat, sleep and work during the crossing. If sailors started to miss any of these phases, they couldn't perform their duties to the degree needed. So, he tried to encourage everyone as best he could. *If we're going to die, there's no reason to die anxious*, he mused.

The quiet of the day was interrupted. "Captain, I have an active sonar pinging! Bearing three-three-one. Range one hundred thirty kilometers."

"That's pretty far out there," said Sakharov.

"Yeah, that's not likely to pick us up in these conditions." Usatov knew that he could hear the active sonar from a much greater range than said sonar could detect his submarine. "Hold steady and we'll let this play out. They could be tracking another sub, or a whale. Who knows?"

"They could just be sending out a shot in the dark to see if they can scare anything up," said Sakharov.

"Yes, and our reaction could be exactly what they need to detect us."

******

HMS *Bristol*
Denmark Strait

Lieutenant Anderson followed the action on the Action Data Automated Weapons System, or ADAWS, on the *Bristol*'s bridge. There was an unknown submerged contact out there, but from what he knew about ASW, it was just a ghostly shadow at this point. The helicopters would use their dipping sonars to home in on it, and if it was identified as an enemy submarine, they'd send it to the bottom of the strait.

That wasn't a concern for Anderson today. His job was to keep the ship on station in the task force. He looked over at HMS *Invincible*. *Bristol* was tucked in close to the British carrier where her Sea Dart surface-to-air missiles would do the most good if they were needed.

With the fleet looking under the water, Anderson looked to the sky. When he returned his glance to the ADAWS, he noticed that the underwater contact hadn't been verified. It was still an unknown contact.

"Action stations. Action stations." The alarm rang out. "Assume NBCD State 1, Condition Zulu."

"The hell?" said Anderson in reply. He checked the screen again. This time, there was an air contact included. He checked the label on the contact. It was a Soviet "Big Bulge" radar track. That could mean only one thing: Backfires. The ship was being painted by the search radar of a Tu-95RT. The only reason that aircraft would light up the radar is to transmit targeting data to enemy strike planes. *Or that damned Oscar-class submarine*, he thought.

The NATO combat air patrol, or CAP, was breaking off to intercept, but the contact was pretty far north. The F-15s and F-4s in the air would have to carefully manage their fuel state in order to get that far out.

"If that contact is valid, things are about to get exciting," said the petty officer at the helm.

"You've got that right. There's no way that Bear would expose himself if they didn't have something in place to take advantage." As if on cue, four additional tracks were displayed. Then six, then eight...

It took a second for Anderson to put it together. "Blimey, we've got missiles inbound. Flank speed."

All of the ships in the task force started to sprint, looking for any possible aid in surviving the missile attack.

"Missiles approaching starboard side." The ship's alarm let everyone know of the danger.

Anderson watched as streaks of white fired into the air. The Sea Dart missiles from his own ship would be joined by those of the other escorts. There were two Type 42 destroyers between *Invincible* and the incoming threat. They would be the first line of defense. As the missiles closed the distance between the Backfires and the fleet, it was clear that those two ships were also the first two targets.

Given the rudeness of the attack, and the Mach 4.6 speed of the missiles, the ships didn't have a chance. First *Gloucester*, then *Exeter* were struck.

Anderson spotted the explosions in the distance to the North. There were still six missiles inbound. The Soviets had snuck four of those Backfires in for this raid and each fired two AS-4 missiles. The remaining fleet, having been further away from the launching point, had more time to react.

The Sea Darts being launched were finally getting some payback. The next two AS-4s were destroyed before reaching their target. From what Anderson could see, the remaining four missiles were targeting either *Invincible* or *Bristol*. From his starboard-side window, he watched the explosion as another missile was shot down.

Then the world went orange as HMS *Invincible* was struck by the final AS-4. The fireball blew through the ship, coming out the port side, and Anderson winced as though it was going to reach him.

The Backfires were now running like thieves in the night. They had the luxury of lighting their afterburners on the way out. The Eagles and Phantoms raced after them, but the relatively short legs of the CAP aircraft prevented them from closing to within range of their AIM-7 Sparrow missiles. Flooding on *Invincible* was severe. The rescue effort was underway, but after several hours the order was given to abandon ship.

The Soviets had managed to take out three Royal Navy ships, including an aircraft carrier, without the loss of a single aircraft. It was the darkest day of the war for the Royal Navy thus far.

****

Minskiy Komsomolets
Denmark Strait

"Sir!" said Senior Seaman Yurasov. "Contact bearing zero-four-eight. Range thirty-two kilometers." There was a pause. "Multiple surface contacts now. I count seven in total. They are making turns for thirty knots."

"Something has them spooked," said Captain Sakharov, the boat's XO.

"Perhaps there's another submarine right underneath them," suggested Political Officer Yermolovo Maxim.

"Helm, take us to two hundred meters," said Captain Usatov.

"Sir, I've detected multiple explosions."

"Any torpedo sounds?" asked Usatov.

"Negative, sir," replied Yurasov.

"Gentlemen," said Usatov, "I believe that this is what an air raid looks like from three hundred meters under the surface." Then he turned to the helmsman. "Make our speed ten knots. We'll take advantage of this chaos."

"Third explosion, sir." The crew stood in silence as their boat continued to the northeast, sliding past the embattled task force to their east.

Chapter 28

15 April 1981
345th Independent Guards Airborne Regiment
Eastern Outskirts of Frankfurt

The 9th Company's BMDs scrambled west along the north bank of the Main River. The 131st Independent Guards Engineer-Sapper Battalion had bridged the river, and elements of the 10th Guards Tank Division had already crossed. The Desantniks of the 345th were hoping to take advantage of the crossing to get out of the hellish artillery bombardment that was threatening to break the attack.

"The lieutenant is pushing us hard," shouted Taras from the driver's seat.

"It won't be long now," replied Misha. "Once we cross the bridge, we'll have to slow down." Misha bounced into the right side of the vehicle as Taras jerked the BMD to the left.

"I've got the bridges in sight," said Taras. Explosions rattled the men in the tank as a fresh round of artillery rained down on them. "*Gavno!*" shouted Taras, and Misha could see why: The bridging unit he was steering toward exploded in front of him.

Everyone was thrown forward as Taras slammed on the brakes. He turned to the right, and as he moved forward, everyone was jostled again as something, probably another BMD, slammed into them. Misha didn't bother to turn the turret to look. It didn't matter, and Tisha, the gunner, would need the gun pointed at any Germans or Americans in front of them, not Soviets on the flanks.

Taras guided the vehicle onto the bridge. They were bumped again from behind as the regiment surged across the bridges. Misha watched as Aleksenko's Second Squad BMD in front of him took a rocket to the left tread, turned, and pitched over the side of the bridge into the Main River. He hoped that the rocket hadn't breached the watertight integrity of the vehicle. His limited field of vision prevented him from seeing.

"I have infantry in those buildings to the southwest," called Tisha, just before the report of the tank's 73mm gun.

I guess they were hiding when the tanks came through, thought Misha. *I don't blame them.*

"First Squad, you're falling behind," said the lieutenant over the squad network.

"Taras, what's going on?" asked Misha.

"*Chego blyat'?*" replied Taras. "The engine is going haywire. The RPMs are all over the place!"

"What can we do?" asked Misha.

"Grab your ass, because the engine is going to die, and even if it doesn't, we're sitting ducks. The enemy is going to pick on the slow-moving target." The cannon boomed again.

"Steer for that group of buildings. Tisha, lay it on as fast and heavy as you can."

"This is Saber Two-One, we're falling out due to catastrophic engine failure. We're going to clear the buildings to our southwest." The cannon hurled another 73mm haymaker at the enemy.

"Everyone get ready to deploy," ordered Misha. He was well aware that everyone was simply waiting for the order.

"*Yebat!*" said Taras as Misha heard the engine die.

"Everyone out! Now. Now. Now," ordered Misha. The sounds of hatches popping were followed by the sounds of bullets ricocheting off the tank's armor.

The squad assembled on the right side of the vehicle, keeping the tank between themselves and the enemy. They were still twenty yards from the side of the buildings they were trying to take refuge in.

"We can't stay here," said Misha. "Tisha, you know best where the enemy concentrations are. Get with Andrusha and point him in the right direction. Get the machine gun on them. Then we'll provide cover for you once we're in the building." Misha had no idea what his men thought of the plan, but they didn't seem to have any better ideas. "OK, you two move to the front of the tank. Everyone else, on me."

As soon as they heard the chittering of Andrusha's machine gun, they bolted. Halfway to the building, Misha heard one of his men go down. He didn't have time to look back. Once they were clear, he'd see if there was anything he could do. His heart pounded as he sprinted. Andrusha's gun went quiet, and for a second Misha feared the worst. It resumed after a few seconds, and Misha realized that Andrusha just needed to reload.

The squad reached the side of the building and crouched while they scanned for any enemy troops. It seemed that they were clear for now. Misha looked back and saw the prone body of a Desantnik in the field. He couldn't remember the kid's name and kept thinking it was Valya. Either way, this trooper and Valya were both dead.

"We need to move around the back and get access to this building. They're going to be expecting us." With that, he started to inch along the wall toward the rear of the building. He took a knee and turned to view the backside of the building. There was a soldier in green running at him. Misha squeezed the trigger and fired a burst of 5.45mm rounds.

With the man down, Misha rose and sprinted to a door. He didn't have time to consider his options. He simply hoped that there wouldn't be anyone on the other side of that door as he threw himself into the room.

There were no soldiers waiting for him. Misha looked around. This was clearly a small office. If he had to guess, he'd say it was for an auto mechanic.

There was an interior door about halfway down the length of the room, and he slid over to it. There was a square window in the door. Looking through it confirmed his suspicions. In the room next to him was a two-man machine-gun team. They were firing, but Misha couldn't see their target. He signaled to his shooters to bring it in.

"We don't need to get creative on this one. The next time they start shooting, I'm going to open that door, and you two are going to kill them." He pointed at Zlobin and Silivanov.

Uralets. Uralets is the dead man, he realized as he got low and put his hand on the doorknob. When he heard the machine-gun burst, he jerked the door open. It was locked. He looked at Zlobin with panic in his eyes, but the Desantnik simply fired at the two through the window. When the glass blew out, he approached and fired a few more rounds into each of the dead Germans. He then nonchalantly reached through the blown-out window and opened the door from the other side.

Misha and his squad cleared the garage and motioned Andrusha and Tisha to make the dash. With his squad once again collected, if down a man, Misha tried to figure out what the rest of the battle was going to look like. How long could they hole up in the garage?

"OK, men, we're going to get some rest. But we've got to press on soon. We don't have our BMD, but we're still Desantniks, and we still have a battle to fight."

"None but us!" shouted Taras.

"Glory and Honor!" shouted the rest of the squad.

Looking back toward the Soviet column, Misha could see more BMDs and T-72 tanks passing on their way to the heart of the attack. He needed a plan for the next few hours. First Squad was down, but they were by no means out.

"Tisha, over here," he called as he pulled his city map out from his pocket. Both Tisha and Taras were junior sergeants, and while Misha was personally closer to Taras, he knew that Tisha was more of a tactician. If you wanted to overhaul an engine, Taras was your man. If you wanted to figure out your fire and maneuver, you were going to want to talk to Tisha.

"Comrade Sergeant," said Tisha.

"We need to find the enemy. Generally, we can assume that we need to advance south and west. If you look here"—he pointed to where they were on the map—"we can expect enemy resistance from any point after about here." He pointed to an open area just over a kilometer away.

"In order to get there, we're going to have to pass this village to the south," said Tisha. "There could be any number of infantrymen hiding in there waiting for an opportunity like a straggling VDV squad."

"That's my fear as well," replied Misha. "How do we overcome the danger?"

"Maybe we don't," said Tisha.

Misha raised an eyebrow at that.

"Maybe we lean into it. Hear me out. If you were setting up a defense and you wanted to station infantry in town, where would you put them?"

Misha looked at the map.

"I would put them here, along the eastern and western edges of town, to give them the best chance of engaging the incoming attack with their rockets."

"That's what I would do also. That means our best route is right down the middle of the village."

"That's a terrifying thought, but I don't have a better plan. Let's give the men ten more minutes, then we'll spell out the plan. No sense in scaring the hell out of them any sooner than we need to."

"Sergeant, you need to see this," said Taras, looking back at their BMD.

"What is it?"

"Someone is trying to start the tank."

"What?"

"Look." Misha looked back at the BMD, and sure enough there were soldiers climbing into the vehicle while others crouched around it.

"Everyone, stay low. I don't want those fools to shoot us thinking we're Yankees." Misha continued to watch as the visitors realized the BMD wasn't going anywhere.

"Easy now, they're heading this way," said Taras.

Misha looked as three men approached the building while four others covered them from behind the disabled BMD. As they approached, Misha suddenly recognized the nearest man.

"Sergeant Aleksenko, what have you done with the BMD that the Soviet people provided you with?" Misha yelled, just out of sight near the window.

He watched as Yuri held his hand up to slow his Desantniks. He didn't lower his rifle as he called out, "Misha? Is that your tank over there?"

"Get in here before some German goat sees you and shoots your ass off," said Misha.

Yuri and two of his Desantniks ran up to the door and slipped into the garage before signaling for the rest of the squad to follow. Before the war, Misha and Yuri had had a relationship that bordered on hatred. But since the outbreak, they had become brothers.

"What happened to your BMD?" asked Yuri. "I didn't see any holes in it."

"The engine died on us," said Misha.

"Something died in the fuel system," added Taras.

"What happened to you?" asked Misha. "I saw you take a hit coming over the bridge, then fall into the river."

"We hit the water," said Yuri, "and right away we started to flood. I don't mind saying it, but it scared the hell out of me. From there, it was a race between getting across the river and going under it. I had the boys pop open the meatbox in case we had to abandon her, but we just made it to shore when the water got to something in the engine and killed it." He paused, reflecting. "We laid low until the heavier fighting moved away from the bridging, then headed here."

"I'm glad you made it with all of your men. We've secured this garage and haven't encountered anything from the surrounding buildings. We were just about to head out, but let's give your men a few minutes to catch their breath."

"Thank you, my friend. I assume you have a plan?"

"It's not a good one, but let's go over it."

With that, First and Second Squads of the 9th Company 345th Independent Guards Airborne Regiment started their journey to rejoin the battle.

****

20th Polish Armored Division
Southeast Outskirts of Frankfurt

Sublieutenant Alfons Knopik hadn't missed combat. During the lull, he'd never once felt the desire to be throwing himself at the Yankees and their German puppets. As the T-55 pushed on toward Offenbach, all of the stress and pressure of the first night of the invasion came rushing back, as though he'd never done this before. *Of course, in a sense, I have never done this... Not as the platoon leader*, he thought. *At least we're not crossing a damned river today.*

Instead, their mission was to support the 4th Motorized Infantry Division of the German Democratic Republic as they pushed the Americans into the Main River. The 20th Polish Armored Division would maneuver outside Offenbach and bring their 100mm guns to bear on any enemy vehicles they could find. They were the southern force in a pincer attack. Elements of the Soviet 3rd Shock Army would conduct a surprise river crossing north of Offenbach, thereby cutting off all NATO forces on the east side of the Main.

Division intel believed that a die-hard resistance made up of units front the 42nd Panzergrenadier Battalion of the Bundeswehr, the West German Army. The 42nd had been shattered when the Red Army had smashed through Kassel. It seemed to Lieutenant Knopik that these men were determined to die on the banks of the Main River in order to keep the Soviets from crossing the Rhine, twenty-five miles to the west. *So be it. We'll gun them down or drive them into the river. It doesn't matter to me*, thought Knopik.

"Sergeant," said the tank's gunner, Borna Kohutek, forgetting his friend's recent promotion. "Target, wheeled vehicle, bearing three-two-four."

"Engage," replied Knopik. The round exploded out of the barrel of the tank, and the delicate ballet of reloading immediately followed. The platoon was keeping with their tradition of firing armor-piercing rounds unless and until a high-explosive round was called for.

Better to just rattle the enemy APC than one of those damned new Leopard tanks, thought Knopik, referring to the main battle tank of the Bundeswehr. The Leopard 2 had been a surprise for the Soviets and their allies. It was on par with the Pact's T-72 tanks and was light-years ahead of the T-55 they were currently riding into battle. The Poles hadn't encountered them yet. However, East German and Czechoslovakian armored units had been badly mauled when they had the misfortune of contact.

"Keep an eye out for any more leakers," said Knopik to his gunner. "Our German communist brothers should be pushing into Offenbach as we speak. As they push in, we're going to see more of this." The West Germans were now being pushed toward the river. Knopik believed that the Lynx armored scout that Borna had destroyed must have understood that there was no way out across the river and sought to test his odds, heading to the south and into the waiting arms of the 20th Polish Armored.

****

3rd Battalion, 69th Armor

Sergeant First Class Don Mackintosh knew his way around the 105mm M68 cannon. He'd been working with one since the summer of 1960, when his unit had first transitioned to the M60A1 tank. In the twenty-one years since then, he'd become an expert. As it stood, he was the master gunner for B Company, 3/69 Armor. Today he rode with the company commander, Captain Jackson Henderson, as his gunner.

3/69 had drawn a bold mission. In the town of Offenbach, a battered battalion of West German infantry were holding out against an expected charge. 3/69 had secreted across the Main River under cover of darkness and were perched to make a counterattack on approaching

Soviet forces. They had gone through painstaking efforts to ensure the Russians believed that the West Germans had been abandoned. They had been ordered to retreat but refused to go, proclaiming that the only chance West Germany had was to stop the Soviets and their allies on the east side of the Rhine. The Soviets were licking their chops at the thought of taking this piece off the board.

As expected, the attack came. The Soviets came at the West Germans with three divisions, intent on finishing the 42nd Panzergrenadier Battalion. The surprises started early for the Soviets. As part of the subterfuge preceding the battle, the 3rd Infantry Division ordered the 41st Artillery Brigade to withdraw to the hills twenty miles west of Frankfurt. Mackintosh smiled at the thought of American artillery dropping in on the unsuspecting Russians.

AH-1 Cobras from the 12th Combat Aviation Group would tear into Soviet armor. And just when Ivan figured it couldn't get any worse, 3/69 was going to ruin their day. The regiment would slam into their flanks and break them.

"Get ready!" said Captain Henderson. He didn't need to. Everyone in the tank, or for that matter, the regiment, was as ready as they would ever be.

"Target, BMP, eleven o'clock," said Mackintosh, firing an armor-piercing fin-stabilized discarding-sabot round at the enemy IFV. "Reload sabot."

All around them, rounds burst from barrels, then reached out to smash enemy vehicles.

"We must have caught a mechanized infantry unit in the open," said the captain. Mackintosh agreed. He knew that the Soviets would have a tank regiment within the division, but he had yet to see any of the tanks. That was a mistake by the enemy commander. That armor should be defending their western flank as they drove north. *So much the better for us*, he thought.

"Up," said PFC Noah Wright, the tank's loader.

"Target, BRD, twelve o'clock, firing," said Mackintosh. "Reload sabot." From his view port, he could see antitank missiles streaking back at the regiment as the enemy infantry tried to dash to the east. That was when he saw the first tank. He was pretty sure it was a T-55.

"Up."

"Target, tank, one o'clock!" He squeezed the trigger and continued to scan the battlefield for the next target.

"They're falling back—we need to press the attack," said Captain Henderson. This was a textbook spoiling attack. They needed to kill as many of the enemy as they could before withdrawing to the safety of their own lines.

"Up."

"Target, BMP, eleven o'clock." 3/69 continued to prosecute the enemy as they pushed south. Mackintosh lost track of how many rounds had gone out and how many enemy vehicles he had destroyed. It was just the rhythm of battle. Until it wasn't.

"Holy hell," said Mackintosh.

"I see it," replied Henderson. There was a wall of armor pressing toward them. It had to be more than the regiment attached to the MI Division.

"Target, command tank, eleven o'clock, firing."

****

20th Polish Armored Division
Southeast Outskirts of Frankfurt

Sublieutenant Alfons Knopik could feel the battle falling apart. The Soviet forces to his north were being plastered by artillery and attack helicopters. According to the intelligence briefs, neither of those weapons should have been present. But he kept his platoon advancing on the enemy, wondering what surprises might be in store for the 20th.

Because the Pact forces didn't believe there was an armored threat, they deployed their tanks inside (to the south of) the East German 4th MI Division. The tanks were to engage withdrawing vehicles but to stay clear of the village. Leadership was worried about losing tanks to ATGMs and tank traps in the town. Better to send the infantry in to deal with the enemy on a more personal level. Knopik turned white when the word came through his radio.

"This is Tiger Command. We have NATO tanks advancing on us from the west. We are taking casualties. Withdrawing to the east. We need all available Ulhan units to cover our withdrawal."

"This is Crusader Two. All Crusader Two units, form on me, heading two-eight-zero, speed forty." Knopik didn't know what he was heading into, but he knew that the East Germans were being annihilated, and his tank could help stop that. "Borna," he called to his gunner, "load M8. There is NATO armor ahead."

"Understood, Sergeant," said Borna out of habit. Knopik didn't mind. He would always be a sergeant at heart. The chaos and destruction of the battle had created a literal fog of war, with the smoke from exploding shells and burning vehicles limiting visibility. But it didn't matter. He had to relieve the infantry.

"Any second now." They blew through the smoke and into the open. Borna didn't even say a word. The tank was rattled by the booming of the main gun.

"Reload," shouted Borna as he elevated the gun to allow Private Krok to slide the next M8 shell into the breach. The tank shook, and Knopik felt heat all over. He was slammed forward, his harness keeping him from breaking his face on his view port. Suddenly he was aware that he couldn't feel anything. He was numb.

And then he was nothing.

****

345th Independent Guards Airborne Regiment
Offenbach, West Germany

Misha and his light platoon were fighting their way west. They had advanced deep into the suburb of Offenbach Ost, encountering light resistance. But for every meter they advanced, the chance of running into a desperate West German unit increased. The closer they got to the Main River, the less likely their next breath. To make matters worse, they were now in the last row of houses before a large open field.

"What do you think?" asked Sergeant Yuri Aleksenko. "One hundred meters?"

"No way. That's one twenty-five at least. I've run across enough football pitches to know that."

"That's a long way to go in the open," said Aleksenko.

"Obviously, Yuri," replied Misha. "But the fighting is over there, and we need to get to it. We'll deploy by squad. I'll take First Squad over, then we'll cover your crossing."

Misha turned to address his men when Yuri called out, "Wait!"

Misha turned and looked across the field. A T-72 burst out of the neighborhood to the west, taking out the corner of a house as it did. To emphasize the urgency of the situation, the T-72 fired to its rear before exploding. More Soviet vehicles came crashing into sight, furiously firing at an unseen enemy to the west.

"This isn't good," said Yuri.

"What is it with you and stating the obvious today?" asked Misha, more frustrated with their situation than the sergeant. "Everyone, take defensive positions and get ready to fall back. If we get separated, make your way back to the garage." He paused as his men nodded their understanding. "None But Us!" he shouted.

"Honor and Glory!" replied the Desantniks.

Misha knew that there wasn't much they could do. They'd have to keep watch across the field and look for any ATGM teams advancing. But whatever had scared the 10th Guards Tank Division out of the village would have to be more significant than some missileers. Whatever fighting was going on mostly stayed on the far side of the field. Soviet vehicles retreating from the meat grinder were coming across unmolested now.

"I think that first T-72 was hit by one of those TOW missiles," said Yuri.

"I think that's right," replied Misha. "And just think, we were just about to run right into that position."

Yuri grimaced at the thought. Before they could continue their conversation, a fleeing BMD broke free of the village and seemed to be running straight for them.

"He's going to turn," said Yuri.

"I don't think so," said Misha. He held his breath as the vehicle continued unabated. "*Govno!*" he shouted. "Run!"

The Desantniks scrambled out the rear of the house they were in just as the BMD slammed into the front porch. The vehicle came to a halt and its engine died. Within an instant, Misha was climbing onto the turret and opening the commander's hatch.

Misha pulled the man out of the crippled IFV as the rear hatch popped open, and more men spilled out. After a quick second to orient themselves, they ran into the houses on the edge of town, taking cover from an unseen enemy. The gunner's hatch next to Misha slammed open and another man scampered away. Misha started for the driver when the vehicle commander grabbed his arm.

"He's gone," said the man. Both he and Misha hit the ground and trotted behind the house.

Once they were safe, Misha asked him, "What the hell happened?"

"It was a trap," replied the sergeant. "Intel said the Panzergrenadier unit that was holding out was unsupported. They told us that even the enemy artillery had pulled back to avoid counterbattery fire and hold the line on the west bank of the Main." The man struggled to catch his breath. "When we got into the village, the fighting was exactly what we'd expected. We were clearing houses, and the tanks were holding off as we dug out the infantry, when out of nowhere, artillery was falling *inside the village*." The man was incredulous that the enemy would act in an unexpected manner.

"The radio came alive with reports of an armored counterstrike to our southern flank. There was a Volksarmee rifle unit down there that got torn apart. Panic set in. We were taking wounded everywhere. Men were scattered and running. I collected up what I could. Pasha"—he gestured toward the abandoned BMD—"was shot trying to help get the wounded into the tank... He bled out getting us out of that hell."

Misha had heard enough. "Everyone, get whatever gear you can. Tisha, Vasya, check the BMD and get anything of value, then spike the gun." The two men nodded and headed around the house. "We're falling back to the garage. My men will take the lead. Everyone stick together, but don't clump up. If this plays out like it looks like it will, we're sitting on the soon-to-be front line of a tank battle."

The Battle of Frankfurt wasn't going to be won today.

Chapter 29

19 April 1981
20,000 feet over the Gulf of Mexico

George Bush felt the plane buffet in the air as he executed a gentle flat turn. It had been years since he'd flown an F-102 Delta Dagger. He couldn't say it was like riding a bicycle, but the instincts of flying the interceptor returned quickly. He straightened his wings and flew level on a course of one hundred eighty.

Bush's radio crackled to life, "Longhorn Five, this is Tower Control. You are cleared to execute your high-speed dash."

Bush pushed the throttle forward with his left hand. The jet leapt forward, pushing him back in his seat. When the throttle hit the wall, Bush pushed it slightly to the left, lighting the afterburner. The plane again leapt forward.

Bush watched his altimeter spin as his slight angle pushed him higher and higher. He saw the speed indicator push past Mach 1. Then he noticed his fuel flow indicator. He couldn't keep this up long, but then again, he didn't need to. He executed the same flat turn he'd performed at low speed, then leveled off and throttled back. The aircraft slowed in response.

"Longhorn Five, Tower Control. Good maneuver. Note the increase of the area covered when maneuvering at high speed. You can go fast, or you can turn tight. Finding the right balance is important. You should never find yourself in a dogfight, but this is important in finding and achieving the correct angles when making an intercept as quickly as possible. The sooner you shoot down the bad guys, the safer the country will be."

"Roger that, Control," replied Bush.

"Go ahead and bring her in. Control out."

Bush altered his course to enter the landing pattern, then worked with the air traffic control to bring the Delta Dagger back to the air base. Once on the tarmac, he turned the interceptor over to the ground crew and headed for the locker room to get out of his flight suit and grab a shower.

"Good flying up there, Bush," said Colonel Lane as Bush was pulling on a shirt.

"Thanks, Colonel," replied Bush. "It's not my first rodeo," he continued with a wry grin.

"Nevertheless, it's coming back to you quickly. To be honest, I wasn't sure what to make of you when you showed up here."

"How do you mean?" asked Bush, concerned with where this conversation was going.

"The children of accomplished men tend to come in two varieties. They're kind of like preachers' kids. They're either devout believers or absolute rascals. Looking at your service record, I had you pegged as the latter. You have a lot of praise in there for leadership and bearing, but your drill schedule leaves a lot to be desired. What's the story there?"

Bush smirked, turning on his "aw shucks" charm. "To be honest, I was a lot more of the rascal than the believer. The last time I came through here, I was a bit of a nomad. I was restless and couldn't settle down. I guess it took me a lot longer to find myself than most of my peers."

"All right, Nomad, that makes as much sense as anything else. Right now, you're one of the top students in this program. If you keep this up, I have no doubt that you'll come out with captain's bars."

"I'm just here to do my duty for Texas and the country," said Bush, demurring from the compliment.

"Let's get you into one of the F-106s so you can do just that. If you liked the Dagger, you're going to love the Dart," said Colonel Lane, referring to the interceptor that had replaced the F-102. "We're going to transition the top students to the Dart. That'll free up the Daggers for the lower end of the class. There are a few of you that are showing enough promise that we think we can accelerate the program and get you out to the wing sooner than expected."

"That would be great, Colonel. I really appreciate the opportunity."

"Don't forget, that's all this is: an opportunity. You've earned a chance, but that's it. It's up to you to take advantage of it."

"Roger that, sir," replied Bush. "I won't let you down."

"I don't reckon you will, son," said the colonel before taking his leave.

Bush finished getting dressed and headed back to his room in the bachelor officers' quarters, or BOQ. He sat at the small desk and picked up a letter from his youngest brother, Marvin. He smiled as he thought about Marvin in Marine Corps Officer Candidates School. He recalled a time back in 1972 when Marvin was sixteen and Bush had taken him out on the town in D.C. They'd had a great time, but when they'd gotten home, his father had been so mad they'd almost had come to blows.

He opened the letter and read:

Dear George,

I'm sorry I haven't written sooner. I wanted to stay focused on the OCS course and becoming a Marine officer. Those ten weeks were full of learning and training. Even when I had time off, I usually just hunkered down to study and learn everything that I could. Everyone here is just as competitive as I am, so every little bit helps when you're trying to be the best.

The physical training wasn't too bad, to be honest. I was in pretty good shape when I got here, but now I'm in the best shape of my life. It was the mental aspect that was the hardest to get used to. I think that's why I didn't write sooner. Getting used to the idea that I was no longer an individual person was a real challenge. I have now voluntarily subjugated myself to the Corps. I don't have any regret, but for a private and independent person, that was a lot to take in.

I hope that everything is going well with the Air National Guard. I know that you'll be a great pilot, just like Poppy.

I'm heading out for the basic school tomorrow. I'll be sure to stay in touch while I'm there. I hope to hear from you soon. You can use the return address on this letter.

—Marvin

Bush folded the letter and put it back in the envelope. He was proud of his brother and, deciding that there was no reason to wait, he began writing a reply.

****

23 April 1981
Jacksonville, North Carolina

Nancy Rodriguez pushed Jennifer in her stroller as she walked down the wide-open main hallway.

"I think everyone in Jacksonville is here today," said her friend Becca.

"You'd think nobody had ever been to a mall before," replied Nancy. Today was the opening day of the Jacksonville Mall, and the stores were packed.

When the war had erupted, there had been talk that the Jacksonville Mall wouldn't be completed. In the end, that turned out to be idle gossip. The project was just too far along to stop, and besides, it gave the locals something to take their minds off the fighting.

"It's really strange to see how empty the stores are," said Becca.

"Yeah, I guess it's one thing to finish the building, it's something else altogether to stock it." Despite the limited inventory, there were enough stores and products to make the trip worthwhile. The two made their way to the Orange Julius and stood in line.

"How's Larry doing at the plant?" asked Nancy.

Becca's husband, Larry, worked on the production line at the Stanadyne production facility in town. The facility produced fuel injection systems used in cars and heavy equipment. The government was in the process of working with Stanadyne to convert the facility over to producing the fuel injectors needed for the gas turbine engines used in the new M1 tanks. This was highly disruptive, but necessary.

"He's getting lost with all the new folks coming in. The good news is that he's pretty sure he's going to get a floor manager position in the new facility they're building on the south side of town." The new facility would allow Stanadyne to more than double their output.

"I wonder how many factories are going through the same process all across the country," said Nancy. "I mean, who knew that Larry's plant would be 'vital to the war effort'?" she said, making air quotes with her fingers.

"Who knows?" replied Becca. "I'm just worried about this one right here. If Larry gets the promotion, he's pretty sure he'll be added to the undraftable list."

"Oh, Becca, that would be so good for you," replied Nancy. There were some positions in industry that were deemed too important to be turned over, and the men and women who held those jobs would be spared the draft. "I'm pretty sure I can get a deferment as a single parent. I guess it depends on how bad things get over there. Not that I don't want to do my patriotic duty, but I just don't know how I could leave Jennifer behind."

"I can understand that. My getting drafted would be a disaster. There's no way Larry would let me go, and he'd end up taking my place, even with his undraftable status."

They reached the front of the line and ordered their Juliuses, then found a seat in the food court.

"Have you been following the news on CNN?" asked Becca.

"Yeah, I still watch Cronkite for the evening news, but I'll tune into CNN when I'm home early."

"It's amazing. The coverage they are bringing is really scary. They have journalists right there on the front lines. I'm shocked that none of them have been killed. The craziest part is, you can tune in anytime, and they're covering the news. You don't have to wait until Cronkite comes on. It's just wild."

"I don't know how much I like the idea of having the news available twenty-four hours a day," replied Nancy. "I can see how people could get really depressed by that." She changed the subject slightly. "Have you seen the pictures that Caroline Kennedy has been publishing in the *Boston Globe*?"

"Yeah, they've been reprinting them in the *Daily News*. I can't believe she's out there either. I mean, my God, she's practically American royalty."

"That's a good point," agreed Nancy, "but don't forget that the British lost Prince Andrew when his ship was sunk a few weeks back. It all makes me feel gross for worrying about the draft."

"We all have a role to play," said Becca. "And right now, your role is to be a mommy to that precious baby girl." She motioned to the stroller. "Speaking of roles to play, what's up with Duane?" This was the question Nancy had wanted to avoid.

"Duane's OK. He's moved to Durham. He's working in the GE plant there, making gas turbines."

"Wow, that's a bit of a hike. You can't tell me there aren't any jobs closer?" Nancy winced.

"Yeah, that's what I thought. He's been acting a bit strange since the war started. I think the news just reminds him of Carlos. I also don't think that being a father was quite what he expected."

"Oh, Nancy, that's terrible," said Becca.

"I don't know. It's better to find out now instead of five years and another kid down the road."

"You've got that right. It's better to wait for Mr. Right instead of Mr. Right Now."

"But what if I already had that, and I threw it all away? Becca, I'm so confused about everything, and with the world falling apart around me, I just don't feel like anything matters."

"Oh, honey, you can't think like that. Of course you matter. And like I said earlier, your job is to raise this beautiful little girl to be strong. And I'm here for you. The war is the war, but that doesn't change the reasons you made your decision to leave Carlos. He was never going to see eye to eye with you. You were never going to be truly happy in that marriage. I know that you really wanted Duane to be the answer, but he just wasn't. To be honest, I've always had my doubts about him."

"Then why on earth didn't you say anything?" asked Nancy.

"Really? You were moonstruck. I didn't want you to get mad at me for giving you an unpopular opinion."

"Becca, that's terrible! I would never—"

"What about Ricky Johnson? When I told you he was going to cheat on you, just like he did Helen Paxton, you wouldn't talk to me for a month."

"That was in ninth grade!"

"OK, I tell you what. The next time you bring a new fella around, I'll give you my honest opinion, no matter what, and we'll leave it at that. I'll say it once and never again unless you ask."

"I'll agree to that now," said Nancy, "but I reserve the right to change that arrangement if I bring home another Marine."

The two laughed as they got up to continue their trip through the mall.

****

25 April 1981
Camp Lejeune
Jacksonville, North Carolina

Oliver stood at the position of attention. 3/6 Marines were being introduced to their new battalion commander. He didn't know much about the man, but scuttlebutt was that he was a platoon commander in Vietnam and had just graduated from the College of Naval Command and Staff at the Naval War College. *That's probably the same background as every other battalion commander*, thought Oliver.

They'd been on the grinder for forty-five minutes, and the regimental commander was finishing his remarks.

"…and with that out of the way, let me introduce you to Major Oliver North, commander of the 3rd Battalion, 6th Marine Regiment." There was applause from the review stand as Oliver watched the major take his place at the podium.

"I know how much everyone loves it when these ceremonies drag on, so I'll keep my remarks short." There was polite laughter. "This is the proudest moment of my career. The only times I've ever felt so much pride were the day I married Betsy and the births of our children. But my current sense of pride does not come from my achievements. It comes from yours. I am humbled and honored to join and lead this distinguished unit. It has been a frustrating year for me as a warrior. I have watched your acts of heroism from afar, from the safety of Newport.

"I knew that my role in the Corps was to learn from the Naval War College, so I focused on learning anything and everything that I could in order to be prepared for when my opportunity to return to combat would come. Today, we take the next step toward that destination. And I well know that though I've learned much through experience and education, I will learn even more from you and your experiences. Thank you, God bless, and semper fidelis."

With that, he saluted, turned and withdrew. The ceremony then moved into a pass and review for the regimental and battalion commanders.

Back at the barracks, Oliver was changing into his PT gear when Sergeant Evans approached.

"Whaddya think about the major?"

"Corps doesn't pay me to think, Sergeant." Then, before Evans could scold him for being flippant, he continued, "But he ticks the right boxes and said the right things."

"He got a Silver Star in 'Nam. I've got a friend in admin that ran down the citation." He pulled a piece of paper from one of his blouse pockets and read:

"For conspicuous gallantry and intrepidity in action while serving as a platoon commander with Company K, 3rd Battalion, 3rd Marines, 3rd Marine Division in connection with combat operations against the enemy in the Republic of Vietnam.

"On 25 May 1969, while Company K was participating in Operation Virginia Ridge near the Demilitarized Zone, the lead platoon came under a heavy volume of machine-gun and automatic weapons fire supported by rocket-propelled grenades, directional mines, and mortars.

"In the initial burst of fire, the platoon commander and point squad leader were seriously wounded. Realizing the need for immediate action, Second Lieutenant North rapidly maneuvered his Second Platoon through the lines of the beleaguered unit and personally initiated an aggressive assault against the North Vietnamese Army emplacement, the momentum of which forced the stunned hostile soldiers to withdraw to another hill and enabled the treatment and evacuation of Marine casualties.

"After regrouping his forces, he fearlessly led an attack on the enemy's new position, killing one soldier as his men closed with the enemy, and causing the North Vietnamese Army force to retreat to previously prepared entrenchments on the ridgeline. Again reorganizing his men, Second Lieutenant North, with complete disregard for his own safety, assumed the foremost assault position and, seemingly oblivious to the intense machine-gun fire impacting around him, led his men against the hostile position.

"As the tempo of the battle increased, casualties mounted, and his unit's ammunition supply became short. Unwilling to unnecessarily risk the lives of his men, he halted the attack and, repeatedly exposing himself to the heavy volume of fire delivered by the determined enemy soldiers, boldly directed the resupply of his platoon and the evacuation of the injured Marines.

"After skillfully adjusting fixed-wing air strikes upon the North Vietnamese Army unit, Second Lieutenant North dauntlessly initiated a fourth assault by his wearied men. Calmly braving the intense fire of the tenacious hostile soldiers, he moved from one Marine to another, directing their fire and exciting them to a last bold effort, which, by his valorous perseverance, enabled his men to push the remainder of the North Vietnamese Army force from the ridgeline and to seize the objective.

"His heroic actions and vigorous efforts inspired all who observed him and contributed significantly to the defeat of the enemy. By his courage, dynamic leadership, and unwavering devotion to duty in the face of grave personal danger, Second Lieutenant North upheld the highest traditions of the Marine Corps and of the United States Naval Service."

"Damn, that's pretty intense. Except for the part at the end where he goes around and tells everyone where to shoot. That sounds like some bullshit. I'm sure his men really liked being told they didn't know how to Marine."

"Yeah, that is a little suspect. I bet his company commander added that little bit to bump it up from a Bronze. But get this, he'd already gotten a Bronze Star three months before this."

"Damn," replied Oliver. "I guess I won't hold it against him that he sat out the fun in Nicaragua."

"Yeah, and you can bet your ass we're not going to sit out the action in Korea. We're heading out soon."

"Really?" asked Oliver. "You know something?"

"No, but we've been sitting on our dicks for too long already, and now that the leadership shakeup is happening, there's no way they leave us on the bench."

"I guess we should all appreciate what time we have left in the real world."

"Damn right, Oliver. Damn right."

Chapter 30

15 May 1981
21st Special Air Service Regiment
South of Lübeck, West Germany

Trooper Trevor Pearce's legs were aching under the strain. He and Corporal Ralph Willis were carrying two hundred pounds of ammunition and explosives through the forest north of their MEXE shelter south of Lübeck. They were bringing bags of goodies for the local Stay-Behind Organization, or SBO, in Mechow. The SBO would then use the weapons and ammo to wreak havoc on their Soviet occupiers. The German resistance understood the importance of repelling the Russians. They knew of the horror stories from the east side of the Iron Curtain, and they wanted no part of it.

Pearce thought back to the first time he'd been out here. His first mission of the war, when he and Willis had scouted out a Soviet petrol depot. That mission had been a major success and, in a way, had led to this one. Their scouting had directly led to the destruction of the petrol depot and caused the Soviets to alter their transit route through the area. Before that had happened, they had been unable to cross this section of Germany. The Soviet presence had simply been too heavy.

Even so, they had to move at a painfully slow pace. There were still Soviet and East German troops in the area, and you couldn't rely on luck to accomplish your mission. They'd had a scare earlier in the night when they were crossing Highway 208. Crossing roadways was always tense. That had been over two and a half hours ago. The voyage had gone smoothly after that.

Now they observed a horse stable on the outskirts of Mechow. There had been no activity for the past half hour. Before the war, this stable had produced some of the finest horses in Schleswig-Holstein. Now it produced partisans that would take up arms against the invading Soviets. Once Corporal Willis was satisfied that they weren't under surveillance, the two men sprinted across the open field and into an open stable.

Pearce heard a shotgun racking.

"Halt! On the ground," said a voice in English. In the shadows of the stable, Pearce couldn't tell where it was coming from until a man stepped out of a stall, pointing the aforementioned shotgun at the troopers. "What is the daily pass code?" asked the man.

"Robin's-egg blue," replied Corporal Willis.

The man smiled at that and reached a hand down for Willis. "Get up, son, you look ridiculous down there."

He led the two troopers to the back of the stall he had come out of. There was a door in the back, which, when opened, led to a pitch-black room. When the door was closed, the man opened another door, behind which was a dim light. All three stepped into the hidden room.

"Klaus Köstler, at your service," said the local.

"Corporal Ralph Willis. It's good to meet you at last." Pearce looked about the room as he set his pack down and rolled his shoulders to work out the stiffness. Aside from the three who had just entered the room, there were four... children. He did a double take.

"Eh, what's with the kids?" he asked in English.

"Those are runners," said Köstler as he started to unload the packs of C-4 and put them into smaller satchels.

"Runners?" asked Pearce.

"Yes. We have five more locations where we will store these supplies until they can be effectively used against the Soviets."

"But they're just kids," persisted Pearce.

"They are Germans," replied Köstler curtly. "They are Germans who are facing extinction at the hands of the communists." He finished one of the satchels and held it out. A blond boy, no older than ten, grabbed the bag and headed for the door. Pearce was horrified.

"What happens if they get caught with a bag full of C-4?" he asked.

"They will be shot," replied Köstler.

"That's horrific!"

"Trooper, shut it," said Willis.

"But Corp—"

"That's enough out of you. One more word and I'll put you on report. I'll deal with you back at the outpost."

Pearce went silent and watched as the explosives and ammunition were divided up between the remaining kids and one adult, with a stack of C-4 left in a corner of the secret room.

"Pleasure doing business with you," said Köstler, shaking hands with Willis. He glared at Pearce and gestured to the door. "Remember, close the inner door before you open the outer."

As soon as they were out of the room and back in the stable, Pearce said, "Corp—"

"Not a word, Trooper. We'll deal with it back at the outpost."

Pearce spent the hours of the return trip with a mixture of rage and fear. Rage at the German Stay-Behind Organization for using children and fear for the arse-ripping he was going to get when he returned to his "home." These transits were always conducted in silence, but this one felt more silent than the rest.

Once they were through the forest and inside the MEXE shelter, Pearce braced for impact.

"Look, Trooper," said Willis. "You were technically correct. That was appalling. The use of children is expressly forbidden. Klaus Köstler is a monster for doing so."

Pearce was confused as to why he was the one who was in trouble here.

"But you can't start making a scene like that. Our entire role in this fight is to remain hidden and to screw with Ivan. We can't do that if you bring attention to a clandestine meetup."

"But—"

"Let me finish. If a man is sending ten-year-olds out to face Ivan, do you think that man is particularly stable?"

"Well—"

"No, he's not. That was a terrible situation, and it could have gotten out of hand quickly. You've never been a hothead, but you were on the verge of it tonight. We will get word out to command about this. Klaus Köstler will be taken care of. But we have to play this by the book. If you've learned anything from tonight, I hope that it's that you need to keep calm in the face of the devil."

"So, am I on report?"

"Don't be stupid, Pearce, I only said that to calm down our German devil."

Chapter 31

25 May 1981
Southwest of Gumi
Republic of Korea

Captain Sun Young-ho didn't like the mission he'd just completed. Command had assigned his flight to take out a North Korean infantry emplacement. That wasn't too bad as far as missions went. It was the weapons. Each F-5 Tiger carried six BLU-27 napalm bombs. When the bombs hit the earth, they would ignite a flammable gel that would stick to whatever it hit. Then it would burn.

For Captain Sun, the thought of burning to death was too much. The idea of burning to death by napalm was particularly savage in his mind.

If they didn't want to burn to death, they should have stayed north of the DMZ, thought Sun, reminding himself of the moral justification for the use of napalm. Even worse than the fact that they were using napalm was the location where they were using the stuff. The City of Gumi marked the farthest south that the DPRK had advanced to today.

The counterattacks outside Daejeon offered a brief reprieve for the defenders, but it didn't last. After a pause, the assault started moving again, and now the fighting was happening in and around the city of Gumi.

On the western front, the city of Jeonju was under attack. This was very worrying to Captain Sun, as it meant his own air base at Gwangju was under threat of attack. The four Tigers were returning to base when the radio crackled.

"Magpie One, this is Tiger Control. We need you to return as soon as possible. We have an incoming raid and you're the only unit that can get here in time."

I wonder where the Alert Five fighters are? Sun thought.

"This is Magpie One to all Magpie units. Increase to full military power." Captain Sun pushed his throttle to the wall. His Tiger was now moving as fast as it could without lighting the afterburner.

His flight leader, Yun Il-seong, got back on the radio. "Tiger Control, this is Magpie One. Request intercept course."

"Magpie One, come to course two-two-zero."

"Two-two-zero, understood. Estimated time: eight minutes."

The Tigers streaked to the west to protect their home. Their course carried them north of the air base in order to intercept the strike that was coming in from the south.

"Magpie One to all Magpie units. Prioritize the attackers. Do not engage the fighters unless you have no other choice."

This is the most frustrating part of an intercept mission. You're fighting with only one hand, thought Sun. Colonel Yun ordered the flight to light up their AN/APQ-159 radars.

Immediately, Captain Sun could see the incoming raid. There were two sets of tracks coming in. Unless the enemy had screwed up, the first group of four would be a fighter sweep. He and his men would fly through that and head for the second group of six, which were presumably the attack planes.

The fighters merged at six thousand meters. At the merge, Colonel Yun ordered his flight to engage the afterburners. The Tigers quickly accelerated past Mach 1. At this speed, and taking into account the attack planes own speed of seven hundred kilometers per hour, the two flights were closing at over two thousand kilometers per hour. Sun knew the plan. They would race past the bombers, then cut throttle and dive on them from behind. They needed to get a rear-hemisphere firing solution in order for their Sidewinders to lock. All the while, those MiG-21 escorts would be trying to get a lock on the Tigers.

Colonel Yun ordered the turn, and Captain Sun complied. He pulled his throttle back, rolled his plane onto its back and pulled on the stick. The enemy Il-28s were in a dive of their own, racing toward the airfield. It was going to be a close race.

Sun looked up to see the MiG-21s diving on his flight, just as he had dived on the bombers. Those MiGs could run circles around the F-5s. The F-5s could outturn the MiGs, but that didn't matter at all right now. The only thing giving the F-5s a fighting chance was how painfully slow the Il-28s were.

They were nearing the edge of the airfield when Sun received the tone telling him that his Sidewinder was locked on. He pickled the first of his missiles and adjusted his aim toward one of the other bombers.

Before he could get off his next shot, Colonel Yun's Tiger exploded. He saw his first missile hit, but he had to evade before he too was destroyed. He pulled hard, dumping flares as he did.

To his dismay, he heard his radar warning receiver, or RWR. *What the hell?* he thought. Up to this point, he hadn't run into any MiG-21s fielding radar-guided missiles. He didn't have time to contemplate this change in the battlefield; he just needed to get away from it. The warning was blaring, and he had no idea how far out the missile was. If he started shoveling chaff too soon, the radar wouldn't be fooled by the decoy. If he waited too long, the missile would take him out.

He said a quick prayer and rolled his plane one hundred and twenty degrees to the right, pulled back on the stick and released his chaff. He could see the bright flash behind him, but his altitude was getting perilously low, and he was forced to keep his eyes forward as he pulled out of his dive. His head was on a swivel as he looked for the fighter that had launched on him, but he was nowhere to be found.

He did, however, see fires at his air base. Some of that could have come from the aircraft he and his squadmates had downed, but he could tell there was more to it than that.

With the enemy vanquished, he was cleared to land. Back in the ready room, he learned that the colonel had been killed during the defense. Two of the Il-28s had managed to get their bombs off before they were destroyed. The fuel depot was now burning.

As for the remaining North Korean fighters, the two Phantoms that were on the Alert Five had chased them away after extending to the south to get some altitude. It was a harrowing mission that reminded Sun that the war was coming, and the only easy day was yesterday.

Chapter 32

10 June 1981
Reserva Natural Serranía de Amerisane
Nicaragua

The Reserva Natural Serranía de Amerisane was a dense jungle area east of Lake Nicaragua. The wild nature of the preserve made it a particularly good place for the last remaining holdouts of the Sandinista movement to hide. The departure of most of the US military had emboldened them to begin harassing the remaining American troops and the Nicaraguans who were loyal to the Americans.

Today, Carlos Rodriguez was taking the fight right to the communists.

Some locals had tipped off one of Pedro Gálvez's men that they'd seen men with guns but no uniforms moving in and out of the refuge. A quick call from Langley to Albrook Air Base, and the Air Force had sent an RF-4C to make some photo passes of the area. Those pictures were hard to decipher due to the ground cover, but there was clearly a camp of some kind out there. Carlos and three of Pedro's men were scouting it out to get a feel for the opposition.

Carlos had a map out on the hood of the jeep.

"OK," said Carlos, "we make our approach from this trailhead off Highway 238." He pointed to a spot in the middle of the reserve. "We'll make our way along this ridgeline here. It's pretty difficult terrain, but that works to our advantage."

"How's that?" asked Pablo Sandoval, one of the "Rémoras" who worked for Pedro.

"The more difficult the approach, the less effort the enemy will make to defend it." That answer seemed to mollify the man. "We'll push on to this point and make a dogleg here just northeast of the objective. We'll make camp there. It's only about seven kilometers, but that's some seriously steep jungle. Before dawn, we need to be in position to get eyes on the objective. We're going to be right on top of these clowns, so I don't want to be moving around too much in the daylight. Everyone got it?"

"I think we're good," said Pablo, speaking on behalf of the other two men, who nodded along.

The hike was arduous but uneventful. Moving in the mountainous jungle was never easy, but the patrol didn't run into anything more menacing than the occasional spider monkey or opossum. In the daytime jungle, the flora was far more challenging than the fauna. Hacking through the vines and branches to clear a path while trying to make as little noise as possible slowed the passage to a crawl.

The time alone in the jungle gave Carlos time to think. Everything had been so crazy over the last year. Twelve months ago, Carlos was rotating out of the Corps, and starting out in his new career with the Agency. Six months before that he was a married and raising his daughter, Jennifer. *Hell, I haven't even seen Jennifer for the past year,* he thought.

There was a tinge of regret. He tried not to think about Jennifer. It only broke his heart when he thought about her growing up without him. He couldn't figure out a way to make this work. How was he going to be a part of her life, when Nancy didn't want him to be a part of hers? He had no point of reference from which he could make sense of it all.

He missed Nancy. He couldn't pretend otherwise. *She left you, dude. Don't ever forget that,* he thought. He remembered how he'd embarrassed himself trying to win her back before leaving. He'd told her he would change. He told her that things could be different.

But the more Carlos compromised, the further Nancy withdrew. It made the situation even worse. It made him feel even worse about himself. That added a lot to why he felt he needed to leave Camp Leajeune. He needed to reset, and Fred Poole gave him the opportunity.

He'd stayed in touch with Nancy through a series of letters. He found a lot of peace in that correspondence. It was nice to have someone back home to write to. He didn't talk to his parents much. They didn't understand why he'd left to join the Corps, and they didn't approve of the decision.

But Nancy had always been a good listener. The thought of her patiently sitting through his rambling rant about the night Oliver and Estrada got kicked out of a strip club after picking a fight with some townies brought a smile to his face.

What about Clara? he wondered. That was a good question, and one that he didn't have much of an answer to. Then again, maybe it wasn't a question. Clara made it unequivocally clear that she had no interest in Carlos. Even so, Carlos found her captivating. He thought back to the day they met. He was tied up, and she was pointing an AK-47 at him.

As with the memory of Nancy, the memory of Clara made him smile. Oh, sure, he wasn't smiling at the time. But with the benefit of hindsight, he could definitely see how ridiculous the whole scene was. *What if we had met in a café in Managua instead of the battlefield along the Par Par River?* he wondered. *You'll never know,* he thought, and tried to push the thoughts out of his mind.

Hours later, the men were perched atop the downward slope of Piedra Tumbé, the stone face of one of the taller peaks in the reserve, waiting for the sun to come up. From this position, they could see into the valley below, where the communist hideout lay unaware.

"We're about to get some sunlight," said Pablo. "What are you expecting to see down there?"

"We need to figure out how many of them are down there," replied Carlos. "I've got a basic idea of how we're going to approach the assault based on the terrain, but we need to know how many men to bring, and if we'll need to bring out some arty to dig them out. Lastly, we need to know the layout of any structures down there."

"It seems like a terrible idea to put your base of operations in a valley like this. There's only one way in or out."

"Yeah," said Carlos, "my best guess is that they were more worried about detection than defense. Essentially, we couldn't attack what we couldn't see."

"But now that we've found it—"

"They don't even know how screwed they are," finished Carlos.

The patrol spent the day observing the action below them. The comings and goings of the communists weren't particularly interesting, but the counting of the numbers and the observation of patrol patterns were invaluable for planning the assault.

Carlos made observations of areas of approach to the compound, comparing what he saw on the map to what was actually on the ground. This would ensure that there were no surprises when his men maneuvered into place for the attack.

There were several smaller tents that Carlos believed were just individual shelters. Two larger tents nestled right up in the tree line grabbed his attention. That was the real objective right there. By the time the sun dipped in the west, they had everything they'd come for.

The attack came the following day. Given that they only observed a total of five communists at the compound at any time, with a patrol of two, Carlos brought twenty of the Rémoras to take part in the attack. With surprise and a three-to-one advantage, Carlos was confident that they would take the Sandis without major losses. He briefed his team from the town of La Puerta, just to the west of the reserve.

"All right," said Carlos, "we're going to divide into three seven-man teams. Team one will move down into the valley west of the objective here." He pointed to the pass on the map. "Team two will come over the pass northeast. Team three will hit them from this valley to the southeast. With this staging, we should be able to envelop them. They won't be able to defend from all three sides, and we'll be attacking from the very hills that they believe will be protecting them."

"*Señor*," said Pablo, "won't they just retreat to the southwest, where the jungle is flat?"

"*Sí*," replied Carlos, "and we'll let them. Kill as many as you can, but what we're really after is whatever we can gain from their camp." Pablo shrugged, and Carlos continued, "The battle is moving to a new phase, and we need to grab any information that we can so that we can understand what the enemy is planning next."

"They are planning to fight us to the death," replied Pablo. This frustrated Carlos, but he admitted to himself that perhaps his own explanation was causing the problem.

"It's important that we understand what they're planning. How are they going to fight to the death? What tactics will they use? How will it affect the civilian populations? How do we best counter it? These are questions, and my bosses believe the answers are in that camp down there." Carlos gestured with his rifle to emphasize the point. Pablo seemed to accept this.

Carlos nodded and said, "OK, let's move out. The trucks will drop us off at the point of embarkation, and from there, each team is independent. Team leaders are responsible for getting their men in position and on time."

Eleven months ago, Carlos would never have handed off responsibility to a local militia to make such precise maneuvers. The Rémoras had proved themselves over that time. They were a lethal fighting force, and Carlos knew he could rely on them.

Carlos led his team through the jungle to their attack position. He'd built in twenty minutes of buffer to the timeline. Though his team didn't need it, he had no idea if either of the other teams might be waylaid.

Carlos checked his watch. With plenty of time before the attack, he went over his gear one more time. He looked around and saw his men doing the same. As the minutes ticked down to go time, he turned his attention to the objective. As predicted, one of the two men standing guard was leaving the main camp for his rounds. He'd be walking right into Pablo's team when things kicked off.

The seconds ticked down. Right at the appointed time, Carlos sent a 40mm grenade three hundred meters downrange. Simultaneous explosions marked the start of the operation.

Carlos and his team advanced rapidly, seeking targets of opportunity as they closed the distance. It was difficult to tell in the dense jungle, but with the rate of their advance, Carlos believed the enemy was already fleeing. They had no intention of dying here. In the exchange of fire, Carlos heard one of his men scream out.

He took a knee and trained his M16 on the camp. He found one particularly brave communist pointing his AK-47 in the general direction of Carlos's squad. Carlos ended him quickly while one of the other Rémoras tended to his wounded friend. Carlos and the remaining five men continued the advance.

Here's where it gets tricky, thought Carlos.

As the three squads of men converged, they had to be extremely careful not to end up firing on each other. The plan was for the other two elements to hold in place in the tree line while Carlos and his men advanced on the actual building. Using his binoculars and taking in all of the information he could from the battlefield, Carlos decided that it was time for his team to assault the building. He raised a black coach's whistle to his lips and gave it three quick blasts. In return, he heard two sets of two whistles.

He urged his men forward with a hand signal. With more signals, he spread his force out along the line, with short intervals allowing interlocking fields of fire. He then motioned for the Rémoras to his immediate left and right to advance with him, leaving the other two in the forest to protect the flanks of the advancing men. Carlos and his team fired three-round bursts into the tents as they advanced. They weren't receiving any return fire.

All of the window flaps were rolled up in the futile hope of getting some kind of breeze. Without slowing down, Carlos tossed a flash-bang into the tent. As soon as it went off, he and the other two men entered and immediately cleared the room.

There was no active resistance, but there was one wounded communist lying on the ground, trying to hide behind some crates. Carlos turned to check the man for weapons and wounds when Juan, one of his men, shot him in the head.

"Dammit!" shouted Carlos. "You can't just execute people like that."

Juan shrugged his shoulders as the man he'd just shot exploded. The blast of the grenade was largely absorbed by the dead communist's body. =

"Holy hell," said Carlos, "I think you just saved my life."

Again, Juan shrugged.

They cleared the second tent without incident, then whistled for the rest of the team to take up defensive positions while Carlos took stock of the files and supplies that his unit had just captured.

"Pablo," said Carlos as the other man entered the tent. "Have someone to get a count on weapons and ammo that we're hauling out of here. Fred and Pedro are going to want to know down the bullet."

"*Sí*," replied Pablo, who then relayed the orders to one of his men.

Carlos rifled through some of the paperwork in a crate near a folding table. He read through it and a shiver went down his spine. He reached down and picked up another piece of paper. It was the same. He looked down at the crate and realized they were all the same. It was a cartoon drawing of a young child, explaining how to create a *dispositivo explosivo especializado*, a specialized explosive device. Carlos read with horror as the cartoon child, Mateo, built a bomb and placed it on a wall facing the door of a government building. Pulling his eyes away, Carlos went to another crate.

In this crate, Carlos found leaflets of Mateo explaining how to rig an SED to a car so that it detonated upon the ignition being turned on. Another leaflet depicted Mateo showing how to break down and clean an M16. Each of the actions was being done "for the people of Nicaragua" and "for the greater family of Nicaragua."

Carlos had started the day desperately wanting to know what the enemy was up to. He was now ending the day desperately wishing he didn't.

****

16 June 1981
White House
Washington, D.C.

Secretary of State Jeane Kirkpatrick was furious. She'd already given Zbig both barrels, and now she was about to take it to President Carter. She pushed the door to the Oval Office open to see Dr. Brzezinski already meeting with the President.

"Trying to get your excuses down before we start?" asked Secretary Kirkpatrick.

"Of course not, Jeane—" began Zbig.

"Spare me your protests, Zbig. You know how colossal this failure is, and you know that I've been railing against the exact policies that have led to it."

"Dr. Kirkpatrick, please," said President Carter. "We're on the same team here."

Jeane relaxed a bit. The President was right. They couldn't move forward unless they were all willing to cooperate.

"I apologize, Mr. President. I have been warning of this for months, and my frustration has gotten the better of me. Please, Zbig, I'd like to hear your assessment of the situation in Nicaragua."

"Thank you, Jeane," replied Zbig. "Mr. President, there's something brewing in Nicaragua. As we've discussed in this very room, we've expected the Sandinistas to go underground once the leadership in Managua was toppled. That's exactly what's happening."

"If that's the case," said President Carter, "what are we doing here?"

"Because, sir," said Secretary Kirkpatrick, "the form that this underground movement is taking is ghastly."

"How so?" asked the President.

"The Soviets have taken a page from the Palestinian playbook. They're no longer trying to defeat us. They're trying to terrify the population to prevent support for our presence in the region. In the past three days, there have been four separate school bus attacks. Over one hundred children have been killed. That doesn't even begin to cover it. Here." She slid a pamphlet across the desk for the President.

"What am I looking at?"

"That, Mr. President, is a pamphlet that teaches children how to build bombs and blow themselves up for the greater Nicaraguan family."

"That's barbaric," said President Carter.

"It is," agreed Zbig. "But we have to be measured in our response. This is horrific, but the Sandinista response doesn't change the facts that we were looking at when we withdrew the Marines and the 101st Airborne."

"We needed them in place longer, to get the situation stabilized," said Secretary Kirkpatrick.

"Those forces are needed in Korea and Europe. There's no tell—"

President Carter cut him off. "We've already had this discussion, and we have already made this decision. We can't change the past, so how do we move forward?"

"We need additional forces sent down there to get the situation under control," said Secretary Kirkpatrick.

"I don't disagree, sir," said Zbig. "But I think the issue is going to be a question of scope."

"How do you mean?" asked the president.

"We need to know what we can spare from the other theaters—"

"That's exactly the thinking that got us here," Secretary Kirkpatrick interrupted. "We need to give this the priority it deserves. If the Soviets can foment enough hatred in Latin America, we could find ourselves on the outside looking in not just in Nicaragua, but everywhere from Panama to Mexico."

"Surely, you're exaggerating," said the President.

Secretary Kirkpatrick took a deep breath. "Sir, I am not. With open warfare in Europe, the Soviets are no longer restrained by trying to keep the peace. They can be as provocative as they want without fear of any real retaliation. It's clear to me that this has been the plan all along."

"What makes you say that?" asked President Carter.

"The Soviets were clearly behind the attack on the 38th Marine Amphibious Unit. I don't think anyone would dispute that. They knew it would trigger our invasion. They were well aware that the outcome of that invasion was never in question. Now they're switching it up, and forcing us to deal with these uprisings while they themselves can spend very little time and treasure printing out trash like this." She motioned to the pamphlet on the desk.

"I agree," said Zbig. "We've often compared the true believers of Marxism to holy zealots. And now we're seeing this spread at an alarming rate. We need a solution that addresses this." He looked to his colleague. "Jeane, let's get with Harold and the Joint Chiefs to come up with our best plan here."

"Very well. Let's get on this today. I'm sure we can get on Harold's calendar." Jeane knew that this was the best outcome she could hope for, and she'd take it.

****

President Carter was surprised by Dr. Kirkpatrick's vehemence. She's always been vocal, but this was on a new level. There was a knock at the door and Hamilton Jordan entered the Oval Office.

"Good morning, Ham," said the President. "What do we have today?"

"Well, sir, we need to talk about the draft again."

"What now? I thought we had the list of military occupations and the facilities prepared—what could possibly be the problem?"

"It's the protestors, sir," replied Jordan.

"The protestors for or against?" asked the President.

"Both, sir. They've been clashing at the gates of the female recruit training facilities. We've been able to keep a lid on it, but it's just a matter of time before the press has footage."

"This is a disaster. What are our options going forward?" asked the President.

"We're backed against the wall on this one," replied Jordan. "We can push out the perimeter to move the protestors farther away, but no matter what, there will always be a point of entry where they can gather."

"How are the crowds being managed?" asked the President.

"Right now, it's mostly local law enforcement. The military security forces don't engage unless and until someone tries to breach the perimeter."

"I don't know how much good it will do, but get with Civiletti and see if we can produce some federal guidelines specific to the situation. And make sure the DoD is looped in. We want everyone coordinating on this."

"Understood, sir," said Jordan.

"Anything else?"

"No, sir, that was the only real fire to put out."

Chapter 33

20 June 1981
Soviet Battle Cruiser *Kirov*
Mid-Atlantic

Captain of the First Rank Fyodor Mikhailovich Serebrov knew that the success of his first mission would only make follow-on operations more difficult. After resupplying in Luanda, Angola, the Soviet fleet command was adamant that Serebrov should return to hunting in the Atlantic.

"I have some bad news, Comrade Captain," said his executive officer, Captain of the Second Rank Grigoriy "Grisha" Vasin.

"Well, let's have it. Stale bread doesn't get any fresher," said Serebrov.

"Command has informed us that without a doubt, the Americans have placed several satellites in orbit on their new space shuttle."

"Wonderful," replied Serebrov. "We won't be able to hide this time. I can't imagine what the High Command expects us to accomplish out there."

"I'm afraid," said Vasin, "that they don't know what else to do with us. We'll never be able to return home. We can't transit into the Mediterranean to join with the Black Sea Fleet. They could order us to transit around the Cape of Good Hope so we can transfer to the Pacific Fleet, but to what end? Besides, I don't see how we could get past Japan without being detected."

"Indeed," said Serebrov, "*Kirov* may be the greatest warship afloat, but he is still only one warship."

Two days later, they were crossing the equator in the mid-Atlantic when the Ka-25 reported a sighting of a single vessel.

"What do we have?" asked Vasin.

"It looks like a refrigerated transport," replied Serebrov. "I believe it's an Argentine beef transport."

"What's it doing out here?"

"I believe that it's transporting beef to NATO," replied Serebrov with a laugh.

"Well, obviously. I meant, what's it doing out here all alone?"

"I suppose they weren't expecting trouble this far south, so they tried to sneak this one by. Who knows, this could be the twentieth Argentine beef ship to make the transit. The good news is that we're going to put that ship on the bottom, adding to our tonnage. The bad news is—"

"That every fleet in the world knows where we are," Vasin concluded for him.

"That's right. We'd better make this count."

Kirov ran down the Argentine vessel *Isla de los Estados* with ease. They pulled to within one hundred meters, and over the loudspeaker, they ordered the crew to abandon the ship.

A boarding party of Marines then escorted the ship's mess chief on a raid of the ship. They procured as much meat as the ship could eat before it spoiled and returned to *Kirov*.

As the sun was setting, the twin-barrelled 100mm cannon on the aft of *Kirov* opened up on *Isla de los Estados*. The punishing hits slammed into the ship along the waterline, opening it up like a can of tuna.

"It's a shame we can't send a crew over to take possession of her," said Vasin. "What a terrible waste."

"*C'est la guerre*," replied Serebrov. "With our current situation, we may be looking at the last meal of a condemned man. Or, in this case, seven hundred and forty-five condemned men."

****

USS *America*
Mid-Atlantic

"Whoa, shit," said Lieutenant JG Richard Rogers, reading the piece of paper in his hand. "Sir, we just received this flash alert. We need to get it to the skipper on the double."

"Whatcha got?" asked Lieutenant Edward Diaz, the ship's intel officer.

"Looks like they've found *Kirov*, and she's in the neighborhood."

"All right," said Diaz, "run this down to the CIC. You get to give the old man the good news."

Rogers set a personal best in getting from the SSES to the CIC. He entered the dungeon, and it took a second for his eyes to adjust.

"Captain Ingram, sir," Rogers said as he approached the skipper. "Message from Fort Meade, sir." He handed the paper to the captain.

Ingram scanned the note, then turned to his yeoman. "Jackson, get me CAG and the squadron commanders to the briefing room ASAP." He pointed at Rogers. "Go get Diaz and meet us there."

"Aye-aye, sir," replied Rogers.

When they had assembled, the CO started the meeting.

"Gentlemen, we are getting another bite at the apple. *Kirov* has graced us with her presence. She's sitting just under nine hundred miles to our southeast. A lone Argentine cargo vessel was trying to run the pond unescorted and paid the price. Her loss is our gain, though. How are we going to take this piece off the board?"

"I suppose I need to put my money where my mouth was," said Commander Glen Hopkins, the CO of VA-95. "The last time we were trying to crack this nut, I opined on the need for Harpoons. Now we've got 'em, we might as well use 'em."

"We have to assume that they've made repairs to any radar damage we inflicted last time," said Commander Dave Stevens of VA-192.

"You have a thought on that?" asked Captain Ingram.

"Yes, sir," replied Stevens. "The Corsair squadrons could fly in with the Drumsticks, carrying a load of Shrikes."

"I don't know," said Ingram. "I don't like how close you'll have to get those Shrikes off. On the other hand, even if we don't manage to take out their radars, the Shrikes will still provide a lot of additional targets for *Kirov* to prosecute. We don't want a repeat of the Eastern Med out there."

"I think it's bold and not brazen, sir, just like last time," said Stevens, reminding Captain Ingram of his own words the last time they'd put an attack plan together.

"OK, we're going to have to find her first, but I think we have the loose plan here. You knuckleheads work out the details and let me know when you have something solid."

With that, the room broke up and Roberts and Diaz headed back to the SSES.

It was several hours later before the call came in. *Kirov* had been located and the carrier air wing was ready for her. The Intruders, Prowlers and Corsairs lifted off and formed up to the southeast of *America*. Diaz explained the plan to Rogers.

"The whole strike group is going to drop to minimum altitude well outside of detection range. Those bad boys will be hauling ass right over the ocean. They'll be scaring the hell out of the sharks. The first flight of Intruders is going to launch their Harpoons at sixty nautical miles. This will force *Kirov* to light up her radars."

"What if she doesn't?" asked Rogers.

"If she doesn't, then the Harpoons will home in and sink her without a fight."

Rogers nodded his understanding.

"The remaining Intruders," continued Diaz, "and the Corsairs will stay low, trying to get as close as possible before engaging. The Intruders will launch from thirty-five nautical miles, and the Corsairs will pop up to fire at twenty-five nautical miles."

"That's well within the range of the SA-N-6," said Rogers.

"That's right," agreed Diaz, "And if everything goes to plan, *Kirov* will be so busy shooting at incoming missiles, she won't have a chance to prosecute the aircraft."

"That's a really big *if*," said Rogers.

"It is. That's what Commander Stevens was telling the skipper when he said it was bold but not brazen. He believes that this will work."

"I guess we're going to find out... One way or another."

****

Soviet Battle Cruiser *Kirov*
Mid-Atlantic

"Sir." Captain Vasin knocked on his CO's door. "It's time."

After the filet dinner in the wardroom, Captain Serebrov had retired to his stateroom. He knew he would have a fight soon, and he wanted to spend some time with his thoughts before it came. He thought of how lucky he was. He had a beautiful wife, Irina, and a fine son, Pyotr. He was in command of the greatest warship of all time. He didn't believe in God, but for a moment, he questioned that.

"On my way, Grisha." He rose from his desk, straightened out his uniform and headed out to the control room. He looked at his crew when he closed the door behind him. He could sense that they were worried. He wondered how many of them knew how bad their situation really was.

"What do we have?" asked Serebrov.

"Sir," replied a radarman, "an American search plane has illuminated us with his radar."

"What type of plane?" asked the captain.

"An E-2, sir."

"OK, so we know what to expect. There is at least one American aircraft carrier out there. We've faced one of them before, and we will face them down tonight." There were nods of agreement throughout the room. He moved closer to his executive officer and spoke in a low voice. "We're really at the disadvantage right now. They know exactly where we are, and we have no idea about them."

Equally low, Vasin replied, "What I would give to be able to shoot down that spy plane."

"This is the hand we've been dealt. We need to play it out." Then, louder, Serebrov continued, "Captain Vasin, what do you expect from the Yankees?"

"I expect something similar to the last attack. They will attempt to disable our radars, then try to pick us off once we are helpless."

"I'm not so sure," replied Serebrov. "That was a good plan and well executed the last time we met. Yet it still failed. If you were the Americans, what would you change to make sure you succeeded this time?"

"They need to take more risks," said Vasin. "I would order my aircraft to get closer to the target before firing their missiles. This will give us less time to react, and give them a better chance of achieving a hit."

"I agree," said Serebrov. "We need to anticipate that. How do we counter it?"

"It comes down to detection, sir. We cannot let them get inside our missile shield undetected. To achieve this, we're going to need to send up the Kamov to paint the ocean with her radar."

"That's right. Order the aircrews to launch the alert chopper, and get the second one ready to go. We're probably going to need both tonight."

"Understood," replied Vasin, who then went to his station to make the proper orders.

Ten minutes later, the Ka-25 was airborne and gaining altitude. Once he maxed out, the pilot turned on the radar. The surface search radar would detect any incoming aircraft that were at a lower altitude. This would prevent the Americans from sneaking anything in on the deck. The radar showed nothing. Just the open ocean.

"Sir," said a radioman, "the Kamov is being engaged by an enemy missile. He's evading." There were several minutes of silence. "Sir, we've lost contact with the Kamov."

"What the hell was that?" asked Vasin.

"I believe that we just encountered the American Phoenix missile. They must already have a fighter screen penning us in."

There were worried glances shared throughout the command room. Serebrov was stuck. Sending up his second Ka-25 would result in the exact same fate. However, if he could time it right, he might at least get a hint of when the second attack would come. "How long until the second helicopter is ready?"

There was a pause as the question was pondered and answered.

"Twenty minutes, sir," replied Vasin.

"Please impress upon the air crew that sooner would be better," said Serebrov. The minutes ticked as the crew waited to see if the helicopter would launch before the American attack arrived.

"Contact!" yelled one of the radarmen. "Four unknown air contact—wait… Multiple unknown contacts bearing three-zero-zero, range one-hundred kilometers. Twenty contacts total."

"Energize the target acquisition and fire control radars. Engage the aircraft as soon as they are in range." There really wasn't any other order he could give. Serebrov couldn't just wait for the incoming aircraft to strike his ship. He watched on the computer screen as missiles streamed out of *Kirov*. It was an impressive show of force.

"Sir, four of the contacts are turning back. The remaining sixteen continue to advance." At first, Serebrov thought that four of the enemy pilots had broken under pressure. But as he watched the screen, he considered another option.

"I believe we are looking at antiship missiles. I wonder why they didn't use them the last time we met?"

"It could have been their arrogance," replied Vasin. "Perhaps they didn't think they needed them."

"Perhaps," replied Serebrov. "I think it's equally likely that we're looking at a new weapons system. Regardless, we must engage those incoming contacts. See if we can get the Kamov launched."

"Negative, sir, they are still fueling."

"Sir, more contacts. Twenty unknown contacts bearing zero-four-four degrees."

"They have us in a pincer," said Vasin.

"No matter," replied Serebrov. "Our vertical launch system doesn't need to rotate. They're wasting their efforts with these games."

Inwardly, Serebrov was worried. The Americans were popping up inside his missile umbrella. They were coming in too low, and there was no way for the Soviet radars to pick them up before they were well within range. This reduced the amount of time he had to intercept the incoming missiles. If just one of those got through, who knew how much damage it would cause? "Prosecute the incoming contacts based on range."

More missiles poured out of *Kirov* and more of the incoming contacts were blotted from the map.

Panic broke out in the control room as the radarman announced, "Sir! Twenty-four contacts, bearing three-six-zero, range forty kilometers."

Before Serebrov could engage the new contacts, the radarman continued, "Now counting thirty-six contacts."

Serebrov turned to his friend and executive officer. "Grisha. How was your steak tonight?"

"It was worth it, sir. It was worth it." It was clear to anyone looking at the display that they would not be able to intercept the incoming missiles before they hit the ship.

"Sir, the computer reports that the latest contacts are antiradiation missiles."

Kirov fired missile after missile in the dim hope of stopping the attack. In the end, Serebrov felt the first impact. The small warheads of the ARMs didn't cause much structural damage, but each one would damage or destroy the radar that it had homed in on.

"Sir, fire control radar unit two is off-line!" said a damage controlman. Several more radars were reported to fail before the first antiship missile struck *Kirov* on the port side.

"Counterflood to starboard," commanded Serebrov. He'd been anticipating the order since the first missiles had been detected.

Smoke started to fill the room as the ship shook from a second, then a third hit. The lights went out and the control room was plunged into darkness. Alarms blared and the emergency lighting lit the room. The intercom was filled with chatter as damage control parties raced to stop the flooding and fight the fires.

Serebrov desperately tried to get a feel for what was happening on his ship, but more smoke was filling the room. Then he noticed the heat. It wasn't just smoke—it was fire.

Serebrov coughed as he tried to move to the far end of the room, away from the fire. But there was nowhere to go. The watertight door on the far side of the room was dogged. He was trapped with the fire as it raged.

He coughed again and dropped to the floor, hoping to find some oxygen. It was no use. The fire had sucked the room clean. From the floor of the most powerful warship in the world, Captain of the First Rank Fyodor Mikhailovich Serebrov drew his last breath, thinking of his wife, and his son.

Chapter 34

25 June 1981
15,000 Feet Over Galveston, Texas

Captain George "Nomad" Bush looked over the Gulf of Mexico. *You can't beat the view*, he thought, looking at the horizon where the dark blue of the water met the bright blue of the sky. The perfect smattering of clouds rounded out the perfect Texas morning.

"Lonestar Two, Kelly Control," said a voice in his helmet.

"Kelly Control, Lonestar Two, I read you," said Bush's wingman, Captain Mike "Weezer" Olson.

"Hey, Weezer, I'm handing you over to Coast Guard Station Sabine Pass. They've got something for you to check out."

"Understood, switching to the intercept net," replied Weezer. Before he did, he called over to Bush. "Tell you what, Nomad, why don't you take the lead on this?"

"Roger that, Weezer," replied Nomad. He switched his radio and called, "Station Sabine, this is Lonestar Six."

"Copy, Lonestar Six. We've got something odd going on out there. Two unidentified contacts, over the Gulf."

"Station Sabine, roger that. Guide us in and let's see what we've got."

The woman on the other end of the radio read out the speed, bearing and altitude they wanted Nomad to take on the way to the target. Bush eased the plane into position and considered the past six months.

The training had been intense. He thought that he'd had a slight advantage over most in the course, since he had F-102 experience. Most of his class had experience in some of the other "Century Series" aircraft, such as the F-100 Super Sabre, or the F-101 Voodoo, but he was the only Dart Driver.

Right now, Nomad was one of only two from the original class to already be placed in the newly redesignated 182nd Interceptor Squadron. Colonel Lane had given him his new call sign "Nomad" in reference to the brief conversation the two had had regarding the captain's past. He'd been flying patrol missions for the past three weeks, but this was the first time he'd been vectored out to investigate something.

As he continued the flight, his mind wandered to his brothers. With the accelerated training brought on by the war, his brother Jeb was finishing up his basic intelligence course at Fort Huachuca. Jeb was pretty certain that he'd be sent to Nicaragua when he was done. The word around the base was that they were putting together a special unit to work on the "Nicaragua Problem" and he'd impressed his instructors with his knowledge of the region and cultures of Latin America as well as his analytical abilities.

Nomad wondered if the latter was a bit of embellishment on his brother's part. Then again, he knew that he himself had been given consideration because his father had been a combat pilot, a member of the House of Representatives, and an ambassador. Surely, Jeb would get some extra attention because Poppy was the director of the CIA.

Marvin had finished the Marine Corps Basic School and was awaiting assignment as an infantry officer. That worried Nomad. He watched the news. He could see the Marine combat casualty numbers coming out of Korea. Sure, flying an interceptor had an element of danger to it, but it was nothing compared to what Marvin would be facing when he hit the beach.

"Lonestar Six, Station Sabine."

"Station Sabine, copy," said Nomad. "Whaddya got for me?"

"Lonestar Six, I need you to come to a course of three-three-zero, angels twenty."

"Copy, three-three-zero, angels twenty." The course change was nearly a reversal of the course he'd been flying. He was now heading northwest. During the transit, the ground controllers informed him that they were bringing him around so he could approach the bogeys from behind.

"Lonestar Six, contacts are moving at four hundred and fifty-nine knots, on your course and at angels twenty-five. You should slide in right under them."

"Understood, Sabine Station." Nomad scanned the skies, looking for the contacts. He squinted a bit and wiped his hand across the canopy to make sure he wasn't just seeing things. "Tallyho, Sabine Station. I have a visual on two airborne contacts, heading three-three-zero, angels twenty-five."

"Copy, Lonestar Six, let us know as soon as you can make a visual identification."

"Roger that, I'm approaching from their low six o'clock." *Might as well have a little fun with this*, thought Nomad as he advanced the throttle to full military power.

The tiny dots grew rapidly, quickly taking shape. "Sabine Station, I'm lookin' at two Tango Uniform One-Sixes." He was sweating a bit. He'd known from the start of the intercept that these could be Soviet bombers, but the reality of it hadn't really hit him until he could see them.

"Understood, Lonestar Six. Remember, you do not have authorization to engage. Get close enough to see if you can identify their nationality. If they have Soviet colors or designations, you may engage. Otherwise, your orders are to establish radio contact and stay with them. We're launching support to take over when you're bingo."

"Roger that, Sabine Station." He was closing on the Badgers at over two hundred miles an hour, and he hadn't even lit his afterburner. Nomad looked at his instrument panel to ensure his radar was in standby mode. He pulled back on the throttle, slowing his Dagger to match speed with the bombers. He waved at the pilot of the leftmost Tu-16, while Weezer, who remained behind, painted them with his radar. "Sabine Station, Lonestar Six, you're not gonna believe this, but I'm looking at a pair of Cuban Badgers."

"Unidentified aircraft," said Nomad, "this is a United States interceptor. You are approaching United States territory."

"American interceptor," replied the Cuban pilot in English, "we are conducting air operations in international airspace. We are of no concern to you."

"Unidentified aircraft, be advised: if you cross inside twelve nautical miles of United States territory, I'll be obligated to shoot you down." To emphasize the point, Bush flipped the switch controlling his weapons bay doors.

The Cubans didn't bother with a response; they simply kept flying toward the United States. Nomad switched to the squad network.

"Weezer, have you ever heard of a Cuban Badger?"

"Sure have, Nomad. The Russkies sold 'em one back before this whole thing kicked off. Rumor around the ready room is that they used it to feed targeting information to the Nicaraguans when they waxed our Marine task force. But I don't think that's what we have here. These don't look like maritime patrol planes. They don't have the big radar bulges."

"I guess I need to brush up on my enemy aircraft identification," said Nomad.

"After this engagement, I think we all do," said Weezer.

The two continued to escort the Cubans right up to fifteen nautical miles off the coast of Beaumont, Texas, before they made a slow turn to the east, then southeast. Another set of F-106s picked up the escort and followed them deep into the Gulf of Mexico.

****

25 June 1981
White House
Washington, D.C.

The past year had aged President Carter considerably. The lines on his face had deepened, his eyes always looked tired. His election victory seemed a million years ago. He'd been a president at war when he'd won, and things had escalated again and again since that point. Now he was a wartime president on the losing end, and he needed to know what could be done to reverse the trend.

"Please tell me you have some good news Harold," said Carter to Secretary of Defense Harold Brown.

"I'll go so far as to say that some of this isn't bad news," replied Dr. Brown. "We're finally getting the new M1 Abrams tanks into France and Belgium." Carter frowned, remembering how the Soviets had sunk the transport that had carried the first wave of M1s in the opening weeks of the war. "That's going to make a difference," continued Dr. Brown.

"Will it be enough?" asked Carter.

"On its own, no," replied Dr. Brown. "But everything we can throw at this problem is going to be a part of the solution. The engineers at Northrop have some very good news."

The President tilted his head at the prospect of good news.

"The first batch of F-5Gs are coming off the assembly lines. Those are equipped with the AIM-7 Sparrow radar-guided missile. It will significantly improve our ability to control the skies over Europe, and especially Korea. Additionally, they're incorporating additional changes to the airframe. With the F/A-18 getting sidelined, there's a surplus of General Electric F404 engines. Northrop believes they can substantially increase the performance of the F-5 by converting new aircraft to the F404."

"Is that going to slow production?" asked the President.

"Northrop is telling me that the factory downtime will be minimal. They have a plan in place to create the tools and machinery for the conversion while they continue pushing out F-5Gs. There's also talk of gutting the avionics and converting the F-5 to fly-by-wire—"

"I'm sorry?"

"Sorry, Mr. President," said Brown. "It's an electric control system, like we've implemented on the F-16 Falcon. Right now, that's all in-house. We're not pushing for it, we just want the Sparrow, and if they can pull it off, the up-engined version."

"Will the new engine make that much of a difference?"

"Yes, sir," said Dr. Brown. "These numbers come from Northrop, so take them with a grain of salt, but they estimate that the new F-5G will be as fast as or faster than the MiG-21s the Soviets and their allies are fielding. All this without sacrificing the agility of the plane. It would be a very potent weapon, and it can be in the field in months, not years."

"Well, you're right, that isn't bad news. What else are we looking at?"

"*Ticonderoga* is about to set sail on her first escort mission. Her shakedown didn't show any major deficiencies, but there are still Raytheon contractors aboard tweaking the systems. If she performs as advertised, she'll be a game changer for the Atlantic crossing."

"That's more not bad news," said Carter.

"The recommissioning of the *Iowa*s is underway. It's a slow process, but it's amazing what you can accomplish when you're running port and starboard shifts."

Carter smiled at the memory of having two twelve-hour shifts running constantly on the USS *Seawolf*.

"We don't have an estimated time of completion, but the yards are doing everything they can. We've also increased our frigate output considerably. We're not quite replacing our losses there, but it's close."

"We'll need to reverse that if we want to come out ahead in this thing," said Carter.

"I agree. And that concludes the 'not bad' portion of the briefing."

Carter frowned.

"Our spoiling attacks," said Dr. Brown "at Frankfurt bought us enough time to pull back across the Rhine River, and the Soviets had to pull up and tighten their lines. That gave us a bit of a lull, but they're moving again against Mainz. We're massing in Bad Kreuznach for a counteroffensive. We're going to trap them on the west bank of the Rhine, and destroy them. That will buy us more time to get reinforcements in place to keep them from completely overrunning Germany.

"Things aren't much better in the north. Despite early successes, the NORTHAG has been taking a beating. Soviet and Pact forces have overrun Hamburg, and the Soviet Baltic Fleet successfully landed naval infantry at Flensburg, cutting off any retreat into Denmark. On the Southern Front, the Italians are holding their own against the Yugoslavian troops. That's not a surprise, but we honestly believe that the real goal there is to keep the Italians busy until Germany is cleared, when the Soviets will turn more attention there."

"I can't believe it's come to this," said Carter.

"It's not over yet, sir. We're still in the fight, and West Germany is still with us. It's not too late to turn this around. Don't forget, the Nazis made it to within fifteen miles of Moscow before being turned back."

"By the Soviet Union," said Carter, ruining Brown's point.

"Yes, of course. Be that as it may, things have bogged down in Korea. We're about to add the 2nd Marine Division to the mix, and we're standing up another division to send to Korea as well."

"What about the Japanese?" asked Carter. "Will they relent on their insistence that we not use their bases for attacks on North Korea?"

"At this point, sir, no," replied Brown. "The Chinese have made it clear that they will intervene on behalf of the North Koreans if Japan enters the conflict. Japan believes that the use of our bases would be enough to trigger a Chinese response."

"What does Stan say about that?" asked Carter, referring to Stansfield Turner, the head of the CIA.

"He agrees. Right now, the Chinese are willing to let the DPRK lie in the bed they've made. Kim Il-sung knew he was facing the ROK and the US. They seem willing to let him hang out to dry as long as it doesn't escalate."

"Until we push them across the 38th parallel anyhow," said Carter, referencing the Chinese intervention in 1950.

"Well, yes. There is always that. But I can only report what's happening, not what might happen."

"Fair enough, Harold, I apologize. It's just hard to hear so much bad news every day."

"I understand, sir. I sincerely believe that things are going to turn a corner soon."

"I pray to God that you're right, Harold," said the President as he turned his chair and looked over the South Lawn.

Chapter 35

26 June 1981
Kremlin
Moscow, USSR

The weight of the casket was considerable, but Minister of Culture Pyotr Demichev was surprised by how little he felt it. *Many hands make light work*, he thought.

There were another nine men carrying the body of Leonid Brezhnev to his resting place in the Necropolis on Red Square. Brezhnev had been in bad health for years. Since the start of the war, the decline increased dramatically, resulting in the heart attack that had killed him. *At least, that's the official story*, thought Demichev. He tried not to allow himself such thoughts, but sometimes they still broke through.

The gray Moscow sky accented the solemn occasion of the funeral. The eulogies began. Andropov went first, praising Brezhnev for his years of service and recounting how well he'd handled the Western menace since taking power. He lauded Brezhnev's service in the Great Patriotic War. As was usual with Soviet state funerals, the man was a saint who had never done wrong in his life.

Demichev dutifully stood at the front of the assembly, listening as Andropov concluded by tying Brezhnev's legacy to the war being fought twelve hundred miles to the west.

The rest of the affair ran through the motions. Once the official proceedings ended, the real work began. The top echelon of the Politburo assembled in the Kremlin. As the father of the plan to bring NATO to its knees, and to revitalize the Soviet economy through conquest, Andropov was the clear successor to Brezhnev. Konstantin Chernenko received polite consideration, but for a nation at war, the KGB Director was a shoo-in. Given how much control he was already exerting during the final year of Brezhnev's reign, it was easy for him to assume the title of General Secretary of the Communist Party of the Soviet Union.

"Gentlemen," said Andropov, "I appreciate that it has been a long and solemn day, but we have work to do." There were nods and murmurs around the table, but nobody contradicted him. "Minister Ustinov, what news do we have from the battlefield?"

"Thank you, Comrade General Secretary," said Defense Minister Dmitriy Ustinov. "We have known from the beginning of our planning that this would be a long-term effort. With that in mind, we are moving according to our original timelines, with only a few hold-ups. We have crossed the Rhine and are preparing to push our assault into the Low Countries. Our current intelligence sources indicate that NATO is preparing a major regrouping to save Belgium and Luxembourg. They aren't conceding the Netherlands, but they aren't in as strong a position there.

"In the south," continued Ustinov, "our Yugoslav brothers, with the help of some Romanian units, continue to hold down the Italians. Bulgarian and Romanian units are keeping Greece bottled up, and I believe that Minister Gromyko will have more on that." Gromyko nodded and Ustinov continued, "Once we have completed operations in the Low Countries, we will pivot toward France."

"Why are we not simply engaging France directly now?" asked Pavel Finogenov, the Minister of Defense Industry.

"I'll let Minister Gromyko handle that question," said Ustinov, turning the meeting to his friend.

"To be blunt," said Gromyko, "the French have informed us through back channels that any trespass onto French soil will result in an immediate atomic response."

There were a few quiet gasps before the room went silent as the members let the nuclear threat settle.

Inwardly, Pyotr was horrified, not only at the fact that atomic weapons were being considered, but by the casual attitude Gromyko displayed. Outwardly, he said, "We've known that an atomic escalation was a possibility," said Pyotr. "We shouldn't be shocked by this."

"That is correct," said Andropov. "The only surprise is that it has taken this long."

"What, exactly, are we talking about here?" asked Finogenov, clearly uncomfortable with the conversation. "What kind of exchange are we looking at?"

Ustinov took the question. "We believe the French will fire between three and six Pluton missiles. These are tactical weapons of fifteen to twenty-five kilotons. They will be directed at troop concentrations or other tactical targets of opportunity. Our planned response will be a matching number of R-17 missiles. Once the smoke has cleared, we'll declare a halt to nuclear operations to prevent this from escalating."

How many people will die in this exchange? wondered Pyotr. Keeping his emotions hidden was a real challenge. He focused on professionalism to keep his voice even as he asked, "How confident are you that the Americans or the British won't join in when the French launch?"

"The Americans under Carter won't dare. They would only use their atomic arsenal in the face of an all out attack against the homeland. Thatcher is more of a wild card, but we don't believe that she'll act independently without US cooperation. They must know that one of our weapons will be aimed at Devonport. She won't risk that unless she feels she has no choice."

"It's a risk, but an acceptable one," said Andropov, turning to Gromyko. "What is your proposed next move, Andrei?"

"I have a twofold strategy, Comrade Secretary General. First, we are negotiating with the French socialists under François Mitterrand. We believe that if there is a nuclear exchange, they can use the ensuing chaos to seize power. Once in charge, they'll declare a separate peace whereby the French will agree to neutrality and the expulsion of NATO forces from French territory."

"And we'll have a socialist France?" asked Finogenov. "That's hardly better than what we have today."

"We will have a socialist France that is aligned with the Soviet Union," said Gromyko, losing patience. "We can introduce central controls once the war is over."

"And the second part of your strategy?" asked Andropov.

"I need Comrade Ustinov and the Stavka to create a plan for holding NATO at bay along the French border until we are ready for this nuclear exchange."

"We need," said Ustinov, "a holding force strong enough to keep the French, or any NATO members for that matter, from crossing into Germany. At the same time, we need sufficient force to engage and defeat NATO in the Low Countries." He thought for a beat. "That is a difficult task, but not impossible."

"Very well," said Andropov. "What about our operations in the Americas?"

Gromyko smiled before continuing, "The operation in Nicaragua couldn't be going better. We suffered minimal casualties. We kept two divisions of Marines and their airmobile division occupied for the first three months of this war. Now the operation is moving into its final phase."

Pyotr raised an eyebrow. He hadn't been updated on the long-term details of this plan.

Gromyko continued, "We are now fostering the revolution through propaganda and terrorism. The Latin American people—not just Nicaragua, mind you, but every nation between Colombia and the United States—will come to see the Americans as their ultimate enemy." A sly smile crossed Gromyko's lips. "And because the Americans have occupied Nicaragua, it will be simple to paint them as the imperialist oppressor. They have been exploiting these people for centuries. It won't matter who is conducting the bombings—the people will blame the Americans for the casualties. The only thing the Americans will be able to do about this is leave. When they do that, we will have won."

As Gromyko continued, Pyotr observed the intensity with which the Minister of Foreign Affairs spoke. This wasn't a "pie-in-the-sky" fantasy. The Minister truly believed that this was inevitable. "

We will be able to set up communist regimes throughout the region," continued Gromyko, "and the Americans won't be able to stop us, because every person in Central America saw the naked aggression of the Americans when a successful communist government threw off the yoke of their American masters. Our success in Europe will embolden them further. It may take a decade, but we will have a communist bloc in the Americas."

There were smiles around the table as each member took this in. *And when we start stationing our Air Force in Mexico City, what will the Americans think of that?* thought Pyotr.

Chapter 36

30 June 1981
82nd Airborne Division
Chièvres Air Base, Belgium

The journey from Iran to Belgium had been a long and frustrating one. The men of the 82nd Airborne Division needed to get into the fight. The taste of battle they got in Iran simply whetted their appetite.

Marlon Reeves felt the frustration just as much as anyone in the division. Command had explained the situation to them, and they knew it was true. The 82nd Airborne was not a blunt instrument. They had too much training and too much experience to be re-tasked as ground pounders and sent out with the mechanized infantry.

In fact, Reeves's own company commander, Captain Patrick Foster, summed it up best when he said, "When an army folds their airborne forces into the general infantry, that army is losing, and badly."

Sergeant Becker, the Russian translator, told Reeves that at the start of the Second World War, the Soviets had one of the largest airborne forces in the world.

By 1942, as the Germans pushed the Soviets east, the Soviets converted them all to rifle divisions. It wasn't until they turned the tide against the Nazis that the airborne units were reconstituted.

The more he thought about it, the more Reeves was relieved that they hadn't been thrown into action. It would have been a very bad sign of how poorly the war was going, and he wanted to contribute as best he could—and that would be by jumping out of a C-130 and killing communists. There was going to be a major counteroffensive, and the 82nd Airborne was going to be a big part of it.

Now, six months after the war started, Reeves was standing in formation waiting for word on their next combat drop and hoping nothing changed from the previous brief they'd received about one in the works.

"Gentlemen," said the Division Commander, Major General Corey Duran, "this is the big one. We have assembled every available airframe for this jump. The plants in Georgia have been cranking out Hercs in an effort to keep up with losses, but this may be the last major jump of the war unless things change. They're calling this one Operation Fullback, and this is our best hope for turning the Soviet forces back. If we fail at our objective, we may well lose the entire war."

I hope he's exaggerating, thought Reeves.

"That is no exaggeration," said the General. "Our mission will be to occupy the airfield at Bitburg. Once we have established control of the airfield, we will prevent the enemy from bringing reinforcements westward. We will be mutually supporting Infantry and Armored forces that will break out to the east. If we can keep Soviet reinforcements away from the armor, the armor will get to Bitburg to relieve us before we run out of ammunition."

"Your unit commanders will pass down the particulars, but this operation will commence within the next forty-eight hours. You are the best warriors in the United States Army. You're descended from the men who jumped into Sicily and Normandy. Our division fought with honor and distinction in Market Garden and we hung tough in the Battle of the Bulge. When historians look back on this war, they will know that Operation Fullback was fought as tough and tenaciously as all of our previous actions, and you will be honored as heroes... Dismissed!"

****

27 June 1981
3rd Battalion, 69th Armor Regiment
Diekirch, Luxembourg

Sergeant First Class Don Mackintosh looked out of the picturesque fields of eastern Luxembourg as he leaned on the track of his M1 Abrams and ate his C ration peanut butter.

"Damn, Sarge, how long before we get thrown back in it?" asked Specialist Cameron Fletcher, the tank's new driver.

"Best I can tell," replied Mackintosh, "we're gearing up for a big counteroffensive. There's no way they would pull us back and reequip us unless they had something big in the works."

In the over two months since the Battle of Offenbach, the 3rd Infantry Division had fought a retreating defensive action. It had taken the Soviets another week to take Frankfurt, after which they'd halted to regroup before crossing the Rhine. A month ago, 3/69 AG had been pulled off the line and sent here to Luxembourg. Nobody understood the orders until they'd arrived and found eighty-five brand-new M1 Abrams tanks, and replacements to help crew them. Since that day, they had been training on the new tanks and getting acquainted with the new faces.

Mackintosh looked over at the kid. They hadn't had a lot of small talk during their rushed training. "Where you from, Fletch?" he asked.

"Plano, by God, Texas," replied Fletch.

"Oh no, not another one," chuckled Mackintosh. "You Texas nationalists are something else."

"Ain't nothin' wrong with having some pride in your heritage," replied Fletch.

"That's fair enough. But once you've been around a world a bit, maybe you start to see that everywhere has something to be proud of."

Fletcher thought about that. "Is that so? Where are you from, if you don't mind my asking."

"Ahh, one of the things I most appreciate about you Southerners is your manners. I was born and raised in Canada. In fact, that's where I started soldiering. I got my first combat experience in Korea with the 27th British Commonwealth Brigade."

"I didn't know Canada had tankers in Korea," said Fletch.

"They didn't," replied Mackintosh. "We were an infantry unit. And if there was one thing I learned from my combat experience in the infantry, it was that I would rather be in a tank."

"Amen," said Fletch. "How'd you end up in the US Army?"

"Stick around in this business long enough, and you'll hear this story a hundred times. When I got back from Korea and came home to my wife, things were just... different. I can't really put my finger on it, but maybe I was different, maybe she was different. We just didn't work anymore. I needed a change of pace and figured I'd make a go of it in the States."

"Did you end up in Montana, or Wyoming?" asked Fletch.

Laughing, Mackintosh replied, "Oh no, son, I'd had enough of the cold and snow. I moved to Florida to thaw out for a while. I dabbled with journalism for a while but decided 'what the hell?' and enlisted."

"But this time, you knew enough to get a tank billet?"

"That's right," confirmed Mackintosh.

The commander's hatch of the M1 popped open, and Captain Henderson popped his head out. "All right, men, break's over. Police up your trash and mount up! ASAP!"

"That's what I like to hear, Captain," said Mackintosh, climbing onto the Abrams. He slid into his seat at the main gun and asked, "We heading back to the range?"

"Negative, Sergeant," replied the Captain. "We're heading out to our jump-off point. Looks like we have orders to move out. We're finally taking the fight to those Godless bastards."

Mackintosh checked his gun, verifying that everything was in order before asking, "What are we expecting, sir?"

"Their calling it Operation Fullback," replied the Captain. "We're part of a multi-divisional force striking out for Bitburg."

"That's a big push," said Mackintosh.

"You're not wrong about that. We'd better hope that the brass understands what they're asking from us. Even with these new tanks, this is going to be a real challenge. The word up and down the line is that this is just one of several assault points. We're going to keep Ivan from being able to focus his defense. Hopefully that'll soften things up for us."

Mackintosh considered the desperate task ahead of him. Within the next twenty-four hours he'd be involved in NATO's first significant counter-offensive. He was certain that it would be one of the biggest tank battles in history, and he couldn't wait to make the Russians pay for starting this war.

From Alex Aaronson

Wow! I can't believe we've gone through two books together! It seems like just yesterday I was sending the first draft of a short story titled: "Eagle Claw:1980" to my buddy Caveman and asking if he thought it was ass, or what? So many things have happened, both in our world, and in the world of the Soviet Endgame. I really hope that you're having as much fun with this as I am.

The next book in the series is already available for preorder. Simply click on the following link, and you'll receive the third installment of Soviet Endgame, *Pursuit by Fire:1981*, on your Kindle as soon as it is released.

If you can't wait for the next book to come out, please consider joining my mailing list. This will give you access to additional "Soviet Endgame" content, as well as updates and notices for new books, audiobooks and other projects. To join the mailing list, just click visit: https://frontlinepublishinginc.eo.page/alexaaronson

I love interacting with the readers, so please join me on:

Twitter (@alexaaronson80)

Facebook(https://www.facebook.com/alexander.aaronson.102)

Facebook group (if you don't want to be Facebook friends with a stranger!) https://www.facebook.com/groups/833777043807871

Instagram (https://www.instagram.com/authoralexaaronson/)

Or YouTube (https://www.youtube.com/channel/UCCulp1Ru2EkO3pknPcGkb_Q)

If you have a chance, I would greatly appreciate it if you could stop by Amazon, and/or Goodreads and leave a review of this book. It's a very competitive market out there and ratings and reviews are a tremendous help in bringing in new readers. Unless you thought the book sucked, and you just skipped to the end to find out how to contact me to blow up my accounts with hate posts—in that case, please don't review the book.

Finally, if you enjoyed this book, and you haven't checked out the rest of the Frontline family, please takes some time to do so. I'm partial to the Monroe Doctrine series, since I helped write Volumes IV and V, and the Crisis in the Desert series, since I did a little ghostwriting on those. Check them out on Amazon.

Thank you so much for taking the time to read this. Writing this novel has been a dream come true and I hope you stay with me as we continue the journey together.

From James Rosone

I have really enjoyed working with Alex Aaronson over the last two years. It has been exciting to see one of my fellow veterans take wings and fly. He has embodied everything that I had hoped would come true when I started this project to mentor other vets in this writing business.

If you'd like to be added to my personal mailing list, you can do so by clicking on this link. This will help you keep informed of any new releases as well as any upcoming promotional deals.

I enjoy connecting with my readers online. If you'd like to connect, you can find me on:

Facebook (https://www.facebook.com/groups/803443733408830)

Twitter: @jamesrosone

Facebook private reader group (https://www.facebook.com/groups/803443733408830)

Our YouTube page is (https://www.youtube.com/channel/UCCExLcHFoPmwC8IKikNsVvg/videos) if you'd like to listen to some author interviews I've conducted of some fellow writers as well as some of our thoughts on the Ukraine war and the performance of the Russian military and how this plays into China, Taiwan, and other topics.

You may want to see what other books I have written. To find a full list, visit frontlinepublishinginc.com

Abbreviation Key

1MC	The main communications channel on a US Warship
4MC	The Damage Control channel on a US Warship
AA	Anti-aircraft
AAV	Amphibious Assault Vehicle
AC/DC	An Australian rock band
ACV	Amphibious Combat Vehicle
ADCAP	Advanced Capability Torpedo
AEGIS	Advanced Electronic Guidance and Instrumentation System
AFB	Air Force Base
AGM	Air to Ground Missile
AIM	Air Intercept Missile
AK-74	Standard Infantry Rifle for Soviet and Soviet aligned forces
AKS-74	A Combat Rifle used by Soviet Paratroopers
ALICE	All-Purpose Lightweight Individual Carrying Equipment
AMTI	airborne moving target indicator
AN/PAQ-1	A Laser Designator used by the US Military
AN/PRC-77	A man portable radio used by the US Military
AN/PVS-5	Night vision goggles
AN/SPS-59	Surface search radar
AN/VRC-12	A medium sized radio used by the US Military
APC	Armored Personnel Carrier
ARM	Anti-Radiation Missile
ASAP	As Soon As Possible
ASW	Anti-Submarine Warfare
ATGM	Anti-tank Guided Missile
AWACS	Airborne Warning and Control System
BLUF	Bottom Line Up Front
BMD	Russian Paradropped infantry fighting vehicle
BMP	Russian infantry fighting vehicle
BOHICA	Bend Over, Here It Comes Again
BTR	Russian armored personnel carrier
C & C	Command and Control
CAS	Close Air Support

CIA	Central Intelligence Agency
CIC	Combat Information Center
CCP	Casualty Collection Point
CIWS	Close-In Weapon Systems
CNO	Chief of Naval Operations
CO	Commanding Officer
COMSEC	Communications Security
CRT	Cathode-ray tube
DLAB	Defense Language Aptitude Battery
DMZ	Demilitarized Zone (area along the border of North Korea and South Korea)
DOD	Department of Defense
DOJ	Department of Justice
DPRK	Democratic People's Republic of Korea (North Korea)
ECM	Electronic Countermeasures
ERA	Equal Rights Amendment
ETA	Estimated Time of Arrival
FARP	Forward Arming and Refueling Point
FBI	Federal Bureau of Investigations
FSO	Foreign Service Officer
FUBAR	F***ed Up Beyond All Recognition
GAU-8	A very large rotary cannon fielded by the A-10 Thunderbolt II
GOP	Grand Ole' Party. The Republican Party in the United States.
GQ	General Quarters – Battle Stations
GRU	Soviet Military Intelligence
HE	High-Explosive
HEAT	High-Explosive Anti-tank
HQ	Headquarters
HUMINT	Human Intelligence
IBM	International Business Machines
ICBM	Intercontinental Ballistic Missile
ID	Infantry Division
IFV	Infantry Fighting Vehicle
IR	Infrared
JP-4	A type of jet fuel

KGB	Soviet Intelligence Service
KH-11	An American Photo Reconnaissance Satellite
KIA	Killed in Action
KPA	Korean People's Army
LAW	Light Antitank Weapon
LCAC	Landing Craft Air Cushion
Lieutenant JG	Lieutenant Junior Grade
LT	Lieutenant
LZ	Landing Zone
MAC	Military Airlift Command
MANPAD	Man-Portable Air-Defense System
MAB	Marine Amphibious Brigade
MAU	Marine Amphibious Unit
MD	Mechanized Division
MP	Military Police
MRLS	Multiple Rocket Launch System
NATO	North Atlantic Treaty Organization
NCO	Noncommissioned Officer
NMCA	National Military Command Authority
NSA	National Security Agency
NTDS	Naval Tactical Data System
NVG	Night Vision Goggles
OPEC	Organization of Petroleum Exporting Countries
PA	Public Address
PFC	Private First Class
PI	Philippine Islands
PLA	People's Liberation Army (Chinese Army)
PO2	Petty Officer, Second Class
POL	Petroleum, Oil and Lubricants
PR	Public Relations
PT	Physical Training
PVO	Russian Air Defense Forces
PVV-5A	Soviet explosive compound. Similar to C-4
QRF	Quick Reaction Force
R & R	Rest and Recreation
RAF	Royal Air Force
RF	Radio Frequency
RHAW	Radar Homing and Warning

RIM	Radar Intercept Missile
ROE	Rules of Engagement
ROK	Republic of Korea (South Korea)
RM3	Radioman, 3rd Class
RP	Rally Point
RPG	Rocket-Propelled Grenade
RPKS	A Soviet Light Machine Gun used by Paratroopers
RSO	Regional Security Officer
RTB	Return to Base
RTO	Radio Telephone Operator
RWR	Radar Warning Receiver
S2	Intelligence Officer
S3	Operations Officer
SACEUR	Supreme Allied Commander, Europe
SAG	Surface Action Group
SALT	Strategic Arms Limitation Treaty
SAM	Surface-to-Air Missile
SAS	Special Air Service (British Army Special Forces)
SEAD	Suppression of Enemy Air Defense
SEAL	Sea-Air-Land (Naval Special Warfare Development Group)
SF	Special Forces
SIGINT	Signals Intelligence
Sitrep	Situation Report
SM	Standard Missile
SRBOC	Super Rapid Bloom Offboard Countermeasures
SSES	Ship's Signals Exploitation Space
TASS	Tactical Air Support Squadron
TOW	Tube-launched, Optically tracked, Wire-guided
TRAM	Target Recognition Attack Multi-sensor
UN	United Nations
USSR	Union of Soviet Socialist Republics
VA-##	Naval Attack Squadron
VADS	Vulcan Air Defense System
VDV	Russian Airborne Infantry Forces
VF-##	Naval Fighter Squadron
VLS	Vertical Launching System
VP	Vice President

VTOL   Vertical Take-Off and Landing
XO   Executive Officer

NATO Equipment

A-6e Intruder	US Navy Heavy Attack Aircraft
A-7e Corsair II	USN/USAF Light Attack Aircraft
AH-1 Cobra	Attack Helicopter
Austin Class	Amphibious Transport Dock
AV-8A Harrier	VTOL Attack Aircraft
Blue Ridge-Class	Command Ship
C-130 Hercules	Medium Transport Aircraft
C-141 Starlifter	Heavy Transport Aircraft
CAR-15	Colt Automatic Rifle. Used by US Special Forces
CH-46 Sea Knight	Medium Transport Helicopter
CH-53 Sea Stallion	Heavy Transport Helicopter
Charles F Adams	Guided Missile Destroyer
E2C Hawkeye	USN AWACS Aircraft
E-3 Sentry	USAF AWACS Aircraft
F-14 Tomcat	USN Fleet Interceptor
F-4 Phantom	US Built Multi-Role Fighter
F-5 Freedom Fighter	US Built Multi-Role Fighter
Iwo Jima-Class	Amphibious Assault Ship
JetRanger	Civilian Passenger Helicopter
Leahy-Class	Guided Missile Cruiser
M113	Armored Personnel Carrier
M16	US Military Standard Combat Rifle
M-163	VADS Air Defense Vehicle
M1911	.45 Caliber handgun
M2	.50 Caliber Machine Gun
M203	40mm Grenade Launcher
M60	Squad Automatic Weapon
M60a1 Patton	Main Battle Tank
M72 LAW	Single Use Light Antitank Weapon
Midway-Class	Aircraft Carrier
Model 37 Shotgun	Tactical Shotgun used by US Special Forces
Nimitz-Class	Nuclear Aircraft Carrier
RF-8 Crusader	Reconnaissance Aircraft
SH-2 Seasprite	ASW Helicopter

Spruance-Class	Destroyer
Tarawa-Class	Amphibious Assault Ship
Thomaston-Class	Dock Landing Ship
UH-1	Utility Helicopter

Warsaw Pact Equipment

A-90 Eaglet	Ground Effect Vehicle
AKS-74	Compact Combat Rifle used by Soviet Paratroopers
An-12 NATO Codename "Cub"	Medium Transport Aircraft
An-72 NATO Codename "Condor"	Heavy Transport Aircraft
BMD	Airlift Capable Infantry Fighting Vehicle
BMP	Infantry Fighting Vehicle
BRDM	Combat Reconnaissance/Patrol Vehicle
BTR	Amphibious Armored Personnel Carrier
KM	Prototype Ground Effect Vehicle
Mi-24 NATO Codename "Hind	Attack Helicopter
Mi-8 NATO Codename "Hip	Transport Helicopter
MiG-23 NATO Codename "Flogger	Multi-Role Fighter
MiG-25 NATO Codename "Foxbat"	Interceptor/ Reconnaissance Aircraft
MiG-27 NATO Codename "Flogger"	Dedicated Attack Version of the MiG-23
Osa Class	Missile Patrol Boat
RPKS-74	Light Machine Gun used by Soviet Paratroopers
SA-8	Surface to Air Missile
Su-20 NATO Codename "Fitter"	Multi-Role Aircraft
Su-25 NATO Codename "Frogfoot"	Medium Attack Aircraft
T-72	Main Battle Tank
Tu-16 NATO Codename "Badger"	Medium Bomber

Printed in the USA
CPSIA information can be obtained
at www.ICGtesting.com
CBHW071334290324
6073CB00043B/883